FEAR ITSELF

It's the late 1930s. Whilst America pulls itself out of the Depression, war threatens in Europe. But there is pressure to stay out of the fight in America, with its forty million citizens of German ancestry. Special Agent Jimmy Nessheim, in the fledgling FBI, is assigned to infiltrate a new German-American organisation. The *Bund*, ardently pro-Nazi, is conspiring to sabotage President Roosevelt's efforts to stop Hitler's advance. Nessheim's investigation probes deeply into the *Bund*, revealing something more sinister at work, seemingly in connection with the White House. Drawn into Washington's high society, Nessheim becomes tangled in a web of political intrigue. But as he moves closer to the truth, an even more lethal plot emerges, one that could rewrite history in the most catastrophic of ways . . .

Books by Andrew Rosenheim
Published by The House of Ulverscroft:

STILLRIVER
KEEPING SECRETS
WITHOUT PREJUDICE

ANDREW ROSENHEIM

FEAR ITSELF

Complete and Unabridged

CHARNWOOD
Leicester

First published in Great Britain in 2011 by
Hutchinson
The Random House Group Limited
London

First Charnwood Edition
published 2011
by arrangement with
The Random House Group Limited
London

British Library CIP Data

Rosenheim, Andrew.
    Fear itself.
    1. United States. Federal Bureau of Investigation- -
    Officials and employees- -Fiction. 2. Intelligence
    officers- -United States- -Fiction. 3. Undercover
    operations- -United States- -Fiction. 4. German
    Americans- -Fiction. 5. United States- -Race relations- -
    Fiction. 6. United States- -History- -1933–1945- -
    Fiction. 7. United States- -Foreign relations- -Germany- -
    Fiction. 8. Germany- -Foreign relations- -United States- -
    Fiction. 9. Suspense fiction. 10. Large type books.
    I. Title
    823.9′2–dc22

    ISBN 978–1–4448–0874–2

Published by
F. A. Thorpe (Publishing)
Anstey, Leicestershire

Set by Words & Graphics Ltd.
Anstey, Leicestershire
Printed and bound in Great Britain by
T. J. International Ltd., Padstow, Cornwall

This book is printed on acid-free paper

For Clare

Part One
1936–38

1

August 1936
Klagenfurt, Austria

Schellenberg crossed the square quickly, avoiding the Town Hall, three storeys of pale quarried stone and a mansard roof that had originally been the house of a minor Hapsburg. Banners from a recent rally were still up, their red and black a vibrant contrast to the sombre grey slate of the paving stones. At the east end of the square, trencher tables stood in the bright sun, covered in crumbs from the platters of *Schwarzbrot* and *Wurst* that had been laid out for the attendees. Though there was no need to lure them with rewards.

He was tired from his trip, and had slept badly — but what could you expect from a railway hotel? He shuddered at the memory of his grim room, but the very pleasant accommodation he was used to when travelling might have led to questions — *Are you here on business, Herr Schellenberg? Do you have relatives in Austria? What is your view of the 'situation'?* Questions required answers, and answers helped people's recollections. On this trip he did not want to be remembered.

His colleagues thought he was in Linz, further north and the boyhood home of the Führer, meeting with members of the Austrian Nazi

3

Party, helping to plan for what was now a certainty in one, maybe two years' time — the *Anschluss*, when Germany came in and the two countries were united. Even his family thought he was there, for it was crucial that there be no slip, however unintended, that would link him to the man he'd meet today.

Klagenfurt was not a large city, but the train station was crowded: it was market day, and people came from all around to buy the local specialities — *Speck*, the slabs of smoked marble-white pork fat streaked by dark strips of lean, and produce from the Rosental, the Slovene-speaking valley that was the most fertile in the region. He was leaving town while the market visitors were coming in, so the carriage of his local train was deserted.

It was a short trip, just twenty minutes, the train gliding west along the north shore of the Wörthersee, a lake shaped like a thin elongated worm running east to west. On every side the land rose rapidly into foothills covered by firs, and in the further distance separate ranges of mountains loomed, which in the clear air of this summer day looked much closer than they were. On the shore itself sat a series of resort hotels, some gathered in clusters to form the core of several small towns — including Pörtschach, where Schellenberg left the train.

The main street was the same road that ringed the entire lake, and he walked west along it, past shops and cafés, and two grand hotels that faced the water. From their grounds he could hear the sound of tennis balls struck softly on clay courts,

4

and across the road on the lawns running down to the water hotel guests were stretched out in deck chairs to catch the high midday sun. It must be nice to have a holiday, he thought — without resentment, for he knew his mission was potentially crucial for the Reich.

To the south he saw the range of the Karawanken Mountains, which formed the border with Yugoslavia. Behind them reared the Julian Alps, jagged and snow peaked. Here was the Dreiländereck, the corner where the three countries of Austria, Yugoslavia, and Italy met in an uneasy nexus. There had been fierce fighting near there in the last war, the Austrians and Italians locked into a system of battlements as complicated as any of the famous labyrinthine trench works in Belgium and France. His own father had fought there, as part of the German reinforcements sent to help the Austrians in the 1917 breakout at Caporetto. Much of the fighting had been waged almost invisibly, at the very top of the range of mountains Schellenberg could see now in the distance. *We were fighting nearer to God*, his father was fond of saying with a tart smile. *Not that he seemed on our side by the end.*

On the outskirts of Pörtschach a garage sat back from the road, with a solitary petrol pump, several cars parked to one side of the lot, and a shed that functioned as the office. Inside, a man in oil-stained overalls stood behind a counter, adding up figures on a scrap of paper.

'*Guten Tag*,' said Schellenberg.

'*Grüss Gott*,' muttered the man, without looking up.

'Herr Schmidt has left a car for me, I believe.' He didn't give his name.

The man nodded, still intent on his sums. He reached with one hand under the counter and brought out a small brown envelope, which jingled as he pushed it across the counter. 'The Mercedes-Benz,' he said.

Schellenberg nodded. 'Much obliged, I am sure,' he said, and went out the door with the keys. He stopped for a moment and pulled a pair of tan driving gloves from a coat pocket. They were small-sized and tight; he had to stretch the leather over each finger until he could clench his fists.

The car was almost new — a 170 DS sedan. It started up with a roar, then purred like a spoiled cat. Thank you, Herr Schmidt, thought Schellenberg as he drove away, whoever you may be. A sympathiser of course, but then many Austrians were, especially here in Carinthia.

He drove into the hills, along winding paved roads, through small farms and past the occasional *Gasthaus*. Once he had to slow for cows on the road. The paved surface gave way to gravel as he climbed higher, then to rough track, and as he entered deep forest he turned off onto an old fire road. From the absence of tyre marks he could see that no vehicle had come this way for months.

The track moved laterally across the side of the hill, and after a mile he turned onto a small spur that ended abruptly in a cul de sac carved from a copse of towering spruce; here his car could not be seen from the track. He got out and locked it, then set off through the woods, moving quietly but quickly along the soft ground which was covered by dried pine needles that had accumulated over the seasons, scenting the air with a mild resinous perfume. After walking less than half a mile, heading down the mountain, he stopped and stood on a ledge of rock that perched over a small clearing, not even the size of a tennis court. He stayed here for a moment, listening carefully. Satisfied, he hopped down and stood waiting in the clearing.

He didn't have long to wait. Within ten minutes he could hear someone coming uphill, along the faded remnants of a trail. Moments later a man emerged from the trees. He was dressed in a loose-fitting green hunter's jacket, with leather hiking shorts, knee socks and climbing boots; on his head sat a felt hat like those worn on Bavarian postcards. He was the incarnation of a hiking visitor, though the man was perspiring heavily and did not look as if he had enjoyed his climb. When he saw Schellenberg he raised a hand and gave a timid wave, then came across the small clearing.

'Herr Werner, I presume,' said Schellenberg cordially. The man nodded. 'It is good of you to come.'

The man named Werner shrugged. 'And you are?'

'Schellenberg of the SD.' He proffered a gloved hand, explaining, 'Urticaria. Hives bother me terribly in this heat. But tell me, Werner, where did you travel from?'

'Venice, of course,' said Werner, looking

7

slightly surprised. He took off his hat. 'As you instructed I changed at Villach. Though my way here was pretty roundabout. I believe it would be thoroughly impossible for anyone to reconstruct my journey,' he said with a touch of pride.

'Excellent. Did they stamp your passport at the border?'

'No.'

Schellenberg nodded. 'It would have helped that your passport is American. If it had been Italian you'd have had a harder time. The Austrians round here are still sulking over the loss of the Kanaltal. Another injustice of Versailles we'll need to sort out when we get here.'

'I don't understand why we couldn't have met in Berlin,' Werner said with a note of complaint.

'It's safer this way. Right now Berlin is crawling with foreign agents because of the Olympics.'

'But Kuhn's there. He claims he's going to get to meet the Führer.'

'Your work is more important than his.' Especially since Kuhn is a fool, thought Schellenberg. 'And it's vital that there be no known link between us and you.'

Werner seemed pleased to hear he mattered more than Kuhn. 'I am ready to brief you on the American developments,' he said.

'You've brought a report?' demanded Schellenberg. He was alarmed that all his precautions might have been endangered by simple stupidity.

But to his relief Werner tapped his temple with a finger. 'Just here.'

'Ah, good. Proceed.'

'We are preparing for the election. Naturally, if Lemke wins, we will not have anything to worry about.'

Lemke? Why was he talking about him? A fringe candidate surely. 'What about the Republican?' he asked.

'Landon has no chance,' said Werner confidently. 'Lemke, on the other hand, has the support of all right-thinking groups — Gerald L. K. Smith and Father Coughlin both support him unequivocally. And their followers number in the millions.'

'And what happens if Roosevelt wins?'

'That won't happen — '

'Yes, I'm sure you're right, but we need to cover all possibilities, however remote.'

Werner shrugged, as if he were humouring the German. 'Then we will mobilise. The *Bund* has over 600,000 members; by the end of the year it will be a million.'

'Really?' said Schellenberg. 'That's impressive.'

'We have set up three camps, as you approved. By next spring there will be six more.'

'What about our special friend in America?' he asked casually, though this was the most significant part of the conversation, indeed the only significant part.

'You mean — ?' asked Werner, his eyes widening slightly.

'Yes, the *Dreiländer*,' said Schellenberg. 'Tell me, why did you give him that code name?'

Werner shrugged a shoulder. 'He picked it

9

himself. He knew you and I were meeting in this part of Austria, so it seemed appropriate.' Werner swept an arm around them, taking in the woods and the distant mountains too, spanning the three countries whose borders converged at a point less than fifteen miles away.

'That makes sense,' said Schellenberg approvingly. '*Drei Völker*. And three loyalties. American on the surface; German deep down and true. And then, the inevitable allegiance to himself.'

Werner looked a little shocked.

'All agents have to have their own interests at heart,' explained Schellenberg, as if he were talking to a much younger man. 'As long as they coincide with their controller, it is a good thing.' He suddenly asked with a sharp voice, 'I take it no one else knows the *Dreiländer* name?'

Was there hesitation in Werner's face? It was hard to tell, and he said emphatically, 'Only me.' He added jokily, 'And *Dreiländer* himself, of course.'

Schellenberg nodded thoughtfully. 'Tell me, is he well placed? You indicated he would be by now.'

'Exceedingly. His patron has people in half of Washington, of course. He has access to everyone.'

'I wasn't thinking of everyone,' said Schellenberg with a hint of steeliness. He softened, asking, 'Is it really true that Roosevelt is confined to a wheelchair?'

'Yes. He had polio as a young man. He cannot walk unassisted.'

'To think a cripple's at the helm of such an

emerging power. It seems quite incredible.'

'It makes him an easier target.'

'Perhaps. Though that man killed the Mayor from Chicago instead of Roosevelt.'

'Was the assassin one of ours?'

'Certainly not. He was an Italian, as you well know,' said Schellenberg sharply. 'Now tell me, Herr Werner, did you bring the weapon we sent you?'

'Yes. Though I was rather surprised you wanted me to bring it here.'

'We need to ensure you are well equipped,' said Schellenberg flatly. 'May I see it, please?'

Werner reached into his jacket and brought out a pistol, handing it over grip first. The gun was short-barrelled and handsome — with a royal blue metal finish, and walnut checking around the rubber of its distinctive sloping butt. 'It's a very nice Luger,' said Werner. 'Be careful: it's loaded.'

Schellenberg held the gun, barrel down. 'It's very light,' he said approvingly. He smiled at Werner, then suddenly his face grew alarmed. 'Did you hear that, Herr Werner?' he asked tensely, pointing towards the woods on one side.

Werner turned to look, and Schellenberg lifted the pistol and shot him in the head.

In the thin mountain air the noise of the gun reverberated as Werner fell to his knees. His hand gradually released his green felt hat as he toppled over, his head falling with a heavy thud on the thin grass.

Schellenberg reached down and calmly placed the pistol on the grass. The noise of the shot wouldn't travel far — not in this dense foliage and thick forest. And there was virtually no blood to speak of, just a dark maroon hole the size of a pfennig in Werner's temple.

Kneeling down, Schellenberg went through Werner's pockets, taking off the dead man's watch and extricating his wallet and passport. He found a few coins — schillings and some lira — and took these as well. Grabbing Werner's jacket by both shoulders, he stood up and dragged the corpse across the ground to the edge of the forest, where he stopped and caught his breath. Then he propped the body to sit against the base of an enormous spruce, next to the boulder he had stood on just half an hour before. He spent a few moments brushing off the grass and earth on the knees of the man's trousers.

He went back into the clearing and retrieved the pistol, then came back to the corpse, where he took Werner's right arm and let it flop to one side, so the hand trailed on the bed of dead needles that carpeted the ground. He placed the butt of the pistol flush against the still-warm palm, then closed the fingers gently until they encircled the gun.

Stepping back, he examined his handiwork. It would do. An observant eye might notice the grass stains on the man's knees and wonder how they got there, but it seemed unlikely — it was too obviously a suicide to let doubts creep in very easily. Even if someone went to the lengths of checking the prints on the gun, they would only find Werner's — the driving gloves had seen to that.

12

When the Austrian police arrived (if they ever did; it didn't look as if anyone had been here for ages), they would be more interested in establishing the identity of the corpse than in questioning how the man had died. Good luck, thought Schellenberg. No wallet, no passport. It could be months before they even discovered Werner wasn't Austrian, much less that he had come from the United States. And if they ever did succeed in establishing his identity, what of it?

Werner had clearly been a fantasist. For all the many million German descendants in the United States, they seemed ill-placed for power — located in communities hundreds, even thousands of miles from Washington, in places like Wisconsin and Texas. There were German communities closer to the hub, of course, especially in Baltimore and New York, but in these cities there were also many outlying ethnic groups. Jews by the thousand, especially in New York; the Irish, filling up Boston and never very reliable; even Negroes. A mongrel kind of state, which might make for a weak body politic in Schellenberg's view, but it didn't make that body pro-German. Werner's idea that a popular uprising against the American government might take place, in support of a foreign power to boot, was misconceived nonsense. Schellenberg would leave that, as well as straightforward efforts at espionage, to the *Abwehr* — military intelligence, staffed by strait-laced officers of the old school. Most of them hopelessly antique.

Not that it would matter any more, thought

13

Schellenberg, looking at Werner's corpse, propped up like a dummy against a tree. And most crucially, the identity of this 'Dreiländer' was safe. Only Schellenberg knew the man's 'real' American name — no, he corrected himself, strictly speaking that was not the case. Heydrich knew, of course — it was he who originally briefed Schellenberg on his mission, one-to-one, making it clear without actually saying so that he was keeping it from his direct superior, Himmler.

None of these others knew. Not Himmler or Goering or Goebbels or Bormann. Röhm had known, for it had been Röhm who had drawn in Werner, as an American liaison he thought helpful. Fortunately Röhm was dead. Perhaps that was the reason he had been murdered.

The thought was chilling. Could not the same thing happen to him?

No, Schellenberg told himself, not unless he got in so much trouble that it was decided to silence him in case he talked to save his skin. Well, he would just have to make sure that didn't happen, so that he would still be there to give the signal, when and if the moment came, for 'Dreiländer' to act. Hitler himself would give the order; it was Hitler who had already likened the position of the Dreiländer to that of a bat — eine Fledermaus — that had hung unseen for years, unnoticed while people moved around him, until the command came, the bat's wings stirred, and the creature swooped down to attack.

2

March 1937
Milwaukee, Wisconsin

Milwaukee had no sky. Nessheim parked on a small side street and got out of the car, searching in vain for stars in the black canopy above him. A pungent aroma filled the air, a rich nutty smell of malt and burnt hops. It was early spring, but the evening held the vestigial chill of winter. When he exhaled, curled feathers of breath hung in the air.

He took off his suit jacket and swapped it for a dark duffel coat on the back seat, quickly wrapping the coat around him to hide the .38 that hung in a holster from his right shoulder. Smith & Wesson — Model 10, apparently; not that he had any idea of what models 1 to 9 had been like. He unknotted his striped tie and laid it on top of the jacket, then pushed the lock down and closed the door. Turning around, he looked at the two houses on this side of the street. One was boarded up, the other run down and unlit.

As he went around the corner he saw four grain silos looming like bleached minareted towers a quarter-mile away. The air turned thick and strangely moist, then Nessheim realised it was dispersed steam, floating over from the malt-house chimneys. Across from them was the bottling plant, which had a neon sign — *Pabst*, it said, glowing like a purple trail of wax above the open iron gates. The second shift had started an hour before. How many factories had a second shift these days? Though if anything sold in the Depression, it was movie tickets and beer.

It took him ten minutes to cross the vast complex of buildings and traverse an empty lot, where a group of men in one corner were huddled around a small fire. Tramps. Milwaukee was meant to be a red town, a Socialist-leaning city, though it had its share of down-and-outs — but then what city in America didn't? The only difference was that here the cops didn't chase them out of town.

He passed two blocks of brick row houses, the light from their living rooms spilling like yellow gas onto the sidewalk. Then he came to a wider commercial avenue, where cars were parked on both sides of the street, most of them black and old, Model Ts and As. The stores were a smorgasbord of retail business — a pharmacist, a baker, a Chinese laundry, a greasy spoon — but their shop fronts were dingy and worn. Most were now shut for the day, though the drugstore, more in hope than real expectation, was open for any after-work trade.

Ahead of him a new-model Dodge was parked by the kerb. Passing it, he noticed that the driver was inside, his feet propped on the dashboard with a fedora pulled halfway down his face. An awkward way to snooze. On the corner he saw the flashing sign — *Reno's*. Nessheim didn't know if the bar was named after its owner, or for the city in the one state where you could get a

16

divorce in six weeks. He stopped outside its entrance, and casually looked around. No one along the sidewalk seemed to be paying him attention, so he went into the bar.

Inside, a group of men in working clothes stood holding bottles of beer while another guy chalked up numbers on a board. The horses? College basketball scores? Nessheim didn't stop to watch, but walked towards the bar itself, a long worn slab of dark mahogany, fronted by a row of padded bar stools with thin chrome legs. Behind it, the bartender was drying glasses with a cloth; he looked at Nessheim with careful, non-committal eyes as a bakelite radio played soft swing piano.

'Hiya,' said Nessheim, as he stood and propped a foot against the low brass rail of the bar. On the bar top a pig's foot sat on a plate in a congealed pool of jellied fat, a leftover from lunch, part of the nickel Beer & Eats offered by a sign on the wall behind the bar.

The bartender nodded grudgingly. The music stopped, and the announcer's voice declared, 'That was Count Basie, live from the Grand Terrace Ballroom in Chicago.' Nessheim gave a small smile; he had heard Basie play there three weeks before.

'Eddie Le Saux around?' he asked.

The bartender gave a quick jerk of his head towards the rear. Wooden booths ran along one side wall in the back area of the bar, which was suffused by smoke and the dim light of a single ceiling bulb. Through the gloom Nessheim could just make out a solitary figure sitting in the last

17

of the line of booths.

'What's he drinking?'

'Beer and a shot.'

'Give me another round for him, and a regular coffee for me.'

The bartender filled a mug from a tin coffee pot and added a slurp of cream. Then he poured a big shot of whiskey and put it, the coffee, and a bottle of Pabst on a small tin tray. 'Forty cents,' he said.

Nessheim put two quarters on the bar, then took the tray and walked to the last booth. He set the drinks down on the table, and sat across from the man already sitting there.

'Well, if it isn't Christmas come early,' said Eddie Le Saux, and he lifted the fresh bottle of beer in greeting. 'My thanks to the FBI.'

'We missed your birthday and wanted to make up for it.' Nessheim had half a dozen informants in Chicago, but he didn't trade banter with any of them — probably because they were too frightened of the Bureau. Le Saux, by contrast, didn't seem scared of anything.

He was in his late forties, more than twenty years older than Nessheim. His hair, black and straight and shiny, was long in front, and he flicked it back now with his hand when it tumbled over his mahogany face — he could have passed for an Indian, or a man with Mexican blood. In fact he was French Canadian, and though only average height, he cut a powerful figure, bulked out by years of pulling hand saws through timber — he had worked as a lumberjack through pine plantations from

Halifax to Seattle, before arriving (he never said how or why) in Milwaukee, where he'd met his wife, taken a job in the brewery, and settled down.

Le Saux was a Party member, and had been since the mid-1920s. He was quick and quick-tongued, and a natural leader of men. He was too savvy, sometimes even cynical, about human nature to be fanatical, and though his politics were always reflexively on the side of 'the workers', his attitude towards them was benign rather than expectant, as if he'd learned that high hopes suffer the biggest bump on landing. Still, Nessheim felt confident that if push ever came to shove, Eddie Le Saux would always storm the Bastille rather than defend it, and however friendly he may have acted, would if ordered happily put Nessheim up against the wall with the other counter-revolutionaries to be shot.

Which made the man's willingness to inform on his 'comrades' mystifying to Nessheim — Le Saux was paid to do so, but not that well, and he had never asked to be paid more, a diffidence not shared by any other of Nessheim's informants.

'Have you got the minutes?' asked Nessheim, trying to keep to business. Never easy with Eddie Le Saux, who would prefer to yack about anything under the sun rather than deal directly with what Nessheim was there for.

'Not yet.'

Nessheim stirred uneasily — Ferguson, his boss, had been showing signs of impatience with Le Saux's failure to deliver. Or rather,

Nessheim's failure to deliver info from Le Saux.

'I thought you were the branch secretary — can't you even get the minutes out on time?'

Le Saux just grinned. 'Too busy. Minutes can wait; it's money we're trying to raise. I've been selling raffle tickets until they come out of my ass.'

'What for?'

'I told you we had a guy head for Spain at Christmas with the first bunch of volunteers. Now we got two more trying to go over there and help defend Madrid.'

'They can't get there on their own steam?'

'Even a steerage ticket to Europe costs more than a wort master's pay runs to. Or do you think they've got first-class cabin tickets courtesy of Moscow Central?' Le Saux gave a weary shake to his head. 'I've told you, you've got it all wrong. There isn't any pipeline from the Soviet.'

'They're happy enough to send instructions.'

Le Saux shrugged. 'Instructions are free.'

'Sure. And Zinoviev and his friends got a fair trial.'

'They were traitors to the state,' Le Saux said, but the ironic tilt to his lips hinted at a lack of conviction. 'Don't pretend you're some kind of Trotskyite — I know you played football at college.' He gave a short laugh. 'But what's the point of my arguing? You probably think it's right that your countrymen are helping Franco.'

It took him a second to realise Le Saux meant the Germans. 'They're not my countrymen.'

'Nessheim? Don't try and tell me it's a Norwegian name.'

'I'd like to think it was American. And actually, I think we should stay out of it. That's what Roosevelt says.'

'You and your Roosevelt. Can't you see he's as bad as the rest? I wouldn't mind his wanting to sit it out if Germany and Italy were doing the same. But they're not.'

'Russia's helping on the other side,' Nessheim said. When Le Saux started to lecture him, he felt compelled to argue back. He knew it was unprofessional, but he couldn't help himself.

'Why shouldn't they — when the Fascists are intervening on the side of the Falange? Britain and us should be doing the same. Don't forget, the Spanish government was elected.' Le Saux shook his head, as if stuck with a recalcitrant child. 'You don't get it, do you, Jimmy? We can't stay on the sidelines for ever.'

He picked up the fresh shot glass of whiskey and drank it down in one fierce gulp, wincing slightly from the harshness of the cheap booze. He wiped his mouth with one hand, then said, 'There's something else I wanted to talk to you about.'

'What's that?' asked Nessheim, wary of more runaround.

Le Saux leaned forward confidentially, even though they had the row of booths to themselves. 'I've got a boat. Nothing fancy, just a little skiff, hardly bigger than a row boat, though when I stick the outboard on it I can get around just fine on the big lake. I keep it down on the shore, just outside the downtown harbour; there's a little hut I built where I can store it during winter. A couple more weeks and I'll bring it out.'

Nessheim wondered what this had to do with the Communist Party's branch in Milwaukee.

'There're other guys down there — a few from the brewery. By and large I keep to myself, but you can't help getting to know each other.'

'Right,' said Nessheim, thinking only of the missing minutes he knew Special Agent in Charge Ferguson was going to chew his ass out for not obtaining.

'One of these guys was named Heydeman. Big fellah, with buck teeth. Blonde as sauerkraut, and Perch-crazy like me — that's how I got to know him. Heydeman was a newcomer. He said he was born upstate somewhere — maybe Fond Du Lac.' He spoke as if the town were five thousand miles from Milwaukee instead of a hundred.

'We never talked politics; it was fishing we had in common. To cut a long story short and keep you from asking me to get to the point' — Le Saux gave a knowing smirk — 'Heydeman hasn't been around for a couple of months. Nobody seemed to know where he'd gone. But then last week there's a knock on my door; this was Thursday night. Must have been ten o'clock — I was about to go to bed. When I opened it there was Heydeman. He'd never been to my house, I wouldn't have bet he even knew where I lived, but he says he's got a favour to ask — could he store some stuff for a couple of days in my hut by the harbour? He says he's got no place else — he's moved away, and he's only back for a day or two.

'I was a little surprised to see him, but I said sure — why not? No skin off my nose. I wasn't gonna be around — my wife and kids and me were going to Racine for the weekend to see my old lady's parents. So I gave Heydeman my spare key to the hut.

'But we didn't go to Racine after all — one of the kids got sick. That Sunday I went down to the harbour like I always do. When I opened the hut I got one hell of a surprise. This 'stuff' of Heydeman's turned out to be guns.'

Nessheim stiffened. 'What kind of guns?'

'That's the thing. It wasn't a couple of shotguns, or a pair of deer rifles. These were submachine guns. Thompson sub-machine guns.'

'How did you know they were Thompsons?'

Le Saux gave him a look. 'Come the revolution we'll need to know our weaponry.'

Nessheim let this pass. 'So how many guns are we talking about exactly?'

'There were eight of them.'

'What did you do?'

'Nothing. I'm too old to get killed out of curiosity. I locked up and went on my way.'

'You could have called the cops.'

Le Saux looked at him scornfully. 'Of course I could have. I'm sure they'd have been pleased as punch to see me — five gets you three they'd have my confession by now, too. Think of the headline — 'Guns Found in Red Subversion Plot.' He shook his head disgustedly.

'Okay,' said Nessheim. 'I get it. But are the guns still there?'

'No. I went back to the hut on Monday morning before work. They were gone.'

'Did you hear from Heydeman again?'

Le Saux shook his head. 'Not a peep. He left the key for me at the brewery. But no note with them, nothing.' He added wryly, 'Not even thanks.'

'So where do we find him?'

Le Saux shrugged. Nessheim asked impatiently, 'Did he give any idea where he'd moved to?'

Le Saux shook his head, but there was a knowing look to his eyes. He asked, 'Ever heard of the Friends of New Germany?'

'Sure,' said Nessheim. In fact Nessheim's uncle Eric, husband of his mother's sister Greta, was a member. A social thing mainly, full of recent immigrants from Germany. They spoke German, sang songs of the old country, played pinochle and strange card games using wooden boards carved in Bavaria. It all seemed harmless enough, though Nessheim had wondered why these people had not embraced their new country uninhibitedly. That was the point of America, wasn't it? To join in the great adventure.

Le Saux said, 'The *Bund* is the new name for it. They've renamed themselves — I guess to sound even more like Krauts. No offence, Jimmy. And most of them are Nazis — sympathisers anyway. They'd like to spread the word over here.'

Nessheim nodded curtly; he wasn't there for Le Saux's views on Hitler, he wanted to know

24

about these guns. Le Saux saw his impatience and bristled slightly. 'They have *camps* now — like the ones in Germany.'

'So? Kids go to them. They swim and play ball and do all the things kids do — just with a German-American coating.'

Le Saux ignored him. 'There's one ten miles north of here, another in Michigan and I think there's one in New York. For the little kids it's harmless, I agree, if a little weird — yodelling away, wearing those funny shorts and hats. But they're not all kids. And the older ones aren't spending their time singing Christmas carols. More like *Deutschland Über Alles*.'

'What's this got to do with Heydeman?'

'I asked around the harbour. Nobody seemed to know for sure where he was, but one guy said he thought Heydeman's gone to Michigan, to do training in a camp over there.'

'Training for what?'

'Whatever you need a tommy gun for, I guess.'

This could be serious, thought Nessheim, or it could be malarkey intended to compensate for the missing Party meeting minutes. He looked hard at Le Saux, searching for any sign that he had made this up. But the French-Canadian returned his stare with unwavering eyes. Nessheim asked, 'Can you find out anything more specific?'

'I can ask, though I can't promise I'll get anywhere. Heydeman kept to himself pretty much. I seem to have been his only friend, which isn't saying much — I don't know anything about the guy.'

'Do your best.' There was a Pabst beer mat next to the ashtray on the table and Nessheim picked it up and turned it over on its blank side, taking a pencil from the inner pocket of his duffel coat. He wrote a number down — the phone in the hallway of his boarding house. 'You've got my office number in Chicago. This will get me after work. Phone me if you learn anything, okay? And even if you don't, I want to talk again. Say a week from today, same time.' He looked around the empty back of the bar. 'This place will do.'

'I get extra for the extra meeting?' asked Le Saux flatly.

This was unlike Le Saux. 'I guess so,' Nessheim said slowly.

Le Saux nodded, then drained his beer and stood up. 'See you in a week then. I'll go first.'

Nessheim nursed his coffee for ten minutes before leaving the bar. When he came out he saw a new car parked across the street, its back half lit up by a street-lamp. Another Dodge, or was it the same car he'd seen before? He stood and studied it for a moment — it was unoccupied, but he saw a fedora on the dashboard, sitting like a marker left to keep the driver's place.

Looking both ways, he crossed the street and stopped behind the car, putting a shoe up on the chrome bumper to tie his laces. The licence plate was from Michigan. In the streetlamp's semi-halo of light he could read its numbers. He was memorising them for the second time in his head when a voice said coldly, 'You're on my car, bud.'

Nessheim put his foot down and stood up

straight. Ten feet away a man in a long wool overcoat stood on the pavement. He was as tall as Nessheim and had both his hands in his coat's pockets. The man stepped forward until Nessheim could see his face in the streetlamp's light. His eyes were deep set, dark as raisins, and he had a tight, mean-looking mouth. But what Nessheim noticed most was the strawberry birthmark, stretching like an ink stain from just below his left eye to the corner of his mouth.

'Just tying my shoe,' said Nessheim. He pointed at the car's bumper. 'I didn't scratch your chrome.' He gave a witless smile.

'So beat it, in case I decide to scratch yours.'

Nessheim stiffened. There was nothing to worry about — he had a badge under his coat that should calm this man down, and if that didn't do the job, he figured his .38 would. But the last thing he needed was an altercation: putting this guy in the local hoosegow would drag in higher-ups from the Bureau — he could hear Ferguson's complaint already. He said with a feigned sense of hurt, 'Okay, no need to get tough about it, pal.'

'I'm not your pal. Like I said, beat it.'

The man took a further, threatening step towards him. Nessheim backed out into the street, his hands up in surrender. 'Take it easy, take it easy,' he said, sounding as feeble as he could. He turned and walked away fast, looking back over his shoulder to make sure the man wasn't following.

As he headed back towards his own car, he wondered what the guy was doing here. And why had he moved his car until it sat directly across from Reno's? Probably a coincidence, he told himself, then mentally recited the licence plate numbers again, since he'd decided he'd check them out after the weekend, back in Chicago. If they'd been Wisconsin plates he probably wouldn't have bothered. Not that a Michigan car in Milwaukee was all that unusual.

Unless you'd had another mention of the state already. What had Eddie Le Saux's harbour friend said? *Heydeman's gone to Michigan.* Too many Michigans for me, thought Nessheim.

3

Jimmy Nessheim was twenty-six years old and had been an agent in the Chicago Field Office of the FBI for two and a half years — by accident, as he remembered each day that he went to work. This morning he was dressed in his best suit, a three-piece grey worsted one from Brooks Brothers. It had cost more than his father made in a month, and Nessheim had bought it for days like this one, when he needed to look professional and experienced, since he knew his boyish face made people think he was younger than he was. It also meant they tended to underestimate him — not always wisely, for there was an inner steeliness in Nessheim of a kind usually found in older, jaded men. The hardness had been forged by a personal disappointment that he thought he had got over — he knew he was fortunate to have landed where he had. There weren't many people who could say the same, not with so many lives damaged in the eight years since Wall Street committed suicide.

He had stayed up late, writing up his notes, trying to summarise as tightly as possible his conversation with Eddie Le Saux. Concision was at a premium with Warner Ferguson, the Special Agent in Charge (SAC for short), who made a point of doing everything as differently as possible from his predecessor, the legendary and loquacious Melvin H. Purvis.

Nessheim dropped the pool car he had taken to Milwaukee back at the Bureau's garage on Wabash, across the street from the sludge-filled Chicago River. In the early sunshine, the air was gradually warming as Nessheim walked across the Loop to the FBI offices. They were curiously anonymous, an entire floor of a new building located on the corner of La Salle and Adams, in the heart of Chicago's famous Loop, almost next door to the Board of Trade, where the agricultural futures of the country — corn and pigs and soy beans and wheat — were traded, these days still fetching prices lower than a decade before. Known as the Bankers Building, the forty-storey tower had been designed by the Burnham Brothers ten years ago, one of the skyscrapers for which both they and the city were now renowned.

In the lobby, a two-storeyed lavish galleria of marble and brass, he bought a copy of the *Tribune* from Leo, the one-armed owner of the news kiosk, then walked across the polished floor to the bank of elevators. He got in with several other early birds, and pressed the button for his floor — the building owners crowed about these automatic elevators, a heartless kind of boast when they could have filled each job of elevator operator a hundred times over. As the doors closed, their rubber edges met with a jolt, and Nessheim took a deep silent breath as the steel box started to rise with a gradual, growing *whoosh*. As always, it made him slightly dizzy, and triggered another mental replay of the moment his life had changed.

They'd been Fourth and Six on the Michigan 42-yard line. Too far for a field goal, though Northwestern were behind by only two points. There were ninety seconds left, and in the huddle Beckerbaugh the quarterback told him to go long. Nessheim had lined up wide, on the far touchline, and with the hike he sprinted to the 25-yard line, planning to curl in for the pass. But the safety was slow to cover, so Nessheim kept going, turning his head on the 10-yard line to see the ball floating towards him, in one of Beckerbaugh's wobbly spiral passes. He timed his leap and jumped with both hands fully extended, and as he felt the pigskin on his fingertips he knew the ball was his.

Then the safety showed up.

They told him later he'd landed directly on his head. He woke up in the locker room, with Coach Goetz looking on anxiously while a doctor, summoned over the PA system from the stands, stood over him.

'What happened?' Nessheim asked groggily.

'You got decked,' the doctor said, and Jimmy saw he was wearing a Northwestern scarf.

'Did I hold onto the ball?'

The doctor shook his head. 'I wish to hell you had — I had twenty bucks riding on you guys.'

Nessheim had missed the last two games of the season, for his immediate concussion was followed by headaches so excruciating that he couldn't walk more than a block at a time. After Christmas they receded, but then the dizzy spells began. They would attack him out of the blue, a vertiginous imbalance that made him fear he would fall down — once, buying gum in a Walgreen's Drugstore, he actually did. When spring practice started he didn't make it through the first day, and the coach had called him in.

'You look kind of shaky.'

'I'm all right,' he'd insisted.

'I want you to see the doctor before you come back to practice.'

It was not a request. Dutifully he had gone down to Michael Reese Hospital on the near South Side to see a specialist, Dr Morris Abrams, a Northwestern graduate who waived his fees in return for season tickets. Abrams had given him a thorough physical, then asked a battery of short, penetrating questions. To his eternal regret Nessheim had answered them all truthfully, and four minutes later Dr Abrams had ended his football career.

'Another knock could be fatal,' he had declared. 'You can't take that risk.'

He remembered the meeting that followed with Coach Goetz. It hadn't lasted very long: Coach had said, his voice sympathetic but firm, *If you can't play, we can't pay. Sorry, Jimmy.*

★   ★   ★

Now when the elevator in the Bankers Building opened on the nineteenth floor and Nessheim stepped out, it was just seven-thirty; only the night security man sat yawning at reception. Nessheim could see Ferguson's office, down the hall at the front of the building, its door wide open. He walked down and snuck a look inside;

32

it was empty, so he went and stood by the window, taking in the view of the lake, which spread like a blue tablecloth, unruffled and calm this sunny morning. He never got tired of this view, and he loved to look out across the high buildings of the Loop — until he'd come to Chicago, the highest man-made vantage point he'd known had been the bell tower in the Bremen Wisconsin Lutheran church. He pulled back from the window, remembering where he was. One day I'll have an office like this, he told himself, half-defiant, half-joking. He returned to reception, then down the carpeted corridor that ran the other way along this floor. The small agent offices that lined one side of the corridor were empty; on the other side the fingerprint and forensic lab was still locked.

He walked into the Bullpen, an open area of half a dozen desks. It was separated by a half-wood, half-glass partition from the typing pool, where a woman sat at one end, facing the small tables where the secretaries worked.

'Morning,' he said as he went to his desk.

'Hi, kid,' the woman said without turning her head.

Her name was Eloise Tate, but everyone knew her as Tatie. She was a slim woman with sharp features punctuated by a sliver of dimple in her chin, short black hair, and a tart mouth which spoke as if words were burning her tongue. She smoked any kind of cigarette that didn't have a filter, and dressed in the dull uniform — white blouse, grey skirt, black heels — of a woman who made it clear she wasn't going to push the boat out in an effort to impress you. With Tatie, you either took her as she was, or left her well alone. Attractive in a Girl Friday kind of way, she was probably in her early forties and definitely unmarried, and in the absence of a known boyfriend everyone assumed she'd stay that way. Some of the agents said she had to be a lezzy; others claimed she'd had a thing for Melvin Purvis when he'd been Chicago Special Agent in Charge. Either way, no one had the balls to try their luck.

It was Purvis, the legendary G-Man, who had plucked Tatie out of the ranks. He made her head of the typing pool, but she did a lot more than hammer a keyboard — she'd already been in the bureau for a dozen years by the time Nessheim started, and she knew where the bodies were buried, and just as important, where the files were stored. Her formal rise through the organisation had reached the dead end imposed by her sex, but Purvis relied on her to handle most of his communications with HQ in D.C., and whenever a crisis arose — with Purvis that was at least once a month — it was no accident that Tatie was always around to help. For all the flamboyance that got him in the papers — this was the man who'd arrested Ma Barker — Purvis was careful, and he confided in no man. But Tatie wasn't a man; though she could type 95 words a minute and take shorthand as fast anyone could talk, with Purvis her most important job had been to listen.

Nessheim walked over to her now, holding the

notes he'd written the night before. 'You busy, Tatie?'

She looked up at him sourly. 'No, I'm here this early because I like the place so much. What do you want me to type?'

'This,' he said, giving her the handwritten pages. 'It's important. It's for the SAC.'

'Everything's important, kid. Even documents that never reach the eyes of Warner Ferguson.' She turned back to her typewriter. As he walked away she called over her shoulder, 'I'll have it by noon, okay?'

He stopped. 'Have you heard from Mr P. lately?'

'Postcard from Hollywood. It's 78 degrees there. Lucky bastard.'

He spent the morning writing up his other recent meetings with informants — Mike Louis, at the meat-processing factory, who claimed there was a plot by Trotskyites to take over the union, and asked for an extra ten bucks a month; 'Domino' Reading, a mulatto piano player who doubled as a Pullman waiter and kept tabs on political dissidents in the jazz world (this month Nessheim was glad to see there weren't any); and Dankiewicz, first name unknown, who warned of trouble ahead with the steelworkers out in South Chicago.

When he was through he checked with Tatie in the Bullpen and she handed over a sheaf of carbon typed pages with a shake of her head. 'I'm flattered you asked me to do this — and I can see why you did. I just hope you know what you're getting into.'

35

'It's just a proposal, Tatie,' he said. 'He can always say no.'

'He'll say no all right, believe you me. It's what else Ferguson says that worries me.'

'It can't be that bad.'

'Oh, kid, you're green as chartreuse. This isn't a football game, and if it was, you'd be on your own goal line.'

'Thanks a lot. Listen, do you think I can get in there after lunch? I want to leave early because I'm driving up to my folks' house in Wisconsin.'

'Oh, he'll see you as soon as he's read your report. I wouldn't worry about that. I'll put it on the top of his stack for when he gets back from lunch.'

★　★　★

And right after lunch Ferguson called him in. He was standing stork-like (for he was six foot three) at the window of his corner office, looking down at the small figures far below heading back to work on La Salle Street. He turned as Jimmy entered and signalled for him to sit down, then took his time before sitting down himself, pushing his chair back from his desk to give his legs room to extend.

Where Purvis had been cock of the walk, Ferguson was strictly Sears and Roebuck, conventional, nothing flash — he wore a blue three-piece suit, a white shirt, and a tasteless brown striped tie. Purvis had commanded respect, in the words of one senior agent, 'the way sand soaks up water'; by contrast, Ferguson

36

was an ex-inspector of taxes who'd originally joined the Bureau out east. He had none of Purvis's flair — he'd once barked at a hapless agent, 'I like my men to do things by the book. That way we all know how the story's going to end.' Nessheim wished he still worked for Purvis, but Purvis was in Hollywood, capitalising on his new-found celebrity — he had become as famous as Hoover, and Hoover had not liked that at all.

Now as Nessheim sat down stiffly, his legs uncrossed, Ferguson said neutrally, 'We have a few things to discuss.'

'Have you read my report?' asked Jimmy.

'Oh, yes, I've read the report all right.'

'So you saw my proposal then?' When Ferguson didn't respond, Nessheim went on: 'About putting me in undercover.'

Ferguson shook his head. 'The Director's made it clear we're not going to use our own agents undercover. And in this case,' he pointed at the typed pages on his desk, 'I don't think it would be worth the effort.'

'You don't?' asked Nessheim. He couldn't have predicted Ferguson's precise reaction, but he had certainly expected his recommendations to be taken seriously.

'I think you've been taken for a ride, Nessheim. Le Saux's a Party member, yet he never provides us with information of value. Why, he can't even supply the minutes of the Party meetings.'

'Okay,' conceded Nessheim. 'But what about the *Bund*?'

'What about it? A few Krauts get together every once in a while to drink beer and sing folk songs and wear *Lederhosen* — I'm supposed to get excited? I'm supposed to put you undercover for *that*?' His tone was acid.

'They're dangerous people,' Nessheim said, but it sounded weak.

Ferguson was already shaking his head. 'Exactly what have you got? A Michigan licence plate — could be anybody's who happened to drive round the lake. Christ, they might have even taken the car ferry. Then there's a mysterious German who's disappeared. And supposedly some tommy guns, which have also conveniently gone west — I'll believe that one when my Aunt Minnie takes up bowling in the nude. Come on, this guy Le Saux is spinning you a yarn. Can't you see that?'

No, he couldn't, because Nessheim trusted Eddie Le Saux. But this was not a reason he could offer to Ferguson — you were supposed to run your informants, not become their support-ers. He said, 'Why would he do that?'

'Why do you think?' Contempt poured from the man. 'To distract you from the true gen. He didn't want to talk about the CP any more, I noticed.'

'You mean about Spain? Why's Spain so important?'

'Why? Because these are American citizens trying to fight for a foreign government. That in my book is *treason* — what's it in yours? Just what hymn sheet are you singing from, Nessheim?'

'The Bureau's hymn sheet.' There wasn't anything else he thought it safe to say.

Ferguson pursed his lips to show he wasn't satisfied. 'Sometimes I wonder.' He clasped his hands and set them on his desk; not a good sign, in Nessheim's experience. 'Here's the point. You're way in left field on this one. I know you're kind of green, but you should know better. Part of me feels maybe I should turn this over to another agent. Like Stapleton.'

Stapleton was a clapped-out veteran, who drank his lunch in the Berghoff Bar most days, and was simply counting the time until he took his pension. He'd joined when J. Edgar Hoover was still in short pants and the Bureau had a different name; he would never have passed through in this day and age. If Ferguson was trying to insult Nessheim, he was doing a good job.

Nessheim swallowed his anger and tried to sound level-headed, saying, 'I think you should keep me on Le Saux. Continuity's important with an informant, and Le Saux doesn't like change.'

Ferguson nodded — he could not have expected Nessheim to agree to the switch. 'Okay. But time for you to get back in the game. I want you to go see Le Saux next week and get these Party minutes. Understood? Tell him if you don't have them by a week from today then . . . ' He paused.

Then what? thought Nessheim. We won't use Le Saux any more? We get to save a lousy hundred dollars a month and lose a Class A informant — he didn't know of many other secretaries of CP branches on the Bureau payroll.

Ferguson saw the dead end of his own argument. Annoyed, he thrust his jaw out like a real-life Dick Tracy, and barked, 'Just get me the minutes.'

4

On the way north to his parents in Wisconsin, Nessheim stopped on the outskirts of Milwaukee to fill up with gas, pump the tyres, and check the oil and water. With Ferguson's orders still ringing in his ears, he was tempted to go into the city and try to find Eddie Le Saux. But he didn't even know where he lived, and besides, he wouldn't get the minutes any faster that way.

So he kept going towards home, heading north on the Oshkosh Highway. He could do an easy 40 mph in the Ford pickup truck he had bought two years before, and he made it to the edge of Fond Du Lac by eight that night, then turned west onto the smaller roads of farm land. It was dairy country, with far more cows than people, and the biggest buildings were barns. Not that he could see in the pitch black of a moonless night. He felt rather than saw the flat terrain of the southern part of the state give way to gentle rolling hills, and could only imagine the shock of green peeking out beneath the melting snow. The car's headlights were feeble, half-charged as if the battery was paying more attention to getting him there than lighting the way. He didn't know what he would do if he had a puncture, except pray his flashlight held out long enough to let him see the lugs he'd have to turn.

He always felt half-sad heading home, through the landscape of his childhood, now home only for his nostalgia. Because he knew he had left it behind for good.

He was also nervous. He had been brought up to tell the truth, so to lie to the people — his parents — who had taught him not to was uncomfortable and then some. As far as his folks knew, he still worked for a bank on La Salle Street, in an unspecified position that paid okay and, most importantly, had prospects.

It was not entirely invention, for he had worked there for the first six months after dropping out of college. But the job itself had almost killed him from its boredom — he'd once spent four straight days collating serial numbers of Treasury bonds. He'd been rescued by Purvis, by then already a local legend — even before he had led the shootouts with the Barker gang. Purvis had taken him on as an assistant, halfway in the pecking order between the (all-female) typing pool and the FBI agents reporting to Purvis.

'You're going to have to learn fast, young man,' Purvis had said, in the velvety tones of the Deep South. 'Ah haven't got time, nor the patience, to be teaching you. But if you're half as quick thinking on your feet in an office as I hear you were on the gridiron, you should do just fine.'

He must have done all right, since it was Purvis who after his first two years pushed him to apply to be an agent. He'd needed every bit of Purvis's clout even to be considered — he was under the minimum age of twenty-five, and he'd never got his BA, much less the law degree or accounting qualification the Bureau liked its agents to possess. There were enough irregularities to his application, in fact, that Hoover himself would have to approve it. But Purvis had been reassuring: 'You're applying from the inside, Jimmy, which helps a lot. And there's a dispensation for athletes — not official, but it does exist. Hoover's nuts about them. When he sees you were second team all-American in your sophomore year, he won't care if you were twelve years old and never graduated high school.' Though not even his football stardom would have saved him if he had been caught lying after filling out the medical questionnaire. It wasn't his only omission; he also hadn't listed his sometime girlfriend Stacey Madison on his list of close acquaintances, knowing her former membership of the Communist Party would not go down well with his vetters.

He'd got through, and after training received his badge — and his gun. Not that he ever expected to use the latter outside a firing range. For all its gung-ho reputation, the Chicago office had only a few agents who had ever drawn their weapons in anger. And none of them boasted about it, or acted like it was a notch on their career bedpost others didn't have. There had been one agent, a certain Mueller, who had been known to be too eager to use his gun (two of the robbers he'd cut down had been shot in the back). He'd been transferred within a month of Purvis taking over — the SAC told Tatie that he didn't want trigger-happy agents on his staff.

Nessheim's luck with his tyres held, even on the sharp gravel of the road north of Green Lake. Two miles south of Bremen he came down the hill into the small valley, where white snow banked on one side of the road helped light the way as the dusk moved close to dark. He pulled onto the rough drive that moved left around the old farmhouse, set back a hundred yards from the road. It was two storeys, white pine, built by a farmer in the 1880s, with an attic and basement, four bedrooms, and the standard layout of Midwestern farmhouses everywhere — big kitchen, pantry, small dining room, formal parlour, and the second smaller sitting room where he had spent evenings as a boy reading and listening to the radio with his parents.

He came into the kitchen through the back door, to find his mother at the stove. She heard the outer swing door slam behind him and looked up, beaming. Wiping her hands on her apron, she held out both arms and he crossed the room and enveloped her in a hug.

'Oooh, don't crush me, Jimmy,' she said with a laugh. She was a small woman, with thin arms and a brittle frame; her hair, once a rich chestnut brown, was starting to grey. She was a worrier.

'You made good time,' she said, looking at the clock on top of the wall cupboard.

'Not bad. Where's Papa?' he asked.

'He's resting,' his mother said, trying to sound matter of fact.

'Is he all right?' It was just after eight; his father never went to bed that early.

'Sure he is. Just a bit tired. The car's in the

shop. The walk takes it out of him.'

So his father was walking two miles into town and two miles back to work in someone else's store.

'You should have told me, Mom. I'd have paid Karlsen to fix it right away. You know that.'

His mother gave a resigned smile. 'You know your father.'

'He's just being stubborn.' His father was reluctant to let his son help, not that Nessheim had been able to do much when it really mattered. Like save his store, or the farm.

'I'm making good money now. You know that. I hope you're using the money I send you.'

She avoided his look. 'You should save your money. There's night law schools I've read about. Why — ' she was starting to say, when his father appeared from the back stairs.

'Hello, Papa,' said Nessheim, as his old man ducked under the old low doorway and came into the kitchen. He was tall, almost as tall as his son, and broader — with the wide shoulders that came down from generations of Swabian farmers. His hair was the colour of bleached wheat, cropped short with none of his wife's curls or his son's waviness, and his features were unwittingly handsome — he seemed to have no idea how he appeared to others. Unusually in these parts, his eyes were brown. They shook hands, as awkward a greeting as a kiss on the cheek. His father was not a cold man, his son had long since realised, just an uncomfortable one, his feelings held in check by a caution based on experience. As a boy Jimmy had found his

45

father a pillar of quiet strength; now he just seemed tired, even after a nap that was meant to refresh.

'*Schlaf gut?*' his mother asked, and his father nodded quickly.

They had *Spätzle* and *Hassenpfeffer* for supper, fried rabbit his mother made with chopped onions and sour cream. The heavy German comfort food of childhood; in Chicago Nessheim's meals were snatched affairs — sandwiches and hot dogs and diner food, except when his landlady, Mrs Schneiderman, bullied him into one of her suppers.

While they ate they talked, though Nessheim was reluctant to say much about his 'job'. His mother described a letter from Nessheim's sister, Kathy, who lived in the northernmost reaches of Upper Peninsula of Michigan with her husband, a Lutheran minister, and their three children. They were effectively snowbound up there each year from November until April, and Kathy was planning to visit the following month, snow melt allowing.

While Nessheim cleared the table and his mother put out an apple cake, he asked his father how business was at Merlin's store. His father sighed. 'Not too good. Money is tight again. Alberg at the bank says they've cut back their lending fifteen per cent in the last three months. Not that I'm looking to borrow,' he said with a smile that contained a wince, like a sweet apple enveloping a worm.

★ ★ ★

In the morning he went with his father into town, for Nessheim's aunt and uncle were coming to lunch and they needed supplies. They drove in silence, punctuated only by his father's laconic remarks on the neighbouring farms they passed — the Enschafts were selling up, Godberg's daughter had polio. It was the local news — and these days it seemed news was never particularly good.

Bremen was a pretty town of late-nineteenth century establishment, with high-gabled white pine houses, and shady maple-lined sidewalks. The main street was three blocks long, and had threatened in the prosperous twenties to expand, but had now contracted, with six or seven *For Sale* signs hanging over the windows of unoccupied shop fronts. Nessheim stopped by Stimpson's hardware store but didn't park.

'I've got a couple of things to do myself,' he said.

His father arched an eyebrow. 'Your mother wants some special rye bread from the bakery,' he said. 'Your uncle likes it,' he added, the flatness in his voice suggesting what he thought of Nessheim's uncle. 'You want me to get it?'

Nessheim knew his father was trying to make it easy for him, but he shook his head. 'I'll go get it, then pick you up here.'

He stopped first at Karlsen's, where he paid eighteen dollars to have Henry Karlsen fix and return his father's car. Then he walked towards the bakery, two blocks down the street. Town was always busy on a Saturday morning, and after the anonymity of city life, it was a jolt to know most of the people he passed. Even those he didn't recognise seemed to know him, saying, 'Hey, Jimmy.' He'd forgotten that once he had been a Big Man in a Small Town, thanks to a game he'd never play again.

As he neared Kretchmer's he could see people lined up for bread and sweet rolls — the cinnamon pecan ones were a speciality. He stayed outside, staring through the big pane window until he caught Lou Anne Fisher's eye, and saw the big-boned girl nudge Trudy.

He walked around the side of the bakery into the small yard behind the building and waited until Trudy came out, hurriedly but empty-handed — in the past she would have been carrying a warm *cruller* for him, fresh from the oven. Her blonde hair was tied up and covered in a headscarf, accentuating the size of her blue eyes and the crooked pout of her lips, which were cracked from the heat of the bakery. Nessheim noticed flour marks streaked across her lilac baker's blouse, and felt as if they were meeting on business. But then, in a way they were — unfinished business.

'I didn't know you were coming,' she said.

'I wasn't sure myself,' he said.

She looked around to see if anyone was watching, something she had never done in the past. It was he who had always been nervous, ducking out of sight when Mrs Fosdick came out to hang up the wash in her yard.

'I'm glad to see you,' she said, and for a brief moment he wondered whether maybe things hadn't changed after all. But of course they had.

'It's good to see you too.'

'You still working for the F . . . B . . . I . . . ?' She gave a small titter, though she had been proud when he had first told her where he was going to work.

'I am,' he said.

'Your folks know yet?'

'No,' he said wearily. 'I'll have to tell them, but — '

She interrupted with a knowing laugh. 'I know — the time's not right.'

He shrugged. 'I'd be grateful if you'd keep my secret.'

She looked at him, uncertain whether to agree or take offence.

'Well,' he said, thinking of what to say.

But she wasn't listening to him. 'There's something I want to tell you.'

'What's that?' He didn't think she was going to announce she was pregnant, since in five years of going out together she had never slept with him. He remembered Stacey Madison's louche reaction when he'd told her that: she'd said, wheezing with laughter, 'What do you expect from a girl named Trudy?'

'I've been seeing someone, and it's serious.'

'I see,' he said. He couldn't claim the news was unexpected. She was lovely, *ziemlich und zaftig* as his mother had been too fond of saying, a real catch for any man willing to spend the rest of his life in a small Wisconsin town.

'The thing is, Jimmy,' and he realised she was covering one hand in a pantomime of coyness, 'I'm engaged now.' She blushed as her hand

49

slipped down and he saw on her finger a single stone, fiery ruby red, set on a thin gold band. He knew he shouldn't have been surprised, but he was. Not dismayed, just startled. He had always assumed he would be buying her an engagement ring, though he had never got as far as imagining what it might look like.

'Congratulations,' he said, trying to put energy into it. 'Who's the lucky Joe?'

'It's Alex, Jimmy. Burgmeister. I know you were never friends, but I hope I have your good wishes.'

'Of course you do,' he said mechanically, but he was taken aback by the news, though it made sense: Alex Burgmeister was a big, beefy fellow who'd gone to high school with Nessheim and Trudy, where he'd followed a work ethic noteworthy for its admirable intensity and less attractive joylessness. He didn't have sick days, he never flunked a quiz, and he didn't make jokes. His father ran the local grain cooperative where Alex worked now; one day he would take over that farming hub. He was a safe, good bet. Nessheim smiled at Trudy now with authentic goodwill, along with some regret. Not much regret — he knew he had escaped.

★　★　★

When they got home Uncle Eric was sitting in the parlour in the rocking chair, laughing in the loud way he had. A relatively recent émigré, arriving in the early twenties rather than starve in Kaufbeuren, he showed neither gratitude nor admiration for his new country, remaining a reconstructed German burgher at heart and, bosomed by a German-American community, unafraid to show it. His deprecating views of his adopted land were expressed with gusto. By implication he seemed to regard his wife's relations, grateful for their Wisconsin lives, as hopelessly timid.

Nessheim pecked the cheeks of his aunt, a shy woman who seemed to shelter in the large shadow her husband cast, and then shook hands with his uncle. They were drinking iced tea, and Nessheim held back when he poured out a glass for himself, since he knew Uncle Eric would want a refill before lunch was served.

The meal prepared by Jimmy's mother was immense even by her German standards. There was schnitzel, with fried potatoes and sauerkraut, and two kinds of sausage (liver and spiced pork chopped roughly), and a basket of the bakery rye bread passed around with butter churned at Dreigenberg's dairy farm down the road. Once it would have been their own butter, but the cows had been sold three years before. There was corn relish, too, pickles in a glass dish, and green beans in brine, all bottled the summer before by Nessheim's mother.

'So how is the life in the Big City?' asked Uncle Eric as he tucked in. Fifteen years in America had only partly subdued the fruity yodel-like tones of his native Bavaria, and his occasional difficulties pronouncing W gave an oddly child-like cast to his booming cadences.

'It's good,' said Nessheim and kept it at that.

He knew Uncle Eric's views of the metropolis.

'We weren't sure what you might be bringing back with you. Were we, Greta?' said Eric, giving his wife a sly look. 'A *Schwartzer* for Easter maybe. It could help your mother with the house-vork.'

'Eric!' said Greta, trying to sound shocked. Nessheim's mother smiled cautiously, while his father did his best to ignore his brother-in-law.

'The boy knows I'm joking,' said Eric without concern, 'But is it true, Jimmy? There are clubs where nigger men dance with white women?'

'Of course, Uncle Eric,' said Nessheim brightly. 'But I gather in Berlin it's been standard practice for years.'

Eric gave a forced, fleeting smile to show he too could take a joke. 'That was the case, I admit. But not since the new regime.'

'Well, we haven't advanced that far in America. FDR has had other priorities.'

'*Ja*. Putting riff-raff to vork while honest men struggle.' He was no longer smiling.

'A lot has been built,' said Nessheim's father quietly.

'Badly built,' Eric declared, puffing out his cheek. 'Of course we Germans are the best engineers in the vorld.'

Nessheim said, 'Americans seem to do okay.'

'Bah!' Uncle Eric crinkled his nose.

'The Empire State Building — there's nothing like that in Germany, Uncle Eric.'

'Bah!' his uncle said again, slapping a fat hand through the air as if swatting a fly. 'Americans have all this space, and yet they want to go *up*.

Ridiculous. There is no *Lebensraum* in a skyscraper.'

'What about the Golden Gate Bridge? It's going to open this spring — the longest suspension bridge in the world.'

'A bridge. Who can be excited about a bridge, when Germany has built the *Autobahn*?'

After lunch they sat and had coffee in the parlour, then Uncle Eric looked at his watch. 'You know what time it is?' he asked rhetorically.

'What's wrong, dear?' his wife asked with concern.

'Three o'clock. Can we listen to the radio?'

'What for?' asked Nessheim's father. He usually had it on in the evening, for concerts broadcast from Milwaukee or Chicago. And he had liked listening to Roosevelt — at least at first, when his fireside chats were cheering.

'Father Coughlin is speaking,' said Uncle Eric, as if they all should have known.

'Must we?' muttered Nessheim, and his mother gave him a sharp look. They'd listened a few times to Coughlin several years back, when he'd been an ardent supporter of Roosevelt. Lately, his politics seemed to be turning slightly kooky — his talks alternated between disquisitions on the iniquity of the Federal Reserve and more conventional pieties about God's purpose in putting men on this earth.

His father said, 'I'm sorry, Eric. The Motorola's not working. It needs a new tube.'

Nessheim wished his father had mentioned this that morning — they could have taken the radio into Bremen and had it fixed.

'That's a pity,' said Eric. 'You know, it is my opinion that if Coughlin had stood for president last year instead of this Lemke fellow, there might have been a surprise.'

'He'd have beaten Roosevelt?' asked Jimmy sceptically.

'Who knows?' said Eric, raising both beefy hands from his chair rests. 'I think people are tired of this Rosenfeld you so admire. He's letting Communists take over everything.'

'I haven't seen many Reds in this neck of the woods,' said Jimmy.

But Uncle Eric waved this away. 'You are absolutely wrong, young man. If you come to the Town Hall tonight you can see one in the flesh. He is travelling from Milwaukee just to show us the errors of our ways.'

'You're kidding.'

'Certainly not. Come see for yourself. I plan to. He's speaking at eight o'clock in the Town Hall — on Spain, it says. He may find us not the dupes he thinks ve are.'

'Or you might be swayed by his eloquence,' said Nessheim, ignoring his mother's disapproving look. She didn't like arguments.

'I doubt he's a Coughlin,' said his uncle.

'Eric has heard the priest speak in person,' said Aunt Greta with pride.

'Coughlin's come to Wisconsin?' asked Jimmy's father.

Greta shook her head. 'This was at his own church. In Michigan. Eric visited there last month.'

'*Stille!*' said Uncle Eric sharply. He seemed uncomfortable now, and made a show of looking at the clock. 'We should take our leave, Greta. We must not overstay our welcome.'

Nessheim went out with his mother to say goodbye as they left. When he came back his father was in the little sitting room, listening to a concert on the Motorola.

'I thought — '

His father answered with a grin. 'I am sure the Radio Priest would forgive me.'

★ ★ ★

Nessheim stayed home that night, and on Sunday morning stayed in bed while his parents rose and went to early service at the Lutheran church in Bremen. It was no longer a point of contention; he had stopped attending in college, and by now there was an unspoken truce not to argue about his decision.

He got up twenty minutes after they left, and went downstairs. He saw his parents had only had coffee — his mother usually made breakfast after church. He went out and with the small hand scythe splintered small logs into kindling, then used the axe to split big logs into small. He filled the bin on the back porch, then carried a smaller basket into the kitchen and fed the wood stove.

He took six eggs from the pantry, also from Dreigenberg's farm, and broke them into a bowl, whisking them with some cream he found in a jug in the pantry. Cutting thick slices from the bacon hanging from a peg, he put them on the stove top to fry, laid the table, made a fresh pot of coffee, and began to scramble the eggs just as his parents came through the back door.

'Good service?' he asked.

'It was 'Save Your Nickels',' his father said, his nick-name for the resident minister, who had offered this helpful advice from his pulpit one Sunday when the Depression had first struck.

'You didn't have to do this, Jimmy,' said his mother, gesturing at the table, then the stove. But she seemed grateful.

'It's okay, Mom. Cut some bread will you, the eggs will be ready.'

They ate at the kitchen table, his parents unusually quiet. 'Lots of people at church?' he asked.

'Quite a few,' his father allowed. 'Mrs Weisborn's ill.'

'Sorry to hear that.' She'd been his third grade teacher.

'And we saw Trudy's parents,' his mother offered. 'They said hello to you.'

This didn't explain why his parents were so subdued — they'd known for months that he and Trudy were no longer going steady.

His father pushed at the last of his egg with a heel of home-baked wheat bread. 'There was some trouble last night,' he said.

'What kind of trouble, Papa?'

'Fighting,' his mother said, her lips pursed in disapproval.

'In town,' his father said, lifting his head. 'At the hall.'

'With the Communist who spoke?' He was surprised. Wisconsin was a progressive state, and this county was no exception — it had voted for La Follette in 1924, when he'd run as a Socialist candidate for President.

'This Communist brought some supporters with him.' His father scraped his plate absent-mindedly with his fork.

'Did they cause the trouble?'

'Not exactly. Some locals went to the meeting; they weren't happy with what the man had to say.'

'About Hitler,' his mother said flatly. For all her vestigial Germanness, she had no time for the Reich's leader.

'*Ja*,' said his father. 'About Germany too. It upset some people.'

Suddenly he understood. 'Like Uncle Eric? And these *Bund* friends of his?'

His father nodded wearily. Jimmy said, 'So what happened then? Is Uncle Eric okay?' Not that I care about the fat son of a bitch, he thought to himself.

'He's fine now. They were heckling this Communist, and one of the Milwaukee men pushed him. Alex tried to help him out. The biggest bruise your uncle has is his pride, but Alex has a broken jaw.'

'Alex Burgmeister?'

His father looked at him with surprise. 'Of course. He's the leader of the *Bund* here.'

★   ★   ★

He spent the morning clearing junk out of the barn, shifting the heavy items his father couldn't

57

move alone any more. They had chicken dinner at two, then Jimmy packed up and got ready to go. He wasn't going to trust his luck twice and wanted to reach Chicago before dark.

He helped clear the table, then went and stood on the porch while his mother did the dishes. He gazed out at the land that ran from the back fence down through mixed grass meadow to a small pond. The forty acres had been theirs once, and he felt an ineffable sadness that it was gone — his father said the bank hadn't resold it yet, but that was just a matter of time. Nessheim wondered, if he felt this morose himself looking at the forty, how his father must feel, having to see it every day. Then he realised his father was standing next to him, his forearms propped against the rail.

His father broke the silence. 'I know you don't work at a bank, son.'

Jimmy was going to protest, but he saw the resolution in his father's face. 'How do you know?'

'I keep my 12-gauge shells on the shelf in your closet. When I went to get a box, I knocked off one of the hangers, and your holster fell on the floor.' He snorted. 'I don't think a bank job usually requires a gun, so unless you've gone to work for Mr Capone *robbing* banks, I think you must work somewhere else.'

There was no point denying it. He said, 'I work for the Federal Bureau of Investigation. I'm a Special Agent; that's why I carry a gun. I'm required to wear it when I travel, even coming here.'

His father nodded, but remained silent. He said at last, 'I didn't bring you up to lie.'

'I don't know what to say. I'm sorry, Papa.'

His father put a hand on his shoulder. 'I think maybe we'll say nothing to your mother. She's taking it hard enough that you're not going to law school.'

Jimmy gave a grateful nod. His father added, 'I hope they've taught you how to shoot straight. Your Uncle Eric almost blew my head off when he took me target shooting.'

They both laughed, but then his father said more seriously, 'You're a true American.'

'Do you think that's wrong?'

'No, not at all. It's just that in the past they didn't allow it for the likes of me.'

'Who was 'they'?'

His father shrugged. 'You name it. The government, the newspapers, the police, the local folks — anyone who wasn't German. Some of them were even my friends — so I thought, until the night they came after me in my own house. I should have guessed they were coming after they'd written *Kaiser Lover* all over our front door.'

'Did you get hurt?'

'I was lucky. They took me and a few others with funny German names down to the Town Hall and had us swear an oath of allegiance. Then they made us get on our knees and kiss the American flag. You were five years old and sound asleep in bed, thank God.'

'I can't believe it.'

'My cousin Alfred — you never knew him, he

went back to Germany — he got it worse. They beat him with sticks like he was a dog.'

His father put both hands on the rail of the porch and stared intently out towards the back field, at the dark saucer-like dip of the soil which held part of his past.

He turned his head to look at his son. 'As I say, you're American in a way I wasn't ever allowed to be.' Through the screen porch Jimmy could hear his mother moving around the parlour, plumping the pillows on the sofa. His father said quietly, 'But I'm worried there's going to be another war.'

'There already is one in Spain,' said Jimmy.

'That's just a rehearsal for the main event.'

'I hope we can stay out of it.'

'Me too,' said his father. 'But the Communists, even the Liberals say we will have to act. You must know people like that,' he added slyly.

Jimmy thought of Stacey Madison and her circle. He said, 'If anyone can keep us out of a war, it's Roosevelt.'

'You believe that? Uncle Eric and his Nazi-loving friends think it's Roosevelt who'll drag us in. That's why they hate him so much.'

5

Nessheim made Chicago by dark, helped by not having any flat tyres. As he passed through the northern suburbs twilight was descending, and ahead of him the low slant of setting sun painted the thirty-nine floors of the Palmolive Building a rosy pink, like a sandstone obelisk. Going by Lincoln Park, he wondered if Stacey was home, and could just see her apartment building by craning his neck.

He had met her at a party on the Near North Side during his spell at the bank. She'd been with a former Northwestern student who'd seen Nessheim play football and greeted him like a conquering hero; Stacey had been amused. She was a graduate of the University of Chicago who didn't seem to have a job — not because she couldn't find one, but because she didn't want one. She was rich (the daughter of a paper manufacturing magnate), clever, and funny, and, he realised soon enough, infinitely flighty, losing interest in her passions, especially men, as soon as something more arresting hoved into sight. She'd picked him up — he still felt guilty thinking about the look on the Northwestern guy's face when she'd asked Nessheim to drive her home — and for three weeks after that they'd seen each other every night. Then he didn't hear from her for a month: she'd gone to Mexico, she told him breezily on her return.

And she was a Communist — no, an ex-Communist she claimed, since she had transferred her affections from Stalin to Trotsky. It seemed an infinitesimal distinction to Nessheim, and one that would be lost on his bosses at the Bureau, but Stacey saw it as a gulf, and hated the powers at the Kremlin with an intensity to rival that of J. Edgar Hoover. She talked politics all the time but didn't seem to mind Nessheim's comparative lack of interest.

'You're the only right-wing lover I've ever had,' she declared one afternoon, as they lay in the bedroom of her apartment on the edge of Lincoln Park.

'I'm not right wing. I like FDR.'

'Sometimes I can't believe your politics are so naive.'

'You're just saying that because I don't believe in Socialism.'

'That's what I mean — you're so naive.'

★   ★   ★

There was a smell of fried meat and cabbage in the front hall of his boarding house, drifting in from the kitchen where the landlady, Mrs Schneiderman, liked to hold court while Tillie the black cook made supper. Meals were extra for her boarders, a peripatetic bunch who rarely stayed more than a few months. Three years on, and Nessheim was the longest-serving lodger.

He stuck his head in the kitchen door. 'Hi, Mrs S. I'm back. Any messages for me?'

'Carole Lombard forgot to call,' she said, and

looked up from the comic section of the Sunday paper. She was a broad-shouldered woman of indecipherable age — she could have been sixty-five, or forty, since the fullness of her face kept wrinkles at bay. On the stove top Tillie was frying pork chops.

'You want supper?'

'No, thanks. I ate already,' he fibbed.

'Suit yourself,' she said equably and turned back to her comics. Nessheim went upstairs.

He knew that with the salary he was making he should be looking for a place of his own. But there was something comfortable about life at Schneiderman's, which even after three years kept him there. He had a large sunny room, he could come and go as he pleased, and the rent was $6 a week, a savings on the rental of a 'proper' apartment that he could send home. He wasn't allowed to have women in his room, but right now there weren't any women to invite. Stacey Madison had been the last girl he'd slept with, and he'd been too embarrassed for her to see where he lived, much less come to his room. Stacey might have been a passionate advocate of the workers' rights, but she liked to lay her own head at night on a refined kind of pillow.

★   ★   ★

'*Jimmy!*' came a shout from the hall and he woke with a start, realising he had dozed off. The wind-up alarm clock by his bed said nine-thirty. He opened the door and saw Mrs Schneiderman peering up from the bottom of the staircase.

63

'Phone,' she said unhappily, since she discouraged calls after eight o'clock. He quickly went downstairs to the phone on the wall by the kitchen door.

'Hello,' he said into the mouthpiece, pressing the receiver firmly to his ear.

'Is that Jimmy Nessheim?' It was hard to hear — the radio was on in the kitchen.

'Who's that?'

'It's Mary Le Saux. Eddie said I should call you if there was ever a problem.'

'What's happened?'

'He hasn't come home, Mr Nessheim.'

'It's not that late, Mrs Le Saux,' he said with a trace of impatience. 'Maybe he got held up somewhere.'

'You don't understand. He hasn't been home since Thursday night.'

'What?' He had met with Eddie on Thursday. Three days before.

'It's not like him at all, Mr Nessheim. I'm worried.'

'Have you talked to the police?' Through the earpiece he could hear a child crying in the background.

'I called them yesterday morning. They told me to sit tight — they said Eddie was probably on a bender. But Eddie's never stayed out all night, Mr Nessheim. He isn't like that.'

'Could he have gone somewhere? You know, left town for a reason — maybe gone somewhere he couldn't get in touch with you.'

'He'd never do that.'

I know, he wanted to say, but he held back

— it would just worry her more.

'I'm sure he'll show up soon, Mary. He'll have a good reason for having been away.' Trying to soothe her, he sensed he was not doing a good job. 'Why, he'll probably be home tonight. If he's not, you should phone the police again in the morning. And call me when you have news.'

He gave her the number of the Bureau in Chicago. She thanked him and hung up, but her voice was as fraught as when their conversation had commenced.

Back in his room upstairs, Nessheim wondered what he should do. He could call the Milwaukee police, but doubted he would get much out of them — they'd be more interested in his recent incursion on their turf. He'd better talk to Ferguson first thing, not that he figured he'd get much help from him.

It was getting late, so he stripped to his underwear and climbed into bed. But even with the light out he couldn't sleep. What had happened to Eddie Le Saux? Jimmy couldn't see him as the type to do a bunk — not with a wife and kids. Could it be something political then? A mission for the Party perhaps, taking him out of town on business he didn't want even his wife to know about. If Eddie were helping those guys trying to get to Spain, for example, he'd know he was playing with fire as far as the federal authorities were concerned, and it would be a fire he'd want to keep his family well away from. That could be it, thought Nessheim with relief.

He went to sleep at last, and the knock came as a complete surprise. He got up and opened the door, groggy but cautious, and found Mrs Schneiderman standing there, wearing a vast cotton nightdress. 'It's the phone again, Jimmy, and it's after midnight. The man said it's an emergency. All I can say is it better be.'

★ ★ ★

The lake was calm, the gently lapping water muted as a baby's bath. Out a few miles from shore an ore boat trudged north under a ceiling of cloud, headed for Duluth and copper country. Nessheim looked up and down the beach, but saw nothing but a vanilla length of sand. It was only as the patrolman pulled back the covering tarp that he looked down.

The face of Eddie Le Saux had lost its knowingness. His cheeks were creased slightly and the skin around his strong jaw seemed curiously puffy and soft, but otherwise his immersion in the water had left him looking entirely peaceful. And dead, thought Nessheim with a jolt.

'When was he found?'

'Two hours ago,' said the cop, whose name was Otis. He had blond hair but dark eyebrows, and he seemed to resent Nessheim's presence. 'We were going to move him, but Sarge said you had to see him first.'

Nessheim nodded. He'd come up at first light after the late-night phone call, from Mary Le Saux's brother, telling him they'd found Eddie's boat drifting five miles outside Milwaukee's harbour. The boat had been towed in by the

66

Coast Guard. Nessheim had just seen it — a small dinghy with only a five h.p. outboard engine — when he'd been told they'd found a body on the shore.

'Any idea how long he was in the water?'

The cop shrugged his shoulders. 'Doc said at least a couple of days.'

It was Monday, less than ninety-six hours since Nessheim had seen him. 'Is there anything to show what happened?' It seemed odd to speak of Le Saux like this, when he lay four feet away.

'He didn't hit his head, if that's what you mean.'

'He just drowned?'

The cop looked at him incredulously. 'You know how cold the water is this time of year? 50, maybe 55 degrees.'

'So how did he come to be in the water?'

The cop snorted. 'He's the only guy who knows the answer to that. Why don't you try asking him?' Nessheim shot the cop a look, and he moderated his tone. 'Maybe he lost his balance. It happens, you know. This isn't the first guy we've fished out of the lake. Chances are he couldn't swim. He falls in somehow, a wave carries the boat out of reach, and Jiminy Cricket, one more ticket for the morgue gets sold.'

'No life jacket, eh?'

'No. He looked just like this when he was found.'

'Anything on him?' He had turned to face the cop, though really only so he wouldn't have to look at Le Saux.

'Just a wallet. Not much in it. Five bucks, a

Pabst ID card, and a snapshot of his wife.'

Nessheim took a deep breath. 'Get me her address, will ya? I'm done here.'

★   ★   ★

The Le Sauxs lived in one of a row of brick houses, half a mile from the brewery on its downtown side. Inside, it was tidy and depressingly small. To Nessheim's relief a policeman had already been round to break the news, and when he arrived Mary Le Saux had stopped crying. She was a small woman in a kitchen apron, with black hair that curled around her ears, and thin lips which she kept pursing, tic-like. She took him into the front sitting room, then closed the door. The children were upstairs, she explained, sitting upright on the front edge of a sofa while Nessheim sat down in a broad-backed rocking chair.

'Do they know what my husband was doing out on his boat?' she asked him.

'I don't think so,' he admitted. 'He might have been fishing.' There had been rods in the empty skiff, two of them, but they were stowed neatly under the plank seats, with no signs of recent use.

'He sometimes fished at night,' she said. 'But never without telling me. It wasn't like him, Mr Nessheim.'

'Did he ever mention people he went fishing with?'

She shook her head. 'He liked to fish alone. 'My thinking time', he called it.'

'So you wouldn't know the name Peter Heydeman?'

'No. Did he mention him?' When Nessheim nodded she said, 'Maybe he knew him from work. He had friends there — lots of friends. My husband was a popular man, Mr Nessheim.'

He could believe that; he'd liked Eddie Le Saux himself, but was trying not to let that get in the way. He saw Mary Le Saux hesitate, so he didn't say anything, and waited.

At last she said hesitantly, 'I guess now that Eddie's gone you'll have to stop paying him.'

'I'm afraid so,' he said, masking his distaste, telling himself that it was only natural she'd be worried about money, even this soon after her husband's death.

She nodded, and stood up. As they went into the hall, a child brushed past him — a boy, on his way out the front door. There was another noise behind him, and when Nessheim turned he saw a little girl. She was no more than five or six, and stood in the doorway of the kitchen, illuminated by the harsh light of its bare bulb. She had red hair that flared out from her temples like wings, and a big gap between her two front teeth which he noticed when she smiled at him. But what he really took in were the two braces on her legs, and the crude walker she leaned on with both hands for support.

'Izzie,' said her mother, 'Go back and sit down.' And though Mary was clearly keen for him to go, Nessheim watched as the little girl gradually turned the walker, and stumped slowly back into the kitchen.

'You'd better leave now, Mr Nessheim. She'll be showing you her letter from FDR if you don't.'

So it was polio. Suddenly he understood Eddie's willingness to act as an informer. It had been the money all right, but not for himself or the Party. For his daughter. Even the diehard old-style Communist had put family first. Good for you, thought Nessheim, in what was as close to a blessing as he could supply to the dead Le Saux.

He was about to say goodbye when Mary Le Saux spoke again. 'There's something I don't understand, Mr Nessheim.' She spoke abstractedly, almost dreamily, and he decided she was still in shock after all. 'How can you drown with a life jacket on?'

'The water was very cold.' Then he realised what she'd just said. 'Eddie wasn't wearing a life jacket, Mrs Le Saux.'

There was nothing vague about her voice now. 'I don't believe that for a minute. He may have loved fishing, Mr Nessheim, but Eddie was scared of the water. Absolutely terrified. He wouldn't even get into his boat on the shore without putting a life jacket on. The police must have taken it off before you got there.'

★　★　★

When he arrived back on the nineteenth floor of the Bankers Building he headed straight towards Ferguson's office, but Tatie intercepted him in the corridor. 'I wouldn't barge in right now if I

70

were you,' she said.

'Why?'

'Something's up. Go calm down and I'll try and get you in.'

When he went back to the Bullpen he found no one working — the typists were in small conspiratorial conversations which they broke off when he walked by, then resumed. The senior agents had deserted their offices and stood in a group, smoking at the back of the floor next to the small kitchen, which held a kettle and mugs for coffee, and a cupboard for the harder stuff that came out for leaving parties, promotion parties, birthday parties — any occasion providing an excuse for a drink. But no one was drinking now.

Nessheim was in no mood to stand around speculating, so he went to his desk and started his report on the death of Eddie Le Saux. It seemed important to get that done, though he wanted to tell Ferguson in person what he'd discovered. He had just finished when Tatie stood at the edge of the Bullpen and gave him the nod. As he got to Ferguson's office, two stiff-looking men in suits were leaving.

Ferguson sat at his desk, looking harried. For a flicker of a moment, Nessheim felt sorry for him, then the SAC looked up and snapped, 'Make it quick.'

'My informant Le Saux is dead. They found him floating in Lake Michigan. I think his death wasn't an accident.'

'He got bumped off? How interesting,' he said blandly.

Nessheim explained about the life jacket — its absence, and what Mary Le Saux had said about her husband's fear of the water. 'He didn't drown by accident, and I'd bet ten to one it has to do with the information he gave me about the *Bund*.'

'Would you now?' asked Ferguson. Nessheim was surprised; he had expected more resistance.

'You see — ' Nessheim started but Ferguson cut him off.

'See what exactly? A man drowns and you say he must have been murdered because he *wasn't* wearing a life jacket. That's supposed to make sense to me?' He waved a hand in disgust. 'Anyway, save it for Stapleton — I've assigned Le Saux to him, and you can tell him all about it.'

'But — '

'No 'buts'. The decision's final.'

He knew better than to argue; he was off the case. 'My report's being typed; I can talk Stapleton through it. In fact, it might help if I could still keep an oar in. After all, I ran Le Saux. I knew him pretty well, and the set-up there in Milwaukee.' He was trying not to plead.

'Sure, kid, if that's what you want.'

He looked at Ferguson curiously. There was pleasure in the SAC's face now which Nessheim could not decode.

'You see, you're not going to be in Chicago much longer. Three months maybe, six months max. Orders of the Director himself. He wants all of Purvis's people out of here. You're being transferred.'

6

October 1937
Washington D.C.

Harry Guttman had a hard roll and a hard pencil on his desk, and in his fury was half-inclined to chomp the pencil. He might have, too, had he not just finished eating a lot of crow. What am I supposed to do? he wondered, settling for the pencil and holding it in both hands. He could usually control his temper, but he was glad to be alone now.

The meeting could not have gone worse. Hoover hadn't said much until the end, letting Tolson do most of the talking. But when he had intervened he had done so decisively.

Looking down now, Guttman saw he had snapped the pencil in two. He stared for a moment at the pair of wood stubs, then looked out the window at Pennsylvania Avenue, where people were still rushing for the trolley as the rush hour ended — say what you liked about the Depression, federal employees were still in plentiful supply.

If I just forget about it like they want me to, he told himself, I will always regret it. But if I act on it, and they find out, my goose is cooked.

★ ★ ★

Harry Guttman was forty-four years old but felt a hundred. As a boy in New York City he had always wanted to work in law enforcement. He couldn't have said why — comic books, maybe, which featured good guys and bad guys, or a neighbourhood beat cop named Keane whom he'd admired. Who knew? Even when he'd graduated from CCNY, along with umpteen other striving Jewish boys, then taken a night-school law degree while working all day for a Midtown jeweller, he had still wanted to be some kind of cop. He didn't like the thought that he was an avenging angel, but he knew that deep down he yearned for the power to keep good people from being harmed, and to punish those harming them.

He'd joined the Bureau precisely to fulfil these aspirations, though he never expected to rise so high through its ranks — he was an assistant director in charge of an investigative division in the D.C. headquarters of the whole shebang. He even reported to Tolson, who was Hoover's right-hand man (maybe even more than that, a few snidely liked to suggest). Yet he had never expected to spend more time fighting his corner than fighting crime.

He ran an absent-minded hand through the few strands of hair remaining on his head and tried to remember when last he'd had a good night's sleep. His stomach rumbled, but he ignored it, just as he ignored the weight he'd put on in the last few years. As a boy he'd been active, sporty, playing handball with his pals on the Lower East Side, running everywhere, as if walking was a jail sentence meted out to grown-ups. Now his physical activities were restricted to taking the garbage out at his Arlington tract house, and passing up dessert at lunch.

He wondered how Isabel was right now, and if she'd managed to light the stove burner this time to make supper. It made him nervous — stuck in a wheelchair, how would she get out if she accidentally set fire to something? — but his wife insisted on doing whatever she could around the house. If he'd had more money he'd have help in for more than two hours each day, but then if he had more money he wouldn't be sitting here, sweating about his unproductive encounter with the boss.

He thought back to the original break. It had seemed astounding at the time — and still did, whatever the Director thought. He'd had the call on Saturday night at home, from Kevin Reilly, a contact he'd made with the D.C. police — they'd met on a blackmail case that had gone nowhere. Reilly had asked if he could come down to the station in Northwest; there was someone he thought Guttman would want to see.

He'd had to leave Isabel with the spaghetti half-cooked, and only the radio for company, but he knew Reilly wouldn't have called unless it was important. He'd driven in, across the bridge and through Georgetown, until he came to the station house, a low cheap pile of brick due for demolition whenever the municipal coffers perked up.

The desk sergeant nodded him through, and

he found Reilly outside the captain's office. 'What's the panic?' asked Guttman.

'Ever heard of Big Ma Thornton — as in Big Ma Thornton's Establishment?'

'Sounds like a cat house.'

'Got it in one.' He paused. 'The thing is, usually we leave it alone.' Meaning Big Ma, whoever she might be, paid the police to stay away. Reilly continued, 'Anyway, there was a raid tonight. No big deal — I mean, we weren't out to arrest anybody — ' He stopped awkwardly, realising he'd effectively admitted that the cops had gone in to shake down Big Ma. He went on more carefully, 'There were a dozen or so guys in the place, and we took IDs. Probably half of them gave phoney names, and most were smart enough to have left their wallets at home. But one guy stuck out. He was a Kraut, and a noisy one — he started shouting that he had diplomatic immunity.'

'Maybe he does.'

Reilly shrugged. 'He got lippy with O'Doyle, the sergeant, and O'Doyle hauled his ass in here, immunity or not.'

'So you've got a Kraut from the embassy caught in a whorehouse. For this you called me into town?' He hoped Isabel had left the spaghetti alone — he should have made her a sandwich before he left.

'Keep your shirt on, Harry. I'm just trying to help you out.'

'What's this guy's name?'

'Bock. Emil Bock.'

'Did he say what he does at the embassy?'

Reilly shook his head. 'No. But I figure he's pretty senior, Harry. He drove to Ma's in a Lincoln.'

Guttman whistled appreciatively. Unless he was a chauffeur, Herr Bock had to be pretty high up to own such a fancy set of wheels. But so what? he asked himself, then repeated the question to Reilly, adding, 'I mean, I can't believe this guy's going to tell me his state secrets because you caught him with his pants down. Who knows? His ambassador might even approve — fraternising with the natives and all that.'

'It's not quite that straightforward, Harry. Let's get a coffee and I'll explain.'

★ ★ ★

Twenty minutes later Guttman watched as the door to the interview room opened and a man came in, stepping into the garish circle of light thrown off by a naked overhead bulb. Behind him Reilly closed the door and stayed outside.

Bock was average height but stood ramrod straight, with blond hair combed straight back, pale lips, and the square unmoving jaw of an alabaster statue. He wore an expensive-looking charcoal suit that hugged his shoulders, a white dress shirt that looked handmade, but no tie — possibly his one sartorial concession to the informality of Big Ma's House. Bock's composure seemed complete but contrived, for his eyes blazed revealingly at the indignity of his situation.

'*Sitz bitte, Herr Bock,*' said Harry casually, pointing to the chair across the interview table from him. Bock's eyes widened. Harry added in English, 'This shouldn't take too long.'

'This shouldn't take any time at all,' Bock declared, angrily pulling out a chair and sitting down. 'I am a diplomat with the German Embassy.' *Cherman* Embassy, he said, which reminded Guttman of his father, an immigrant who had never mastered his new language.

'The policeman who arrested you seemed to think you were a chauffeur.' He wanted to prick the man's bubble of pride fast.

Bock bristled. 'I am the Principal Secretary to the Ambassador. And I demand my instant release.'

'I just have a few questions and then you can go.'

'No,' said Bock, adamant. 'I will answer nothing. I want my release.'

Harry scratched the crown of his head with bemusement. 'I could do that, Herr Bock, and if you really want me to I will. Only I'm not sure what you'd want me to tell your superiors.'

Bock pursed his lips and spoke through clenched teeth. 'My superiors are quite beside the point.'

Guttman sat forward, and put both elbows on the table. 'Maybe you're right. We don't usually press charges for this sort of thing. Maybe release it to the press — you know, to make the humiliation a public one.' Though even then, thought Guttman, most people could buy their way out of that. Fifty bucks to the desk sergeant and the original booking sheet had a funny way of getting lost.

'I do not believe your newspapers would take an interest in this.'

'Normally, I'd agree with you. I mean, a man has his needs, now doesn't he? And I'm sure it's not easy, being a foreigner and all, to meet ladies your own age. It's only natural — I bet even His Excellence, or whatever you call your boss, would understand.' He was sounding like Reilly, he realised, but there was no point matching the German's starchiness with any of his own.

And indeed Bock started to relax for a moment. But then he caught himself, as if something in Harry's tone belied the reassurance he was offering. He said suspiciously, 'The policeman said you were from the Federal Bureau of Investigation. Is that true?'

Guttman took his shield and flipped it on the desk between them. Bock looked at it briefly, and shook his head. 'For a federal official, you act in a most unorthodox fashion.'

You aren't alone in thinking that, thought Guttman. 'Let's stick to the point. There was nothing natural about what you did, now was there? Or to put it another way, would the Ambassador really understand?'

'I don't know what you are talking about,' Bock said quickly. Too quickly. He was tenser now, perched on the edge of his chair.

'Oh, I think you do, Herr Bock. Like I say, there are times when a man needs a woman. And he goes out and finds whatever he can. A tootsy, a tramp, a floozy, a broad — funny how many words there are to describe what a man has to have, almost as many words as there are women.

79

But the funny thing is, I can't think of an alternative way to describe what you got up to tonight. What's a different way to explain that you paid six bucks to sodomise a sixteen-year-old coloured boy? For the life of me, I can't think of one. Maybe your Ambassador could.'

Guttman stared at him, but Bock wouldn't meet his gaze. He seemed suddenly deflated, his hauteur gone. In a quiet voice he said, 'Do you have any cigarettes?'

'Sure thing,' said Guttman cheerfully. He reached into his jacket pocket, and pushed a crumpled pack of Lucky Strikes and his Ronson lighter across the table. Bock shook out a cigarette, lit it with the Ronson, then sucked the smoke fiercely into his lungs. He didn't look at Guttman as he said, 'What is it you want from me?'

★   ★   ★

I didn't know myself, thought Guttman now, looking out the window as the first streetlamp lit up on Pennsylvania Avenue. Having turned the German, he'd found himself at a loss how best to run him, especially when the information Bock began to provide at their monthly meetings seemed so low-grade. Either the Ambassador's activities were as humdrum as Bock's reports suggested, or the Principal Secretary was holding out on Guttman.

Assuming the latter, Guttman decided he had better turn the screws. 'I think we have a pretty good idea of what the Führer thinks about your kind of man,' he'd said menacingly. 'Remember what happened to Röhm and his Brownshirts. I'd hate to see your career ruined by one indiscretion, you know. But you're not giving me much choice — who knows, it might be more than your career that's in jeopardy if we deport you to Germany. People there don't seem very tolerant about that sort of thing — my own superiors wanted me to have the book thrown at you. You've got to give me something to keep my bosses off my back, or it's back to Berlin for you, my boy.'

And it worked — at their next meeting, in a remote park near the Potomac, Bock had given him several pages of handwritten notes.

'They're in my handwriting,' he explained, 'but I have copied down the drafts the Ambassador makes for his weekly cables.'

'Cables?'

'Yes, to the Ministry in Berlin. He reports every week. He writes them out, then has them encoded by one of the cipher clerks first thing Monday morning. He has the clerk come to his office to transcribe them, on security grounds.' He smirked slightly. 'I meet with him Monday afternoon, and he's always late. Often the papers are still sitting on the table in his office where the clerk comes in to work.'

Most weeks in fact the notes were still there for Bock to read — and memorise. Consequently Guttman was meeting with Bock most weeks as well, at rendezvous arranged in the city's suburbs for safety's sake. But the information remained uninspiring. After a while Guttman had started

81

to feel he knew Ambassador Luther personally — a vain peacock of a man, intent on magnifying his own importance by inflating the most casual gossip into reports from 'high-placed' sources. A few words with an Argentinian chargé d'affaires at a reception were transformed for his superiors' benefit into a fabricated report on South American views of neutrality. An invitation to a Rotary Club lunch in Virginia led the Ambassador to claim half the businessmen in Alexandria would have voted for the Führer if somehow he could have run against Roosevelt the year before.

Again, Guttman grew impatient. The time his meetings with Bock took up was not being justified by the results. 'Jesus, Emil,' he had finally said, 'does the son of a bitch have to embellish everything? I'd fall over if just once the Ambassador said he'd had a corned beef sandwich at his local lunch counter, or stayed home with the missus and listened to the radio.'

But it was not actually the inflation of the Ambassador's reports that was the real problem; it was that nothing he did seemed worrying. And that was worrying in turn for Guttman. But then maybe the Nazis didn't really trust the Ambassador, Guttman mused, since Luther had been Chancellor long before Adolph Hitler showed up on the scene. Perhaps America was too unimportant for the Nazi regime to require an ambassador they could trust.

It occurred to Guttman, who had learned to keep all options open in his head, that maybe Bock was still holding out on him, hoping to string the FBI man along and thus keep his forays to the likes of Big Ma's house and the world of coloured busboys secret from his own superiors, without doing anything to betray them either. It didn't work that way, however, so Guttman had pushed him again, this time harder.

'You got to do better than this,' he'd told Bock angrily, waving a valueless sheaf of transcript notes in front of the startled German's nose, as they sat on a park bench in Arlington, Virginia, while rain dribbled down. 'Otherwise this time I *will* leak word of your little misdemeanours to Ambassador Luther.'

'You can't do that,' Bock had protested.

'Try me,' said Guttman.

★   ★   ★

And whether through coincidence or this coercion, suddenly something had come up.

Where is Werner?

And then just a week later:

I repeat: Where is Werner? He was due back in this country two months ago.

It was the first time Guttman could remember the Ambassador asking anything. *Where is Werner?* It piqued his curiosity, but Guttman didn't get carried away. Werner might be Luther's valet for all he knew, and the Ambassador was merely lamenting his absence.

He asked Bock, but the German shook his head.

'I know no one of that name,' he said. 'He is

83

not with the embassy.'

'Could he be with one of the consulates? Like a trade officer or something?'

Bock drew himself up to his full height. 'Absolutely not. I know them all. I would recognise the name.'

'Okay. But do me a favour — check the staffing lists, will you?'

And reluctantly, Bock had. There was no Werner on any of them.

So who was the guy? Guttman had plenty else to think about, but the miniature mystery wouldn't leave him alone. He consulted the original notes Bock had made of the same cable, and realised they had been focused on the German-American *Bund*. Ambassador Luther had wanted to attend a rally in Baltimore the month before, but it seemed he had been told by Berlin not to. And his query about Werner had immediately followed. Could Werner be American then?

He ordered a search through the files he had compiled on the German-American *Bund*. When the results came in a day later, he had asked for an urgent meeting with the Director and his associate director.

★   ★   ★

'I think you're getting a little overexcited,' Tolson told him in his flat Missouri voice. Trust Hoover to pick a number two who acted even less human than he did. Tolson was a well-built, handsome man, a smart dresser (tie pin, starched collar; Guttman had felt even more slobby than usual) and former college athlete who had parlayed his friendship with the Director into a small FBI fiefdom of his own. There was something curiously bloodless about him, a coldness Tolson seemed to pride himself on but which Guttman found creepy. Even Hoover got excited at times.

'We're not at war with Germany,' Tolson had added, to which Guttman had wanted to say, *not yet*. 'After the last one, it's hardly surprising that German-Americans don't want a repeat performance. They're entitled to their views. I know the Nazis are giving your people a hard time, but this is America.'

'Your people' — how Guttman hated that phrase. No one had to tell Harry Guttman that Hoover didn't like the Jews, but Guttman wasn't at the FBI to be a Jew, he was there because he was an American. And it didn't matter a jot to him if people were German-Americans or Eskimos; if they were bad guys, he'd go after them.

They were in the Director's office, a large corner room on the fifth floor of the Justice Building, site of the Bureau's headquarters. It would have had a fine view down Pennsylvania Avenue, but the drapes were almost fully drawn — as usual, ever since an anonymous postcard had arrived the year before, suggesting Hoover might find himself in a sniper's sights. In a corner away from the windows, the three men convened around a round maple table which the Director used for small meetings. A chandelier of candle-shaped bulbs cast a thin synthetic glow over the room. Tolson and Guttman sat across from each other, while Hoover occupied a high-seated padded leather chair at one end. He had no papers with him, and Guttman snuck a look over at his desk, bare except for an ink blotter, a miniature American flag on a stick, and a file.

And then Hoover spoke. His lower lip pushed up when he talked, reinforcing the bulldog image cartoonists liked to sketch. He wore a crisp white shirt and a blue suit, double-breasted and buttoned, which reinforced his squat fireplug build. A silver tie ballooned like a snake between his lapels, and from his jacket's breast pocket a paisley handkerchief peeked out.

'Agents of the Federal Bureau of Investigation,' he declared, letting the words roll sonorously, 'represent the American people. They have to maintain the highest possible standards — in dress, demeanour, and personal conduct. You know that, Assistant Director. It would be damaging to have them scurrying around like rats under the floorboards.'

Damaging to what? Guttman thought, but he knew enough not to argue. You could sometimes get the Director to change his mind, when the benefits of doing so were overwhelming, and when he could take credit for your idea. Otherwise, it was pointless arguing, unless you thought a spell in the Wichita Bureau a reasonable price to pay for speaking your mind.

'Informants are necessary,' Hoover went on, his eyes moving back and forth between

Guttman and Tolson. 'Even if their motivation is sometimes questionable. Your handling of this fellow Bock, for example, has been exemplary. I can tell you the President himself is aware that we have suborned a man in the German Embassy — I've shown him some of the transcripts myself.'

Guttman tensed, since praise from Hoover was usually a prelude for bad news. 'But the agent has to stand aloof from criminal elements; he has to keep his hands clean, be whiter than white. He can't lower himself to the criminal's level. And for that reason, I cannot agree to your recommendation that we place a man surreptitiously in the . . . ' He seemed unsure of his words for the first time.

'The *Bund*.' Tolson supplied the word, like an assistant handing his boss his glasses.

Hoover was displeased. 'I was going to say, the German-American community. And I emphasise *American*. We have no reason to suspect their fundamental loyalty to this country. Though of course we are alert to the dangers extremist movements pose to this country.'

'Well,' said Guttman sceptically, for he had supplied along with his request a full dossier on the activities of the *Bund*, and their increasingly vociferous support for Hitler. There had been several recent ugly incidents: gangs in Baltimore and New York had set upon innocent passers by — Jews in two cases, Negroes in another. There had been an FBI investigation of the *Bund* the year before, instigated by the President himself, but it had been cursory, crippled from the start by Hoover's manifest lack of interest.

But Hoover was not in the mood for demurrals from Guttman. 'Our priority in detecting subversion is the Communists. I have the President's full backing on that,' he added.

'I know, sir,' said Guttman.

Hoover looked ostentatiously at his fob watch, which hung from a small chain pinned to his suit jacket. 'Clyde, seems to me we're running a little behind.'

Was that it then? Guttman saw Tolson raise his eyes, and reluctantly he took the cue and rose. As he made to go, Tolson whispered something and Hoover gave a little laugh. When Guttman looked puzzled, Hoover said, 'You could always use Sidney.'

'Sidney, sir?'

Tolson was struggling to keep a straight face. He said, 'Sidney had himself a snortful at some roadhouse on Saturday night and managed to flip over his car. He's lost his licence for a year. He's not going to be driving for a while, so there's a guy you could send undercover.'

Hoover laughed more loudly, a high cackle at odds with his husky voice. As he left the room, Guttman didn't know which was more unpleasant — Hoover's laugh, or what he was laughing about.

As the Negro struggle for equality advanced, Hoover had taken to proclaiming that he was happy to employ people of colour in the Bureau. And true enough, there were Negro agents in the FBI — three of them to be precise.

One, Nathaniel Davis, was strictly a 'field

operator' — he was Hoover's gardener. The second, Anita Gibbons, had the unusual distinction of being both coloured and a woman. She was Hoover's cook. Finally, Agent Sidney Washington was an expert in evasive driving techniques, having been extensively trained at the FBI school at Quantico. Until he'd had his 'snortful' on Saturday night, he had been Hoover's chauffeur. Easy to sneak him into the *Bund*, thought Guttman bitterly.

★　★　★

He turned away from the window now, having made up his mind. He knew what he'd be in for if he got caught, but it was worth the risk. Back at his desk, he turned to the files again, this time with a different objective. Flipping through them, their contents awfully thin, he decided to start with the reports from the Midwest.

7

Three days later Guttman was in the Bureau's Chicago office talking to the SAC, a man named Ferguson he'd never met before. Guttman had arrived in the nick of time at the tail end of a purge of former SAC Purvis's appointments. Not content with driving out Purvis, Hoover was clearing out his protégés too, posting them to the remotest offices of the FBI. Many had resigned instead, which was the intention.

Guttman didn't cotton to Ferguson, a buttoned-up yes-man who wouldn't have had a choice but to follow Hoover's orders — not unless he wanted to move to Butte Montana too — but who seemed unduly eager to carry them out. And now Ferguson wasn't happy about the exception being made for one name on the purge's list.

'I don't get it,' he said, pulling at a starched white cuff. 'All these guys getting sent to the back of beyond, and you want this kid to live the life of Riley out in Frisco.'

'We've got plans for the guy,' said Guttman, without elaborating. He was happy for Ferguson to think he was just the messenger for Hoover himself.

Ferguson shook his head and looked out the office's glass panel fronting onto the hall. 'There he is now.'

A moment later Nessheim walked in. He

looked startlingly young, with the easy gait of an athlete but — Guttman was glad to note — none of the usual cockiness. His face had good features, just this side of handsome, and Guttman sensed women would like him without other men getting jealous. Some guys made enemies without opening their mouths; this guy would have to do a lot before pissing anybody off.

Yet the young man looked wary now. 'I'm Agent Nessheim, sir. SAC said you wanted to speak to me.' It was a quiet voice, deep and resonantly Midwestern.

'Close the door and take a seat,' said Guttman. He wanted to put the guy at his ease. 'Smoke?' he said, holding out a pack of Lucky Strikes.

Nessheim shook his head. 'I don't, thanks.'

'Me neither,' said Guttman, with the trace of a smile. 'I carry them to break the ice. It can help in an interrogation.'

Nessheim seemed to stiffen at the word.

Guttman said, 'You seem a little nervous, Agent Nessheim.'

'I guess I am,' he said, glancing at the clock on the wall behind Guttman's head.

'Why's that?'

'Maybe I'm for it. Like the other guys.'

'Why, because Purvis hired you?' He gave a wry smile. 'That could happen to anybody. Relax — you're not in trouble.' Guttman put his hand on the desk with finality, asking, 'Tell me, can you swim?'

'Yeah, I can swim.' Nessheim looked puzzled.

'Well?'

'Well what?'

Guttman gave a small chuckle. 'I mean, do you swim well?'

'Oh. Yes, sir. I've got a Senior Lifesaver's badge.'

'Excellent. And you can run?'

'Like the wind.'

Guttman laughed out loud. 'I forgot, you were a football star.' He reached for the file on the desk. 'You didn't finish college, I see.'

'I dropped out when I lost my scholarship. I got hurt and couldn't play ball any more. It was an athletic scholarship.' He shrugged.

'You couldn't work your way through?' asked Guttman.

Nessheim looked a little piqued. 'I was already working — I bussed tables, waited tables, cleaned tables, washed dishes and delivered laundry for the cleaning service. But it wasn't enough to cover tuition *and* room and board. I got offered a job so I took it.'

'I suppose the salary was tempting,' said Guttman.

Nessheim flushed. 'I had to help my parents out. My dad had lost his store, and his farm.'

Guttman nodded indifferently, but he liked this kid's answers. 'You ever going to finish?'

'I've thought of law school,' he ventured. 'Maybe.'

'Don't you need a BA first?'

'At Northwestern you do,' he conceded. 'But not at the University of Chicago.'

Guttman raised an eyebrow. 'Good school. If a

92

little bit Pinko, eh?'

Nessheim shrugged, but his expression looked uneasy again.

Guttman watched him for a moment, then said, 'What about politics? Do they interest you?'

'I was a Politics and Economics major.'

'Have you got views of your own?'

Nessheim didn't blink. 'None that I bring to the office. Sir.'

Guttman gave a half-smile. 'You think there's going to be a war?'

'I hope not.'

'Why's that?'

'Who would want a war?' he replied, sounding perplexed.

'The Nazis are itching for a fight — to fulfil their destiny, I guess. The Russians — well, they see it as a function of historical inevitability.'

For the first time Nessheim smiled. 'I'd say a plague on both their houses.'

'So you didn't mind when the Nationalists rebelled?'

'Well, the government there was elected — I'm not sure Franco has any right to overthrow it. But I figure that's up to the Spanish.'

Guttman looked down at the file on his desk. Suddenly he asked quietly, 'If you were hurt badly enough to lose your scholarship, then how'd you pass the Bureau medical?'

Nessheim sat frozen in his chair. He wouldn't look Guttman in the eye. At last he said, 'I guess I recovered.'

Guttman stared at him, then fiddled with a pencil in his left hand, looking down at the yellow stick as if it were a barometer. Or a lie detector — they were now using the gizmos at the Bureau headquarters in Washington. Not that he needed it now, for his own internal lie detectors — his gut instincts — were swinging wildly. He'd remember this moment, but moved on. 'So tell me, who's your hero?'

An odd question perhaps, but Nessheim replied immediately. 'FDR.'

'Me too.' Guttman's mind was made up. He would take a chance with this kid. 'Tell me, do you enjoy life out here?'

'Yeah. It's swell.'

Guttman made a cricket noise with his tongue. 'That's too bad.'

'What do you mean?'

'Only that it's a shame you like it, because you won't be here much longer. What do you think?'

'I'm not paid to think, sir.' He hesitated, seemingly unable to read Guttman's expression. 'I guess I'd like to know if it's a promotion or I'm being kicked in the can.'

Guttman shrugged a shoulder easily. 'That depends on how you view working for me. I imagine there are some guys would give their eye teeth . . . not to. In your case, it should be interesting — I can guarantee you that. It's conceivable it might also get you killed.'

'That's what they pay us for,' said Nessheim with a breeziness he clearly didn't feel. But there was eagerness as well as relief on his face now.

'I'm thinking of having you go in. That is, if you're willing.'

'Go in?'

Guttman paused, weighing his words carefully. 'Go undercover. I want to place you in the ranks of the German-American *Bund*. You see, I think the *Bund* will do anything to keep us out of a war in Europe, and then when Hitler's taken over that continent, he'll turn his sights on America. It will be our turn to become part of the Great Fatherland. And that's what the *Bund* wants.'

'Do you really believe that?'

'I sure do. Let me tell you how I got this far.' And he explained how he'd received a report, alarming in itself, of a theft of guns from a US Army armoury in Detroit.

'A few guns get pilfered in Detroit and you come all the way to see me?'

Guttman looked at him sharply, but he saw Nessheim was genuinely puzzled. Guttman said, 'At first I thought it could have been anybody — the Purple Gang, or Communists, or just plain thieves. But then I got another report — yours. Your source Eddie Le Saux bumps into a guy from Michigan. A guy who stores eight guns in Le Saux's fishing shack without telling him. And a guy who we know is active in the *Bund* in Detroit.'

He focused his deep dark eyes on Nessheim. 'One coincidence I can live with; two might keep me awake at nights. Three gets me on a train.

'I read your report,' Guttman continued, 'then I looked at your file. You're young, and that will cover a multitude of sins. It's also easier to create a dummy history for somebody when it's not very long. You're German-American obviously, which is a good start for someone infiltrating the *Bund*.'

'I don't speak German.'

'I bet you understand it. Your folks spoke it, didn't they?'

Nessheim's silence was tacit affirmation. Guttman said, 'I want you listening anyway, not talking.'

'What do you want me to find out?'

'I don't know yet,' said Guttman, trying to sound unbothered.

'Well then, where are you sending me in?'

'I'm not sure of that either, or when it will happen — not for a year at least. You'll have to be patient.'

'What do I do in the meantime?'

'I want you to go to San Francisco.'

'Golly,' said Nessheim in surprise. But he looked pleased.

Guttman had his reasons for sending Nessheim there. Even if he helped Nessheim to escape the wholesale transfer of the Purvis-appointed agents (and Guttman doubted he could swing that), SAC Ferguson would never let Nessheim work high-profile cases. He'd sideline the agent, put him onto liaison with the Treasury agents working out here, or stick him with the bean counters down the hall. If he stayed in Chicago, Nessheim wouldn't gain the experience Guttman wanted him to have.

Whereas Morgan, the SAC in California (and an old acquaintance of Guttman) had agreed to throw the kid in at the deep end. It also helped that San Francisco was 2,500 miles from D.C., a world away from the suspicious eyes of Tolson and Hoover.

'Better than Butte, heh?' Guttman said.

'I'll say.' Nessheim seemed to think of something. 'Does SAC Ferguson know about this?'

'No one knows. Except me.' He paused. 'And the Director.'

'Mr Hoover?'

'Yes, J. Edgar himself. This was his idea.'

'I see,' said Nessheim casually, but he looked impressed.

'Now why don't we get started.' Guttman pushed the file to one side of the desk to show he was done with questioning him. He looked at Nessheim and gave another half-smile. 'We've got a lot to go through, and I'm leaving in the morning. Let's start with the death of Eddie Le Saux. I don't think it was an accident, either.'

8

April 1938
San Francisco

Simmons and Mueller were sitting in the car this time; it was Nessheim's turn to take the street. He stood against a lamppost, idly turning the pages of the early edition of the *Herald*, trying to look unconcerned while keeping a keen eye on the entrance to the Bank of America branch across the street.

They were waiting for Danny Ho, but with little confidence that he and his associates would show up. Ho was half-Chinese, a San Francisco native who had been a stand-out baseball player at St Ignatius High School. Smartly dressed, a careful planner, Ho might have become an insurance executive, or a stalwart of industry. Instead he had opted to make his living robbing banks, and had shot a bank guard dead only two weeks before in Petaluma; the month before, his sidekick McCosh had pistol-whipped an old lady who'd got in the way when they held up a bank across the Bay in Oakland — her skull had been fractured and she'd died the next day. Ho and his friend were armed and undeniably dangerous, and Nessheim was glad to have his .38 under his arm.

Nessheim had been on four stakeouts in the last week, none of them productive. Three teams

98

of agents were assigned to the case, divvying up the bank branches in town, narrowing their selections to cover any given building only on collection day. Morgan, the San Francisco office's Special Agent in Charge, had been adamant the gang would strike when money was being transferred from a bank's vault to an armoured truck, since these days there was never enough cash in the tills to justify a stick-up.

They were in the downtown financial district, Nessheim's least favourite part of San Francisco. The expanse of the city was lost here; it was a small area, just a few square blocks, but dominated by a dense higgledy-piggledy pattern of new skyscrapers which blocked out the city's picturesque contours and panoramic views, an odd canyon in a city that had its own natural variety of height. After Chicago, this business district seemed both titchy to Nessheim, and also foolhardy — only three decades before, the earthquake of 1906 had levelled buildings without any regard to how tall they were.

He was living in a small rental apartment near West Portal, a new neighbourhood being developed five miles west, not far from the Pacific. He had it on a short-term lease, arranged that way on Guttman's instructions so Nessheim could leave at a moment's notice. From the corner nearest his building he could see the ocean, and on first arriving, he had wondered why the rich people of the city preferred to live east on Nob Hill when they could have erected mansions on an undeveloped coast. But he knew why now, for each day he rose and walked through the chilly fog to the West Portal station to take one of the trolley cars that trundled through the tunnel cut under Twin Peaks, then emerged five miles east into bright sunshine.

From San Francisco Nessheim wrote dutifully each week to his parents, and he heard twice a week from them — though there wasn't much news from Bremen, except the startling revelation that not only had Trudy married Alex Burgmeister but she'd had a baby already. God damn, he thought, doing some counting, she must have been three months' pregnant walking up the aisle. And there he'd been, patiently accepting her insistence that sex could not take place for a good German girl until she'd been wed in a holy Lutheran church. More fool me, he thought, and was glad to find he could laugh.

After six months in Fraud, Nessheim had been moved onto bank robberies, where Congress had changed the law to allow the Bureau to intervene even when no state line had been crossed, in recognition that something had to be done — villains were being turned into heroes, deified by the press, by books, and most of all by the movies. Dillinger, Ma Barker, Bonnie and Clyde — these were names that resonated throughout the heartland, and Nessheim saw how fame cleansed even the dirtiest pair of hands.

The heartland — he had seen it now, after deciding to drive to San Francisco. His early progress through Iowa had seemed familiar, almost comfortable, dulling any sense of adventure. He'd crossed the Mississippi in Dubuque and stopped for lunch in a diner. Two pork chops, a mountain of fried potatoes, string beans, apple pie with ice cream — the bill had been 30 cents, and the waitress had been over the moon at the dime he'd left besides.

In western Nebraska he had got caught between towns, unused to the vast spaces of the American West. He thought he might have to spend the night in the car, which would be cold on the prairie, even in spring. But after three miles and a Burma Shave sign he saw a farmhouse ahead, set back from the highway a hundred yards or so. It had a slender windmill, its spokes lifeless as a dead flower's petals. He pulled into the barnyard next to the two-storey farmhouse, which might have been painted once, but whose boards were now the colour of old silver. A dog lay by the front porch, tied by a chain; it was too tired to rouse itself when he got out of the car.

He looked around, thinking that though he'd seen a lot of hard-luck farms in recent years, this one took the biscuit. A few chickens squabbled in the dust yard behind the house, but there was no sign of other livestock, and the tractor parked in the open bay of the barn was missing its front tyre. Behind the house there was an acre-sized, knee-high patch of corn.

A tall old man came out onto the porch. He was thin and unshaven, and wore faded overalls and a yellowed straw hat, with cracked leather boots on his feet. He stared at Nessheim.

'Hi, I was wondering if I could maybe spend the night here.'

'This ain't no motel.' There was a twang to the

101

voice, like a country fiddle on the radio.

'I'd pay whatever's fair.'

The man studied Nessheim for a moment, then spat, just ahead of one boot, onto the rough planks of the porch. 'Two bits and you can sleep in the hayloft. Four bits gets you the sofa.'

Nessheim looked over at the barn. A cocoon of flies hovered in its doorway. 'I'll take the sofa. Is there a bathtub I can use?'

'Baths are Sunday,' said the man dismissively. 'There's a horse trough half-full of water.'

When Nessheim looked doubtful, the old man gave a creaky laugh. 'Ain't no horses here no more, if that's worrying you.'

'Can I get some supper, too?'

'That'll make it a dollar then. Not that we got a whole hell of a lot to eat.'

Supper was beans with a few scattered chunks of fatback, served on tin plates by the man's daughter. She looked in her twenties, but had prematurely greying hair to which the hot sun of the Great Plains had done no favours. As thin as her father, she had a hawk nose and gaunt, dried-out cheeks. She exuded a sense of inner exhaustion, which people with fewer chores to do might have called despair.

There was no sign of other family. Nessheim and the old man ate in silence in the bare picture-less dining room, while the daughter stayed out in the kitchen. The old man pushed his fork into his mouth without pause, and Nessheim struggled to keep up with the pace of his feeding.

'That was real good,' said Nessheim as the

daughter came and took their plates away. The faintest flush surfaced on the woman's wan cheeks, and her father scowled.

After supper the old man went into the parlour, starkly furnished with a rickety sideboard, several upright chairs, and a moth-eaten sofa which Nessheim just knew was going to keep him awake all night. The old man turned on an ancient radio, the tubes crackling as an announcer declared that the listeners to Cornbelt Broadcasting would be hearing waltz music live from the Lincoln City Auditorium. As the old man sat down, settling in for his concert, Nessheim wondered when he'd be able to go to bed.

'Think I'll have a little stroll,' he said, and went out the front door. The sun had dipped below the horizon line, and ahead of him he could just see the highway demarcated by a sagging line of barbed-wire fence. He turned and headed toward the barn, and was having a peek inside when he heard steps behind him.

'Never seen a barn before?' Her voice was throaty, low; he realised he hadn't heard her speak once during supper. He didn't have any idea how to answer.

'I reckon you're allowed to look inside,' she said, walking past him and entering the bay of the building.

He followed, and stood beside her on the rough dirt floor, which was littered with loose straw. Through the darkening gloom he saw stairs at one end that led through an open trapdoor to the loft.

103

'We're not on the electricity here,' she said.

'That's okay,' he said, and an awkward silence ensued.

Suddenly she asked, 'Ain't you gonna kiss me then?'

He was surprised, but complied out of politeness. Leaning forward to give her a peck on the cheek, he immediately felt her lips pressed like clamps on his, as she wrapped her arms around his shoulders. She hung on ferociously, until at last he managed to break his mouth away and breathe.

'We could go upstairs,' she said, her eyes lifting to indicate the loft above them. She paused. 'If we do, will you promise to take me with you when you go?'

To his relief she didn't seem surprised when he said no, as gently as he could. He realised this was not the first time she had made the offer.

In the morning he wasn't given breakfast, and when he left the daughter stayed inside. The old man stood on the porch watching while Nessheim drove off, as if suspicious he might not be going after all.

★   ★   ★

He liked his colleagues in San Francisco well enough, except for one, Jake Mueller, who turned out to be the same man shunted out of the Chicago office by Melvin H. Purvis for being too eager to use his gun. Large and balding, Mueller was aggressive, quick to spot weakness, and an accomplished bully. He couldn't have been much older than Nessheim, but he acted as if he had been an agent for years. He had played tackle both ways at the University of Southern California, and liked to boast that he could have played pro ball. He mocked Nessheim for having played a 'sissy' position, until someone told him that Nessheim had been second team all-American. This temporarily lifted Nessheim in Mueller's estimation, and after they worked well together on one fraud case — breaking up a Chinese crime ring which bilked members of their own community, desperate to be buried back in China, into paying way over the odds to have their remains shipped home — Mueller even invited Nessheim to come along to a party east of the Bay one Saturday evening.

It had not been a party per se, as Nessheim discovered after Mueller had driven him in his old jalopy over the new Bay Bridge, then across Oakland and into the hills rising east of there, until after almost two hours' drive they descended into arid valley land and reached the outskirts of the town of Livermore. Here they stopped outside a saloon, fronted by a large wooden sign that said *Plumholtz's*. They went inside, into a large high-ceilinged bar room, where only a couple of dusty-looking farmers sat drinking steins of beer. In a back room they found more people — all men, Nessheim realised, wondering where the girls were. Chairs were lined up in four rows at one end of the room and a flag hung on the wall which he recognised as an emblem Uncle Eric also had hanging from his porch in Wisconsin. He suddenly realised he was present at a meeting of the German-American *Bund*.

His face must have shown his surprise, for Mueller suddenly grinned and slapped him on the back. 'Cheer up. The formalities never last long. Then we can get good and *schnockered*.'

A thin man with a goitre and a string tie stood up and convened the meeting. Mueller was right: the proceedings were peremptory — minutes approved, officers elected, dues set for the following year, and an application from a local Jewish storekeeper unanimously turned down. The meeting was then adjourned and the boozing began.

Four hours later, after too many German drinking songs and too many toasts, a remarkably sober Nessheim piled a semi-comatose Mueller into the back seat of the jalopy, then somehow drove them both west over the foothills, the way lit by a gibbous moon that threw out about as much illumination as Mueller's headlights.

On Monday at work, far from being embarrassed, Mueller acted as if Nessheim had let the side down by staying relatively sober, and Nessheim's subsequent unwillingness to attend any further *Bund* get-togethers soured things between them again. They still worked together and both were transferred at the same time to bank robberies, but Mueller was now barely civil. When one night after work, Mueller had started badmouthing Purvis to a bunch of other agents, Nessheim had felt obliged to defend his old boss, who had given him his big break. The argument grew heated, and other agents had intervened to calm things down — to Nessheim's relief, since he didn't fancy a fistfight with a former lineman. After that Mueller made it clear he was Nessheim's enemy, an unnerving proposition since Nessheim was not the sort of guy who had them.

★　★　★

Nessheim noticed the car because it was slowing down, looking for a parking place. A Chevy Olympus, four-door, with a powerful engine. They came in all colours, but this one was black — the inconspicuous choice. The car slanted over to the kerb and stopped. After a moment the driver got out — a fireplug figure of a man, hatless in a charcoal suit with thin white pinstripe. This must be Arthur Lee.

Nessheim looked across the street to the car where Simmons and Mueller were sitting. To his consternation neither noticed him: Mueller was fiddling with the radio and Simmons was working on a hoagie — Nessheim could see the lettuce spilling out of one end. *Look up*, he commanded, but telepathy didn't work.

The back doors of the Chevy both opened. A tall man in a summer suit and a Panama hat stood on the pavement, brushing the shoulders of his jacket. This was McCosh. The other passenger walked around the back of the car, then stood next to him. He was medium height, black-suited, and wearing a grey homburg. Danny Ho. The two of them looked around carefully while Nessheim stuck his nose deeper into his newspaper.

At last Simmons put his hoagie down and looked at Nessheim, who tossed his paper into a metal bin, and took a couple of casual strides, cutting across Montgomery Street. Out of the corner of his eye he saw Simmons poke Mueller, and a few seconds later they got out of their car. He figured they would be right behind him when he flashed his badge and pulled his gun.

He was approaching the other side of the street when he spotted the trio of robbers mount the kerb and move along the pavement towards the bank entrance. Suddenly Danny Ho stopped and pointed to his right, then said something to his two companions. Nessheim looked across his shoulder and saw Simmons and Mueller standing still in the street, forced to wait for a cable car to pass. Mueller had his gun out. Idiot, thought Nessheim. He would have to make his move now — too early.

'FBI!' he shouted. Danny Ho immediately turned and took off west across Montgomery, just as Simmons and Mueller arrived at last on the east side of the street. McCosh and Arthur Lee stood for a moment, like deer in a headlight, then they also ran, following Ho.

'Stop!' shouted Mueller, and lifted his gun.

Nessheim punched his arm and Mueller lowered the gun. 'Are you crazy? There're people all over the place. Come on,' Nessheim said, and ran into the street, dodging a cab, until he made it to the far corner. He saw the robbers running up Clay Street, Ho well in the lead. He sprinted after them on the bone-jarring concrete, and he cursed his stiff leather Florsheims as he ran.

He was soon gaining on the second two, but when he reached the corner he saw that Danny Ho was a hundred yards ahead. Nessheim poured it on now and was only fifty feet or so behind Arthur Lee and McCosh when they got to Kearney Street. The lights were red and they kept running; he did, too, narrowly avoiding an old Model T which gave a squeaky outraged honk of its horn.

He was only just behind them now, and getting ready to pull his gun, when at last they did what they should have done from the beginning — separate. McCosh zigged diagonally across the tree-lined plaza and the fat Arthur Lee cut sharply left. Nessheim hesitated, then decided to leave them both for Mueller and Simmons. It was Ho he really wanted, not these sidekicks, and Ho was running hard — he would be uncatchable if Nessheim stopped to nab either of the other two.

So Nessheim took off up Clay, just in time to see Ho turn south into Chinatown. A labyrinthine network of shops and restaurants and tiny, dingy apartments, inhabited by foreign people speaking a foreign language. There were even tunnels: the whole neighbourhood was virtually replicated underground, in a parallel network of gambling rooms, opium dens, and subterranean bordellos.

Nessheim turned at Grant Avenue and scanned the street. It ran slightly downhill, and

109

several blocks along he could see the brown brick of the Episcopal church looming at the corner of California. Then halfway down the street he glimpsed a homburg.

He knew the area only at night, when he and his colleague Devereux sometimes came to eat at the Golden Palace. Now the red-and-green painted wooden front to the restaurant seemed dimmer in the harsh sunlight. Smells of sizzling beef and fried rice filled the air. He swerved around a squat Chinese woman carrying a wicker basket in each hand and realised he had lost sight of the homburg.

He slowed down. He was looking for anything out of the ordinary — hard to do when it all seemed so strange. A grocery store, unnameable vegetables in boxes out front; a takeaway restaurant — he could see the kitchen at its rear, two Chinamen in grease-stained T-shirts chopping away; a tourist shop, full of brass ashtrays and lamps with rice-paper surrounds; a fortune cookie factory he remembered from a post-Golden Palace walk with Devereux — he could see the old lady behind the table that held a complicated wire contraption.

He stopped short of the church. Wait a minute. The fortune cookie factory — the woman there, spied through the open door. She had looked at him momentarily, then quickly looked away. Nothing probably, but the one sign of something awry.

He walked up the street to the doorway of the small factory — which was actually one big room. This time the woman behind the table

110

didn't even look up, attending to the thin wire that ran in a loop between two metal boxes at either end of her table. On the wire hung spaced strips of warm dough. Across from her two Chinese girls were packing cookies into cardboard boxes. Behind them, another woman stood holding a pair of scissors, reaching out with a metronomic rhythm to snip individual segments from an endless stream of white tape — the 'fortunes'.

He entered the shop, squinting as the bright daylight of Grant Avenue gave way to the half-darkness inside. A sickly smell of sweet dough filled the room. The women ignored him.

A man bustled forward from the rear, Chinese with a pockmarked face, in an open-necked white shirt and black cotton trousers.

'What you want?' he demanded, blocking Nessheim's path.

'I'm looking for somebody,' said Nessheim, deciding not to show his badge. He pointed to one of the girls at his left, packing boxes. When the man turned to look, Nessheim brushed by him, heading for the back of the building.

'Hey!' the man shouted, but Nessheim didn't stop. He swept aside the curtain covering the rear doorway and found himself in a short corridor.

He drew his gun. Yanking open the door on the left, he found a toilet and a sink — both filthy. On the other side of the corridor there was a tiny kitchen, with a hot plate and a tall cabinet with a saucepan on a shelf that held ancient chicken necks in putrid water. Nessheim gagged slightly at the sudden stench and closed the cabinet door.

He tried the back door, and found it led to a small brick courtyard, no bigger than a swimming pool. A door in the far corner opened into the back yard of another building. If Ho had come this way, he would be long gone.

Damn it, he thought with a sinking feeling. He turned, expecting the Chinese owner to have shown up, angry at this intrusion. Why hadn't he? He turned back quickly into the factory building.

As he went through the curtain, pushing it brusquely aside, he saw Simmons standing in the front doorway. Nessheim raised a hand but Simmons was staring at someone else. A man in a black suit and homburg, standing by the table where the old lady had been stationed. There was no sign of her, or of the girls, or of the owner.

Danny Ho's back was to Nessheim, his arm extended straight towards Simmons, pointing a pistol.

Nessheim stopped and slowly started to raise his own weapon. Something in Simmons's face must have given him away, for before he could fire Danny Ho announced, without glancing back, 'You shoot and this guy's had it.' He gave a faint jiggle to his gun, but kept it levelled at Simmons's chest.

Nessheim took a silent step forward.

'Do you hear me, Mr G-Man?' Ho's voice was flat and accentless, nothing like the singsong caricature of Chinamen you heard on the radio. 'I know you're there; I saw you come in.'

He must have been hiding under the table. Nessheim cursed himself for not stopping to check.

He took another step forward, keeping his gun aimed directly at Ho's back — it was too far for a head shot. The problem was that if he fired Ho might himself fire reflexively; at such close range he couldn't fail to hit Simmons, who had both hands raised, his arms quivering like half-set gelatine, his eyes fixed fearfully on Ho, like a man who'd encountered a cobra.

Nessheim tried to assess the situation calmly, but his mind was blank. He could only take in what he saw: the grey-suited Ho nearest to him; Simmons sweating tensely in the background. Then out of nowhere an internal voice whispered, *Never let the criminal take charge*. He recognised the words from his training.

Before Ho could speak again, Nessheim declared in as firm a voice as he could manage, 'You plug him, Ho, and you're a dead man. I think you know that. Put the gun down now and you'll live.'

Silence at first, except for a faint wheezing sound from Simmons. Then Ho said, 'Sure I'll live — in Alcatraz, if you call that living.' He paused. 'Can't see it myself.'

There was a small splat, like bird guano hitting a windscreen, and Nessheim realised Ho had spat on the floor without moving his head.

Ho said, 'I tell you what — you put down your gun and this sucker lives. I want a car, and he comes with me. But nobody gets hurt.'

It almost sounded appealing; Nessheim

realised there was nothing he would rather do than put his gun down and wash his hands of the whole thing, leave Ho to his own devices. Only the sight of Simmons, petrified and helpless, kept him from considering this. *Don't be lulled* — another training precept.

He took another small, silent step, and it was then that he felt a slight sense of imbalance, which didn't go away even when his shoe felt rock-solid on the floor. Oh no, he thought. He blinked, and blinked again, but his eyes were teary, moistening perversely, letting him down when he needed them most.

He realised that Ho had moved a foot or two towards the wall to Nessheim's left. Why was he doing that? And why couldn't Nessheim see him clearly? He started to inch forward again, but stopped when Ho barked, 'One more step, G-Man, and your friend's a goner. I'm not bluffing.'

Nessheim tried desperately to pull himself together. He could make out that Ho had moved some more — until he was close to the wall. Nessheim knew he should shout at Ho to stand still, but the dizziness was taking him over now. He felt his legs quivering; his raised arm felt unattached to the rest of his body; an aura of fuzzy lilac blue was starting to colour the scene before him. He struggled against feeling that he was about to faint.

'*Jimmy!*' he heard Simmons shout, and in a split second he realised Danny Ho's arm was turning, and he could see the gun now that had been shielded by Ho's back. As it moved around in a sweeping arc in his direction, he heard an enormous bang.

Am I dead? That was his first thought as he lurched back a step, barely managing to hold onto his gun. In the doorway he saw Simmons stagger forward and he wondered if he'd been hit. The door swung open behind Simmons and two men rushed in from the pavement outside: Mueller and a uniformed cop. Both had their weapons drawn.

He saw Ho, his face creased with surprise as he sagged back against the wall, still standing, his arm down, though he had dropped his gun. Blood was spreading like water squeezed from a sponge across the front of his shirt, and his eyes went vacant with the onset of death.

It was only then that Nessheim realised he had just killed Danny Ho.

★   ★   ★

The next day SAC Morgan himself interviewed Nessheim, then told him to take a couple of days off. He tried, spending a day reading in Golden Gate Park and walking along the beach on the Sunset side of the city, searching the onrushing breakers and wondering if this was going to change him. He had killed a man, but he still ate breakfast, read the *San Francisco Chronicle* (which to his relief didn't mention his name in its account), and thought about how to get a girlfriend. He even slept just fine, and wondered if this meant something was wrong with him.

115

That night he drove down to the Embarcadero, to a bar tucked away on Lombard Street, where agents often gathered after work. Sure enough, he found half a dozen of them sitting at a long table, drinking pitchers of beer. Their greeting was friendly enough, and even Mueller nodded, but he sensed an unease, the way people treated a colleague after a family bereavement. After a while, he got up and took an empty pitcher back to the bar for a refill.

He could hear Mueller's voice now, lowered but still resonant. There was an awkward laugh that made Nessheim turn around, and he saw that Mueller was standing up now, acting out some scene. He had his hand out and then put the other hand on top of it, mimicking a man with a pistol. His hand started stuttering, then shook openly until Mueller, in a parody of fear, shouted '*Bang!*' in a booming voice and staggered backwards. The others laughed, but hesitantly, and Nessheim turned around to spare them the embarrassment of knowing he had watched.

Nessheim took the pitcher, brimming with cold beer, back to the table, which went quiet as he approached. He put the glass pitcher down in the middle of the table, and stood behind Mueller.

Nessheim put his hand on the big man's shoulder, and said in a loud voice, 'At least I didn't shoot him in the back, Jake.'

Mueller flushed, and Nessheim flipped a folded ten-dollar bill onto the table. 'Here's a sawbuck,' he said. 'Beer's on me.' Then he walked out of the bar.

116

Nessheim returned to work the next day, and found himself taken off bank robberies. He hoped he might be assigned at last to the counter-subversion team, where even if he'd spend most of his time chasing Communist longshoremen, he might also get to investigate the local *Bund*. Natural preparation for what Guttman said he had in mind.

But instead he was assigned to join the accountants working with the Treasury Department on counterfeit currency. He didn't like it: desk-bound phone calls, and the only field work was collecting the bogus bills passed in stores and banks. He missed the possibility of action. It wasn't that after shooting Danny Ho he was eager to shoot anybody else, but not even remotely needing a firearm in the course of his work was stultifying. The only good news that came through was that Mueller was being transferred to the Washington Bureau.

Two months later Nessheim was assigned to Fraud again; mail fraud this time, which meant he spent most of his time interviewing people — both victims and suspected conmen. Sometimes the victims were conmen too, lying about the amounts they'd been swindled out of when insurance claims were involved. After five months of this, Nessheim prided himself on his ability to spot liars before they even opened their mouths — there were body-language telltales which, like an expert poker player reading faces round a table, Nessheim had come to recognise.

He became skilled at interviews as well, finding that he could draw out confidences from even the most taciturn types, and spot the holes in any shaky story.

But all the while he was conscious that this was temporary work, and the longer he waited for Guttman to summon him the more impatient he grew. By Thanksgiving he felt at the end of his tether; he'd even tried to sound out his SAC, David Morgan, though he got nowhere. 'Just do your job, Nessheim. I'll let you know if any new orders come in.' Morgan was old school and didn't look happy himself with the situation.

Spring came, with the lilacs out in West Portal and the fruit trees all in blossom, and Nessheim started to lose any confidence that he would ever hear from Guttman again. It had been nearly eighteen months since he'd met the man. So when he came back from lunch one day to find a message to see Morgan right away, he assumed it was about his latest fraud case, which included the Mayor's sister among its victims.

'Where you been?' Morgan growled as Nessheim came into his office. Before Nessheim could reply, Morgan said, 'I've got marching orders for you, kid.' He flipped a folder at Nessheim.

'Your ticket's in there — you catch the *City of San Francisco* tomorrow afternoon. Make sure you're on it. You are under strict orders not to break your journey in any way, is that understood? No calls either, no telegrams, don't even post a letter. And I'll need your gun.'

'My gun?' He felt suddenly proprietary about his weapon.

'Don't ask me. It's orders.'

'Guttman's?'

Morgan looked at him stonily. 'Who else? If you got a problem with it, you can always miss the train. Though I have to say you'll lose a lot more than your gun if you do.'

'Okay,' said Nessheim, acknowledging defeat. He took his holster off his shoulder and handed it over.

'One more thing. Guttman wants to know your mother's maiden name.'

No gun, no calls, his mother's maiden name. What was going on? He realised Morgan was waiting for an answer. 'It's Rossbach.'

Morgan nodded and stared pointedly down at his desk. Nessheim stood there bemused. The SAC looked up irritably from his desk. 'What are you waiting for?' he snapped.

'Nothing, sir.'

As he turned to go, Morgan said more softly, 'Nessheim, look out for yourself.'

Part Two
1939

9

May 1939
Berlin

The café at the corner of Friedrichstrasse was filling up. Schellenberg sat at a table for two under the awning outside, enjoying the coolness of the evening after a hot day — unseasonably hot for springtime Berlin. On the Unter den Linden, the pavement was a moving tableau of couples out for a stroll after dinner, local residents walking their dogs, and the odd *poule de luxe* looking for custom.

Schellenberg wondered if these happy Berliners had any sense of what would happen next. So far the search for greater *Lebensraum* had progressed without a shot being fired: Austria had been happy to succumb to the *Anschluss*, and Czechoslovakia, so recently annexed, had conceded without a fight. But did people really think the Führer would be satisfied with the annexations of minor neighbours?

The future made Schellenberg nervous, far more than he would be prepared to admit, even to his fiancée Irene. He knew that the world thought the Germans ran things with impressive machine-like efficiency. Yet the scales would have fallen from their eyes had they seen the inner workings of the Reich: the remorseless jousting among even the most senior men for Hitler's favour, the cliques that made personal favour the chief criterion for advancement, the bullying and duplicity and toadying. It took all his competence and all his wiles to stay afloat in such a cesspool's maelstrom.

He had been waiting half an hour. Realising it might be an hour more he lifted an arm for a waiter. One of them, moustachioed and wearing a black jacket with a white apron tied around the waist, swooped balletically through the nearby tables and stood before him expectantly. '*Bitteschön?*'

Schellenberg was glancing hungrily at the menu — he hadn't eaten since lunchtime. Better not overdo it, he told himself, since he was here on business, not for a three-course meal. 'Thüringer, please,' he said shortly.

The waiter nodded. 'Anything to drink?' he asked hopefully.

Schellenberg hesitated. After the day he'd had he would love a drink — he'd spent the afternoon listening to Müller, that pig from the Gestapo, outlining his plans to crush the few dissidents left in Prague. But he checked himself, and pointed to the empty bottle of mineral water he had just finished. 'Another of these.'

The waiter gave a second nod, curter now, making it clear he didn't see much of a tip coming from Schellenberg's sobriety.

Schellenberg looked around at the other tables. Some of the people seemed mildly familiar — but then, he was discovering that in many ways Berlin was the world's largest small town. There was one sharp-nosed man, as young

124

as Schellenberg, sitting in a corner with a coffee and a copy of the *Völkischer Beobachter*, the Party paper. He wore a pale cotton suit, and a neatly creased brown derby sat on the table next to his coffee. His eyes strayed from the paper every few seconds, scanning the pavement. Schellenberg could have sworn he had seen him before.

Just as his Thüringer came, with a small helping of Kartoffelsalat, a Duesenberg suddenly halted in front of the café. At the wheel sat a regular soldier in the uniform of the *Wehrmacht*. The back door opened and Heydrich got out, crouching to leave the car, then stretching to his full height. He was in uniform, with a holstered Luger on his hip. He wore the peaked hat of an SS officer, and black driving gloves of thin calf's leather on both hands.

Heydrich possessed the regular features of the handsome, though close up his nose was rather long and his lips slightly too full. He carried himself with a correctness that managed to seem natural rather than acquired. Schellenberg felt certain that if Hollywood should ever want to cast the real thing to play a Nazi officer, Heydrich would sail through auditions.

He spotted Schellenberg and crossed the pavement to join him at the table. The waiter appeared at once by his side.

'*Kümmel und ein Kaffe,*' he said, drawing his gloves off. He peered at Schellenberg's plate. 'A better dinner than I've just had,' he announced.

'Oh,' said Schellenberg. 'Where was that?' He was trying not to sound nervous. He'd found

125

that Heydrich was best handled with a show of confidence, since the *Gruppenführer* had a predator's nose for weakness.

'At the New Chancellery. In the Führer's private quarters,' he added casually, and Schellenberg stiffened slightly. Heydrich elaborated. 'You may know that our leader doesn't eat meat, and although he is happy to serve it to others, it is not exactly a priority with his chef. I had schnitzel that reminded me of a pair of boots I once ruined crossing a stream. The Führer's pancake looked positively delectable by comparison, which perhaps explains why he ate it with his fingers.'

Heydrich gave a muted shudder, and Schellenberg allowed himself a small smile; anything more overt might be interpreted as laughing at the Führer, a prerogative he would leave to superiors like Heydrich. But he could picture Hitler's rabbity teeth nibbling away under the cover of his bristle moustache, butter oozing down the small pear of a chin. There was always the unspoken discrepancy between the Führer's vaunted ideals of manhood — blond, blue-eyed, wide-shouldered Aryans — and his own dark diminutive form.

The waiter came and put down a demitasse and a small frosted glass full of clear liquid. Heydrich took an appreciative sip of his drink. Putting it down, he said, 'The Führer was in a good mood this evening. That isn't always the case.'

Schellenberg said nothing, chewing on his sausage. This meeting had only been arranged at the end of the afternoon when Heydrich's secretary had called and said it was urgent, and he waited now for Heydrich to tell him why. Was the dinner with the Führer the reason? It must be. Otherwise Heydrich would have seen him the next day in his office.

But Heydrich seemed in no hurry to get to business. 'He was very mellow; you'd almost think he'd had a couple of beers. Not that he had,' he added, and Schellenberg nodded. Everyone knew Hitler neither drank nor smoked. Nor, despite having a putative girlfriend . . .

'Anyway, I had an interesting phone call this afternoon. It was from Ausbach in Vienna. He's in charge of counter-espionage now.'

'What happened to Colonel Ronge?' The Austrian had offered to work for the SS following the *Anschluss*, which had seemed sensible to Schellenberg, since Ronge would know the ins and outs better than anyone coming in from Berlin.

'He was sent to Dachau for a spell after his loyalty came into question. I believe Canaris had him released, though he won't be getting his old job back. But as I was saying,' he added pointedly, and Schellenberg told himself to refrain from interruption, since Heydrich liked the sound of his own voice, 'Ausbach rang to tell me there'd been an inquiry about a missing man. An American of sorts. I think you knew him.'

'I did?' asked Schellenberg in surprise. He was not aware that he knew anyone in America, German or not. His own family had stayed without exception in Germany — even in the

127

mass emigration of 1848 none of them had left for the New World.

'His name was Werner.'

Schellenberg sat stock-still, silent. The high meadow grass, and the pines that stood like sentries around the small clearing. It had been almost three years since his encounter in Austria with the man of this name. After he'd returned from the operation and told Heydrich that the mission had been satisfactorily accomplished, Heydrich had seemed to lose all interest in the matter.

'Yes, apparently people are looking for him,' Heydrich continued.

'What people?' asked Schellenberg, unable to picture these researchers. He could only envisage the clearing, the thick tree trunk he had propped the body against, the way sunlight had slanted through, like nature's insistent witness. 'Did Ausbach say who?'

'He wasn't altogether sure, though he thinks they said they were Swiss. The inquiry came to someone in the district office in Lienz in the Ost Tirol. It's quite a few miles west of Klagenfurt,' he added, giving Schellenberg a knowing glance. 'An organisation no one had ever heard of was asking questions of the local police. Trying to see if any dead bodies had gone unidentified. They claimed they were a humanitarian organisation, whatever that means,' said Heydrich in deprecating tones. He made a face. 'Probably Jews.'

'Jews? Werner wasn't one.'

'Of course not.'

'Then why were they poking their noses into

things?' He felt both resentful and afraid, as if what had been acted out in that small clearing had been private business, and should remain that way.

'I suppose they were operating on the principle that any enemy of ours must be a friend of theirs,' Heydrich speculated blandly.

'But why should they think Werner was our enemy? He was a member of the German-American *Bund*.' Schellenberg realised his voice was rising.

Heydrich gave him the appraising look Schellenberg was learning to live with — it made him feel like a milk cow whose capacity was constantly assessed by the farmer who owned it. He could only hope he continued to look worth his keep — God knows, there were many under Heydrich who failed their reappraisals, and lost their posts.

'They wouldn't think that necessarily,' said Heydrich shortly. 'But they seem to know he disappeared. Anyway, whoever these Swiss people are, it seemed peculiar to the local *Polizei* that they should be snooping around looking for a corpse. Strange enough in fact that it got mentioned in their regular report to headquarters in Vienna. That's how it came to Ausbach's attention.'

'What were these Swiss told?'

'Not a lot. They hadn't gone far west enough in their searches, I gather, so they didn't find a match. And when they widen the net, they'll find the fish long gone — I made it clear to Ausbach that they were not to be assisted in any way by anyone, especially local officials in the area.'

Schellenberg said nothing, waiting tensely.

Heydrich finished his drink and held the little glass in one hand, staring at it moodily. He seemed preoccupied, not at all the usual crisp figure found behind his desk, with a mind like a meat mincer. 'I found this evening a very unusual occasion,' he said, letting his lower lip drop to suggest again what he'd thought of the meal. 'Over dinner, the Führer began to reminisce. At first, I was slightly taken aback. It was my understanding from Himmler that there was something particular Hitler wanted to discuss. Instead he began talking about the *Putsch*. Not the *Putsch* per se,' Heydrich corrected himself. 'But his time in prison afterwards. He did six months, you know.'

'I thought it was longer,' Schellenberg said mildly. Hitler's incarceration had assumed legendary proportions in Nazi lore. History — the Goebbels-directed official history, that is — now painted the *Putsch* as a courageous uprising that had been crushed with autocratic brutality by a decadent regime. The facts as far as Schellenberg knew were that the 'insurrection' had collapsed into farce like a leaky balloon. It had fizzled out almost right away — within twenty-four hours the leaders, including Hitler, had all been arrested, and the hoped-for uprising had been confined to a few hundred Party members marching around Munich for a night.

He wondered when Heydrich would get to the business at hand, though he listened with interest, since it wasn't often that one got to hear a first-hand account of the Führer.

Heydrich explained that when Hitler was sentenced for leading the abortive rebellion, he had been sent to jail in Landsberg, outside Munich. His conditions had been anything but spartan — he had a large room to himself, with a view no less, and both the guards and most of his fellow inmates were sympathetic to his cause. One guard in particular had made it his duty to look after Hitler. His name was Seitz, and he was Austrian, which put Hitler in his favour already; he'd also been impressed by Hitler's audacity in leading the attempted *Putsch*. And he was a friend of Ernst Röhm, who had participated in the *Putsch* too, but managed to escape doing any time.

Schellenberg must have raised an eyebrow, for Heydrich looked at him. 'Not that kind of friend,' he said sternly, effortlessly reading Schellenberg's mind. 'They served in the war together.'

Like Hitler, Heydrich went on, Seitz had been an enlisted man, and like the former corporal he held the same bitter view of the leaders who had let them and their country down. It was natural, therefore, that Seitz did countless small favours for prisoner Hitler, including supplying him with pens and paper.

'For writing letters?'

'For writing *Mein Kampf*,' Heydrich said, raising a reproachful eyebrow.

'Of course,' said Schellenberg, and studied his plate.

Doubtless Seitz would have become just

131

another of Hitler's followers, joining the Party in time, possibly rising to a middling rank in the SS which would have seen him now patrolling the old Czech border. But then something had happened.

'Some prisoners were transferred to Landsberg from the city jail in Munich. Among them was a young radical named Driberg. A Bolshevik of sorts, though not a very brave one it seems — he had sat out the war in Switzerland rather than fight. In Landsberg he was shunned by most of the other prisoners; the rest liked to torment him — pissing in his food tray, banging on the walls when he tried to sleep. Driberg seemed to think the Führer was responsible for this, that he incited the other men to make his life hell.' Heydrich shrugged, which suggested this might have been the case. 'Then something snapped in the man, and he broke into Hitler's room and attacked him.'

'Really?' Schellenberg tried to picture this, but couldn't — it seemed the equivalent of a Christian punching Jesus.

'Yes, but not with his fists,' added Heydrich, as if to say the man wouldn't have dared. 'He took the coward's approach, and used a knife.'

'*Mein Gott.* What happened?'

'The guard Seitz was passing and intervened. He disarmed Driberg, but not before sustaining wounds, terrible ones in his chest apparently.'

'Did he die?'

Heydrich shook his head. 'No, not then at any rate. The Führer said he seemed to make a full recovery, though he was in hospital for a time.

When the Führer's sentence was up and he left, he found among all the guards lined up to say goodbye Seitz standing there, in uniform, as good as new. But six months later, he did die, from an infection in his chest — it wasn't hard to link it to Driberg's attack. Funny,' he said dispassionately, 'even after all these years the Führer was very moved remembering him.'

'Did the Führer feel guilty about Seitz?' Schellenberg ventured, putting down his fork as he swallowed the last morsel of potato salad.

'Guilty?' demanded Heydrich, seeming to enjoy the flicker of panic on his younger associate's face. 'Certainly not. The Führer thought Seitz was lucky to have had the good fortune to die for our cause.' He added with a trace of amusement, 'As he was, of course.'

'Of course,' said Schellenberg, avoiding Heydrich's eyes. They sat in silence as the waiter approached. Schellenberg suddenly wanted a large glass of Riesling to help him through this mystifying meeting. What precisely did Heydrich want? Had Schellenberg really been called to this night-time rendezvous to listen to him show off his knowledge of Hitler's personal history? But when Heydrich ordered another kümmel, Schellenberg thought better of it and gestured to the waiter that he was fine with his water.

'That would normally have been the end of the story,' Heydrich said, with a tantalising undertone. Schellenberg knew enough to wait. And soon Heydrich went on.

A year later as the financial crisis continued to grip the Weimar Republic, Hitler had been in

Berlin when Röhm came to see him. Seitz was long dead, but Frau Seitz was still alive. Though only just — she had been diagnosed with cancer, and had only a few months to live. A sad story, but one which Röhm himself would normally have dealt with — a small cheque in gratitude for her husband's bravery, perhaps, but nothing more.

Frau Seitz wasn't looking for money, however, at least not directly. Her concern was for her son, still just a boy and about to be left all alone in the world — she didn't elaborate, but it was clear that there was no family close enough to take the lad in. He'd probably end up in a state *Waisenhaus* — orphanages that condemned you to a meagre life at best. What she wanted, she explained to Röhm, was to send the boy to America. Would he, or Hitler (for it was Hitler really, even then, she was asking) help provide the fare?

Rather dismissively, Röhm had spoken to Hitler about the request, but surprisingly the Führer had ordered him to help her at once; Heydrich said Hitler seemed to enjoy recalling his generosity. Then as if to counter any suggestion that he had simply been soft, Hitler told Heydrich that he could see the use of a German in America who would always owe a debt of gratitude to the Fatherland. And the Party would have a middleman there, a contact, who would keep in touch with the boy and make sure this was the case.

Heydrich sipped from his new glass of kümmel, smacking his lips as he put his glass down. This gave Schellenberg time to venture a question. 'Why was Werner made the contact?'

Heydrich sighed, suggesting to Schellenberg that he thought it had been a mistake — otherwise, why had Werner been killed? But then Heydrich surprised him, saying, 'Actually, he wasn't the contact originally. It was Jahnke.'

Jahnke? Schellenberg was even more startled. The son of a Pomeranian landowner, Jahnke was a veteran member of the intelligence service, recruited long before the rise of the Party. Recently he had been running intelligence for the Foreign Service under von Ribbentrop. For this, he had earned the distrust of Himmler and, Schellenberg assumed, Heydrich.

But Heydrich's voice stayed neutral. 'Jahnke had been in America a long time when this occurred. He had a business there in the West before the war; during the war, of course, he proved invaluable.'

Schellenberg remembered the stories — how Jahnke had helped foment industrial disorder in several American cities; how, more damagingly, he had planned the bomb that had gone off in Philadelphia towards the end of the war, killing ten and wounding scores. It was hearsay, of course, but then that was always the case in the espionage business: in a trade that was by definition secret, there was no such thing as a reliable history.

'Jahnke placed the boy with a family of sympathisers, who'd moved to America many years before. When Jahnke came back to Germany, he handed over liaison duties to

Werner. That wouldn't have mattered — it was because Röhm retained a personal interest in the boy. But quite coincidentally, the boy grew up to become very well placed. It was then that the Führer saw an opportunity.'

'Remarkable. But why wasn't he spotted by the Americans? I mean, if he was placed with a German-American family over there.'

'The boy got to America early enough to lose any trace of a German accent. And the link was with Jahnke at first, and for all I distrust Jahnke, I have never thought him an agent of the Americans. In any case, he was back here by then, and Werner was made the point of contact. Not by Jahnke — he knew Werner was a fool,' he added, sniffing slightly, then gave a small sigh. 'It was Röhm's choice. Hitler left him to sort out the details.' He sighed again, probably at the thought of how much unnecessary trouble had been caused by the captain — bully, predatory homosexual, leader of the SA, all in all the worst aspects of the Party's military side. Then Heydrich seemed to pull himself together. 'Once it became clear that this boy had managed to establish himself as an American, and in a privileged position to boot, it became necessary to protect his secret.'

Which was why Werner had to die, thought Schellenberg. But it hadn't been that simple, had it? Heydrich confirmed this when he said, 'The problem was, Röhm arranged for Werner to communicate with us via the embassy. It should have only been a conduit, but Werner couldn't keep his mouth shut. I suppose he felt he needed to explain himself, justify why he was allowed to send transmissions back. Whatever the reason, he talked. Which meant someone else knew as well.'

Schellenberg looked at him questioningly, and Heydrich answered impatiently, 'The Ambassador. And when Werner disappeared, we received a cable from the Ambassador asking where he was.'

'Oh, no.'

'Quite. We recalled Ambassador Luther right away.'

Schellenberg remembered this. Eyebrows had been raised when the former President of the former Republic, made Ambassador as a sop to the old-style diplomats still in place, had been brought back from Washington peremptorily.

Now Schellenberg knew why, but the satisfaction of solving that small mystery was far outweighed by the chilling realisation that this American plant, fruit of a guard's brave intervention years before, must be more important than even Schellenberg had sensed, since in order to protect his hidden identity a man as distinguished as Herr Luther had been humiliated.

'You see what is missing?' Heydrich eyed him keenly.

It wasn't clear to Schellenberg whether he was supposed to know or not, so he simply said truthfully, 'I'm not sure if I do. Except that if Werner was the connection, and he only told the Ambassador, then no one in America knows this man is there.'

'Exactly.' Heydrich seemed delighted. 'I knew

your lawyer's training would show through. No one knows at all.'

'What about our Washington friend?' The other contact at the embassy. 'Can we not use him as an intermediary?'

Heydrich shook his head emphatically. 'As far as he knows, he is simply there to help the *Bund*. Since the Führer himself has publicly forbidden German citizens in America from joining it, he will think he has a highly secret mission. He won't suspect that he's serving any other purpose — the best way to use a decoy is to plant one who doesn't realise that's his role. Which is particularly true in this case, since this embassy fellow is no more reliable than Röhm.' He added drily, 'And with the same deviant predilections.'

Schellenberg must have looked surprised, for Heydrich explained, 'Not that this is known. He would have been booted out of the Foreign Office if it were.'

Schellenberg nodded thoughtfully. Heydrich was famous for his knowledge of the personal peccadilloes of his colleagues, subordinates, and sometimes even superiors — Heydrich had hinted more than once in Schellenberg's presence that Field Marshal Göring had a private fondness for opiates. Still, it seemed remarkable to Schellenberg that Heydrich would know of the sexual preferences of a middle-ranking member of the Foreign Service staff based in Washington. 'You must have a very good source,' he said now, trying, not altogether successfully, to sound complimentary.

'I do,' said Heydrich simply. 'But then, I am paid to know about people. Even people working directly for me — perhaps I should say especially for people working for me.' He had put his glass down but still stared at it. Schellenberg tried not to show the agitation he was starting to feel. Heydrich went on, with a calmness that seemed contrived, 'Say, for example, that a member of my staff wanted to get married. Normally a matter of congratulations, but in this case there's a problem: his bride-to-be has something irregular about her. Spitzer my adjutant is awfully good at flushing these things out.'

'Spitzer?' The name rang a bell. Slowly a picture formed in Schellenberg's mind like a sketch under construction by a police artist, until suddenly it corresponded with the face of the man he had noticed earlier here in the café, sitting with his eyes darting around him, a creased brown derby on the table before him. Schellenberg instinctively looked over at the corner of this outside section of the café, but the man was gone. 'Was he . . . ?' he started to ask, staring at the now-empty table.

Heydrich shrugged, then smiled broadly, like a cat who knows his mouse has backed himself into a corner. 'Spitzer is everywhere,' he declared. 'That's the point of having a man like him around. But back to my little story. Perhaps the fiancée has a dubious antecedent — a mother with some foreign blood. Something *lumpen* and normally unacceptable. Slav, perhaps, or even Polish.'

Schellenberg was trying not to flinch. How

had this man learned about Irene? Even she hadn't known until the last month that her mother had Polish blood.

'Marriage of that sort would be out of the question for your average Party official. But for a valued member of my organisation a waiver could be arranged.' He paused to let this sink in. 'Or not.'

The message was clear: Heydrich had a hold on him, despite all Schellenberg's best efforts to avoid putting himself in that position. It didn't matter now, perhaps, since he had not crossed Heydrich in any way he knew of. Indeed, it sounded as though he was being given dispensation to marry Irene. But he would be beholden to Heydrich ever after — like almost everyone else who worked for the man.

Schellenberg tried to collect his thoughts. *Stick to business*, he told himself, as he always did when meeting with the *Gruppenführer*. 'If the man in the Washington embassy is not to be involved, then how do we make contact with the *Dreiländer*? Assuming we wish to.'

'Oh, we may well wish to,' said Heydrich knowingly. 'Though the Führer says that will be up to Roosevelt. If he finishes his term and bows out gracefully, then there will be no need to contact our friend over there. No one else is going to drag America into the war. But if Roosevelt lets the Jews persuade him that he's needed, then that will be a different matter.'

'So how — ' began Schellenberg.

But Heydrich cut him off with a short chop of his hand. 'The answer lies abroad.'

'Abroad? Why there?'

'If the link comes from here in Germany — either written or radio transmission — then we are just asking for trouble. The Americans are innocent in many ways, but they seem to have a natural aptitude for technology. I am convinced that half the transmissions coming from our people over there are either overheard in Washington — or actually controlled by the Americans. I wouldn't be surprised if they've turned over most of our agents. We can't afford that to happen with *Dreiländer*. So I've chosen a different route for our communications, which are strictly one way. You see that, too, I take it?'

Schellenberg thought for a moment. Yes, of course he did, but he was wary, in case his view differed from Heydrich's. There was always an agenda, wasn't there? Sometimes ideological, sometimes personal, but always *political*. Which meant truthful replies were often more dangerous to express than bromides; highly intelligent men, capable of the most complex manoeuvres and intrigues in private, were impotent to speak the truth.

Taking his silence for assent, Heydrich went on, 'We need a trigger in his case and we arranged that with him, even before Werner was removed. It was a backup channel precisely in case something happened to Werner.'

Schellenberg thought about this for a moment, and then said at last, 'How do we contact the *Dreiländer* then?'

Heydrich smiled again, pleased that Schellenberg had got there in the end. But he didn't answer the question directly. 'I need you to make a trip. How are you fixed?'

Schellenberg thought of his office, the dizzying pile of reports that sat like Sisyphus's rock on his desk — the more he read, the more there was to read. If he went away, the pile would be twice the height on his return. 'Not so well,' he said.

Heydrich was shaking his head already. 'Take your time, and take your new bride with you.' He saw the surprise on Schellenberg's face and suddenly clapped him on the shoulder. 'Excellent cover for your mission. But you need to go well before the end of summer. You wouldn't want to find yourself stuck there if war broke out, now would you?'

'Stuck where?' asked Schellenberg.

'In England. That's where I need you to go. If we want *Dreiländer* to make his move, the message will come from England. No one in America would expect their President's death warrant to come from that small, presumptuous island.'

10

Nessheim took his copy of the *Deutscher Weckruf und Beobachter*, house organ of the German-
American *Bund*, and shoved it into the trash.
What a mouthful, and what a terrible paper.
Amidst its unread pages he had placed torn-up
bits of the letter he'd received from the post
office. C/o P.O. Box 172 — the address made
him feel transient, as well as phoney. Phoney
went with the job, he supposed. If there was a
war, and he was starting to think there couldn't
help but be one in Europe soon, would he really
have to go through it under the name *Chug?*
That was what all the girl campers called him.
For Christ's sakes, it was as bad as Chip.

Membership in the *Bund* gave him a subscrip-
tion to its newspaper. Joining had been at Guttman's
insistence, as had Nessheim's adoption of a phoney
name — this time a surname. He couldn't really
fault the logic when Guttman said, 'We can't
have you up there under Nessheim, just in case
somebody's seen you play football.'

At least he'd been allowed to keep his first
name. Guttman had said, 'That way, you'll react
if somebody shouts 'Hey, Jimmy'.'

Only nobody did. They shouted, 'Hey, Chug'
instead.

If Nessheim didn't like the subterfuge much, God knows what his mother would make of it. She must have been puzzled to be writing to a P.O. box, and mystified that his new employer, which he'd told her was the US Treasury Department, had him working in Vermont. Small-town Vermont, to boot, though from what he gathered there wasn't really anything *but* small-town Vermont.

★   ★   ★

He turned the corner onto Central Street, a straight stretch of neat shops that were well-preserved and freshly painted. There was money in this town, though from what Nessheim had seen, it was a different story in the countryside. For all the picture-postcard beauty of Woodstock — the elegant Episcopal church, the town green with its iron railings, the quaint covered bridges — the country around it was poor farming land, rocky and too broken up by mountains to allow large crop conversions. It was as green as Wisconsin but without its lushness, and there was a flint resilience to the people here that suggested the good life for them would always have to be a hard life. It seemed fitting that the place was full of quarries.

Now Nessheim saw the girls gathered on the pavement outside the drugstore, excitable as moths. They wore the camp uniform of green shirts, brown skirts, and green socks. He could also see the gangly figure of Frances Stockton, hair pulled back, corralling them, and he went to

144

help her herd the girls onto the camp bus. There Emmet Hale, who drove the local school bus during the rest of the year, sat yawning in the driver's seat as they trooped aboard.

Nessheim plopped down next to Frances in the front row, from which they could both turn and stare down any misbehaviour in the rows behind. Not that there was much to deal with — the 'campers' ranged in age from eight to twelve. They were all German-American, and likeable kids for the most part, though Nessheim didn't even pretend to understand the ways of young girls — all giggles one minute, tears the next.

He found Frances hard to make out, too. She was not much older than Nessheim, but acted like she had a decade's worth of living experience over him. Assertive, often prickly, Frances was a modern woman — smoking cigarettes, professing a fondness for gin (though there was no drinking allowed at Camp Schneider), and always wearing trousers. She was a sharp-featured Yankee from a genteel family that had fallen on hard times, and she made it clear she found the sheer Germanness of Camp Schneider repellent, and was working there only because it was close to her parents' home in New Hampshire. Nessheim was for some reason exempted from her disdain for German stock, though he failed to meet her high standards on other counts — especially education. She let him know early on that she had graduated from Wellesley, and viewed 'Rossbach's' failure to graduate from college with ill-disguised compassion.

145

If she could be cutting to Nessheim, she could also be coy. 'Some people say I look a little like Katharine Hepburn,' she'd confided one evening, but though Nessheim had watched the movie *Holiday* the year before he couldn't see the similarity himself. True, Frances was also tall and uncurved and wore her hair up, but except on the tennis court, she moved awkwardly, with legs and arms that were all sharp angles. Sitting next to her he was always worried he'd get clocked by an elbow.

'Get your business done?' Frances asked now, slightly peeved.

'Yes, thanks. Had to mail a letter.'

'You always do.' She paused but didn't let it go. 'Who's the lucky girl, then?'

He smiled with a dutiful amusement he didn't feel. 'My aunt, actually.'

'Good boy,' said Frances, managing to sound as patronising as an older sister. 'You're on the aisle, so you can do the count.'

He got up and faced the back of the bus, counting quickly to himself. A minute later he declared, 'I'm one short.'

'You can't be. Everybody was with me outside the drugstore.' Suddenly the bus door opened. Nessheim turned and saw Emmet gesturing at someone outside. Nessheim saw to his surprise that it was Adele Kugel, running towards the bus, looking pale as a sheet. She was a nice girl, if a little docile — this was unlike her.

He went down the steps. 'Where've you been?' he asked, more in relief than anger.

She avoided his questioning eyes, saying,

146

'Sorry, I had to buy something.'

'Okay, hurry up and get on the bus,' he said. He turned to follow her on board when something caught his eye, and he stared down the street to where a car was parked in front of the post office. It was a Dodge Roadster, and its driver sat in front with his feet up on the dashboard. The pose was familiar to Nessheim, as was the fedora tipped down over the driver's eyes.

'You comin' then?' Emmet shouted out crankily.

'Just a minute,' said Nessheim, his eyes focused on the car. He took a few steps towards it, feeling adrenalin start to surge through him. He remembered the menacing voice back in Milwaukee — *Like I said, beat it*. Then as he peered at the car he relaxed. The plates were green and white — Vermont plates. Besides, there were plenty of Dodges around, and plenty of fedoras.

Nessheim went and sat down next to Frances as the bus started up. They moved north onto Route 12, passing a vast mansion on the outskirts of town, its bricks the colour of burnt oranges. He felt jumpy about the fedora false alarm, and realised it was the first true nervous moment he'd experienced since arriving in Vermont. What an anti-climax this assignment was proving to be, for all of Guttman's strictures on secrecy and his insistence that this undercover work was of critical importance. It was hard to see anything critical about teaching little girls how to swim. Just why had Guttman placed him in this backwater?

11

The trip east had seemed to take for ever. Nessheim had left early in the morning, taking a ferry over to the station in Oakland — the only trains out of San Francisco went south along the peninsula. The *City of San Francisco* was a long string of gleaming cars, yellow and grey with red trim. He hopped on the rear first car and walked down the middle corridor of the train, looking with envy at the luxury of the Pullman sleepers, then took a seat in the chair car. The Bureau had bought him a berth, but he had cashed in his ticket for an upright seat, and in Cheyenne, Wyoming, defied orders, wrapping the $50 he'd saved in tissue paper and mailing it to his mother. In Chicago he had changed stations; when at La Salle Street he looked in a phone book to see if Stacey was still living on Lincoln Park, he discovered she was, but this time he obeyed Guttman, and didn't call her.

He'd had plenty of time to think on the train, though his situation seemed persistingly unreal. After all, it had been eighteen months since his sole encounter with Guttman, the man who was pulling his career strings like a marionette. Nessheim remembered the afternoon of their encounter vividly. He had been standing around shooting the breeze with Ferguson's secretary and agents Lithgow and Franklin.

Lithgow jerked a thumb towards the SAC's

office, where Ferguson was talking to a stranger. 'Who's the sheeny?'

Franklin shrugged. 'Some big shot from D.C.'

'What, a Congressman or something?' asked Lithgow.

'No,' said Franklin. 'He's from the Bureau.'

'Really?' said Lithgow, who liked to wear starched collars and gold tie pins. 'Jeeze, what must Hoover make of him?'

Nessheim turned to look through the half-window of the SAC's door. He saw the man talking with Ferguson. He was wearing an ugly chocolate-brown suit, with a wide tie that had a knot the size of a pastry. He had receding hair and a sweaty forehead and eyes the colour of cocoa, and this late in the day his cheeks were sprinkled with iron filings that shouted their need for a second shave. Short but heavily built, he looked like an oversized bowling ball.

Then Ferguson had come out, and pointed at Nessheim. 'There's an assistant director from Headquarters sitting in my office. Name of Guttman. He wants to talk to you.'

And eighteen months later, when Nessheim had started to wonder out in San Francisco if Guttman's plans for him were real, he'd finally received his second set of marching orders from the man, with a train ticket and a large dossier on the German-American *Bund* which he read on his journey east. Nessheim's existing view of the organisation, shaped by Uncle Eric and the drunken get-together out in Livermore with Mueller, was soon and sharply changed by its contents.

149

Originally founded as the Friends of New Germany (and renamed the *Bund* in 1935), the organisation had grown rapidly at first. But that had been a time when right-wing groups had sprouted like weeds across America, growing in the dessicated soil of the Depression, fed by populist fears and populist hopes for a strong leader. Most notably, Father Coughlin of Detroit had for a time enjoyed a popularity that threatened the traditional institutions of the country.

But Uncle Eric's favourite had fallen from his peak, after an ill-conceived attempt in 1936 to back an independent presidential candidate through his *Social Justice* newspaper. The campaign had failed pathetically; far from strengthening Coughlin's National Union movement, it had crippled it. Coughlin was losing his audience — literally, since radio stations across the country were dropping him.

Threatened with the worst enemy of all — obscurity — the priest had become shriller in his pronouncements. The latently anti-Semitic tirades against the banks were now openly anti-Jew. His hatred of Roosevelt seemed almost pathological. His latest venture, the Christian Front, represented the desperation of a man who had reached out for the chalice of national power only to see it slip through his hands.

The *Bund* had also lost much of its membership — the Bureau report had it under 8,000 — even as Nazi Germany went from seeming strength to strength. Perhaps that was the problem, for after 1936, Hitler and his bunch said they wanted nothing to do with German-American imitations, fearing that goose-stepping swastika-wielding burghers on the streets of Baltimore, Chicago, and New York would only drive most Americans into the arms of a war-wishing President, whose sympathies — or antipathies — were all too clear.

You couldn't blame the Nazis for stepping away from the *Bund*, thought Nessheim as the train chugged halfway across Nebraska, since even a cursory inspection of the organisation showed its members to be an unimpressive lot. Some of them were little more than clowns, including their leader, Thomas Kuhn (German-born but like Coughlin living in Detroit), who claimed an intimacy with the Führer based on nothing more than shaking his hand at the Berlin Olympics in 1936.

* * *

Guttman greeted him at Grand Central. Even at night the ticketing hall was busy, with late commuters in suits and woman shoppers in heels crossing the marble floor under the vast vault. Guttman led him out a side entrance onto a street hazily lit by sulphur lamps. Along the kerb yellow cabs were lined up, and Nessheim expected they'd take one to the Bureau offices, but Guttman walked right past them. Nessheim followed him uneasily, as they moved north a couple of blocks.

They turned off Lexington onto a side street, a block of six-storey brick buildings that were a mix of storefront and apartments. Nessheim could see it was not a classy part of town. They came to a small hotel with a tarnished plaque on the wall that said *The Stanley*. The dowdy ground-floor lounge was deserted except for a clerk with a pencil tie who sat with his eyes half-shut behind the reception desk. Guttman ignored him and walked to the elevator, where he jabbed at its bakelite button. When it arrived they ascended slowly to the fifth floor, and Nessheim followed Guttman down a dusty corridor until the older agent unlocked a door at the end of the hall.

It was a suite — Nessheim could see a small bedroom through the open doorway on the room's far side — and the sitting room held two flattened sofas positioned at right angles and a small dining table of badly cut maple, with four chairs around it. Guttman hit a switch, and light the colour of smoky caramel illuminated the dingy quarters. On a bare pine sideboard a black telephone sat like a squat toad. There was no external view — the yellowed blinds on the windows were pulled down. The room smelled stale.

'Have a seat,' said Guttman, as he double-locked the door and sat down himself. 'It's not the Waldorf, but relax, it's only for a night. Was your trip okay?'

'Not bad. Morgan didn't seem too happy about my leaving.'

Guttman gave a small smile. 'Maybe he's pissed off to lose a good agent.'

Nessheim nodded perfunctorily at the compliment, unconvinced.

'You hungry?' asked Guttman and Nessheim shook his head. 'Then let's get started. First of all, here's the new you.' He flipped a small card at Nessheim. It was a driver's licence issued by the State of Illinois for James Rossbach, resident at 1472 N. Kedzie Avenue, Chicago Illinois. The small photograph in one corner of the card was of Nessheim.

'Where did you get this?' he asked, pointing to the mugshot.

'The Bureau files.'

Nessheim looked again at the licence. Something about the address seemed familiar. He looked quizzically at Guttman. 'What happens if somebody goes and checks out this street number?'

'They'll be told that a Mrs Ethel Rossbach lived there for the last few years, with her nephew — a nice orphan named Jimmy. When she passed away, this Jimmy fellow moved on. That's your ID, now let's talk about your job. Do you know how to canoe?'

Was Guttman serious? 'Yes,' said Nessheim slowly. In fact, he had learned on the pond at home, and on the small lakes that dotted his Wisconsin county like raisins.

'You said you were a good swimmer. That still the case?'

Nessheim could not suppress a laugh. 'I don't think it's something you lose. It's like riding a bike.'

'I wouldn't know. Can't swim a lick myself.'

'What's this about?'

'Your new job,' said Guttman. 'Ever been a camp counsellor?'

'Nope.' He'd worked summers closer to home;

camp counselling didn't pay well enough.

'There's a first time for everything. I'm trying to place you at Camp Schneider. It's a new *Bund* camp.'

Suddenly Nessheim forgot about this grim suite of rooms, the letdown he had been starting to feel after the excitement of his trip across country by train. He knew the camps were indoctrination centres for the *Bund*, focusing on the military training of young male volunteers. Places like Camp Siegfried in Long Island, Camp Norland in New Jersey — he'd learned about them in the papers he'd read on the trip east. Behind the cheery front of German folk songs, bratwurst, and steins of bock beer, proceeded more sinister training of the thuggish OD — the *Bund*'s counterpart to the German Nazi Party's paramilitaries.

Suddenly Guttman coughed harshly. A cough full of phlegm. He pushed a clenched fist hard against his mouth, as if to stop himself from retching, but coughed again, almost uncontrollably.

Nessheim looked at him with concern, but Guttman shook his head. 'I'm okay,' he said, gasping a little for air. 'Just a chest cold. Worst thing in the world to have in summer. Anyway, you're going to need some training of your own first. I know you can swim, but that doesn't mean you know how to teach other people to swim. So I've arranged for you to be taught in the Catskills. You'll go up by train tomorrow.'

'Not Quantico?' The training facility outside Washington where all new agents were trained in

154

firearms and self-defence.

'No. We can't take the risk of a leak. The only people who know where you're going to be are you and me.' He paused, seeming to weigh his words. 'And the Director, of course.'

This *was* important then. All the waiting had been worth it.

Guttman reached for his briefcase, an old beat-up satchel with a leather tongue that wobbled as he lifted its latch. He rummaged for a minute, then brought out a small sheaf of papers, which he placed on the table between them. 'This is more background stuff on the people you'll be working for. You can't take it with you tomorrow, so try and read through it tonight. It shouldn't take that long.' He looked at his watch. 'On the top page there's a bunch of names. Have a look, will you?'

Looking at the list, Nessheim recognised one right away. 'Heydeman. That's the name of the guy Eddie Le Saux said stored some guns in his fishing shack.'

'That's right. Recognise any of the others?'

He looked again, and managed to keep his eyes from widening:

Adolph Bauer
Peter Heydeman
Dieter Fischer
Konrad Werner
Henry Koch
Jerry Eisenlaur
Bruno Pfeffer
Bernard Ganz

'I knew a Koch and a Schwab back home. These are all pretty common German names.'

Guttman sighed. 'Take one more look, will you?'

'Sure,' he said, trying not to show his anxiety. He pretended to scan the list, thinking hard. It seemed pointless to dissemble. He said, quietly, 'I've got an uncle named Maier. He's married to my mother's sister.'

'Eric?' asked Guttman, but it was friendly enough.

Nessheim nodded.

Guttman said mildly, 'Well, who knows? There may be a lot of Eric Maiers.'

'He's in the *Bund*,' said Nessheim.

'Ah. I see.' When Nessheim didn't say anything Guttman sighed again, then clapped his hands and said, 'I think you better get some sleep. You've got a busy time ahead.'

'What about you?' asked Nessheim, wondering if he was going to have to sleep on the couch. He couldn't see Guttman letting him have the bed.

'I'll be back in the morning. I'm staying downtown.' He pointed to the tiny kitchen at one end of the sitting room. 'There's some stuff in the fridge if you get hungry. No booze — I want you clear-eyed tomorrow. I think the bedroom's got a radio.'

'I might take a walk round.' He had seen nothing of Manhattan, and tomorrow he was leaving.

But Guttman shook his head. 'Not a good idea. Lot of bums in this area.'

'You think I'd get rolled?' demanded Nessheim, confident he could look after himself.

'A powerful all-American like you?' said Guttman with amusement. 'Of course not. But I don't want you hurting anybody and ending up in the papers. I'll see you tomorrow.'

* * *

After Guttman left, Nessheim sat in the soft armchair, with the window open as high as it would go. It was as hot as Chicago here. Turning on the radio in the bedroom, he listened to a live broadcast of the Harry James swing band from Radio City Music Hall, only blocks away. He went into the living room and put the blinds up, but the view was uninspiring — in an apartment across the alley a bald man in boxer shorts sat in front of a fan, reading the paper and scratching his arms. Nessheim envied him the fan. Down the street a neon sign on a bar at the corner started to flicker, throwing blue light in melancholic streaks across the windowsill.

He was starting to feel melancholic himself, reading the material Guttman had given him. But he was satisfied he was doing the right thing infiltrating the *Bund*. Any qualms had been dispelled by Guttman's dossier and by his own growing sense that Hitler *was* a menace — not a buffoon, not a lunatic who could be ignored, and certainly not the admirable leader of a reinvigorated nation.

He poked around the icebox, hoping for a beer, but could find only a ham roll with a browning lettuce leaf and a bottle of soda. He tried the soda, then made a face. Looking at the label he saw it was something called Dr Brown's Cel-Ray Soda. Celery? Probably some New York invention. Yuck.

He poured himself a glass of water from the sink and decided to go to bed. There he discovered that the walls' gimcrack construction meant he could hear every footstep in the corridor outside. He was nonetheless just managing to doze off when he heard more steps in the hallway, muted ones, which paradoxically called them to his attention. They stopped just outside his door. Nessheim listened carefully; there was another step and a key jingled, then a lock turned, and a door opened and shut. Was it his front door? He sat up, listening tensely, wishing he had his gun with him. Then there were more steps, and he realised they came from the apartment next door.

After a moment he heard a man speaking in low tones, the voice coming through the thin walls. The man sounded calm, almost soothing, and Nessheim gradually relaxed. He must be speaking to a woman, he thought, though he could not hear another voice. Then he realised the man was talking on the phone.

The man coughed, and Nessheim froze. He sat up again, listening hard. A minute later came more coughing. Its timbre was very familiar.

So Guttman was next door. But he had said he was staying downtown. Why had he lied?

It was only as he lay down again and pulled the pillow under his head that the answer came. *Because he doesn't trust you.*

* * *

In the morning, Guttman led him the few blocks to Grand Central, where Nessheim would take the next train north into upstate New York. As they walked, Guttman reviewed their communication procedures. 'You memorised the number, right?'

'Yes,' said Nessheim, and said it out loud.

'That's only in emergencies. How about the names? You know those too?'

'*Adolph Bauer,*' he said. '*Peter Heydeman, Dieter Fischer . . .* '

'Okay, that'll do. I'll call you.'

* * *

Mesinger Brothers, where he went for 'training', wasn't an FBI facility at all, but a resort — famous on the east coast, Nessheim soon learned. Five miles from the nearest town, it sat on over 500 acres of mixed woodland and pasture. Wealthy New Yorkers came here to enjoy themselves, sometimes for weeks at a time, and give their families a vacation away from the city. They paid a lot to stay at Mesinger's, and expected a lot in return. Besides entertainment, recreation of all kinds was on offer — with good reason, since the dining room's buffet was open from breakfast until midnight. There was a championship golf course, a roller-skating rink (frozen over for ice skating in the winter months), seven handball courts, twelve tennis courts and an Olympic-sized swimming pool.

It was in this last, vast basin that Nessheim spent most of his working day. He'd been met at the station by Sammy Mesinger himself, a mirthless fat little man who seemed to take against Nessheim at once. 'Welcome to Sullivan County,' he said sourly, throwing down his cigar. He muttered, 'Christ. Harry didn't say he was sending me *goyim*.'

Fortunately Nessheim wasn't there to work under him, labouring instead under the veteran eye of the swimming director, an ageing Swede named Alvo Svenson who claimed to have been a stand-in for Johnny Weissmuller in a Tarzan movie.

At ten o'clock kids appeared at the poolside, and Alvo taught classes until lunchtime. In the afternoon he gave private lessons. He soon had Nessheim helping with both. Alvo would stand by the poolside in a terry-cloth robe he wore over his old-fashioned striped swimsuit, with straps like suspenders on his lope-shouldered frame, trying to soak up the weak spring sun; all the while giving encouragement as Nessheim held the kids one at a time in the shallow end of the pool, centring their little frames like Archimedes's levers, putting one hand on top and one hand on the bottom of their stomachs, while they kicked and moved their arms simultaneously. Then he'd let go, with an encouraging push through the water, while Alvo

160

boomed a mantra *Chug! Chug! Chug!* Soon Nessheim found himself shouting *Chug! Chug! Chug!* as well.

Mesinger discouraged Nessheim from contact with the paying guests, and the staff kept their distance when they learned he had a room in the main resort, not in the barracks they inhabited tucked behind the tennis courts. The exception was a waitress named Peggy Rourke, with shoulder-length auburn hair and a gutsy laugh, who paid deference to nobody. She started talking to Nessheim during one of her cigarette breaks underneath the big spruce trees behind the kitchens. Soon he found himself looking forward to their daily conversation. Ten years older than Nessheim, she had been married three times and worked most of the year in New York city hash joints; every summer she came up to Mesinger's.

On the one day off Nessheim was allowed by Alvo, she drove him round the Catskills, then stopped at a tourist court, where she took a room, and took Nessheim to bed.

Later as she lay smoking, half-covered by a sheet, he said, 'I hear you come to Mesinger's every year.'

'That's right. The Jewish Alps,' she said, blowing a smoke ring.

'You must like it.'

'I do. I love the Yids. They make me laugh,' she said with a fond smile. Then she looked at him, curious. 'But I wouldn't have made you as a friend of Mesinger.'

'I'm not.'

'Glad to hear it. I can't stand him myself.'

'He's doing a friend of mine a favour, letting me stay and help Alvo.'

'But why — ?' she started to ask, then seemed to catch herself. She reached out and lay a calloused finger on his stomach. 'You don't have to tell me anything,' she said. Her hand moved slowly down. 'I'll take you as you are, Rossbach. Or whatever your name is.'

★   ★   ★

Three days later, Mesinger came to his room. 'Harry phoned me. He says it's time for you to go.' Mesinger looked pleased. 'I've got instructions in my office.'

He'd left early the next morning, now knowing where he was going next. He went to say goodbye to Peggy and found her putting down a breakfast tray of dishes in the kitchens. She touched his cheek with her hand. 'You're a sweetheart, kid. Look me up if you ever get to the city. I'm in the book — West 37th. The only P. Rourke there.'

12

Frances jabbed him sharply in the ribs. 'Two bits for what you're thinking.'

'That's a lot of dough considering I wasn't thinking much at all.' He let Peggy Rourke recede from his thoughts as the bus turned off Route 12 and rattled up the gravel road to Camp Schneider. They were in forest now, a mix of thrusting maples and thinner birch. Then they bucketed over a disused cattle grille, and the trees stopped. The bus pulled up to the lodge, Emmet braked sharply on the gravel, then pulled the lever for the door. Once outside the girls scampered off like mice.

'I'm going back to my cabin,' said Frances, and he wondered if he was supposed to walk with her.

'See you later,' he said, and went into the lodge.

It sat on the crest of a hill overlooking the camp's small lake. As Nessheim walked inside, he saw through a long line of windows the view of the mowed grass that ran on a gentle slope down towards the water. On the far side of the lake the woods stretched to the base of Coolidge Hill, over a mile away. Above the lodge there was another field, farmed only for its hay, and an ageing apple orchard with gnarled, spidery trees. Otherwise the camp was surrounded by woods.

In the big rec room two girls had begun a game of ping pong, but the rest played outside. A piano sat in a corner, where on Sunday nights they would gather for a singalong after supper, and Mrs Grumholtz played old German favourites which the girls sang dutifully, then sang with more enthusiasm a few American songs ('Five Foot Two Eyes of Blue' was the campers' favourite). He noticed one of the window frames was rotting, and cursed. His duties included making minor repairs — and they were constant.

He passed by the camp office, empty since Herr Schultz, the camp director, was away. In that room Nessheim had been interviewed on his arrival — a formality, since he had been officially offered the job, but still a daunting one since it was the first time he had posed under his assumed identity.

A man named Beringer had collected him at the train station in White River Junction. Slim and elegantly dressed in a blazer and Panama hat, Beringer had made a few polite queries about his journey, and then they had driven in silence to the camp.

On arrival, Beringer had said Schultz wanted to see him in his office. When Nessheim asked to use the bathroom first, he was disconcerted that Beringer had followed him in. There was a line of six urinals placed there by a CCC corps expecting mainly male residents, and when Nessheim took his stance at the furthest one he found Beringer standing next to him, staring with such interest at Nessheim's exposed organ that Nessheim felt as if he had pulled a snake out of his fly.

The interview itself hadn't lasted long.

'You come recommended to us by Herr Bock from the German Consulate in Washington,' Schultz said. He had a harsh metallic voice and a pie-shaped face made mean by startling eyes. Short but compact, he wore a tight-fitting jacket and tie. The effect was slightly military, enhanced by hair that was short, bristly, and cropped by a straight razor on sides and back. He looked like a smaller, older version of Agent Mueller.

'That's very nice of him,' said Nessheim, trying to look appreciative.

'How did you come to know Herr Bock?'

Nessheim knew the script by heart. His résumé included a fictitious stint as a lifeguard at the Oak Street Beach in Chicago — the man in charge during the pertinent years was now dead, which would make it hard to check — and a stint at Mesinger's, which in a sense was real enough. 'I don't know him personally — we've never met. But his family and mine were neighbours in Germany.'

'Where was that?'

'A village called Dasbach, near Neidernhausen. It's outside Frankfurt.'

'Not my favourite city. Too cosmopolitan for my taste.' Schultz made a face. Then he said, 'I am surprised your last job was working for a Jew.'

'I needed the job. Though to tell you the truth, I couldn't stand it. Filthy kikes; they tried to cheat me out of a week's salary.'

'You are surprised by that?' asked Schultz with a knowing smile. '*Der Jude ist ein Laus.*'

Beringer nodded as if it went without saying.

Then they questioned him on his politics, his feelings about National Socialism, and what he thought of Germany's recent expansion. Guttman had instructed him that though he should hew to the line of the *Bund* and show allegiance to Nazi Germany, he mustn't go overboard. He was to come across, Guttman reminded him, as easy-going rather than fervent, tending on the dumb side rather than smart. 'An athlete not a thinker,' Guttman had said, then laughed.

And despite the vagueness of his replies, Nessheim must have satisfied Schultz, for the camp leader seemed to tire of Nessheim's unsophisticated answers to his pointed political queries, and began describing his duties instead. He would teach swimming and canoeing, and each weekday afternoon lead the campers on a hike (Schultz was big on hikes, and said the mountains of Vermont reminded him of his native Bavaria). And once a week, Nessheim would take the kids into the nearest town, Woodstock, where the campers would be allowed to spend their pocket money.

Schultz said, 'You will be there to supervise the girls, both on the bus and in town. You may find some of the inhabitants not so welcoming. We try and keep a low profile. There are not many Germans here, and the Yankees are an odd breed.'

'Oh?'

'*Ja.* They seem to think they are the true

Aryans. Everyone else is *Untergebene*,' and he gave a pointed thumbs-down.

'I'll remember that,' said Nessheim.

★ ★ ★

Past the office sat the staffroom, from which Ernst Kessler now emerged. He was Nessheim's cabin mate, a middle-aged German who taught the language to the girls and never laughed. Nessheim nodded to him and took a short cut through the kitchen, where the Negro cook stood over an enormous range.

'Hey, Smitty. Cooler today.'

'Not in here,' he replied with a grin. Nessheim liked the man, but couldn't make out if his reflexive smile was sincere, or the product of years knowing it was safest to act happy to white men. Smitty slept in a tiny room, not much bigger than a closet, behind the kitchen toilet; at one point Nessheim had thought of suggesting he share the roomy quarters of his own cabin. But when he'd raised it with Kessler, the German had been horrified. '*Ein Schwartzer?*' he'd said with disbelief, and that was the end of that.

'What's for supper?' he asked now.

'Fried chicken,' said Smitty with a smile. 'With *Hefeklösse*,' he added in pitch-perfect German that made Nessheim wonder about him again.

He came out of the kitchen and around the lodge to the back, where he could see the girls already playing, scattered along its ragged lawn. This was one of the few times when he was without duties — Mrs Grumholtz was in charge until dinner. Sixty minutes of freedom, and he walked down to the lake and then around it to the far side, where his own cabin lay at one end of the line of twelve, each with a pitched roof and screens for windows on both sides. Inside the Kessler-free cabin he lay down and read for an hour. He'd finished a collection of Hemingway stories, and the only English-language books he'd found in the lodge were a book of poems by Robert Frost and an ancient history of Vermont. A century before, he discovered reading the latter, the hillsides around him had been denuded of trees and grazed by sheep. Would wonders never cease, thought Nessheim sourly, wishing he'd joined the library in Woodstock.

He thought of his recent mail: there had been nothing from Guttman, and he was tempted to call him again soon. But each call carried a small but discernible risk of getting caught; he knew too that Guttman was impatient with Nessheim's impatience, which he'd expressed even in their first phone conversation.

Guttman had ignored him then, asking instead, 'Have you found a rendezvous point yet?'

'Yep. I have.' In the flat pocket of woods that lay between Route 12 and Coolidge Hill, Nessheim had located an old forestry track. Disused, it seemed the perfect location, and in his first note to Guttman, posted beneath the WPA-sponsored murals of the post office in Woodstock on Saturday afternoon, he had drawn a small map locating this track for emergency meets.

Not that it looked as though it was ever going to be used. With just three weeks left to go at the camp, Nessheim wondered what was supposed to happen to him after that. Was he going to be sent back to San Francisco? Or was there some other part of the *Bund* organisation he'd be sent to infiltrate? He could just see it — writing copy for the latest edition of the *Deutscher Weckruf*.

At supper the counsellors split up among the tables, standing with the children as Schultz said grace in German. The campers took turns bringing the food from the kitchen window, where Smitty stood on the other side, handing them the crockery bowls. This evening Nessheim had Mrs Grumholtz on the opposite end of the table, with six girls chattering happily on the benches between them. Then Beringer sat down on his right.

'You have been to town,' he said to Nessheim in his mild German accent.

'I took the girls.'

Beringer served himself from the bowls, then looked down at his plate. Green bean salad dressed in cider vinegar, German dumplings, and a piece of fried chicken with a thick flour crust. 'This looks like *Dreiländer* food,' he said with an amused air.

'What's that? Three lands?'

'*Ja*. A little joke from my part of Austria.' Beringer pointed to his bean salad. 'Here is some of the food these local Yankees like — meagre fare in my view. Then dumplings: German heft,

169

thank goodness. And finally fried chicken — the *Schwartzer* gets to make his own contribution.'

When the plates had been cleared and they sat waiting for dessert, Schultz appeared, and stood at Nessheim's end of the table next to Beringer. The girls at the table were suddenly quiet.

'You have been working hard, young Rossbach, and I have good news for you. Someone is coming to join our staff and he will be helping you with the swimming duties.'

'Great.'

'He will be here tonight. I think you will be pleased to have his help.' Schultz looked at Beringer then back at Nessheim. 'It seems the news from Europe is getting interesting.'

'Oh,' said Nessheim, who had seen nothing noteworthy in the *Bund* paper. There was a radio in the staffroom, but it was rarely listened to. He felt out of touch with events, but he also tried to avoid political discussions with the other counsellors. Schultz often made disparaging comments about Roosevelt and the administration, and about those groups he put under an umbrella he called 'riff-raff', pronounced lovingly with a guttural German emphasis to the Rs. The category included Communists, Democrats, Roosevelt, Jews, bankers, Poles, Italians, French-Canadians, and the local Yankees — in short, much of what constituted the American people.

'The Führer has made it clear that he considers Danzig a natural extension of Germany. With justice, too, I might add. But the British are kicking up a bit.'

Beringer scoffed. 'Ach, Chamberlain kicked up before, you know. But in the event he did nothing. There is no reason to think this will be any different, Max. Why stand up for Poles when you have not done the same for Czechoslovakia? It makes no sense.'

'Maybe not,' said Schultz slowly, and Nessheim felt the man's eyes were on him. 'There was another report too. It said that if there was a war in Europe there might be a draft here soon.'

Mrs Grumholtz was listening from the far end. 'Well, it's always windy, Max. It doesn't do anyone harm.'

Schultz gave an indulgent smile, but his eyes remained fixed on Nessheim. 'What do you think?'

Nessheim shrugged. 'I can't see the point of it myself.'

'Can't you? You have a draft when you expect your men to go to war.' Peach cobbler had arrived, and Nessheim took the stack of small bowls by his side and began doling the dessert out with a large tin spoon. Schultz mused, 'It will be interesting to see the way our people react.'

'How do you mean?' asked Nessheim, then kicked himself for getting drawn in.

'Would you enlist if it meant fighting against your people's homeland? That's what Roosevelt wants Americans to do.'

Nessheim looked at Schultz blankly. 'I've always assumed America would keep out of it. Let the British fight their own corner. Nothing to do with us.'

'Maybe. But what do you think will happen if

171

there is a draft? Will young men put up with it?' He waited a beat. 'Will you, young Rossbach?'

The question dropped like a weight on the table.

Keep it simple, he told himself. 'I couldn't fight against Germany.'

'*Ja*, but if you are drafted?'

'I would refuse to serve.' He was acting, but he didn't like saying the words.

Nessheim handed Beringer a bowl. The German picked up a spoon and inspected the cobbler. 'You would go to prison for that,' Beringer said.

'Not if I were in Germany,' he said.

'You would go there?' asked Schultz, surprised by Nessheim's reply. He seemed to look at him anew. Then suddenly Schultz laughed out loud. 'Fine words. But let me give you some advice, young Rossbach. If you're really thinking of returning to the Fatherland, you had better learn to speak the language first.'

★ ★ ★

After dinner they played softball on the lawn that ran down in a gentle slope to the lake. The girls enjoyed it, and Nessheim pitched for both teams. They used a twelve-inch ball that was soft, with raised seams, and he would gently lob it to the plate underhand. Sometimes Frances would come out and help the littlest girls bat. When dusk came they played one last inning and by then Schultz had appeared, dressed in alpine shorts and stout hiking boots. There was

172

something ridiculous about the man, but something formidable as well.

Schultz insisted on a turn at bat, and hit the second lobbed ball deep towards the lake. Nessheim ran almost to the water's edge and just managed to catch the ball without toppling in. Cheers came from the girls and he heard clapping from nearby. Nessheim looked over and saw a tall man in green work pants and a striped shirt applauding gently. He had the build of a pulling guard, with ragged blond hair that fell across his forehead like strands of bleached hay.

The man said, 'Good catch,' and grinned, revealing big buck teeth that gave his face a childish cast. But his eyes were beady, and examined Nessheim like a tailor gauging his suit size.

He said, 'They tell me you're from Chicago.' When Nessheim hesitated he added, 'Or have I got the wrong fellah?'

'No, that's me all right.'

'Thought I'd say hello, being as we'll be working together.'

This must be the new hire, who would help with swimming lessons and the afternoon hike.

He stepped forward. 'I'm Rossbach. They call me Chug.' He shook hands.

'I'm from Detroit myself. My name's Peter Heydeman.'

13

'They called me.'

'*Again?*' Guttman was unable to disguise his alarm.

Bock nodded. He looked unperturbed as he carefully shelled a peanut. He had developed a fondness for them ever since Guttman had brought a bag along to one of their rendezvous. After that Guttman brought a bag to each meeting, and would suppress his irritation as Bock ate them one by one, carefully tearing a panel from the brown paper bag on which to lay the empty shells.

'Yes, they were asking about Rossbach.'

★ ★ ★

Twelve months before Bock had suddenly flipped from being a grudging informant to an actively helpful one. The trigger had been the sudden recall of Ambassador Luther — one week he was in place, helpfully leaving out the drafts of his cables back to Berlin; the next he had been abruptly recalled. No more cables, no more information. Overnight, Bock's market value in intelligence terms had plummeted like an October '29 share price.

Guttman had expected Bock to be relieved by the Ambassador's departure. Without access to the confidential cables, there wasn't much he could do for Guttman and the FBI. But instead, the German had seemed deeply alarmed, even fearful. When Guttman had tried to reassure Bock that he was never going to inform Bock's superiors about his predilection for boys, the German had cut him off. 'I have access to other information. There is much going on in the embassy that I could report to you.'

Sure, thought Guttman, you've lost your card in the hole, so magically you find another ace. He stifled a groan at the prospect of this 'information': the menus from official banquets, the seating plans — what else could a Principal Secretary provide? Meeting with Bock took up a lot of time, and it wasn't as if Guttman weren't busy with other things — just the week before he had spent seventeen hours investigating a state department employee who had several unde-clared cousins in the Soviet Union, one of them in the Kremlin.

He was tempted to sever the relationship, but something held him back. He had come to know Bock, he realised. He was not a career diplomat by vocation, nor a true Nazi — he had, of all things, been an aspiring opera singer. In the end he told Bock he'd be happy to continue to meet.

And to his surprise, if not astonishment, when he next saw Bock the German had something of value to impart. They met by the banks of the Potomac on the capital side, which meant a shorter ride for Guttman. It was a windy day and they walked for a few minutes in silence, watching as a coal barge made leaden progress through the river's choppy waves.

175

Bock suddenly spoke up. 'Do you remember some time ago, you asked me about a name mentioned in one of the Ambassador's cables?'

'Do you mean Werner?'

'Yes. Did you ever find him?'

'Why?'

'I bet you haven't,' Bock said archly.

'What makes you so sure?' Guttman hadn't expected this at all.

'Because he's disappeared. Even his friends don't have any idea where he is.'

'How do you know that?'

'I told you I could establish good contacts with the *Bund*. And I have — in New York. I have met Kuhn himself.'

'Lucky you,' said Guttman. No orator, Kuhn was so shrill that he was ignored now even by the real Nazis in Germany. Not that Guttman believed this was anything but tactical.

'I agree that Kuhn is not much of a leader. But Schultz is different.'

The name was vaguely familiar, but he associated it with Detroit. 'Why is that?' he asked leadingly.

'Schultz is a businessman — he owns a small printing business in New York, and he is establishing a summer camp for little German-American girls up in Vermont. He is correct in manner, intelligent, clear-headed — unlike Kuhn. Schultz is not so theatrical, or impetuous. He would have made a far better leader, and many people think so. Yet he has absented himself from all public gatherings of the *Bund*.'

'Sulking in his tent maybe?'

Bock shook his head. 'He could have been the leader — without question. Most people thought that's why he moved to New York from Michigan. But he chose not to.'

'What has this got to do with Werner?' he asked.

'Maybe nothing,' said Bock, yet smugness sat on his face like the photographed grin of a golf club champion. 'It was interesting nonetheless to learn that Werner's sister is married to Schultz.'

'What?' Guttman tried to control his sudden interest. 'So where is Werner now?' All Guttman knew was that Werner had once belonged to the Detroit chapter of the *Bund* and been mentioned mysteriously in one of Ambassador Luther's cables. Just who the hell was he?

'He came to this country from Austria almost twenty years ago; he took citizenship here after a while. He lived all over America, I gather, until he settled in Detroit near his sister, who had by then married Herr Schultz. As for his whereabouts now, even this sister doesn't know. He disappeared two years ago: people thought he was going to Germany — the Olympics were on at the time. But Kuhn and the others never saw him in Berlin.'

'How did you find this out?'

'Schultz has an assistant named Beringer. More than an assistant really.' Bock hesitated. 'We have become friendly. He seems keen to establish closer relations with an emissary of the Reich.'

'Doesn't he know the Reich has expressly forbidden that kind of contact?'

'That makes him all the keener. He assumes my overtures must have approval from the highest level of the German government.'

'I hope you haven't let him know that's not true.'

A sly expression crept across Bock's face. 'Of course not. There is one problem, though.'

'What's that?'

'I have nothing of practical value to offer them. Moral support only goes a certain way, does it not? If they are going to trust me completely, they would have to see a commitment on my part, as a representative of the Reich.'

Guttman saw at once what Bock was driving at. If his plan to put somebody in undercover could get him in hot water, what Bock was asking him to do would get him fried in oil. But he couldn't see an alternative.

'How much money do you need?'

Bock was ready for him. 'A thousand dollars to start with would find me most welcome with Herr Schultz.'

I bet it would, thought Guttman, already thinking how to divert the funds from other parts of his budget.

★ ★ ★

It was a month after this that Guttman had travelled to Chicago. Now, thanks to Bock's discovery, Guttman knew where he wanted Nessheim to go. The only problem was, he needed Bock to help him do that, and he wasn't sure he could trust the diplomat. Trust him? He'd never *trust* Bock. No, he just needed to feel confident that Bock wouldn't reveal what he was doing to his Nazi superiors back home.

Curiously, it was Bock himself who allayed his worries, although at first Guttman was made even less confident of Bock's true colours when in mid-October of 1938 the man announced he was going back to Germany on leave. He'd be gone for eight weeks, he told Guttman, who couldn't help wondering if he would ever come back.

But he had, and he'd returned thoroughly shaken. He had arrived in Berlin just in time for Kristallnacht, the orgy of destruction unleashed by Goebbels against the Jewish community after the murder of a German Embassy official in Paris. Bock gave Guttman a firsthand account of what he'd seen himself: the Jewish stores burned and vandalised, the broken glass everywhere (hence 'Glass night'), the torching of synagogues, and worst of all the physical attacks — he had seen an old Jewish man beaten half to death. The outrages had been widely reported in America, and Roosevelt had been swift to respond, immediately ordering Dietrich, the new German Ambassador (and Luther's successor) to be recalled. Now the embassy held the status of a mere consulate. Perhaps that was increasing Bock's agitation.

But he wasn't just shocked, Guttman realised. Bock was also deeply frightened. Why?

'It was terrible what they did to the Jews,' Guttman ventured softly.

'It's not the Jews I'm worried about,' said Bock. 'Other kinds of people are being put in camps as well.'

Guttman tried to look sympathetic. He had heard about the rough treatment of the Roma, the gypsies of Germany. Though they were not the people Bock had in mind either.

'A friend of mine was sent to Dachau. He had to wear a pink star. Can you imagine — a *pink* star? He was lucky — they let him out after two months. He's in Holland now, where people are more civilised. Germany has changed,' said Bock, shaking his head. 'You know, when Hitler first came to power there was a new spirit in the air. People felt optimistic.'

'And they don't now?' asked Guttman sceptically.

'They feel confident — even arrogant perhaps. But it's on the surface. There are too many soldiers around to feel at peace, too many marches and banners. A militaristic society is never a trusting one, that much I have learned. Even private citizens are encouraged to spy on one another.'

'So not a happy visit home?'

'No.' Bock squared back his shoulders and inhaled deeply. 'Tell me, if I chose not to return to Germany, would I be allowed to stay in the United States?'

Guttman felt his heart start to beat rapidly. 'I wouldn't think so. Especially if things get even worse between our countries.'

Bock seemed to expect this. 'But if I had help from the authorities. Perhaps someone from the

180

FBI? Like yourself, Herr Guttman.'

'If our relationship continued to be beneficial to American interests, then, Herr Bock, we might be able to swing it.'

And he saw a satisfied smile flicker momentarily on Bock's face. Gotcha, thought Guttman.

★　★　★

Now they were meeting in a small park in Bethesda, a newly planted construct of the CCC. It was hot, over 90 degrees, the air misty with nectar drops of heat. A small pond with a concrete surround lay at the park's heart, its water level down to mere inches after two months without rain. Birches had been planted randomly across the three or four acres of yellowing grass, and several were looking perilously parched.

Guttman sat next to Bock on a bench. They were out in the open, sacrificing shade for security, though the park was almost empty in the late morning. Only one woman, tall in a sleeveless pink summer dress, slowly walked a terrier near the pond. She wore high heels, which couldn't have been comfortable on the rough asphalt paths.

'What did you tell them about Rossbach?' asked Guttman.

'What I'd said before, of course.' He looked mildly affronted. Bock wore a suit but had taken off his tie, while Guttman kept his on, a striped number he now loosened at the knot. 'That I didn't know this young man, but his relatives in

Germany were friends with my own family there.'

'Did they want to know anything else?' These people were more thorough than their *Bund* colleagues elsewhere.

Bock finished the last peanut, chewing it slowly. 'They wanted to make sure he wasn't a Jew.'

'Rossbach?' It was hard to believe — to Guttman Nessheim was the *goyische* German incarnate.

'It was because he worked at that Jewish resort. Someone tried to infiltrate the *Bund* in New Jersey who turned out to be both a Jew and a Communist. He was lucky not to be killed.' He added as an afterthought, 'They examined your Mr Rossbach very carefully. Physically, I mean.'

Guttman shook his head in puzzlement, and then he understood. 'What, you mean they looked at his *putz*?'

He blushed as he remembered Bock's own proclivities, but the German did not react. Guttman tried to picture the scene at Camp Schneider but couldn't. It would have been comical if it hadn't been so serious.

Bock remarked mildly, 'There are plenty of circumcised Gentiles, but I've never heard of an uncircumcised Jew, so Rossbach passed that test.'

Guttman thought it was best to move on. 'Anything else to report?'

'*Nein*. But there may be in two weeks' time. I am going to New York again.'

'Aren't they all in Vermont?'

'Beringer is coming down for a day.'

Just to see you? Guttman wanted to ask, but he refrained.

Bock asked, 'Is there any news from your immigration authorities?'

Guttman noticed the woman with the terrier had come slightly closer. She looked at her watch, and even from a distance Guttman noticed it had a big face — a man's watch. He turned to Bock. 'I'll chase them up — you know what bureaucracy's like.'

'Not really. In Germany it is very efficient. I would like to think there would be progress soon.'

Guttman stood up to go. 'I'll see you in two weeks. Same place, same time.'

★ ★ ★

'Mr Tolson's looking for you,' said Marie, Guttman's secretary. She was a red-headed French-Canadian divorcée whom he had pulled out of the downstairs typing pool, earning him her gratitude and loyalty — and discretion.

'Is he happy? Or are the waters troubled?' One of the nice things about Marie is that he felt he could speak this way.

'More puzzled, I'd say.'

And ten minutes later when Tolson stuck a big pinstriped shoulder through the doorway, his face still held a look of bemusement. 'So how's life down here in the ghetto?'

Guttman gave a little grimace. It was a stale joke by now, if it had ever been funny. Tolson clearly thought it was — it had been Tolson who'd first come up with the tag of 'Guttman's Ghetto', his soubriquet for the suite of corner offices and small space of open floor Guttman had claimed for himself and his immediate staff.

'How's Sidney getting on?' Tolson asked.

'Good.'

'What you got him doing?'

Guttman tried to sound nonchalant. 'Oh, this and that. Deliveries, messages, that sort of thing.'

Tolson nodded. 'It will be nice when he gets his licence back. Mr Hoover doesn't like the replacement driver. Heavy foot on the gas, he says.'

Guttman wanted to ask if Tolson agreed with this — since everybody knew Tolson rode to work each day with the Director.

'I had a call from Accounts,' Tolson said mildly. Unlike Hoover, he never raised his voice, and his tones were soft and high-pitched. People who'd only talked to the man on the telephone were always surprised by his big athletic frame when they met him in the flesh.

'Oh?' said Guttman, trying to sound helpful while remaining non-committal.

'Yeah, it seems you had a guy transferred into your department here.' He consulted a yellow legal pad he was holding. 'Came all the way from Frisco. Name's James Nessheim.' He looked up quizzically from his pad. 'Why's that familiar?'

Guttman shrugged. 'Beats me,' he said.

'Anyhow, Accounts say he didn't pick up his last pay cheque.' And before Guttman could say anything — his mind was racing to pick a plausible explanation — Tolson added, 'Or the one before that. They just wanted to know if this guy's got any objection to being paid.'

He chuckled, so Guttman gave a forced laugh. 'Nah, he needs the dough all right. But he had to go home — death in the family, so I gave him some leave. He's from the Midwest.'

'Two pay cheques' worth?' There was the first hint of steel in Tolson's voice. Hoover was notoriously impatient with the concept of compassionate leave. They said when his own adored mother had died, the Director had taken just the morning off.

'No, he was only home a couple of days. I sent him to Milwaukee after that, following up some reports we've had of Communist activity in one of the breweries.'

Tolson gave an understanding nod. 'Chicago office know he's there?'

The question hung like a hook in the air between them.

'No.' Guttman added quickly, 'They've reopened the Milwaukee Field Office, remember?' He didn't add that he hadn't told them either.

Tolson slapped a paw against his forehead, in a vaudeville mime of stupidity. 'How could I forget? I'll tell Accounts to lay off.'

'Have them send the cheques to me,' said Guttman, purposely looking down at a report on his desk.

'I'll do that,' said Tolson, already out the door.

★ ★ ★

185

Ask me no questions, I'll tell you no lies, thought Guttman, but he was nervous about this encounter. As he'd long ago learned, Hoover (and by proxy Tolson) loved to poke his finger into the smallest pie, indeed was famous for showing up in the most remote field office and scrutinising everything from the resident SAC's shirt colour to the number of personnel who knew the combination of the office safe. In a saner organisation, Guttman thought angrily, Accounts would have called him first. After all, Nessheim was his agent.

But was he really? He considered the matter for a moment. He liked the kid, though he didn't know if this was because of Nessheim's air of innocence, or despite it. Either way, he wondered if it wasn't a front for a more sophisticated take on things. After all, Nessheim had shot dead Danny Ho, though by all accounts he'd come within an ace of getting plugged himself. That would have sent Guttman's grand scheme down the drain, and he'd had Morgan switch Nessheim to the relative safety of Fraud right away. The kid had done well there, according to the SAC, and developed into a pretty competent interrogator. So whatever his demeanour, Nessheim couldn't be that green.

As for Nessheim's German roots, they made him ideal for placement in the ranks of the *Bund*, but they also made Guttman uneasy. It wasn't that he suspected Nessheim of hidden Nazi sympathies. Guttman simply worried that if there was a choice to be made between duty and some family allegiance, the kid might hesitate.

That was one reason why he hadn't told Nessheim most of what he knew. He hadn't mentioned Werner to him, in particular, and didn't plan to.

★ ★ ★

The following day Marie came to find him down in Files. 'You're wanted on the Fifth Floor, Mr Guttman. The Director's office.'

Oh, shit, he thought. Maybe Tolson hadn't accepted his explanation for Nessheim after all.

Guttman took the elevator up to give himself time to gather his thoughts — and damp down his rising anxiety. For there was no way he could explain Nessheim's presence in Vermont without it being clear that he was working undercover — in strict contradiction of Hoover's explicit orders.

He thought idly of what career he might have to pursue next. Would anyone give him a job after he'd been given the heave-ho by J. Edgar himself? He pictured Isabel, sitting in their Arlington home, relying on him. He couldn't afford enough help as it was, not with the additional drain made on his salary by his ageing mother, living alone in her walk-up flat in Hester Street. His father hadn't left a dime when he died. Not even a will; just a bill.

Pull yourself together, he admonished himself, as the elevator opened and he walked down the hall, where Helen Gandy, Hoover's executive assistant, motioned him to go through. Hoover was already at the corner table, po-faced, with

Tolson sitting next to him, also looking sombre. Oh, well, Guttman told himself, I can always run security at some department store, spend my days managing floor dicks chasing shoplifters, and leave the Nazis to someone else.

'Ah, Harry,' said Hoover. 'Thanks for coming. We've got a visiting fireman and I thought you could help make up the numbers.'

Guttman realised how worried he had been, for he had to struggle not to show his relief. He sat down, while Tolson drummed his fingers impatiently on the table. There was a knock on the open door, and when Guttman turned he saw Miss Gandy in the doorway with a stranger. 'Mr Stephenson,' she announced, and the man came into the room.

He was tall, with a crumpled pleasant face, high cheekbones and a long slightly crooked nose, with brown hair that rose back from a high forehead. His expression was tentatively friendly, as if he were waiting to see if you'd be friendly, too. He wore a suit but it wasn't orthodox wool — it was tweed, the colour of dusty sage, beautifully cut, worn with a cream shirt and a bright vermilion tie. The clothes said this was a man who ran his own affairs.

'Thanks very much for seeing me,' he said as he sat down, giving an affable nod. To Guttman's surprise, the accent was American — well, pretty damn close at least. Stephenson explained, 'I'm here on behalf of the British government. I'm Canadian by birth myself, but a British citizen.' He took an envelope out of his jacket and passed it over to Hoover.

The Director opened it, and quickly scanned the letter inside. Reading aloud he declaimed, 'The Home Secretary asks that we 'extend you every courtesy' . . . You 'have the full authorisation of His Majesty's Government to conduct discussions with our government'.' He looked over at Tolson with mild amusement.

'Here's another note you'd better see,' Stephenson said coolly.

The Director looked at this less tolerantly, probably expecting more embossed stationery from London. But his eyes widened slightly as he read this note, and when he had finished he said stiffly, 'Very well, Mr Stephenson, how can we help you?'

Stephenson looked around the table, as if searching for a friendlier face. 'Gentlemen, I am sure you are as aware of the gravity of the situation in Europe as I am. Given the renown of your intelligence activities,' he added, nodding respectfully, 'possibly even better informed. The recent spate of German aggression seems to many of us on the British side of things very likely to continue. At best, there will be serious confrontations coming; at worst, there will be war. Personally, I fear the latter.'

Hoover said, 'That could be the case, Mr Stephenson, though it's not a conflict I hope we'll get involved with. You'll appreciate that much as we are dismayed by the prospect of war in Europe, it is a different continent.'

'Of course. But we'd like to think that the distance between our two countries is geographical rather than emotional. That in fact there are

189

special ties between us, which mean our involvement in a war would be of more than usual concern to the United States.' He added a little heavily, 'I wouldn't say this if we had not had indications from your government that this was the case.'

He means Roosevelt, thought Guttman, since the President's sympathies were well-known. He had been vocal in his condemnation of the Nazis at every opportunity, to the fury of those who worried he was egging Americans into a fight they didn't have to have.

Hoover was unmoved. 'America is a country of many constituencies, many faiths, many nationalities. The Founding Fathers may have been of English stock, but I think you'll find that there are as many people of German descent in this country as Anglo-Saxons. So naturally, there are differing points of view about what's happening in Europe.'

Stephenson looked taken aback by this. Perhaps he'd been led to believe he would receive a warmer reception, thought Guttman. People often made the mistake of thinking that Hoover was just a big cog in an even bigger wheel. When actually he ran his own wheel with which he brooked no outside interference.

Stephenson said, stony-faced, 'I greatly esteem the diversity of your country. My own wife is Tennessee-born and bred. But I don't think there can be any doubt about the threat that Hitler poses to anyone who believes in democracy, Mr Hoover.'

Hoover gave a shrug, more condescending

than benign. 'I'm sure we're all agreed he poses a threat to Great Britain. It's how that affects us here that's in question.'

'I'm not here to argue politics with you, sir, or in any way to try and influence the conduct of your affairs. I merely wanted to introduce myself in the hope that your organisation and those of my country could cooperate more closely to counter a threat — one which at least some officials here seem to see as common.' He looked down pointedly at the second letter he'd given Hoover.

'Of course,' Hoover said with a brisk smile that conceded nothing.

'In particular,' Stephenson went on, determined to say his piece, 'we thought an exchange of information about internal subversion — Fifth Columnists as they're called nowadays — might be useful. Particularly in those cases where they are receiving assistance from abroad.'

Tolson spoke up. 'Our Fascist subversives are of the home-grown variety, Mr Stephenson. It's the Communists who turn to Moscow for assistance — we have plenty of evidence of that.'

Stephenson shook his head. 'They're not alone, I assure you. We have information indicating financial support for American Fascist groups from German intelligence.'

Hoover shook his head. 'I'd like to see it. All our evidence suggests the German government is at pains to disassociate itself from organisations like the German-American *Bund*. They've expressly forbidden their representatives from being in contact with *Bund* officials, and forbidden German citizens over here from joining. It's hard to see what more the German government could do to distance itself.'

It almost sounded as if Hoover were praising Nazi sensitivity, and Tolson must have sensed this, for he said quickly, 'The Nazis aren't stupid, Mr Stephenson. They realise that if they're exposed assisting the *Bund* it could backfire, and sway opinion even more against them.'

'I have to say I think that's a very optimistic appraisal of the situation.'

'Yes, but it's *our* situation,' interjected Hoover angrily, dropping his initial air of cordiality. The room was silent. Stephenson was pursing his lips and staring at the table top. Hoover continued. 'I think you'll find we have a full command of it as well. There isn't a Fascist organisation in this country we don't know about. Our intelligence on domestic subversion is the match of any intelligence service across the world.'

Stephenson raised a mild eyebrow. 'I hope that's not the case, Mr Hoover. If you can match the efficiency of Stalin's secret police that would be very worrying indeed.'

Guttman wanted to laugh, but didn't dare. He liked this man, his calmness coming unarmed into a lion's den. Hoover was turning puce; for a moment Guttman thought he might explode with rage. He had seen it happen before. But the Director regained his self-control, and Guttman noticed that he had glanced down at the second note again.

'It's good to meet you, sir, and kind of you to come in,' Hoover said in the polite monotone which Guttman recognised as his method of disengagement with people he could not be openly rude to. If the door had ever been ajar for this conversation, it was closed tight now. 'I think a communication flow between your government and this agency might be very valuable indeed. I need to think just who your contact point should be here.'

Stephenson nodded, seeming to sense the rebuff. He said quietly, 'You'll appreciate that time is of the essence as far as we're concerned, Mr Hoover.'

'Of course. Let me give it some thought, and then I'll be in touch.' Spoken like a casting director in Hollywood. *Don't call us; we'll call you.*

★   ★   ★

After Stephenson had left, they held an impromptu postmortem. Hoover was seething. Tolson, as was often the case, tried to calm Hoover down with flattery. 'I thought you handled that exactly right, Director. No point not hearing the man out — he'd just have complained elsewhere. I think it's right that we cooperate on the surface, without of course giving very much away.'

'Yeah,' said Hoover sourly, to show he had heard Tolson but was still angry. 'I don't know who this prick thinks he is, pushing his way in like that. I won't have it. In twelve months' time I won't give him the time of day — let him show me his letters of reference then.'

Tolson said, 'Still, we'd better pick a point

193

man to deal with Stephenson.'

'I'll do it,' said Guttman.

Tolson looked at him curiously. Guttman gave an explanatory shrug. 'If he's got anything useful, it's going to come to me anyway.' Counter-espionage was his bailiwick after all.

Hoover thought about this, his lower lip pushed out like a plate for his mouth to rest on. 'All right,' he said at last. 'You deal with the Limeys. I'll write this jerk and tell him that. But if they try to push you around, I want you to let me know at once. I won't have it.'

'Yes, sir,' said Guttman. Getting up, he noticed the second note Stephenson had given Hoover. It was handwritten on headed paper, and Guttman could read the heading clearly:

**Office of the President
The White House
1600 Pennsylvania Avenue
Washington D.C.**

Now he understood Hoover's grudging politeness to Stephenson, and his outburst once the man had left.

Although Hoover habitually cited the entire American Nation as the people he was acting for, his foremost loyalty was to the Bureau and, Guttman sometimes thought, to himself. It was certainly not to Roosevelt, which explained Hoover's reference to twelve months from now, when the Democrats would have nominated a new candidate for President, and Roosevelt would be a lame duck.

194

But that was only part of it, Guttman realised. Hoover hated Roosevelt because Roosevelt was in charge of him and his beloved FBI; when push came to shove Roosevelt was not afraid to let Hoover know this. It was FDR who had insisted that Hoover's obsession with internal dissidents be widened to include Nazis, specifically the *Bund*, as well as Communists.

But a new President would need Hoover more than the other way round. Knowing Hoover, Guttman was sure that by the time he was inaugurated the new President would already be the subject of a file in the Director's office an inch thick. Any peccadillo, any weakness (alcohol, gambling, girls — these were the usual foibles) would be lodged there.

Guttman happened to know that Roosevelt's file was minuscule — in an indiscreet moment at the Christmas party, fuelled by two egg nogs, Hoover's assistant Miss Gandy had allowed as much. *Not even a whole page*, she'd said, after confessing that she herself was a Roosevelt admirer, unlike her boss. Hoover had nothing of substance on Roosevelt. Guttman knew the Director would give a lot to change that.

★　★　★

Bock called his office three days later, an unheard-of event. Normally Guttman would have busted his balls for breaking security, but there was something urgent about the German's tone. They arranged to meet just south of Franklin Park.

195

They sat on counter stools at one end of a crowded diner while Guttman ate his new-fangled hamburger and hash browns. His weight had been ballooning from too many hours at his desk, but he justified his calorific lunch on the grounds that an order of cottage cheese would be conspicuous in this greasy spoon.

He stopped eating long enough to look around the diner for faces he recognised. The customers were all men, mainly construction workers, except for two women who had just come in, probably secretaries from one of the neighbouring office buildings.

Bock didn't seem himself, and he didn't touch his food — a grilled cheese sandwich sat isolated on his plate, almost begging for a side order. He just sipped from the tumbler of water the waitress splashed down, and spoke as if talking to himself, looking straight ahead at the waist-high mirror that stretched along the wall they faced.

'Listen carefully,' he said in tones as tense as strung wire. 'The Michigan men are moving.'

Guttman struggled to follow him. 'The Heydeman crew?' he asked.

'Ja,' said Bock reflexively. He pushed the plate of grilled cheese to the far edge of the counter top, next to the chrome sugar holder and glass salt and pepper shakers. 'They're coming east.'

'East is pretty vague,' said Guttman, feeling pretty vague himself. Sometimes Bock made him feel like a hopeless fisherman, aimlessly throwing line into the water on the principle that a hook never caught anything on dry land.

'Young Rossbach should get ready. People will be arriving there shortly.'

'At Camp Schneider?'

'Why else do you think I told you to place him there?'

Guttman nodded, but sensed that Bock was very agitated. He signalled the waitress. 'Gimme a piece of the blueberry pie, will you? And my friend wants a cup of coffee.' Anything to keep Bock there.

'When is this happening?' Guttman asked quietly now.

Bock was looking around the diner suspiciously. 'In three days,' he said tersely.

'Drink your coffee,' said Guttman soothingly. 'Tell me what else you know about this, okay?'

Bock's hands were shaking. 'I've told you all I know,' he hissed.

Guttman realised he needed to calm him down. But it was too late: fear seemed to have overwhelmed the German, for Bock suddenly got up and walked out of the diner.

Goddamn it, thought Guttman. He resisted the temptation to follow Bock. The German must be running very scared to leave like that — Bock couldn't afford to alienate Guttman if he wanted to stay in America. Bock had asked for the meeting, moreover, so why had he got so frightened? Anyway, it seemed likely that he had told Guttman all he knew, which made the information the more tantalising for its imprecision. It looked as though anything more specific was going to have to come from Vermont.

Back at headquarters on Pennsylvania Avenue

197

he showed his pass, then joined a couple of agents and a bunch of typists waiting impatiently for the elevator — one of the cars was out of order. At last the door opened, the elevator man slung back the grille and they all got in, Guttman heading for the rear of the car. It was crowded, and they scrunched together until the third floor, where a couple of people got off. As the grille closed again Guttman noticed a woman in front of him. She'd been in the diner, he realised, one of the two women he'd decided were secretaries. Funny place to have lunch with a girlfriend — it was kind of rough and ready, more hard hats than high heels.

The woman lifted her wrist to check the time, and he noticed the face on her watch was very large — too large to be a lady's watch. His heart began to thump. When the elevator man stopped at the fourth floor, the woman didn't move, so Guttman stayed put. At five, she got out with three other women.

'Must have been daydreaming,' Guttman said to the elevator man. 'Take me down to four, will ya?' As the grille closed he noticed that the three others who'd got out had gone left, heading to the typing pool. But the woman with the big watch had gone right. That way there wasn't a typing pool, or a powder room, or any other kind of room that would explain things and reassure Guttman. The woman with the big watch he'd seen five days before in the Bethesda park as he talked to Bock, was heading for the office suites of Tolson and the Director.

14

Heydeman was a strong swimmer, but he couldn't teach. He was too rough with the girls, chucking them about in the water as if they were boys — the man didn't seem to know his own strength. Powerfully muscled, he could have modelled for a Charles Atlas ad in a magazine, especially if they kept his goofy grin out of the picture. He seemed to Nessheim a little like Lennie, the simpleton in a Steinbeck novel he had read in San Francisco. He had to remind himself that this was someone capable of handling stolen weapons and murdering Eddie Le Saux.

Guttman had not shared Nessheim's excitement when Heydeman had appeared. Or at least he hadn't shown it. 'Watch him,' he'd said simply when Nessheim phoned from the Woodstock Inn. 'But he's not a *Macher*.'

'A what?'

'He's not important in the scheme of things. This is a foot soldier, so make sure you don't show your hand. I want the officers.'

Later that week, when Nessheim had brought the girls back from a long walk to Coolidge Hill, he saw Mrs Schultz signalling him from the lodge. He climbed the hill wearily, hoping she wasn't going to ask him to stand in for Mrs Grumholtz supervising the girls before suppertime.

'You had a phone call, Jimmy, from Chicago. It's about your aunt — they want you to call them right away.'

He had told everybody that his parents had died when he was a boy, and he'd been raised by his aunt in Chicago. He tried to look concerned as Mrs Schultz showed him into her husband's office, which held the solitary phone of the camp. Fortunately, Schultz had gone to Burlington for the day.

'You'll call collect, won't you?' Mrs Schultz asked.

It was a party line, and a neighbour was on it talking about a tractor. At last the line was free, and the local operator in Woodstock got through to the Chicago number. He could hear Mrs Schultz creeping around outside — the floorboards creaked slightly each time she passed by the door.

'Hello,' came faintly down the crackly line.

'It's Jimmy Rossbach here.'

'Oh, Jimmy, it's Matilda, your aunt's neighbour.'

'I see,' he said, though he didn't know anyone named Matilda.

'I don't want to alarm you, but your aunt's had a fall. She's in Cook County.'

'Is she all right?'

'They say she'll be fine. They thought she'd broken her hip, but the X-ray looks okay. She said you're not to come out here.'

'How long is she going to be in for?' he asked, trying to sound worried about his non-existent aunt.

'They don't know yet.' There was a pause. 'I tell you what, can you phone again tomorrow? Say, five o'clock. I'll be here then, and I should have more news to tell you.'

'I'll do that. Thanks for letting me know.' He hung up. Guttman had made Chicago the phone contact point, which made sense: that was where 'Rossbach' came from, and it wouldn't be hard for Schultz and Co. to bribe someone at the exchange in Woodstock and discover that the call had come from Washington. But Guttman hadn't told him that he would know the voice on the other end of the line. Now he realised why 1472 N. Kedzie, the address on his driver's licence, had rung a bell. It, and the voice, belonged to Eloise Tate, known to all as Tatie at the Chicago Bureau of the FBI.

★ ★ ★

The next day Nessheim kept the afternoon hike short — too short, perhaps, since both Adele Kugel and the little Schultz girl complained when he made them turn back only halfway along the fern-lined path they usually took to the end and back. Once returned to camp, he went straight to his cabin, where there was no sign of Kessler. He put on a long-sleeved shirt, then slipped out and moved into the woods. Across the lake the campers would be gathering to play before dinner, but under the shade of the trees he was confident no one would spot him.

It took him twenty minutes to cut at an angle through the dense woods to Route 12, where he emerged at a point where he could see in either direction for almost a mile. No cars were coming, and he sprinted across the road, then moved parallel through the woods to the old forestry track. The second-growth trees were almost all maples — he could see the tap marks on the larger trees — and their high canopies blocked enough sun that the ground cover was sparse and easy to move through.

He was early for the five o'clock rendezvous set by Tatie but already heard the soft throbbing of a car along the overgrown trail. After a minute it stopped where the trail had a large turnaround on one side, constructed as a passing place for the lumber wagons of the old days, almost half a mile in from Route 12.

He moved as quietly as he could, but the going was slow now; here the forest was largely birch and the ground cover resultantly dense, a mass of thick brambles and ferns that shimmied with each step he took. At last he could see light ahead of him, where the turn-around had been carved out of cover. The chrome of a bumper came into view.

He wondered if Guttman himself had come. He wouldn't put it past the man, since as far as Nessheim knew, no one else was privy to his work here. Except Hoover, of course, but however important this was supposed to be, Nessheim didn't imagine the Director himself was going to step out of the automobile.

The car's nose was parked away from Nessheim, pointing into the forest, and it took him a moment to see it was a Dodge. He had entered the small clearing by then, and saw that there was a man in the car. He was lying back against the driver's seat with his feet up on the dashboard and a fedora was jammed down over his eyes. *Beat it* — he heard the chilly voice in Milwaukee all over again.

He'd been set up — someone must have been listening to the call to Tatie. Nessheim started to turn, ready to run, his heart pounding, but the man in the car swung his feet down and in one athletic movement jumped out of his seat and faced him with a pistol in his hand that was pointed directly at Nessheim.

Nessheim threw both hands straight up in the air. 'Take it easy. I'm just walking through the woods, buddy. Give me three secs and I'll be on my way.'

To his relief, the man lowered the gun, though he still held it firmly in one hand. Nessheim remembered how hard the man had seemed in Milwaukee. Would he kill him, just like that? You bet he will, thought Nessheim. He wondered how to distract him so he could run far enough away to give himself a chance.

The man in the fedora laughed, a disconcertingly happy chortle. 'Christ, you gave me a scare,' he said. 'Guttman said you'd be waiting for me.'

'What?'

Nessheim must have looked as dumbfounded as he felt. The man said, 'Yeah, Guttman. You think I get my orders from Hoover himself?' He laughed again.

'You're with the Bureau?' asked Nessheim weakly.

'Well, I'm not with the *Bund*, if that's what you mean.'

'But you were in Woodstock the other day.'

'That's right. I didn't think you'd spot me — it's a real pisser in these one-horse towns. You can't tuck into a side street when there aren't any.'

'But what were you doing there?'

'Watching your ass, pal. I've been doing it for four weeks.'

'You have?' The other man just shrugged, and Nessheim shook his head in wonder. 'So what am I supposed to do now?'

Fedora sighed. 'I guess you haven't talked to Guttman. There's going to be a meeting at your camp. The hard guys are coming in tomorrow, and Schultz's going to give them the word sometime after supper.'

'What word?'

Fedora looked at him as if he were an idiot. 'That's what you're meant to find out, fellah.'

'How do you know all this?'

Fedora cupped a hand to one ear. Nessheim said, 'You've tapped the camp's phone?'

'Sure. The Woodstock exchange have been very cooperative. They don't seem too keen on all these Krauts, either.'

'So what's the gen?'

'Beats me. Schultz phoned them yesterday in Burlington — they came in from New York State. I just know that Schultz said he'd talk to them all after supper. As well as some big shot he'd got coming in from outside.'

'Who is it?'

'Don't know. But you've got to figure out

where they're going to speak.'

'Why?'

Fedora came to the back of the car and opened its trunk. Reaching down with both arms he lifted a large gun-metal box and set it on the ground, exhaling from the exertion. He stood up, puffing, and pointed to the box. 'So you can use big Fred there.'

'Where are *you* going to be?' Nessheim asked, wondering why Fedora wasn't going to do it.

'I'll be right here, pal, waiting for you to deliver the goods. If you can't get it out tomorrow night, don't worry — I'll be here in the morning too.' He gestured at the car with his head. 'The back seat's not too bad when you get used to it. Now let me show you how Fred works. You're not gonna like it — the sonofabitch weighs a ton. And I hope you're mechanical.'

★   ★   ★

Half an hour later Nessheim moved back slowly towards Camp Schneider, weighed down by the metal box he was carrying (it weighed over 30 pounds, he reckoned). He stuck to the Forestry fire road, but when he had crossed Route 12, he carried 'Fred' off the gravel track, putting it deep in some brush. He would retrieve it under the cover of darkness that night.

He was familiar with wiretaps. They were an increasing part of the Bureau's armoury — Mueller had used them relentlessly to try and prove the longshoremen's Union in San Francisco was full of paid Soviet surrogates.

205

Nessheim had never tapped a phone himself, but he understood how the mechanics of it worked. It was easy enough to tap a line, on the target phone or on the actual phone line anywhere between the phone and the exchange.

But the box Fedora had given him contained something altogether different. If you wanted to tape conversations in a room, a phone wiretap wasn't any use. A radio frequency bug was best — they were tiny, small as a half-dollar, and could transmit to a receiver where the audio signal could then be recorded on tape. He considered where best to place the bugs. The meeting could only really be held in one place — the lodge. Schultz's rented house had a minuscule living room, and besides there were the other counsellors living there. In the lodge there was ample space for a meeting, though Nessheim was glad he had two bugs — depending on the numbers, Schultz might opt for the rec room, or his office. The problem wasn't placing the bugs — he was sure he could find two discreet places for the small transmitters. It was rather finding places for the receiver and the tank of a tape recorder.

That night he waited until midnight, when Kessler lay asleep, snoring lightly. He went out the cabin quietly, but not furtively — if you needed to take a leak at night you had to go outside, so his absence was explainable. He waited for his eyes to accustom to the dark, and then, helped by a faint trace of moonlight, moved around the lake and down the track to Fred's hiding place in the woods.

Adrenalin meant Fred felt lighter than earlier in the day, and Nessheim carried the box easily enough to the lodge. Smitty would be asleep next to the kitchen, but the staircase to its loft was outside, and Nessheim went up it quickly. Used now for storage, the attic was full of the suitcases and trunks the girls had brought to camp. It had electricity outlets at either end, but he hadn't dared bring a lamp or flashlight in case the light showed outside. He had to feel his way around the luggage and he made a small passageway for himself between the trunks, then deposited Fred in one corner, where it would look indistinguishable from the other baggage. For insurance, he had written a big tag with the camper Adele Kugel's name on it, and now tied that around the handle of the big box.

Descending, he went into the rec room. Here enough moonlight came through the windows to let him get to work. There was a framed photograph of Coolidge Hill on the wall, and he thought for a moment of hiding the bug behind it, then decided it was too obvious. Instead, he felt behind the mahogany top of the upright piano, and placed one bug there, sticking it against the wooden back with tape from a roll of sticking plaster he had brought in his pocket.

Inside Schultz's office he stumbled over a wooden chair that had been placed by the door. He waited, listening, but there was only silence. A coffee table, crowded with magazines, sat next to a sofa, and he placed the other bug under its pine top, securely fastened with another strip of tape.

When he got back to the cabin, Kessler was still asleep.

★ ★ ★

In the morning no visitors arrived, though Heydeman didn't show at swimming class. When Nessheim went up to the lodge for lunch he discovered the school bus was gone, along with Schultz and Beringer. As he served out the meat loaf at his table, Mrs Schultz came over.

'Herr Rossbach,' she said, always formal with the male counsellors, even Mr Grumholtz who was a neighbour in Manhattan. 'Herr Schultz would like you to go to White River Junction this afternoon and pick up someone at the train station. He will not be back in time.' She handed him a car key. 'He said you should use our Chevrolet.'

'Who am I picking up?'

Mrs Schultz looked blank. 'He didn't tell me, I'm afraid.'

'I'll find them,' said Nessheim, looking forward to driving Schultz's car, which was new.

★ ★ ★

The train was coming in from Boston, and Nessheim was late, since there had been a hold-up at Quechee Gorge, where a sightseer, stretching to see the famously deep ravine, had back-ended another car.

At the station a solitary figure sat on a bench on the platform, hands clasped and head down.

Nessheim rushed over. To his surprise, he saw the man was wearing a priest's collar.

'Excuse me, Father. Are you expected at Camp Schneider?'

The man stood up and his shoulders suddenly seemed to widen. Nessheim realised the priest was big, six feet tall, athletic in build. The face, crinkling into a grin, the eyes lively behind a pair of round spectacles, gold-rimmed, and the hair still dark and combed back wet, suggested a vigorous man. And someone Nessheim was sure he had seen before.

'I am,' the priest said, clearing his throat. The voice wavered, oddly familiar.

'Let me take your bag,' Nessheim said, reaching down for it.

'That's not necessary,' said the man, as Nessheim gripped the bag's handle. 'But most welcome. I've come a long way in twenty-four hours.'

Suddenly Nessheim understood why he had encountered the face before — not in person, but on newsreels that trailed the feature movies in picture houses across the land, and in countless newspaper photographs. Nessheim was carrying the suitcase of the once famous, now infamous, Father Charles Edward Coughlin. Wouldn't Uncle Eric have been thrilled?

They walked through the small waiting room to the car outside. Nessheim lifted the trunk lid and placed the bag carefully down. Like someone used to chauffeurs, the priest had already got into the back seat.

He looked tired from his trip, and sat with his

eyes closed as Nessheim drove the Chevy west towards Woodstock and the camp. Soon the priest nodded off, until a bump on the road jolted the car and he woke with a start. His nap seemed to have perked him up. 'Sorry to doze off like that.' He pushed his window down. 'This is lovely countryside. Do you hail from around here, young man?'

'No, sir.'

'What would your name be?'

'It's James Rossbach, Father.'

Coughlin said cheerily, 'You must be one of Max Schultz's fellows then. I wasn't sure if he'd sent one of the local taxi services to collect me.'

'No, this is his car.'

'And a fine piece of machinery it is, too. I take it you're a member of the *Bund*.'

'A fully paid-up one,' said Nessheim.

Coughlin laughed. 'And a good Catholic to boot?'

'I was raised a Lutheran, Father.'

'Still a Christian in the eyes of our Lord. That's what matters. To maintain a united Christian front.'

'Have you come all the way from Detroit, Father?'

Coughlin looked pleased that Nessheim knew who he was. 'I went to Washington first. That hellhole. One hundred degrees in the supposed cradle of democracy.'

Nessheim laughed, but there was a venomous note in Coughlin's voice.

'Tell me, my young friend, how is Max Schultz taking the news?'

'What news is that?'

'You mean you haven't heard.' A newspaper was thrust over Nessheim's shoulder, which he took with one hand. A herd of Holsteins was being led across at the bottom of a hill, and when he stopped to wait for them he unfolded the paper, a copy of the *Boston Herald*. The headline read: **Reich-Moscow Pact Stuns World**.

Disbelieving, he scanned the rest of the article. It was true: Ribbentrop was flying to Moscow to formalise a non-aggression pact between Germany and the Soviet Union.

The cows had gone. Handing the paper back to Coughlin, he said, 'Amazing.'

Coughlin laughed. 'It's stunning news, I'll grant you that. Some might call it a pact with the Devil, but I think the Lord himself understands that sometimes you have to do business with the enemy. And we in the Christian West have no one to blame but ourselves. We've driven Hitler to it; not you and me, but the British with all their posturing, the Jews with their machinations, and Roosevelt.' He pronounced the President's name with a magnificent rolling R. 'He should have kept a million miles away from the English.'

'Well, that will change in a year.'

'What makes you think that?' demanded Coughlin. He was leaning forward now, to hear Nessheim over the noise from the open windows. They were nearing Woodstock.

Nessheim said, 'Well, the new President is likely to hold different views about things, don't you think? None of the candidates you read about seem half as pro-English as FDR.'

'They're not — they're sane men. But who's to say Roosevelt won't still be our President?'

They were in town now and Nessheim turned up Pleasant Street, lined by Federalist houses, then drove through the delicate covered bridge at the end of the street. But Coughlin was paying no attention to his surroundings now.

Nessheim started to say, 'I thought the Constitution — '

'The Constitution says nothing about it.' Coughlin spat out his words angrily. 'It's only tradition that keeps a President from serving more than eight years. That and a sense of restraint. But that's not a word I'd put in the same sentence with the man Roosevelt. He's a menace. Mark my words: he wants a war, and if he has to run again to get his war, he will.'

*   *   *

When they came to Camp Schneider, Schultz and his wife were waiting in front of the farmhouse, dressed formally in honour of their visitor, as if for church. While Nessheim took Coughlin's suitcase out of the car, they led the priest inside. Depositing the bag on the porch, Nessheim walked the few hundred yards to the camp.

He heard the firing from the upper farm field before he got to the lodge. Repeated rifle shots, stinging flat cracks in the air.

'What's going on?' he asked Smitty, who was

212

standing outside the kitchens in his white apron, smoking a cigarette.

'I don't know. The school bus done come back full of these fellahs. Then they all went up to the field with Mr Heydeman.'

'What are they doing up there?'

'Whatever it is, it's not my business. Though that ain't corn popping I hear.' He tossed his butt down and ground it out with his heel. 'They gonna come down for lunch, so you can see for yourself then, but they looks to me like they mean business. And they got a dog — nasty one too, or else maybe it just don't like coloured people. German Shepherd sure didn't like me.'

And at lunch Nessheim saw what Smitty meant. Schultz wasn't there — presumably he and Frau Schultz were feeding Father Coughlin in style up at the farmhouse — when roughly thirty men trooped into the dining hall after the campers had sat down for lunch. Nessheim noticed the visitors were dressed in uniforms of brown T-shirts, grey cotton trousers, and canvas sneakers. They all looked in good physical shape, with cropped hair and arms tanned from hours in the sun. Like tough, experienced soldiers, Nessheim thought. Most were young, younger than he was, but there was none of the horseplay one would expect from males their age. They stood patiently in line for their food, then sat by themselves at trencher tables that had been set up at the far end of the dining hall. They ate quietly, as if even lunch was a matter of discipline rather than enjoyment. These men were from the *Ordnungsdienst* — the Order

Division, or O.D. for short. The hard men of the movement.

After lunch the visitor platoon went back up to the far field, out of sight from the rest of the camp. At hike time, Nessheim tried to lead his pack of girls in their direction, for there had been no more gunfire, but halfway up the slope Beringer called out to him. 'Not that way, Jimmy.'

'What's the problem?'

'There is no problem,' said Beringer. 'Just take them in another direction, please.'

$\star$ $\star$ $\star$

At supper there was still no sign of Schultz, or Coughlin. The visitors had stayed up in the far field for supper, grilling meat — the smell of barbecue wafted down the hill as Nessheim came into the lodge.

He wished he could have placed a bug in the farmhouse, but the receiver's reach was under 75 yards, and there would have been no safe place to tape-record the conversations between Coughlin and Schultz. He could only hope that there would be something of substance to record in the lodge. He knew now that there would be a meeting, for Beringer had circulated among the tables during supper, explaining to all the counsellors that the staffroom would not be available that evening. The rec room would be occupied after nine o'clock.

Nessheim killed time after supper, playing tag with the girls on the grassy slope in front of the lodge. At lights out he helped Frances check on each cabin, extinguishing their kerosene lamps and saying goodnight to the campers. When he went back to his cabin Kessler was reading by lamplight.

Nessheim said, 'One of the girls isn't feeling well. I may need to fetch the doctor. I'll try not to wake you when I come in.'

Kessler nodded absent-mindedly, caught up in his book.

It was starting to rain as Nessheim circled the lake and went up the sloping lawn. The lodge was lit and as he approached he could see the *Ordnungsdienst* men in the rec room, drinking mugs of coffee from two vast canisters Smitty had brought out from the kitchen. Nessheim kept his distance from the lit-up windows and turned towards the end of the building. As he was about to leave the safety of the shadows, Coughlin, Schultz and Heydeman walked by, less than 20 yards from him. He froze, but none of them looked around, their faces down against the rain.

He waited a full minute to be sure they had gone into the lodge, then quickly crossed and went up the steps on tiptoe in the pair of old sneakers he had put on.

The loft was pitch black, but he didn't dare use a flashlight. He knew where he had put 'Fred', and could feel his way there, but suddenly realised in such darkness he wouldn't be able to tell if he had pushed the right switch to operate the machine. He'd probably end up erasing instead of recording.

He needed some kind of light, but it would have to be natural not to be seen outside. At his end of the loft there was a large opening, originally designed for bringing up hay bales on a pulley system — the old wheel sat ten foot in from the wall on the floor, its ropes tangled in a knotted heap. When not in use an immense square of oak slats filled the opening, with a surrounding plywood frame. It opened inwards, but was much too heavy for him to lift, so he worked the big panel out of its frame and let it fall on his extended upraised hands, then slowly brought it down silently onto the loft floor. From the rainy, cloud-filled sky a dark grey layer of light suffused his end of the loft. It would have to do.

He found 'Fred', and opened the box, then carefully lifted out the tape machine. It was heavy, steel-framed with metal components. He set it down near the door, then went back and took the receiver from the metal box. It was about the size of a small desktop radio. He set it on the floor next to the tape machine and unravelled the receiver's cord. Feeling his way, he found the electrical outlet near the staircase door, and after several efforts, and a risky probe with his fingers, managed to fit the two prongs in.

There had not been much noise from downstairs, but then the sound of singing came up to him, bass notes reverberating through the floorboards. It sounded German, a marching song. After each chorus everyone stamped their feet, so hard that even the loft rafters trembled.

Jesus, thought Nessheim, glad he hadn't been put in undercover to join these *Bund* paramilitaries.

He crawled back to the receiver, and flicked its switch. A tiny red light went on, and in its small glow he could make out a needle moving on the central gauge. The RF bug was transmitting, and he breathed a sigh of relief.

Nessheim waited while downstairs they all sang another marching song, then the low hum of chatter he had heard before resumed. But only momentarily. There was a sharp knocking sound, and he realised someone was calling for attention.

A harsh voice began speaking in German; it must be Schultz. After only twenty seconds or so, it stopped, and was followed by clapping. When the applause died down someone else started speaking. It was Coughlin — in the same compelling, mellifluous voice once heard by millions every Saturday afternoon, travelling up and down the octaves like scales played on a piano. Sitting down on the floor, Nessheim turned on the recorder.

Coughlin spoke for about ten minutes, while Nessheim watched the empty reel on one side slowly begin to fill. He had forty-five minutes' recording capability, which should be ample he reckoned. He wished there was a way for him to hear the words himself, but the acoustic signal received from the transmitter was unintelligible to human ears, unless played back in recorded form by the tape machine.

When Coughlin finished, Schultz took over

again. Curiously, his voice projected better than the priest's — he half-shouted his words, but they were clearly enunciated, and by straining Nessheim could almost make them out. He noticed a tiny chink of light coming through between the floorboards, nearer to the staircase door. Perhaps if he lay there, ear down, he could make out what Schultz was saying. It seemed worth a try.

He got up very slowly, taking care not to knock over the receiver or jiggle the tape machine. Too much care, in fact, for he felt his back hit one of the trunks stacked behind him. He stopped moving as soon as he made contact, but the trunk, perilously balanced to begin with, started to slide off the stack. Panicked, Nessheim turned around to grab it, but clunked it with an elbow instead. That did it: the trunk fell backwards onto the floor, landing with an enormous bang.

Shit! Nessheim stood there hoping against hope that the noise had gone unremarked downstairs. He could hear nothing from below, but silence was the most ominous noise of all. Then he heard chairs being pushed back and Schultz shouting orders.

Nessheim grabbed the receiver, and with his free hand yanked as hard as he could on its cord. It popped out of the outlet 20 feet away and came flying through the air, hitting him on the ear. It stung, but this was no time to worry about that. He chucked the receiver into Fred's case, then leaned down, switched the machine off, and lifted the right-hand reel out of its socket. With his teeth he broke off the tape still linked to the other reel, then lifted the machine and dumped it into the big box. Closing it, then hoisting the heavy container with his arms, he set it down amidst a pile of trunks and suitcases. He grabbed the single reel, shoved it under his shirt, and made for the external stairs.

All this had taken no more than thirty seconds, but he was still too late. Voices came from outside the lodge, and they were coming closer; he saw the beam of a flashlight at the corner of the building on the ground below.

There was nothing for it. He turned and moved quickly to the hay opening at the end of the loft. He climbed onto its lower sill and looked down. Even if he didn't break a leg, he'd be spotted before he had collected himself and run away. And on either side of the opening there was nothing to grab onto — just the flat boards of the lodge.

He looked up, and saw that the roof was only a couple of feet above the top of the big square aperture. He grabbed one of the empty trunks lying near him and pushed it over to the edge of the opening. As he got up and stood balancing on it, he heard footsteps coming up the stairs outside.

He turned with his back to the hay opening, on the very edge of the trunk. For a moment he thought it might tip over under his weight, and send him flying backwards, to land on his head on the ground. But the trunk held steady. He decided he had to move before he became mentally paralysed by calculation of the odds.

Jumping up and out, he timed the swing of his arms, and reached for the edge of the lodge's roof. Its surface was shingles, probably cedar, and his hands held firm to their wet but scratchy surface. He swung his legs back into the air, then using all his strength pulled himself straight up, until his chest came to roof level and he could hook his elbows over the edge. Then with another massive effort he drew the rest of his body up high enough to swing a leg onto the roof edge. He managed to roll his other leg onto the shingles, just as he heard a voice come from the loft opening below.

'*Heraus!*' shouted a member of the O.D.

Nessheim lay still for a minute, chest heaving, trying to catch his breath as the rain spattered the shingles around him. The men below would have a hard time getting on the roof, but once Schultz knew someone was up here, he could simply surround the building and wait him out.

He climbed to the central gable point of the roof, scrambling up the shingle tiles as fast as he dared. Then he moved along with one hand on the ridge beam to keep from slipping down the steeply angled sides. Halfway along, he let go and slowly slid his way down to the edge of the roof. He turned over, so that his stomach lay flush against the shingles, and slowly let his legs slide over the edge until they dangled in air. Suddenly his descent accelerated as his jacket, slick from the rain, slid like grease on the wet cedar. He grabbed both hands onto the final line of shingles, and hung on, trying to summon the courage to let go.

He felt a faint dizziness, the same vertiginous nausea he'd last had with Danny Ho. He wanted to retch, but was terrified to make a telltale cough. He heard someone at the far end of the lodge, probably at the hay opening, but there was no flashlight beam. The dizziness was growing; sensing he would fall at any moment, he let go, bending both his legs like a parachutist.

It could not have been more than a twelve-foot drop, and the ground had been softened by the rain, but he still landed with a hellish jolt. He sensed nothing was broken, but there was a stabbing pain in one knee. He ignored it and crouched down against the side of the lodge. The rain was heavier now, and the wind had picked up, throwing the drops like pea gravel against the building's slats.

A dog barked, not far away. Damn, he thought. If they took the German Shepherd upstairs to the loft to catch Nessheim's scent, then brought him down again, the dog would find him in minutes.

He stood up and moved to the end of the building, then slowly peeked around the corner. Half a dozen men were standing in the rain by the back door of the lodge, illuminated by the lights in the kitchen. He could see Schultz, the shortest of the group, pointing sharply around him. There was a lull in the wind, and he heard the metallic voice clearly. 'Search the cabins as well. Check them all. *Schnell.*'

Pulling his head back, Nessheim turned and ran for the safety of the woods, taking care to keep the side of the lodge between him and the men. He had to get back to his cabin before they discovered he was missing.

He moved through a stand of birch nervously, fearing his dark jacket would be easily spotted against the white bark. Moving along he stayed a few yards back from the clearing, heading for the edge of the lake to the point where the semicircle of camper cabins began. If he went deeper into the woods he might get lost in the dark and rain. *The woods are lovely, dark and deep*, according to Robert Frost, but Nessheim would have kept it at dark and deep.

What should he do? He could head to Schultz's farmhouse, try and take refuge there. But if he showed up, rain-soaked and bedraggled, God knows whom he would encounter there or what he would say. Maybe he should stick it out, wait until morning, then appear, claiming he'd spent the night in Woodstock. But that wouldn't wash either. He was never going to dry out by then — no one would believe he hadn't been skulking in the woods.

His only hope lay in getting back to his cabin, and he moved as fast as he could through the low brush of the forest. Once he tripped on a bramble and fell flat, fortunately onto the soft floor of pine needles. Then disaster almost struck — his left leg suddenly dropped sharply, his right followed, and Nessheim found himself in water up to his thighs. He pulled himself out, soaked through, and realised he had foundered on a little creek.

He was near the edge of the pond, and thus near the first of the cabins. Mine would have to be the furthest away, he thought bitterly, but he hoped there was still time to reach it before he was discovered.

Hope ran out as he started to move behind the first cabin. A flashlight suddenly swept across one of the cabins ahead of him, and the dog barked with the jubilant menace of a canine that had been trained to track. Through the overhanging wisps of birch, Nessheim saw that the O.D. had made it to this side of the pond, and were rapidly spreading out to find their intruder. They were heading away from him, but that was no help — they would be searching the cabin of Kessler and Rossbach first.

He waited, wondering what to do, standing near the outermost cabin at this end of the pond. It was Frances Stockton's cabin and its light was off.

A flickering flashlight shone in the distance, revealing three or four shadowy figures in the woods. They weren't moving away, he realised with a start; they were heading in his direction, making sure no one hiding in a cabin could sneak out undetected. Then behind him a twig cracked, and he heard a footstep. Someone was coming, along the same way he had come through the woods. A classic pincer movement. These people were thorough and well-trained; he would soon be completely surrounded.

He could see no way out. Should he wait to be found, or step forward and try to bluff his way out, claiming to be returning from an assignation with a woman, or even from a midnight nature walk by himself? In his heart he knew no story he concocted would be believed.

He moved to hide behind the nearest cabin — Frances's cabin. Suddenly he stopped at the screen door. He didn't hesitate. 'Frances,' he whispered. There was no reply. 'Frances,' he hissed more urgently.

He heard a stirring, then the creak of an iron bed. The screen swung open and Frances stood framed in the doorway. She wore a man's striped cotton nightshirt, and her black hair, no longer tied back, lay in clustered ebony strands on her shoulders.

'Chug?' she said. He heard the dog bark in the distance, and could see flashlights as the men began to work their way through the cabins.

'Can I come in?' he said, and Frances stood aside as he sprang up the two steps and entered the cabin.

He went and stood in the dark by her bed. Frances slowly followed him. 'What's that?' she asked. For he had unfastened the top buttons of his shirt and taken out the 9-inch tape reel. He leaned down and put it on the plank flooring, then pushed it slowly with his foot under Frances's bed.

He took a step towards Frances, visible only by the white of her nightshirt. He could not see her expression, but he had to take the chance.

She said, 'What's going on out there?'

'Just the young Nazis having a party.'

'But what are you doing here?' He couldn't read her tone.

'I sort of hoped that would be obvious.' He held out both arms and waited.

At first she didn't move. Would she slap his face? Shout at him to get out? Even scream?

Then suddenly the white shirt moved forward in the dark and he felt her own arms within his extended ones, encircling him around the chest as her lips moved onto his.

Where they remained, until she broke away to reach down and push back her bedclothes, then moved the two of them onto the bed. She sat next to him there for a moment and sighed. 'I thought you weren't interested.'

'Just shy,' he said. And then her mouth closed over his again.

15

In the middle of August, Stephenson called late one morning. Guttman hesitated when his secretary said who was on the line. He was up to his eyeballs with work, and was waiting tensely for news from Vermont. He had heard nothing from either of his agents there, and could only pray that Nessheim had managed to record the meeting and smuggle the tapes out. How he wanted to nail these *Bund* bastards. And Coughlin — if the priest said enough to be prosecuted — would be the perfect icing on the cake.

He finally took the call. Stephenson said, 'I was thinking that if we're meant to liaise, we should begin the process. Any chance of lunch?'

'Golly, it's a busy time right now.' He wouldn't hear from Nessheim until the next day, but he felt too tense for diplomacy right now.

'How are you fixed tomorrow?'

Tomorrow? You had to admire the guy's chutzpah, thought Guttman, who'd already been impressed by Stephenson's coolness in the face of Hoover's rudeness. Maybe he should get it over with. Besides, there was nothing he could do to help Nessheim by sitting at his desk worrying. 'Okay. Where would you like to meet?'

'Why don't you come to my club? Twelve-thirty if that's all right. Let me give you the address.'

He met Stephenson in a large late-Victorian brick house in Georgetown. Guttman drove past it and parked around the corner, wondering what kind of club would have its quarters in this part of town. Georgetown was coming up in the world — doctors, lawyers, even some of the Congressmen were starting to live here now, fixing up the old townhouses that had not been looked after for years. But it was a residential area, and the only clubs Guttman knew of were nearer the institutions of government, and thus nearer the centre of power.

Stephenson was waiting for him outside. He was in a business suit this day, and Guttman was glad Isabel had made him wear a shirt with an unfrayed collar and had found him an unstained tie.

Stephenson said, 'Delighted you could make it. Let's go in.'

They walked up a few steps and Stephenson turned the large brass handle on the oak door. Inside at the end of a corridor a servant in a white jacket was polishing a side table, and Guttman caught the faint aroma of beeswax.

'Morning, Jason,' said Stephenson. 'Anybody about?'

The black man shook his head. 'Just the Colonel, sir.'

Stephenson opened another door and led Guttman into a long sitting room that had dark green wallpaper and a ruby carpet. Over the fireplace hung a large oil painting showing the

227

Hudson River with a Victorian picnic party (boaters and bonnets) in the foreground. Along the walls, floor-to-ceiling bookcases alternated with dark framed engravings; comfortable easy chairs and two-seater sofas were placed in small groupings throughout the room, little convivial islands which suggested this was a club, not a residence.

The room was empty, except for a solitary old man in a pinstripe suit sitting in a wing chair. From his waistcoat a pocket watch dangled from a fob chain, and his lap was half-covered by a copy of the London *Times*. The old man was sound asleep, snoring lightly. Stephenson pointed to the far end of the room, where a small table had been laid for lunch. 'Let's go down there where we won't be disturbed.' He looked down at the Colonel with a faint smile. 'And he won't be either.'

As they sat down, Stephenson said, 'Good of you to come.'

Guttman grunted. 'What kind of club is this?'

Stephenson chuckled. 'A rather unorthodox one for Washington. It's limited to former officers in the British forces. Army, navy, air force — we're not picky, provided you've served.'

Jason arrived, with a barman's towel over his arm. Stephenson said, 'What will you have to drink, Mr Guttman? I'm going to have a Sidecar myself — it's a bit of a speciality here.'

'I'll just have a ginger ale, thanks.'

'Are you sure? I know Mr Hoover's been known to have a drink at lunch in the Mayflower Hotel.'

'You're well informed. But Mr Hoover doesn't have to answer to anyone when he does.'

Stephenson laughed. 'I suppose he's the Cabot of Washington. What do they say in Boston? The Lowells answer only to Cabots, and the Cabots only answer to God. In this case, is FDR God?'

'Some people have him down as the Devil.'

'I guess they do. Where do you stand on FDR?'

'I think he's a great man.' Guttman felt uneasy, not wanting the conversation to slide into politics. That was never a good idea.

Their drinks came and Stephenson waited to reply until Jason had left the menu and gone away. He took a sip of his Sidecar, then said, 'I happen to agree with you.'

To change the subject, Guttman asked, 'Were you in the British army then?'

'Not quite. I started with the Royal Winnipeg, but eventually did a bit of flying with the Royal Flying Squad. What they call the RAF these days. Made me something of an honorary Brit, I suppose.' He looked a little embarrassed. 'Now, what would you like to eat?'

The food was excellent — Guttman followed Stephenson's lead and had the lamb steak — and Stephenson was an excellent conversationalist, asking Guttman questions about himself without prying, telling amusing stories of his own travels, which seemed voluminous. There was no effort to ingratiate, yet nothing standoffish about him either. Guttman for all his wariness found himself liking the man.

It was only over coffee that Stephenson

brought up business. 'They taught me in school to 'Beware of Greeks bearing gifts', but I hope you won't mind if in order to start our liaison on solid ground, I start with a little gift.'

What did Stephenson have in mind, Guttman wondered? A gold watch, or a case of whiskey, or box seats at a Washington Senators baseball game? Had this man really misread Guttman so badly?

'Don't look so horrified, Mr Guttman. Do you mind if I call you Harry? I'm Bill by the way.'

Guttman nodded, but waited apprehensively.

'We have some good contacts in Switzerland. And they've spotted an organisation that has been looking for someone in Austria. We've got contacts of our own, who so far at least have managed to elude the Nazis. Perhaps they could be of use to you.'

'Austria?' Guttman asked, trying to sound bland.

'If it's any use,' said Stephenson, as if it were a matter of indifference to him.

Guttman thought hard. If he passed, would he be looking a gift horse in the mouth? Equally, if he took the bait, was he being drawn in like a sucker, co-opted by the people his Director had explicitly told him not to get close to? But he had already disobeyed the Director, in a manner far more culpable than this. In for an inch, he told himself.

He said to Stephenson, 'We're looking for a man named Werner. Konrad Werner. He was born in Austria and came to America in 1920, according to our immigration authorities. He settled eventually in Detroit, but then in the summer of 1936 he travelled to Europe — or at least he said he did. His friends and pretty distant family thought he must be going to the Olympics, which of course were in Berlin. But we're not so sure. It seemed likelier that he went home to the Tyrol.'

'Can I ask why you're looking for him?'

'No. Not yet anyway.'

Stephenson nodded evenly. 'I was a bit surprised you had people working on your behalf in Switzerland.'

'Why?' asked Guttman, suddenly prickly.

'How can I put it, Harry? The FBI is famous the world over for its crime-fighting capabilities. I am second to no one in my admiration for your expertise. But America's global prominence is a recent phenomenon — perfectly understandable, you're a young nation after all. One can't expect a sophisticated intelligence network abroad — we've had centuries to develop ours and it still has plenty of holes.'

Guttman didn't argue, for what Stephenson said was perfectly correct. The truth was, the Bureau didn't have anyone working in Switzerland. Guttman had used personal contacts with a Jewish charity organisation, calling in favours he'd performed in a private capacity. Maybe that's why he hadn't got anywhere.

'Anyway, let me see what we can find out. As I say, we have some Austrian contacts your Swiss friends might not have.'

'Thank you.' Guttman meant this, though he was puzzled by Stephenson's unexpected offer.

231

The set-up here was also curious — what kind of club only fed two people at lunch? It wouldn't last long at that rate, he figured.

He pushed back his chair and stood up awkwardly. 'Is there a gents I could use?'

'Of course. Down the hall and just around the corner.'

'Thanks.' Guttman went along the hallway, which was lined with landscape watercolours, and turned the corner. There was no sign of Jason. At the end of the hall he saw an open door. Ignoring the bathroom he walked silently towards it. From the open doorway he saw a girl with a blonde bun standing in a corner, her back to him, pouring coffee into big stone mugs. In the middle of the room four desks were pushed together, each occupied by a man. One was on the phone talking loudly, another sat at a Royal typewriter pounding away with two fingers, while the remaining pair stood poring over papers — newspapers, magazines, typed pages, a sea of print strewn over the desktops.

The man on the phone looked up and spied Guttman outside the doorway. Eyes widening, he gestured to his colleagues and jabbed a finger at Guttman.

'Can I help you?' asked another man, swivelling from his desk. The voice was British, friendly but firm.

'Sorry, I'm looking for the men's room.'

The man raised an eyebrow, then jerked his head towards the hall. 'You've passed it.'

Guttman found the bathroom, and tried to make a lot of noise, flushing twice and running the water at full blast in the sink. Club my ass, thought Guttman as he finished. How many British ex-officers could there be in Washington?

Stephenson was running another kind of operation here, one which must involve lining up American contacts, influencing the American press, doing everything it could to sway American opinion towards the British side of things. Including spinning a yarn to a sympathetic FBI officer? Possibly, though Guttman was struck by the urgency which lay behind Stephenson's relaxed façade.

When he returned to the table, he found Stephenson had poured them both more coffee. This wasn't over yet, thought Guttman as he sat down. But then he hadn't really thought lunch would be free.

'Relax, Harry. If you're thinking I'm going to ask for a favour in return, you're right. But it's one I think could help us both.'

Guttman waited. Stephenson had lost his airy detachment, if not all of his charm, and there was nothing mannered about him now. 'We have some Nazi-lovers of our own in Britain. The most famous is Oswald Mosley, of course. He leads the British Union of Fascists — the Blackshirts as they're known. He is not without sympathisers among fellow members of the upper classes. One of them is a man named Viscount Dugdale. He loathes publicity, and has never publicly come out in support of Mosley. But he has funded him to a worrying extent — we estimate he's given fifty thousand pounds over the past few years to the BUF. That's a quarter of a million dollars.

'Dugdale is married to a woman who shares his views. But it's his second marriage. Ten years ago, he was divorced by his first wife, a woman now named Dove, Lady Dove actually. She also remarried, and lives in Oxford. Her husband is head of one of the colleges there, an eminent law don, and, ironically perhaps, known for his left-wing views. He came to the attention of our services for the opposite reason that Dugdale has. We try and be even-handed in the people we persecute.'

Guttman laughed out loud, and Stephenson seemed happy to see the American had a sense of humour. 'But that's not what really piqued our interest. It was Lady Dove. Despite a bitter divorce, and remarriage to someone decidedly on the Left, we have reason to suspect that she's held firmly to her ex-husband's views and supports the Nazi cause.'

'What does her new husband make of that?'

'He doesn't know their real nature. On the surface, she shares his views — anti-Franco, anti-Hitler, mildly pro-Commissar.'

'But in private . . . ?'

'Her views are very different. And she keeps them to herself. But we have evidence that she is effectively an agent of German intelligence.'

'Effectively?'

'She's not drawing a salary. And possibly not yet doing that much for the opposition. But enough to indicate where her sympathies lie.'

'What has she done?' asked Guttman. He was starting to realise that Stephenson's circumlocutions were precautionary; if you poked his

234

rhetorical balloons, he was happy to talk turkey.

'She importuned a young official in the Foreign Office. Bright chap, an aide to Anthony Eden the Foreign Secretary. A Prize Fellow of All Souls — ' he broke off as he saw the incomprehension in Guttman's eyes. 'Sorry, that's a particularly rarefied college in Oxford. He had rooms there, and went up weekends. Where Lady Dove paid him a great deal of attention.'

'You mean she . . . ?'

'Our intelligence didn't extend to the chap's pillow, I'm afraid.' This time they both laughed. Stephenson said, 'Whatever the lure on offer, she was clearly hoping for inside info about the negotiations during the Munich crisis. Fortunately this chap is no fool, and no fan of Chamberlain's either.'

A snore came from the sleeping Colonel at the other end of the room. Guttman said mildly, 'I don't mean to be rude, but as Mr Hoover might say, what's it to us?'

'Perhaps nothing,' said Stephenson, and again Guttman couldn't help liking the man's candour. 'But there's an American connection you may want to know about.'

'What kind of connection?'

'A correspondence between Lady Dove and an American woman here in Washington. They met in England a few years ago when Dove's husband gave a dinner for Felix Frankfurter — he was in Oxford for a year giving lectures. The American lady was visiting on holiday; she was invited to the dinner because she was a friend of Frankfurter's wife.'

Guttman wasn't surprised. Frankfurter, famously, had married one of the *goyim* — just like me, thought Guttman. It had only been a few months since the Harvard professor had been confirmed by the Senate as a Justice of the Supreme Court, a controversial appointment — there were plenty of people who thought one Jew was more than enough on the court, and Brandeis was still there.

'What's the American woman's name?'

'Sally Cummings.'

'I've heard of her,' said Guttman. His wife Isabel followed the society pages of the *Washington Globe* zealously. She'd read out bits of it to Guttman in the evenings when they sat and had a drink after he got home.

Stephenson said, 'She was married to a senator from Carolina who died young. But he left her very well set up. And I gather she has since established a salon of the Great and the Good — senators, judges, senior members of the government. I believe even your President has graced her portal.'

'Are you thinking she's a Nazi, too?' He couldn't suppress a note of scepticism.

'I honestly don't know. All I can say is that about a year ago her letters to Lady Dove started referring to a project — 'Our project' she called it. The letters after that read like progress reports — 'Prospects look good,' 'Our plan moves ahead,' that sort of thing. It's always put very vaguely — and that's what aroused our suspicions.'

'What about the Dove end of the correspondence?'

Stephenson shook his head, and Guttman suddenly understood. They were intercepting the letters from Cummings to Dove in England, but that would only give a view from one end of the telescope — they wouldn't have any idea what Dove was writing to Cummings.

Presumably Stephenson wanted him to supply the view from the other end. Guttman couldn't see how he could do that. Mail intercepts were not unknown for the FBI, but almost without exception their targets were Communists or known criminals. You couldn't do it willy-nilly, especially to a well-connected society hostess like Sally Cummings. He would need Hoover's permission even to contemplate such a move, and chances of that were precisely zero, especially since the request for the intercepts came from Stephenson.

He tried to explain this tactfully to the Canadian, but the man stopped him. 'That's not what I was asking for,' he said.

Bullshit, thought Guttman, but without resentment.

Stephenson said, 'I think you may want to look into this Cummings woman in any case. You see, something else has come up that seems pretty alarming.' He took a sip of his coffee. 'We keep an eye on Lady Dove herself, not just her correspondence. About two months ago she went to London for the day. Nothing odd there — she often goes for shopping, or to see friends. But this time she didn't go to the West End or Regent Street or any place we'd expect. Instead, she walked to a churchyard north of Paddington

Station. There she talked for a while with a couple. They all acted as if they'd never met before, and perhaps they hadn't — but it still seemed quite peculiar to our chap watching.'

Guttman was intrigued. 'And?'

Stephenson was too smooth to acknowledge Guttman's interest; having hooked his fish, he was going to play him for a bit. 'Fortunately our man had his wits about him. When the encounter ended he didn't follow Lady Dove, but trailed the couple instead.

'They went back into the middle of town to a small hotel off St James's. They were guests there, though the next day they checked out and caught the boat train for the Continent from Victoria. We dug around a bit at the hotel, and it turned out they were posing as a Dutch couple over for a holiday.'

'Posing?'

'Yes. One of the chambermaids said she'd heard them speaking German to each other.'

'Isn't it easy to confuse the two?' asked Guttman, wondering what a chambermaid would know.

Stephenson ignored him. 'We managed to get photographs of them in front of their hotel, waiting for their taxi when they were leaving.'

Stephenson had planned for this moment, Guttman realised, for a Manila envelope suddenly materialised from under the table, which the Canadian handed to Guttman.

Guttman took out a glossy picture, the size of a piece of typing paper. It was a good clear shot, and must have been taken from the inside of a car across the street. In the background was the canopied entrance of a hotel; a bellhop was lugging a suitcase down its carpeted steps. At street level a doorman in the usual absurd hat and tasselled jacket was turned sideways, staring down the street. Next to him a couple were waiting glumly. The woman was medium height and blonde, handsome rather than pretty. She was neat in a long trenchcoat, hat perched at an angle on her head.

The man next to her was lighting a cigarette, and even with his neck craned down to catch the lighter in his hand, was much taller than his companion. He too had fair hair and wore a suit, well-cut but conservative, that made him look just like the Dutch businessman on holiday he claimed to be. There was something rigid in his demeanour; it was that of a man who never relaxed.

Guttman passed the photo back to Stephenson. 'I don't recognise either one.'

'We didn't either at first. That may have been due to the presence of the woman, since we didn't find anyone like her in our files. But we're pretty confident about the man. His name is Walter Schellenberg. Ring a bell?'

'Sorry, no. Should it?'

'Not necessarily. But you might find it useful in the years ahead. He works for German intelligence. He's recently been made head of their counter-espionage department.' He looked with open amusement at Guttman. 'You could say he's your German counterpart.'

'*Counter*-espionage. So what was he doing in England?'

'That's what we found alarming. It had to be something significant to get him there, don't you think?'

* * *

When Guttman returned to the office, he had Marie call down to Research, and ten minutes later a thin file on Sally Cummings sat on his desk.

He noted the basic facts with only mild interest: Born in 1882 in Rutland Vermont, daughter of Franklin Ryerson, a local judge and merchant, her mother, née McHenry, came from a prominent Virginian family. Married 1907 T. Irwin Cummings, a wealthy businessman who after the war was elected senator from South Carolina. He died in 1927 and Sally Cummings remained in D.C., in the large house her husband had purchased in 1924 on the edge of Georgetown.

There were also several newspaper clippings in the file, and gradually a more contemporary picture emerged. She was a society hostess, so he'd been right about that. Gave a famous summer solstice party and a New Year's Day lunch, both attended by senior politicians and members of the executive, as well as by what passed for old society in this town.

So far there was nothing remarkable in the file, and Guttman found himself wondering why this woman had one at all. Hoover loved files, it was true, but except for the higher echelon of elected officials — who automatically got a place

240

in the filing cabinets downstairs — there had to be some past impropriety or ill-judged association (Communist preferably) to warrant the formal attention of the Bureau.

And then he saw it: just a passing couple of sentences in another report, one that had been cross-referenced, copied and pasted here:

> Subject is known as a keen admirer of the Fairer Sex, and though discreet his conquests are legendary. Among the most notable are rumoured to be Mrs Sarah Tydings and Mrs Sally Cummings — widow of the late Senator from South Carolina.

So who was this lothario? Guttman looked at the cross-reference to the subject's file — XFE/35/G01/D1937. The filing system had its own nomenclature, impenetrable to Guttman — the system of acronyms and abbreviations might as well have been Ancient Greek. But he recognised the final 'D' — it stood for 'defunct'. The file had been closed in 1937. He wondered why, even more curious about whose file it was.

Calling out to Marie, he sent her down to Research again. Five minutes later he was staring with astonishment at the file she'd brought back.

Luther, Hans, the side tab read.

An FBI file on the former German Ambassador to the United States of America, who had been suddenly recalled in 1937 just days after Bock had transcribed one of his confidential cables to Berlin. *Where is Werner?*

He thought immediately of Agent Nessheim, working in Vermont for him. At a camp run by Max Schultz, the brother-in-law of . . . Konrad Werner.

Suddenly the world seemed a lot smaller.

16

Late August 1939
New York City

This time he got to see New York. One part of it anyway, since Nessheim's activities were confined to Yorkville on the Upper East Side, where Schultz lived and the *Bund* had its national headquarters.

The cadre of *Ordnungsdienst* had left Camp Schneider after two days. They had continued their manoeuvres in the high field, despite persisting rain, and taken their meals among themselves at the temporary trencher tables in the dining room. Nessheim had avoided them, though he saw them look him over with curiosity and no small contempt — he felt like a conscientious objector in a war, forced to spend time amidst soldiers.

After their aborted encounter in her cabin Frances avoided him. Thank God Schultz and the O.D. had discovered them there before things had gone much further. They had been caught very embarrassingly (Frances had on even fewer clothes at that point than he), but he hadn't had any choice.

The morning after he had managed to sneak back into the cabin while Frances was giving tennis lessons, and retrieve the reel of tape, then make his way through the thick woods to the rendezvous point on the forestry fire road. Fedora was waiting in his Dodge. The agent had been there all night, Nessheim realised.

He held up the tape, saying, 'There's not a lot on here.'

'What do you mean?' Fedora demanded. His eyes were nasty slits.

Nessheim explained what had happened.

'Jesus,' Fedora exclaimed, 'we spent a lot of time setting this up, pal.'

'You think I did it on purpose?' Fedora hadn't been chased by the O.D. and a German Shepherd. Nessheim felt bad enough about screwing up without the dressing down.

He handed over the tape. Without another word, Fedora started the car and drove off.

★ ★ ★

Guttman hadn't tried to disguise his disappointment when Nessheim spoke to him three days later. 'It's not enough,' he said of the contents of the tape.

'Does it give any idea what they're going to do?'

'It sounds like they're planning to take over a building on Labor Day. We don't know which one, just that it's in New York.'

'Can't we just watch Schultz, then grab him when he makes his move?'

'No,' Guttman said testily. 'What good is nabbing Schultz if his thugs go take over the Empire State Building? Or blow up the British Embassy? We need more information. You've got to try and find out whatever you can before this goddamned camp ends.' He didn't sound sanguine.

★ ★ ★

But then they got a break. A week before the end of camp, Schultz called him aside after lunch. 'A word, *Bitte*.'

They went into Schultz's office, where the German signalled Nessheim to close the door, then pointed to a chair. Schultz himself remained standing, looking thoughtful. 'Tell me, when camp ends have you any plans?'

'I thought I'd head back to Chicago unless something turned up out here.'

'You are expected there? Family?'

'Not really. My aunt knows I'll stay if I can find something else to do. When the weather changes there's not going to be much need for a swimming teacher in Chicago.' He managed a wan smile.

'I might have some work for you in New York City. You remember the *Bund* rally in February?'

Nessheim nodded; it had been all over the national press. There had been fights in the hall, bad ones, as Leftists had tried to storm the stage. The police hadn't intervened, leaving it to the *Bund*'s own security to keep peace inside Madison Square Garden. The result hadn't cast the *Bund* in a good light, since their own security force had been more eager to beat up the dissidents than expel them.

'We're holding another one.'

'Really?' In the light of the new Soviet-Moscow pact, this was a surprise.

Schultz said, 'We need to show our strength more than ever. I think record numbers will attend.'

'Where will it be held?'

'In Madison Square Garden again. I wonder if you would be interested in helping out the week before.'

'As a volunteer?'

'Of course not. Same wages as here. You would need to pay for your lodging at the hostel, but we would pay for your meals.'

'I'd like that very much.'

* * *

The hostel, he discovered, was a prim tall building on East 85th, designed for young German males visiting America. He ate supper there dutifully on his first night, sitting by himself as he consumed a solid, flavourless meal of *Spätzle* and minced pork. Looking around him, he thought he recognised some of the young men eating at a long table in the rear. The O.D. Some would have been his pursuers at Camp Schneider.

Upstairs his room was a sullen single cell with a cross on the wall above his bed. Tacked on the inside of the door to his small room was a list of regulations — no women visitors, no liquor, no smoking, no radios.

To hell with this, he decided, and went down to the lobby, where he changed a quarter with the desk clerk for nickels and went into the phone booth, drawing the accordion door behind him. Consulting the phone book he found P. Rourke listed on West 37th. He hesitated for a moment — Schultz had been insistent that he not go out at night. 'Early bedtime. No roistering, *ja*?' he'd said, with a wink that had become a habit since discovering Nessheim with his pants down in Frances Stockton's cabin.

After four rings the throaty voice of Peggy Rourke said hello.

'It's Rossbach. Remember me?'

'Maybe,' she said. 'You in town?'

'Yep.'

'Then I remember. Where are you?'

He told her. 'But I can't exactly wait outside the front door. It's kind of strict.'

'You in a monastery or something?'

'I'll tell you when I see you.'

Twenty minutes later, Nessheim stood on the corner of 2nd Avenue and 86th Street — the German-American Broadway — as Peggy roared up in a jalopy the colour of spring grass. Twenty minutes later, she parked off 125th Street, then led him around the corner where a shimmering marquee had in enormous letters the word *Apollo*. People were milling excitedly in front.

Peggy led him through the crowd. 'Hey, Jackson,' she said, handing a folded sawbuck to the uniformed man at the door. He smiled and palmed the bill, then let the rope down to let them through. They went upstairs to the very top of the theatre, and found two empty seats in the gods. It was between shows, and the overhead lights lit up the vast theatre like a movie set. The audience was almost entirely Negro, and dressed to kill — the men in zoot suits, swaggering and drinking openly from hip flasks, and the ladies wearing brightly coloured dresses.

Then the house lights dimmed, the orchestra in the pit began to play, and a handsome black woman in a dress of electric blue came out on stage. Her face was the colour of caramel, handsome rather than pretty, and she had a garland of white flowers in her hair. Gradually, the audience quieted down, until there was absolute silence in the theatre. Then she began to sing. For the next hour Nessheim could not have told you where he was, who he was with, or even who he was. The voice he heard was mesmerising.

As the house lights went on, the trance was broken. Peggy squeezed his arm and he came back to earth. 'You like that, Rossbach?' she asked.

'She's incredible.'

'They call her Lady Day. Let's go now — nothing's going to beat that.'

As they made their way out to the lobby, Nessheim suddenly stopped. 'I know that guy,' he said, pointing to a Negro man in a wide-striped suit with padded shoulders. He was talking to two women, each wearing bright red lipstick, a taffeta gown and high heels. Where had he seen him before?

He was about to go over and ask when Peggy took his arm. 'Maybe you do, honey, but this ain't the time to find out. We're guests here,

Jimmy. This is their place. If he wanted to know you tonight, he would have come and said so.'

They went back to the car. She drove through Central Park, spooky with shadows this late — it was after midnight. She lit a cigarette with one hand, scratching a match like a bookie against her thumbnail, then rammed the window down and exhaled gaily into the still summer air. 'I hope I'm not taking you back to your monk's cell, kiddo.'

* * *

She lived above a hardware store, between 7th and 8th Avenues, in a three-room railroad apartment. The bedroom overlooked the street, and was lit up by a neon sign flashing *Liquors* on the corner of the block. Peggy fried eggs and bacon on a tiny gas stove, and they ate hungrily on tin plates, squashed together at a table the size of a waiter's platter. As they finished she suppressed a heavy yawn. 'I've got an early start if you're worried about getting back in the morning.' She wiped up the remains of yolk on her plate with a heel of bread and grinned. 'Not that we're going to get much sleep.'

* * *

She dropped him at six the next morning, a block from the hostel. 'It's been great,' she said, patting his knee, but her attention seemed elsewhere.

'How are you fixed tomorrow?'

'Busy tomorrow,' she said. 'All week's bad, to tell you the truth.'

'But — '

'Jimmy, listen.' She was looking at him now, and her expression was level-headed as a teacher's. 'You're a sweet guy — I've already told you that. But I'm thirty-nine years old, three husbands down, and happy enough on my own. You deserve more than that. You need someone in your life, but that someone's not me. Next time you're in town, give me a call, and we'll do the town again. But you ought to get yourself a steady girl. Okay?'

Peggy leaned across and kissed him on the cheek. 'Now beat it,' she said lightly, 'or I'll be late for the breakfast shift.'

Nessheim got out of the jalopy, and watched as she did a big U-turn on the street. Pushing down the window she blew him a kiss. 'Be good, Jimmy. And be safe.'

★　★　★

He went to Schultz's house later that morning. Mrs Schultz opened the door with a frown set like rictus on her face. After being found in Frances's cabin, Nessheim was in disgrace.

She led him through to a spic-and-span kitchen. Through its window he saw a little square of garden, bordered by the high wall of an apartment building behind. The Schultzes' daughter Katrina was playing by an apple tree with a friend — it was Adele Kugel, wasn't it? Both girls looked up, saw him, then promptly looked away. Well, he thought, we're no longer in Vermont. Maybe that's their problem.

Schultz came in carrying a large mug of coffee. 'Young Rossbach, you've made it. *Schlaf gut?*'

'*Ja,*' he found himself saying.

'The accommodation I know is very simple. But healthy, clean,' he added a little insistently.

'It's fine.'

'Then where were you last night?'

'What do you mean?'

'The hostel reported that your bed was not slept in.'

'They're spying on me?'

'I asked,' said Schultz firmly. 'So where were you?'

He wanted to tell him to mind his own business, but he couldn't afford to have a fight with Schultz now. He said with a sigh, 'I was with a friend.'

'I told you not to be in touch with people.'

'I know, I'm sorry. It's a woman I met at the place in the Catskills.'

'I suppose she's a Yid then?'

'Of course not.' He did his best to look indignant. 'Her name's Rourke. She's a waitress.' Schultz looked sceptical so he added, 'You can look it up in the phone book. West 37th Street. That's where I spent the night.'

Schultz still wasn't happy. 'If I were you, young Rossbach, I'd learn to keep your *Pimmel* in your pants. One of these days it's going to get you in a lot of trouble. From now on I want no wanderings, is that clear?'

'Absolutely.'

'Now let me explain what I need you to do.'

The duties were simple, and simple-minded. Ahead of the rally scheduled for Labor Day, Schultz wanted Nessheim to distribute leaflets publicising the event throughout the immediate neighbourhood. House by house, street by street, in all of Yorkville, which as Nessheim discovered, stretched from the East River to 3rd Avenue, and from 79th up to 96th. It hardly seemed necessary, since posters promoting the rally were plastered on every streetlamp and every free wall space throughout the area.

Was it for this that Schultz had brought Nessheim down from Vermont? It didn't make sense; a ten-year-old boy looking for pocket money could have done the job. It seemed odder still when he soon learned that his work was being checked up on — a stout old German woman, whose apartment he'd knocked on one afternoon, saw him an hour later on 2nd Avenue. 'Herr Schultz came round to ask if I had had my leaflet,' she said. 'I told him you had been already.'

He felt sidelined and with five days left before Labor Day, he was getting nowhere fast. Each time he called D.C. — now every day — he could hear the strain in Guttman's voice.

He had to do something. For a lack of alternatives he decided to follow Schultz. To cover the time he would miss from his 'job', he worked late one evening passing out leaflets — he had just about done the entirety of Yorkville.

252

The next day, he watched Schultz's house from a stool in a German bakery on the corner that served coffee. He felt obliged to buy a *Kuchen* every hour, and he had eaten five when Schultz at last came out of the house, accompanied by Beringer. Nessheim gave them a block's head start, and prayed they wouldn't hail a cab. When he caught sight of them two blocks east, he saw that they had been joined by a pack of *Ordnungsdienst* a dozen strong. The paramilitaries now wore shorts, T-shirts, and light boots, a uniform which seemed out of place on the streets of New York.

He followed the group for half an hour, as they walked en masse out of Yorkville, over to the sombre monumental apartment blocks of Park Avenue. There they headed south on the west side of the split avenue, drawing looks from passers-by. Then at 72nd Street on a signal from Schultz they dispersed. Schultz and Beringer were walking alone again, though from his vantage point two blocks behind, looking along Park Avenue as it tilted down towards Grand Central in the distance, Nessheim could see that all the *Ordnungsdienst* were within 200 yards of the pair.

After a few further blocks, Schultz and Beringer stopped at a corner. Behind them, set back from the street, was a massive Victorian mansion of decorated red brick, with a crenellated tower in its centre. Nessheim wondered if it had been the fanciful creation of a nineteenth-century millionaire; it wasn't clear what it was now.

Schultz was looking around with an air of blameless curiosity — he could have been a Kansas farmer on his first trip to New York. Then he turned suddenly and with Beringer began to walk north again, retracing his steps. It seemed strange, and stranger still when at 72nd Street the O.D. regrouped around him.

At 85th they turned east, moving back towards Schultz's house along a thin side street of brownstones. Near Lexington, they passed of all things a synagogue, where two teenage boys were coming down the steps of the building. The O.D., stationed in front of Schultz and Beringer in advance formation, had already passed by, but Heydeman stayed close to Schultz on the street side, like a bodyguard. Nessheim saw that he was wearing a *Bund* armband around one bicep, with a red-and-white blazon that resembled a swastika.

One of the boys, the smaller, imp-like in a little jacket and tie, pointed at Heydeman's arm and said something. His friend next to him laughed. Suddenly Heydeman strode over to the pair of them. The imp fled, laughing, racing up 85th Street towards Nessheim. His friend remained. He was a tall gangly kid with an innocent look on his face.

Heydeman shook his fist at the retreating boy, then turned to the other. Nessheim could see Heydeman square his shoulders and pull his arm back slowly, almost lumbering. It swung powerfully through the air and his fist landed flush on the gawky teenager's nose.

There was a sudden howl and the boy put

both hands to his nose, lowering his face in obvious agony. The imp had stopped running and turned, looking back in horror. The O.D. men had stopped as well, and began to retrace their steps just as the doors of the synagogue swung open and a group of half a dozen grown men came out, all in suits and wearing yarmulkes.

They took one look and rushed Heydeman, swinging. The big man punched one of them, and had lifted another off the ground with both hands when the others overwhelmed him, knocking Heydeman to the ground. But by then the O.D. were back, and they set upon the group of Jews with tactical precision. One of them even came over to push the wounded boy against a wall, where he began to hit him with a rhythmic series of punches — his face, then his body, then his face again.

Nessheim was sprinting forward now, and grabbed the boy's assailant by his shoulder. He was a heavy-set blond guy with a crew-cut, older than the others, and he turned with a look of cold rage on his face. For a moment Nessheim thought the man was going to square off with him.

'I'm on your side,' he shouted. 'Forget the kid, and go watch Schultz.' He pointed wildly towards the melee continuing on the synagogue steps. The O.D. man nodded, and ran back to defend his patron.

The Jewish boy was leaning against the wall, moaning as he held his nose with one ineffectual hand — for blood ran down his shirt in a non-stop stream. His other hand was massaging his lower back, where his kidneys had been subjected to a series of hammer blows. Nessheim leaned forward, and the boy flinched. 'Get out of here, kid,' said Nessheim. 'I mean it. *Run.*' At first the boy only heard the harsh timbre of his voice and not the meaning of his words. He cringed as if Nessheim were about to hit him, too. 'Go on, get going,' Nessheim said urgently, and at last the boy reacted. He stumbled, then ran to join his littler friend, and Nessheim took a half-hearted kick at his backside, and missed.

When he went over to the synagogue's steps he found the Jews had retreated inside. The *Bund* members stood bunched on the steps, blood up. As he approached Schultz looked at Nessheim with surprise, but Heydeman glared at him. 'Why did you let the fucker go?'

'I wanted to make sure they were all right,' Nessheim said, pointing at Schultz and Beringer.

'I don't believe you,' said Heydeman angrily, but Schultz put a restraining hand on the big man's arm. 'Calm yourself,' he ordered. He gave a short cynical laugh. 'You should know by now that young Rossbach is a lover, not a fighter.'

'Should we go in?' one of the O.D. called to Schultz, pointing to the entrance to the synagogue. He looked eager, and Schultz hesitated. But just then a siren wailed from the direction of Park Avenue, then another. They were coming their way.

'No. Now go! *Schnell!*'

And they all ran, Nessheim using the excuse to

peel off, turning up Lexington instead of heading east to Yorkville. Right then he would have happily lived up to Schultz's description of him as a lover not a fighter, but Peggy Rourke had made it clear he shouldn't phone again.

★   ★   ★

He had arranged to go by Schultz's house the next morning, and Nessheim knew he had to stick to the appointment. He reached Guttman at the Bureau, and described the events of the day before. To his surprise, Guttman was less interested in the fight than in the precise details of where Schultz had gone. 'You say they walked down Park Avenue?'

'That's right. Then the squad all peeled off — though they stayed within range, if you know what I mean.'

'Sounds strange. Where was that exactly?'

'I told you. On Park Avenue.'

'*Where* on Park? It's probably five miles long, kid.'

'God, I don't remember. Somewhere just below 72nd Street.'

Guttman was silent for a moment. 'I want you to retrace their steps. Maybe you can figure out what they were doing. It sounds like more than just taking a walk.'

'Okay,' said Nessheim, then looked at his watch. 'I'll do it this afternoon. I have to see Schultz first.'

★   ★   ★

Schultz himself answered the door, and to Nessheim's relief was friendly. 'Come in, come in. There is coffee in the kitchen, and I have a surprise.'

Nessheim followed him through and found Beringer ensconced at the table in the kitchen corner, eating strudel with a fork.

'No leaflets today,' said Schultz, pouring coffee into a mug and handing it to Nessheim.

'What would you like me to do instead?'

'Nothing.' Schultz gave a gnomic smile. 'I thought you deserved a break.'

'Really?' Maybe he would try Peggy on the phone after all. Maybe she'd change her mind. If not, he could go see the Empire State Building.

'*Ja*. We'll all go to Long Island.' There was nothing tentative in his voice. 'You like to fish?'

'Sure,' said Nessheim reflexively. Not that he had fished for years. As a kid his father would take him out to trawl for small-mouth bass on a lake east of Bremen. But not very often.

'Good, I hoped you did. We often go out, right to the tip of the island. It's beautiful, believe me. We catch fish,' he said insistently. 'And then we eat them.'

'What time are we leaving?' asked Nessheim, thinking he had better do what Guttman said first.

'Right now,' said Schultz firmly.

★ ★ ★

Four of them went on the outing — Nessheim, Schultz, Beringer, and Peter Heydeman. No

258

women, for Schultz portrayed it as a boys' day out. 'We will have a good time, and bring the fish home for Mrs Schultz to cook. She can do wonderful things with pollack.'

They caught a noon train from Penn Station. The day was scorching, as if the summer's accumulated heat was making a last stand before fall began. Their railway car was almost empty, picking up only a few early shoppers heading home. Nessheim wanted to look out the window and gather his thoughts — should he start to press Schultz about his plans, or should he continue to play the idiot athlete? — but Beringer unpacked a picnic box with breakfast. A thermos of sweet iced coffee, pastries filled with chocolate, hard-boiled eggs, cheese, and soft rolls stuffed with *Mettwurst*. There was enough food to feed a dozen, but Heydeman demolished what the others could not eat.

It took three hours to reach Montauk. When they disembarked there Nessheim was feeling sweaty and slightly nauseated. The walk from the station to a small harbour on the south side of the island only partly revived him. In the distance the dunes were the pale colour of eggless ice cream, and after days of overcast weather, the sun had taken over the unclouded sky like an avenging god. They passed an inland waterway which held ducks and a dozen pair of honking geese, and Schultz explained that a hurricane the year before had cut off the very tip of Long Island.

They came to a small bay, more a cove really, with a marina in the centre of its crescent curve.

Only a few boats were tied up to its dock: a solitary sailing yacht, a few rowboats with outboards, and a tar-stained fishing trawler that shimmered in the windless heat. 'There she is,' said Beringer, pointing at the trawler. As they approached it along the quay Nessheim saw it was named *The Braunau*.

There was no one on the boat. Following Schultz and Beringer on board, Nessheim stood by the pilot house and watched uneasily as Heydeman untied first the stern rope, then the aft, and jumped back on board. Schultz turned the key at the captain's wheel and the diesel engine rumbled into life. Beringer sat in a deck chair, reading an old copy of *Look* magazine.

At the stern two fishing rigs were set up, the poles reaching high into the air, with a pair of padded chairs set back from the rail. They sailed south and east, into what must have been familiar water, since Schultz did not consult a chart. Nessheim felt queasy again as soon as they moved out of harbour into the irregular chop of the Atlantic, and within an hour he felt deeply seasick, made worse by the scorching glare of the sun and the stench of diesel. They were far enough out now that there was no land in view. Dropping anchor so that Heydeman and Schultz could fish only made things worse, as *The Braunau* tilted and rocked up and down, passive in the ocean swell.

Soon he could take it no longer, and went out of sight to the fore of the boat, where he was violently sick. He stayed there, arms draped over the gunwales, retching for half an hour, until there was nothing left to retch. He felt he'd turned his stomach inside out.

Reappearing at the stern he found that Schultz had caught two good-sized pollack, and that Beringer had laid a small table he'd erected next to the pilot house. The German was taking food from a second wicker picnic box and putting it on plates: more *Mettwurst*, lettuce leaves, cherry tomatoes, a half-pound of butter and a loaf of rye bread. Nessheim found the sight of the food nauseating. When Beringer offered him a bottle of Pilsner he shook his head.

Beringer chuckled. 'No sea legs, Jimmy?'

★ ★ ★

Heydeman and Schultz now joined them. While they ate, Nessheim went and sat in one of the padded chairs, looking out at the horizon and taking deep breaths. The sun was setting and gradually light drained out of the sky, but the air stayed moist and sticky, the temperature at least 80 degrees. A faint moon appeared, and stars began to dot the sky like a series of distant lamps switched on one by one. Nessheim couldn't see the lights of any other boats, and there was nothing dark in the distance that suggested land. They were a long way from Montauk, he concluded, and resigned himself to several more hours of nausea.

After supper Schultz and Heydeman wanted to fish some more, so he vacated the padded chair and went towards the bow. The wind had died completely, and Beringer at the helm had them barely idling. The result was a slow swaying progress through the waves, which were picking up. He managed not to be sick again, and growing drowsy he curled up on the deck, using his shirt for a pillow, since the night air was muggy and warm. Eventually he fell asleep.

When he awoke it was still dark, but he sensed he had slept for hours. For a moment he wondered where he was, then a wave shook the starboard side of the boat below him and he remembered. He got up and made his way back to the pilot house, carrying his shirt.

Beringer was standing at the wheel, smoking a cigarette. He stood in the yellow glow of a small light bulb hooked in the tiny cabin's ceiling. 'Better?' he said without much concern.

'Yeah.' He went out to stand by the padded chairs, where he had to steady himself by grabbing the stern rail. They were moving at a few knots now.

In the far chair Heydeman had gone to sleep with his mouth open, his big buck teeth exposed, and his arms hanging down on each side of the chair. But next to him Schultz was wide awake, watching his line intently.

Schultz said, 'I've been meaning to ask you something, young Rossbach. How did you happen to be there the other night when we had the trouble at the synagogue?'

Caught off guard, Nessheim hesitated. At last he said, 'I saw you and thought you needed help.'

'Yes, but you were a bit far afield, weren't you? If I remember you came down from Park Avenue. That's not Yorkville.'

'I had some extra leaflets so I gave them to the doormen in the swanky buildings. I thought it couldn't do any harm. Was that wrong?'

'Not at all,' said Schultz.

'If it's true,' Beringer interjected smoothly, who had silently appeared in the dark. The boat was idling again.

Nessheim looked at Beringer. 'Why would I lie?' He was trying not to sound nervous.

Beringer said, 'You would if you'd been following us. I thought I saw you earlier down at 72nd Street.'

'I told you, I went over to Park and handed out leaflets to some of the doormen. Maybe you saw me then. What were you doing down there anyway?'

'That's not your business,' Beringer began, but Schultz raised his hand to cut him off. 'I'll tell you. We were looking at the Armory. Scouting the lay of the land, as they say.'

Beringer looked surprised by Schultz's indiscretion, but Schultz's tone suggested it didn't matter in the least. Nessheim noticed that Heydeman's eyes were open now.

'Why the Armory?' he asked. If Schultz didn't mind telling him they'd cased the place, maybe that meant he trusted Nessheim after all. Though it seemed a big maybe.

'He asks, 'Why the Armory?'' said Schultz, turning his head towards Beringer and chuckling.

'What's so funny?' asked Nessheim.

'What do you think they keep in an armoury, young Rossbach? Cat food? Bottles of beer?'

Heydeman was now fully awake. 'Wait until Monday,' he said.

'That's the day of the rally,' Nessheim said.

'What about it?' said Schultz. 'We'll leave that nonsense to Kuhn. There will be 15,000 people there and just as many Jews protesting. That's when we'll take the Armory.'

'You've already got weapons.' He remembered the rifle practice at Camp Schneider.

'Single-shot garbage,' said Schultz scornfully. 'The Armory has powerful repeating rifles and machine guns.' Nessheim could hear the relish in his voice.

Suddenly Schultz tensed and leaned forward, staring at his line. It had gone taut, and when he lifted his reel the rod bent sharply.

'Have you got one?' asked Beringer.

Schultz was reeling in now, and the rod flexed like a bow. Then he stopped reeling. 'Nature calls,' he announced, putting one hand meaningfully to his flies. 'Take over,' he added abruptly, motioning Nessheim to grab the rod as he got up, then headed towards the fore of the boat. Nessheim took his place in the chair, then began reeling the line in slowly.

He sensed Beringer standing behind him, and after a minute Schultz returned and stood there too. He struck a match and Nessheim smelled cigar smoke. Just what I need, he thought, still feeling slightly nauseated. He was reeling in more quickly now, for there didn't seem much drag on the line. It couldn't be a very large fish.

Heydeman had left his chair and come to stand by the stern rail. 'Let me feel,' he said and lifted the rod out of Nessheim's hands. Then Nessheim felt his chair being pushed from behind, spinning him round in the swivel seat to face Schultz. The German was holding a cigar to his lips with one hand; the other held a small snub-nosed revolver which he was pointing at Nessheim. It looked a low calibre of pistol, thought Nessheim mechanically, but it would do the trick.

Schultz took the cigar out of his mouth. 'As you Americans would say, let's talk turkey.'

'What about?' Nessheim had a sinking feeling in his stomach.

'You tell me, Herr *Nessheim.*'

'What do you mean?' he said, but it sounded feeble.

'You collected a letter in Woodstock in that name. It was from your mother in Wisconsin, but you claimed your parents were dead and you came from Chicago. So we started to make inquiries.'

Nessheim coughed, then said croakily, 'Rossbach's my mother's maiden name. I had a bust-up with my dad.'

'Aw,' mocked Schultz. 'A *Streit* with your father. How sad. Did you tell the FBI that when you joined?' He suddenly spat overboard, sending a plug of gleaming saliva out into the water.

Nessheim told himself not to panic. 'The only thing I've ever joined was the *Bund.*'

'That was interesting too. The Chicago branch said you were an extremely inactive member. Too busy with your lawman duties, eh?'

265

'I really don't know what you're talking about. And that gun is making me nervous.' Which was true.

Schultz said, 'I want to know who you work for in the FBI and how you came to Camp Schneider. What did you want to find out there?'

Nessheim shook his head vigorously. 'You have this all wrong, Herr Schultz. Nobody sent me to Camp Schneider; I needed the job. And I've explained to you about my name.'

Schultz ignored this. 'Peter,' he ordered. 'Take hold of him.'

Suddenly from behind Heydeman gripped both of Nessheim's arms. The man's strength was incredible; Nessheim felt as if large manacles had been put around his biceps — he didn't even try to flex them.

He wondered what they were planning to do. If Schultz was simply going to shoot him, he'd have done that already. Perhaps they were just trying to scare him; he had heard that prisoners of war were often threatened before interrogation to make them feel more vulnerable.

But Schultz had something else in mind. Like a nurse passing a scalpel, he handed his cigar to Beringer. Beringer stepped nearer to Nessheim, holding the glowing cigar so close that Nessheim could feel its heat on his chest. When he squirmed, Heydeman tightened his hold, squeezing Nessheim's arms like gelatine.

Schultz said, 'The rules are simple. Tell the truth and you won't be hurt.'

The boat was rocking slightly; the still surface of the Atlantic had given way to a small but discernible chop. It didn't seem to affect Heydeman's hold on his arms in the slightest, but it reinforced Nessheim's nausea, which was mixed with feelings of panic he tried to subdue.

'Who are you working for at the Bureau of Investigation?' asked Schultz.

Nessheim hesitated, wondering how much to admit.

Schultz said sharply, 'We are 20 miles from Montauk, and twice as far from the New Jersey shore, so no one is going to hear your screams. But if you tell the truth you won't need to. Now where are you based?'

'I don't know what you're talking about,' he said.

Beringer suddenly leaned forward and pressed the cigar against his right bicep. Nessheim flinched as he felt intense heat, then agonising pain. Beringer kept the cigar firmly against his upper arm until an acrid smell of flesh filled the air. Nessheim bit his lower lip to keep from crying out.

He could see Schultz's face in the reflected glow of the pilot-house light. He looked dissatisfied. 'Let's get his pants off,' Schultz commanded. 'Peter, hold him tight.'

Beringer came forward and grabbed onto the waistband of Nessheim's trousers. When Nessheim started to kick out, Schultz took a step forward and poked the pistol in his face. Beringer undid his belt and pulled down the khaki trousers until they sat like bags around Nessheim's feet. The German yanked off both of Nessheim's shoes, then pulled his trousers off altogether, tossing them in a heap by the pilot house.

Beringer's expression was intent and all-business, like a surgeon halfway through an operation.

'Who sent you to Vermont?' Schultz demanded.

'I joined because I wanted to,' Nessheim insisted, trying to ignore the pain in his arm and concentrate on his answer. 'My parents are German, so I was interested.'

He hoped this sounded plausible, and was relieved to see Schultz nod. But then he said, '*Wieder.*' This time Beringer pressed the cigar against the inside of his upper thigh. Pain shot through Nessheim like needles, and he only dimly realised he was crying out loud — the odd wailing sound didn't seem to come from him. He gagged, and his gorge rose uncontrollably. Suddenly he retched violently, and vomit shot out of his mouth all over the deck.

'*Yeck!*' Schultz exclaimed in disgust, spattered by the stream of sick. He stepped back reflexively, lowering the gun as he looked down at his stained trousers. Momentarily, Heydeman's hold relaxed, and Nessheim sprang up. Heydeman tried to grab him, but it was too late — Nessheim jumped forwards just out of his reach. Schultz began to lift his gun, but Nessheim took two quick steps and stiff-armed the German, sending him sprawling onto the deck. He sensed Beringer behind him and ran halfway down the boat, then without hesitation dived off the starboard side.

He hit the water in a shallow dive that made his chest and belly burn. He surfaced moments later, sputtering and tasting salt on his lips, and felt the saline sting where Beringer had put his cigar. A wave surged around his shoulders, and he shivered as it unfurled like ice across the back of his neck. *Christ it's cold* was his first thought. He saw that he was only 50 feet or so from the boat, and could clearly make out the figures of Schultz and Heydeman peering from the side. If he could see them, he started to think . . . Then something whizzed at terrific speed past his head and he heard the sound of a pistol firing almost simultaneously.

He jack-knifed into the cold water, desperate to get out of the mild halo of light that would give him away. He swam underwater away from the boat until he thought he would burst. Coming up at last, he tried to break surface gently, doing his best not to gasp for air too loudly. Peering through the dark, he saw that the boat had moved, but in the wrong direction, and was now a longish football pass distant. Beringer must be at the wheel, and Schultz or Heydeman was holding a flashlight on the starboard side, moving the beam back and forth across the water. The light arced wider and wider until it started to come Nessheim's way. He dove again, jacking his legs up and forcing himself down.

He came up gradually, then saw to his alarm that this time Beringer had made a better guess, for the boat was only 20 feet away. Fortunately Beringer had swung the bow round, so the port side of *The Braunau* was facing Nessheim. He could hear indistinct voices from the boat, with the odd comprehensible word or two. Once he even thought he recognised the name 'Le Saux'.

They had shot at him, which meant they weren't interested in hauling him aboard again to make him talk. So why were they searching for him so hard, since they must know his chances of surviving out here in the water were nil? Why were they bothering?

The answer was they weren't. Schultz appeared once more at the stern and shouted out to the indiscriminate waves — '*Schwein haben!*' And Beringer revved the motor, swung the wheel sharply round, and *The Braunau* accelerated away.

No wonder he had heard the name of Eddie Le Saux — Nessheim was going to be left to drown. Nessheim could imagine what had happened to Le Saux, out on Lake Michigan, the night-time water the colour of lead lining a coffin. Eddie's coffin. Heydeman would have taken his boat out and met Le Saux 'by accident'. He'd have tied up to Le Saux's boat and shared a smoke and a beer, persuading Eddie to take off his life jacket for a few minutes, long enough to let Heydeman grab Le Saux and throw him overboard, then drive the tied-together boats away, leaving Le Saux to drown and his body to float ashore without an incriminating mark on it.

As Nessheim's might in time — or else get swept out into the mid-Atlantic to serve as fish food. From Schultz's account, the currents here were capable of anything. Either way, there would be nothing suspicious about his death, just the dark cloud of a tragic accident.

Nessheim tried to shut down these thoughts and collect himself. His body had become acclimatised to the water, which was not as cold as he had first feared — in the low 60s, he guessed, which meant he could stay alive in it for several hours. But the insistent choppy waves made treading water tiring; he found a gentle breast stroke less fatiguing, and it also gave him some sense of moving to the safety of a shore, however distant. Just as he felt he was getting used to the rhythm of the waves, however, one broke out of nowhere and filled his nose with salt water. He snorted, tried to breathe, then another wave struck. He sputtered and coughed and was almost sick again, then slowly caught his breath, frightened by how much effort it took.

He had no idea which way to swim. He needed to go north towards Montauk and the chance of meeting a boat, but which direction was it? He tried to look around him, but the bumpy waves blocked his view of anything but the black curtain of sky. Then as a wave receded he glimpsed to his right the faintest chalk-coloured crack in the dark. Maybe morning was not a million miles away. East must be to his right, so he swam, slowly, steadily, straight ahead, hoping he was due south of Montauk so that he would hit it in time. Time? Three days' worth of swim.

He refused to think about his chances, and focused instead on who had betrayed him back home. It had to have been Uncle Eric, he thought. Though how he'd known his nephew was an FBI agent was a mystery. And always going to stay that way, Nessheim thought in a sudden spasm of fury, suddenly splashing hard through the waves in a furious crawl stroke. Stop it, he told himself, slowing down. He had to keep his emotions under control.

From time to time, he rolled over on his back and tried to rest, floating, but the waves would break over his face, so he could only lie undisturbed for the length of a held-in breath. Sometimes he extended his arms straight ahead — in a double Hitler salute he felt Schultz would have appreciated — and floated on his belly, buoyed by a salinity that was novel to him, for he only knew swimming in fresh water. Then a somnolence would set in, and he would lift up in a jerk, frightened that dozing off would lead to death.

Cramp was developing spasmodically in his feet, then in his hands. He dreaded getting a stitch in his side, since there was nowhere to rest and recover from it. He didn't know if two hours had passed, or two minutes, but he was alarmed by the tiredness he felt in his limbs — and in his mind. There was something peaceful and alluring about the vast body of ocean around him. Increasingly he was putting his head down into the salt water, where he kept his mouth tightly shut so there was no chance of swallowing the cusp of a wave. Each time he did this he found it harder to lift himself up and swim. Once he almost opened his mouth, then some instinct warned him off — he knew he wouldn't survive the coughing fit that a large slug of salt water would bring on.

He felt too tired to fight. If only he could stand on something, just for a minute, he was sure he could go on for the forever it was going to take to save him. He started to dream of a ledge he might find, or a fisherman's warning buoy; anything that would relieve the pressure, even for a few seconds, of keeping himself afloat.

Then, as he lay with his head face down, not even bothering to kick, he thought he heard a low throb reverberating in the water. An ocean liner perhaps, on its way into the Manhattan lower docks. Or a freighter delivering God knows what from Europe to a Jersey port. Lifting his head, he tried to look round, but the only sign of daybreak was far east to his right, where in the distant skyline the chalk-coloured crack had expanded into a milky haze on the horizon. There was no other sign of light, and he was growing too tired to generate a fantasy of rescue.

He heard the throb again when he dipped his head back down into the water. It seemed closer. He stopped swimming, treading water with hands he could no longer feel, and this time there was a pinprick of light in the distance. Or was it an illusion? In any case, it could be many miles away. He realised that the early-morning daylight was creeping in around him, bit by bit, and that the sky ahead was now the colour of smoke, rather than the ebony sheet of an hour before.

The throbbing had stopped, but the light was there — and it didn't seem miles away, after all. He heard nothing now, but the light galvanised him, and he lifted his head and shouted 'Help!'

with an energy he didn't know he had left.

The throbbing started up again, and he realised it was the engine of a boat. For a moment the light flickered, then it came closer again. Closer, and closer; despite himself, Nessheim felt hope stir. The engine cut out suddenly, and Nessheim realised that was his chance. 'Help!' he shouted, sensing it was the last time he would be able to make enough noise. A beam suddenly zipped across the water in front of him, then zipped back again. It was moving side to side, like a scythe whipped against a field of high grass, and finally it reached Nessheim. Terrified it would just keep moving past him, he struggled to lift his arms, and he moved around in the water, trying to make a visible commotion.

But unbelievably, the light moved on, and then went out, followed by the noise of the engine starting up. Despair engulfed him like flu. He wanted to shout out but simply couldn't — he was all but done in by his last efforts.

The noise of the engine was lost in the pounding of his heart and heaving strangled noises he dimly realised were his own sobs. He lay flat on his stomach, floating like a dead man, trying not to think that he would be one soon enough. He only barely took notice of the beam of light when it appeared again, full flush on his turned-down face.

And then he lifted his head and to his disbelief saw the low curved wooden bow of a boat, not 20 feet away. He thought at first he must be hallucinating.

A voice said, 'Hang on, I'm coming.' And then within seconds he felt two hands gripping him by the shoulders and the same voice said, 'Can you lift your arms?'

Somehow he managed to, and found himself hoisted against the gunwales, then pulled an inch at a time, until his weight finally carried him over the side and into the boat.

He lay there on the rough wet planks, breathing heavily. He could hear footsteps on the planks, and a moment later he sensed the man kneeling down beside him. He carried a blanket and sat Nessheim up as he wrapped it around him.

So it wasn't a dream. He looked up and there was now enough daylight for him to see his rescuer. 'Smitty,' he whispered in disbelief, his teeth chattering.

'My real name's Sidney. Sidney Washington,' said the black cook. His voice was different — there was nothing Step 'N' Fetchit to it now.

'How did you find me?' His teeth still chattered, but he had to know.

'Needle in a haystack, really. That boat came past me on its way back to Montauk; I had to duck down pretty quick since those people know me from the camp. But I took a look and there weren't any sign of you. I had a pretty good idea of where you might be, but we were awful lucky just the same.'

'But what were you doing out here?'

'Following the boat. Mr Guttman told me if anything happened to you, he'd see I'd never drive for Mr Hoover again.'

'He sent you to the camp?'

'That's right. Made me go learn to cook first at some Jewish place in the Catskills.'

'Was that you at the Apollo the other night?'

'Hope you liked my suit.' He stood up. 'We best be going. If I give you a hand, do you think you can walk as far as that?' He gestured to the dwarf pilot house in the middle of the skiff. 'I have a little brandy there to keep you warm. We got us a couple of hours' ride, since the last place we want to pitch up at is Montauk. Far as Schultz is concerned, you're drowned. We need to keep it that way.'

'I've got to get to a phone and call Guttman.'

'We've got time.' They were moving slowly across the planks, Smitty holding his arm. 'And Guttman's not going to be too hard to find — everybody's working this weekend.'

'Why's that?' he said, shivering badly. They had reached the pilot house, where Sidney shifted the captain's chair from behind the wheel and had Nessheim sit down.

'You wouldn't have heard,' said Sidney as he turned the key in the tiny wheelhouse. The engine gave a short cough, then caught. Nessheim looked out to sea, east towards Europe, and saw a raw sun the colour of fire looming just beneath the day's low cloud. 'Heard what?' he asked, suddenly overcome by fatigue.

'The Nazis have invaded Poland. There's going to be a war now.'

Part Three
1940

17

January 1940
Washington D.C.

The phone rang three times in the dark before he could find it.

'Guttman,' he said, trying to sound awake.

'It's Kevin Reilly,' said a raspy voice. 'Sorry about the hour, Harry, but I'm pretty sure you'll want in on this.'

'What time is it?' He couldn't see the clock, a wind-up job he'd bought at Hecht's, and he didn't want to switch the lamp on and wake Isabel. Not that she was still asleep. This had better be good, he thought.

'It's three-fifteen, Harry, but I've got the coroner pushing me. Let me give you the address.'

Once he'd put down the phone, Guttman got out of bed, and taking his clothes from the bedroom chair went to dress in the bathroom. When he returned to fumble in the dresser drawer for his gun and holster, Isabel said, clear as a bell, 'Will you be long?'

'Hope not, sweetie. You go back to sleep.'

Outside it was well below freezing, and he winced as he felt his first breath of icy air fill his lungs. He swung open the garage door and climbed into his six-year-old Buick. In good weather, it still ran okay, but it was so cold out that he was relieved when the engine caught. He drove carefully along the icy roads, wishing he had a stronger battery to power his headlights. As he moved onto the bridge over the iced-up Potomac, the car skidded slightly when he touched the brakes. He let the Buick coast the rest of the way across, holding his breath until he reached the Washington side.

Georgetown was asleep, and the houses stood like empty doll's houses in the dark. The road was empty as he moved east on M Street, past blocks of restaurants and stores. The air was turning misty in his headlights and Guttman realised his tyres were a little soft, though that seemed to give them added traction on the packed ice and snow of the streets.

He had never known such a winter in Washington. Usually, snow fell and disappeared within a day; even the largest storms sweeping across the eastern seaboard only made their tail ends felt this far south. But the last snowfall, three days after New Year's, had lasted, unable to melt in frigid air that never even came close to thawing point. He'd turned the heat up at home and instructed the gal who came in as helper to keep a hot-water bottle tucked under the blanket on his wife's wheelchair. It was hard to believe that in ten weeks the cherry blossom would be out.

He turned now onto Pennsylvania Avenue, wide and eerily deserted. As he came to the Eclipse and drove by the White House he looked over at the country's most famous mansion. In the living quarters upstairs the lights were all out

— unsurprising at four in the morning. On the ground floor a corner office glowed from a ceiling light, and at the east entrance the portico was lit up, where he could see a policeman stamping his boots against the cold.

He had been inside recently, after Hoover had managed to persuade the President that the Bureau should help the Secret Service with its duties protecting him. A small team of Bureau agents had been installed in the Executive Wing, in two rooms at the end of the corridor down from the Oval office itself. They reported to Guttman, who had doubts about their mission since the White House was already teeming with Secret Service men.

Continuing along Pennsylvania Avenue now, he passed the Justice Department and his office. He knew Hoover wanted the Bureau to have its own building, but Guttman liked being there — rather than in some newly created monument to Hoover's power. He slid through the intersection with Constitution Avenue, his brakes useless, and he wished that like Hoover he had Sidney Washington chauffeuring him. The Negro was back driving the Director, the latter man none the wiser about Sidney's adventures during his secondment to Guttman's department. Guttman was confident Sidney would never spill the beans about his time spent undercover. Without any words exchanged, the driver seemed to understand that if Hoover discovered what he'd been up to, it wouldn't only be Guttman who'd lose his job.

It had been worth the risk, Guttman thought,

taking satisfaction from the fact that the group Nessheim had infiltrated at Camp Schneider was now safely behind bars. They'd been there ever since their efforts to seize the Park Avenue Armory had been foiled in early September. Once Sidney had telephoned with Nessheim's warning that the Armory was going to be hit, Guttman had put his preparations into effect, then waited nervously all weekend, praying that nothing would tip off Schultz that Nessheim had survived. The Germans themselves had alerted the Coast Guard late Saturday that 'Rossbach' had gone missing, but there was no danger in that, since there were no Rossbach relatives to contact, nothing real behind the bogus identity of Nessheim's undercover life.

On Labor Day Monday at exactly one p.m. a dozen of the *Bund* O.D., led by Schultz and armed with a motley collection of shotguns, pistols, and two deer rifles, entered the Armory building, overpowering the sole, senescent guard left in place, then moving rapidly across the interior parade ground towards the locked arms stores in the rear of the building. Halfway across the packed-dirt ground a voice had erupted through a bullhorn — it was an FBI agent, announcing to the O.D. men that they were surrounded. Immediately from both ends of the parade half a regiment of National Guardsmen emerged, loaded rifles at the ready and bayonets fixed. Unsurprisingly, in the face of such firepower, the O.D. rebels and their leader Schultz had surrendered without a fight.

Outside, Guttman had stationed a dozen

agents armed with Thompson sub-machine guns in buildings within a hundred yards of the Armory. When two trucks had pulled up, waiting to be loaded with stolen weapons, the FBI agents had surrounded both vehicles, seized the drivers and carted them off to jail. Simultaneously, Beringer had been arrested on 2nd Avenue leaving Schultz's house.

No one — from the *Bund* or the Bureau — had been hurt. As Guttman reflected on the events of 4 September, he realised that the only victim had been Jimmy Nessheim.

Plucked out of the water off Long Island by Sidney, he had at first seemed to have survived his immersion unscathed, and was keen to join the other agents when they busted Schultz on Monday. But by Sunday, the day before the assault on the Armory, Nessheim had complained of chills, and spiked a high fever. Occupied with planning the details of Monday's operation, Guttman hadn't paid much attention; when the kid's temperature had reached 105, however, Guttman had phoned a doctor, who in turn promptly called an ambulance and had Nessheim taken to Lenox Hill Hospital. A good thing, too, since within twenty-four hours Nessheim had developed pneumonia.

It had been touch and go after that, the illness developing with an alacrity that made Guttman rue his previous inattention. There had been two days when Nessheim might have died, and it was on the first of them that Guttman had sent a telegram to Nessheim's parents, summoning them east. He wasn't sure whether he was asking them to come and watch their son recover, or to bury him. Nessheim did recover, thank God, and after a week his parents had gone back to Wisconsin, confident their boy was on the mend.

Then Nessheim had a fall. The nurse said he'd been walking the ward as instructed, gathering his strength, when for no apparent reason he'd keeled over. That's when his history of dizziness had come out, admitted by Nessheim while he was still dazed. The hospital consultant insisted Guttman pull Nessheim's medical file from the Bureau, and dissatisfied by its meagreness, the doc had checked out Nessheim's medical history on his own — calling Northwestern University and speaking with the football coach, then contacting the doctor at Michael Rees Hospital in Chicago who'd seen Nessheim after his knock in a football game. None of this was in Nessheim's file at the Bureau.

'This guy should never have passed your medical,' the New York doc had declared.

Guttman had had to break the news to Nessheim: the days of chasing Danny Ho, planting wiretaps in the attic of a Vermont camp lodge, and defying death in the ice-cold Atlantic were all over.

'Look at it this way,' he'd told Nessheim at his hospital bed. 'You've seen more action in your twenties than most agents get to see in a thirty-year career. Why, I've known plenty of agents who've never pulled their gun except in front of the mirror.'

He offered Nessheim a desk job, saying he could put in a word at any field office the young agent fancied. Morgan in San Francisco was coming east soon (Guttman had wangled Morgan the SAC position in the Newark office) but Guttman was confident he could get Nessheim a position out there again.

Nessheim wasn't interested. He'd gone home to Wisconsin before Christmas to recuperate, then wrote in January to say he was planning to head for California to pack up his belongings and drive his pickup truck back to the Midwest. He didn't say what his future plans were, except that they didn't include the FBI. And Nessheim's termination papers were sitting on Guttman's desk, awaiting his signature. One of these days Guttman would get around to signing them.

Now he drove slowly around the Capitol and into the rising streets on the back side of the hill. The houses here were small and run-down, their front steps wobbly, the windows filled with tarpaulin rather than glass. When he reached the address Reilly had given him, however, Guttman found a large Victorian mansion, its wooden cladding painted dark green with black shutters on the windows. It had a rounded turret at one end like a French chateau, and a wide porch with a wooden balustrade and railing. A uniformed cop was standing in the doorway.

Guttman locked the car and went into the house, stamping the snow off his feet in the front hall. To one side a parlour ran towards the back of the house. It was a large room furnished by scarlet velvet-covered sofas and a couple of stuffed armchairs. A French painting of a reclining nude hung above the unused fireplace.

Ashtrays and piles of magazines were neatly arranged on side tables around the room, presumably to help distract waiting customers from having second thoughts.

Kevin Reilly from the metropolitan police force came halfway down the stairs. He said, sounding tired, 'Come on up, Harry.'

Guttman followed Reilly to the top of the house, then down a dark corridor to the back. Reilly opened the door, then stepped aside to let Guttman past. 'Hold your nose,' he said.

The stench was terrible, but Guttman forgot about it as soon as he stepped inside the room. Sprawled on the floor was the body of a young black man — he could not have been more than twenty years old. He was naked, save for a pair of white cotton underpants which hung, obscenely low, on his hips. There was blood on the youth's chest and arms, and his head was thrown back, revealing a long deep gash at the base of his neck. Guttman noted the straight-handled razor lying on the floor, its blade extended and smeared with blood, now the colour of prunes.

This wasn't all. On the far side of the room, an old wooden beam ran between the two walls of an alcove. From it a man in a black suit was hanging by a thick rope wrapped around his neck. The man's tongue was sticking out like a defiant child's, his lips contorted in a painful grimace. But it was his eyes Guttman was most struck by — they bulged as if straining to escape their sockets. About a yard from the body's dangling feet a small wooden stool lay upended.

'It's Bock,' Guttman said, stunned.

286

'I know it's Bock. That's why I called you.'

'Who found him?' he asked.

'One of the girls. She actually sleeps up here — the working rooms are down a flight.'

'Is that the same kid as last time?' He pointed at the dead Negro, noticing that blood had also spread in a coagulating pool onto the room's cheap carpet.

'None other.' Reilly paused. 'Let me get Ma.' Reilly stuck his head out into the corridor and barked an order while Guttman tried to compose himself, and slow the thoughts that were racing through his head. What on earth had Bock been doing here? And why had he killed the kid? A moment of madness, violence fuelled by lust, followed by such remorse that he had hanged himself? It seemed the obvious scenario, but Guttman was mystified. He hadn't read the man that way at all.

After a minute they could hear a slow tread coming up the stairs. Guttman found the stink in the room beginning to overwhelm him, a sickening mix of cigar smoke and faecal aroma. His gorge rose, and he struggled to control his growing nausea.

He said, 'Bock didn't smoke cigars.'

'*I* do,' said Reilly. 'If you think it stinks now, you should have been here an hour ago.'

A creak on the floorboards announced the arrival of Ma Thornton. She was an immense white woman, barely 5 feet tall but looking close to 300 pounds. Her big doughy face was covered in powder, and she'd highlighted her eyes with mascara, her mouth with cherry-red lipstick. She wore a calico dress the size of a tent, and as she crossed her arms now and adopted a world-weary pout, Guttman realised that her biceps were bigger than his own.

'Tell me what happened,' he said.

She shrugged. 'Beats the hell out of me, mister. I haven't seen the Kraut for a couple of years.' She turned to Reilly accusingly. 'That was the night you rousted us.'

'So what about tonight?' Guttman asked.

She pointed towards the black youth without looking at him. 'Anthony asked me if he could use the room up here. I like to keep his business separate — the other customers wouldn't like it.'

'Because he's coloured?'

She looked at Guttman scornfully. 'Half my girls are coloured, mister. No, it's because he was a fairy. Anyway, I told him he could use it. But that was at eight o'clock; I had no idea he'd still be here . . . '

Neither did he, thought Guttman. He pointed to the hanging corpse. 'What about this guy? When did he show up?' he asked.

Ma stared at him. 'How should I know? I didn't see him. Nobody did — like I keep telling your dick friend here.'

'Mind your mouth,' said Reilly.

Guttman said, 'You mean the first time anybody saw him he was hanging like this?'

'That's right. You see, this is Shelley's room. She said she wasn't feeling good, so I sent her up to bed. I'm nice that way — she's a five-dollar girl. And I didn't want her sitting around in the parlour, in case one of the Joes wanted to go with her. It's not fair on a customer to put your goods in the store window, then say they're not for sale. Sort of defeats the whole purpose, if you know what I mean.'

'Let's skip the philosophy of business. So she came up here?'

'That's right. It was after eleven. Anthony should have been long gone by then. But suddenly Shelley screams the frigging house down, pardon my French, and I came running up and found Anthony lying over there and the stiff hanging here.'

'And no one had seen this guy until then?' Guttman couldn't hide his scepticism.

'Not a dicky bird. I swear. He must have come through the back door, up the rear stairs to the second floor, then on up here. Unless one of the girls happened to come out of a room as he was moving along, nobody would have seen him.'

Guttman was trying to take this all in. 'Where's Shelley now?'

'Back to work. She's downstairs in one of the rooms with Mr Huckleby. He's a regular and she didn't want to disappoint him. I could send her up if you're willing to wait a bit — Mr Huckleby can be a little while.'

'That's okay. Tell Mr Huckleby to take his time. You can go now.'

Big Ma Thornton looked at Reilly, who nodded, and she shuffled out of the room.

Guttman pointed to the bureau, where a watch and a small pile of loose change sat on top. 'Those are his?'

'Guess so. He must have emptied his pockets

when he got up there.'

'Where's his wallet then?'

Reilly didn't answer. Guttman walked over to the body. Reaching up, he patted the front of Bock's suit jacket, averting his eyes, and avoiding a long thin streak of blood. He felt something, so there was nothing for it — he took a deep breath and reached inside the jacket. As his hand brushed against the white dress shirt he could feel the dead man's flesh, and he realised it was starting to stiffen. At last his fingers reached the wallet in the inside pocket of Bock's jacket and he brought it out gingerly.

Then something else caught his attention. 'Look at this,' he said with unconcealed astonishment. With his free hand, he held back the jacket on Bock's left side to reveal a holster and handgun. Handing the wallet to Reilly, he said, 'You got any gloves?'

'Yeah. The coroner lent me a pair.'

Putting on a pair of cotton fingerlets, Guttman reached in and extracted the pistol from the holster, then let the suit jacket flap back into place as he moved well away from the corpse. He checked the chamber, and sniffed the barrel. 'It's loaded, but hasn't been fired. What do you think?'

'It's a lady's gun, isn't it? I don't know too many stiffs carrying something that weak. A .22 maybe if they're out to ice somebody, single shot-like. Not a .25.' Reilly shrugged. 'But then, the guy was a fem, wasn't he?'

'That's not my point.' Guttman was staring at Bock now, curiosity overcoming any revulsion.

'Think for a minute. The guy decides to kill Anthony. So why not shoot him? Less mess. How he managed not to get blood all over himself is beyond me — there's only a little bit on his jacket.'

He turned and looked at Reilly. 'But let's suppose he has killed the kid with that razor, and then feels so bad about it that he decides to kill himself. Why noose yourself when you're packing a rod? That would have done it quicker and a lot less painfully.'

'Maybe he really wanted to punish himself.'

Guttman nodded. 'Okay, but I'm not through yet. He gets up on the stool, but only after emptying his pockets first. How tidy of the guy.' He paused. 'But then why doesn't he also take out his wallet and take off his holster?'

'Jesus, Harry, how should I know?' Reilly looked bewildered. 'You might as well ask why he wanted to bump himself off. And why did he kill the shine in the first place?'

Guttman shook his head. 'I don't think he did.'

18

This time the club's sitting room was crowded, though there was no sign of the Colonel. Jason the butler had help now, a young black woman in a dark skirt and white apron, but most of the people at the tables were just eating sandwiches. The monk-like silence of Guttman's first encounter had given way to the steady buzz of people who weren't there to socialise. This club didn't seem to have any stuffy rules about not conducting business in its rooms, but then Guttman remembered this wasn't really a club.

Stephenson was waiting for him, sitting in a chair, reading a copy of the *Spectator*. He was dressed in a Harris Tweed jacket and grey flannels, and his striped tie looked military. He stood up and shook hands. 'Why don't we head for the back?' he suggested, though there was a table free.

He escorted Guttman to the same large ground-floor room that Guttman had peeked into before. Then it had been filled with people working in a newsroom-like atmosphere; now a solitary woman with a strikingly pretty face stood by one of the desks, punching holes in printed pages and placing them into large ring binders. She had her hair up in a blonde bun.

'Everybody seems to be at lunch, Katie,' said Stephenson. The young woman nodded but made no sign of leaving.

Stephenson went to one of the desks and rifled through a pile of paper until he found what he was looking for. He unfolded a large folio and spread it on the desk. 'Have a look,' he said.

It was a map, with foreign place names, and a topographical rendering that showed mountainous terrain, dotted by lakes. 'Germany?' asked Guttman.

'Close. It's Austria.' Stephenson pointed to a town at the end of a long thin lake. 'This is Klagenfurt. Over here is Villach. The blue is the Wörthersee, where the Viennese are fond of spending their summer holidays. Up here,' he said, moving his finger slightly north, 'are hills — some are small mountains really, high enough for skiing in winter.' He pointed to a circle pencilled on one of the hills. 'And this is where I think we've found your man.'

'What man?'

'Konrad Werner.'

'You're kidding.'

'Not at all.' He looked up at the woman across the room. 'Katie, do you think you could persuade Jason to provide a sandwich for our visitor? And possibly one for me as well.'

'Sure thing,' she said, and left the room. Guttman said idly, 'Pretty girl,' though he was really thinking about Stephenson's find.

'I'll let her know you think so,' said Stephenson. Guttman looked mortified and Stephenson laughed. 'Don't worry — she's my niece.'

Guttman was even more embarrassed. He said gruffly, 'Tell me about Werner.'

'Two years ago, a group of walkers found a body on a hillside in Austria, about 20 miles from Klagenfurt. Away from the lakes and walking trails, it's very wild there; it was pure chance they came across it. The body was badly decomposed, but it looked like a suicide — the man had a bullet in his temple, and the gun was still in what was left of his hand. The walkers reported it to the local police, who were at something of a loss because there wasn't any identification on the corpse. The man looked German or Austrian — he was wearing the typical clothes of an alpine walker, but no one had been reported missing, and there was nothing at all that could establish his identity. Unsurprisingly, after a few months of pro forma investigation — they checked with all the districts in Austria, and even made a few inquiries in Germany — the police gave up.'

'How did you find out about this?' asked Guttman, wondering why Stephenson thought the dead man was Werner.

'We had a friend in the Austrian intelligence services. After the *Anschluss* we lost touch — couldn't blame him, really, since any contact with us could have cost him his life. But then the Nazis did us a favour — not intentionally, I assure you. They'd kept on Ronge as the head of the Austrian Secret Service, which was an intelligent thing to do since he was both very good and quite the Nazi himself. But something happened and they stripped Ronge of his post and threw him in a concentration camp for a while. Our chap had always been loyal to Ronge,

294

and he was absolutely furious. That's when he made contact again.

'To cut a long story short, one of the things he told us is that a communication had come from Germany that a Swiss agency was making inquiries about a missing German-American named Werner. Austrian intelligence were told unequivocally not to assist these Swiss people in any way. When our contact dug a little deeper he discovered the police in the Klagenfurt district had been singled out and told not to help the Swiss. That didn't smell right either, and he mentioned it to our officer when they next met. Our chap asked the Austrian intelligence wallah to dig a bit deeper. That's when he came up with our dead friend here.' He suddenly stabbed a finger at the circle on the map.

'But how do you know it was Werner? Couldn't it have been somebody else?'

'Yes,' he said, with an acknowledging nod. 'But consider this: same height, same build. And — we've done quite a bit of work on your Mr Werner — same small scar on his left wrist.' He added breezily, 'Thank God the squirrels hadn't nibbled that away.'

Guttman was impressed. Stephenson seemed to know a lot more about Werner than the Bureau did, and with far less reason. 'All right, I'll accept that it was Werner. So why did he kill himself, and why there?'

'Because he didn't kill himself, and the location of his murder wasn't up to him.' The levity in Stephenson's voice was gone.

295

'Please do go on,' Guttman said, realising he was sounding like the Canadian Brit.

'I don't know about you, but in some cases I find common sense as helpful as evidence. Think about Werner. Here's a man who's a member of the *Bund* — if an obscure one — determined to make America a Nazi state. So what does he do? Travels to Europe. Understandable perhaps if he's going to have a visit — his mother is still alive, apparently. But no, he doesn't see his mother; instead he goes and kills himself in an isolated patch of meadow, having done his best to make sure no one can identify his body. I'm not a policeman or one of these psychiatrists, but that doesn't make a lot of sense to me.

'Also, the gun he used was a Luger, German make. We did a little research and it was a new model — the first came out the previous spring, and they were only issued to senior German army personnel.' He stopped speaking when Katie came back into the room, carrying a plate in each hand. She put them down on the desk, and Stephenson and Guttman thanked her.

'Oh, dear,' said Stephenson, looking at their sandwiches.

They seemed perfectly fine to Guttman. 'What's the matter?'

'Is ham all right?' He sounded concerned.

Guttman gave a wry laugh. 'Sure it is. Just don't tell my wife.'

'Kosher?'

'She's not even Jewish. It's the diet I'm breaking she'd be mad about.'

Guttman took a big bite of his sandwich; he

had skipped breakfast. 'So who killed Werner then?'

'I think the Nazis did.'

'In the middle of an Austrian forest? Why there?'

'They probably thought Werner wouldn't be found for a long time, and when he was, no one would be the wiser. No ID, etc. An obvious suicide.'

'But why did they kill him? The guy was a member of the Detroit chapter of the *Bund*.'

Stephenson looked almost apologetic. 'That, I'm afraid, is where my certainty falters.'

Guttman sighed, and said without thinking, 'They're dropping like flies.' Stephenson gave him a look. What the hell, thought Guttman, there seemed no point being coy. 'One of my informants was murdered a few days ago, here in D.C. He was working at the German Embassy.'

If Stephenson was surprised by this he didn't show it. 'Same sort of business?'

'Yes. Made to look like a suicide. And they almost pulled it off. I — ' He stopped suddenly since the door had been flung open, and three young men came in, talking noisily. They must have worked in the room, for they paid no attention to Stephenson or Guttman, but went to their desks, still talking.

Stephenson looked at the men, then turned to Guttman. 'Let's go to my office. It'll be quieter there.'

And as they went upstairs, Guttman found himself wondering just how much he should tell this man. He liked him, he respected his intelligence, and he was impressed by how forthcoming he had been. But . . . there was no 'but' he realised, suddenly aware of how alone he felt. There wasn't anyone at the Bureau he could share things with. Not if he wanted to keep his job. Part of him wanted to say, *Screw the job*, but every time a fantasy entered his head of telling J. Edgar Hoover just where he could get off, an image of Isabel, cold and ill and in need of care, brought him down to earth.

Now he was talking to a guy who was willing to listen and maybe even help. Stephenson had an agenda — Guttman was not naive — but at least it was an honest one and undisguised.

Stephenson opened a door to a small room that looked like his study. There was a desk with a padded partner's chair, and a polished side table half-covered by two stacks of files. Books lined the back wall, mainly history Guttman saw, reading their spines. The windows had dark drapes, now pulled back, and the carpet was soft plum.

Stephenson put his plate on the desk and pulled over a chair from a corner. 'Have a seat,' he said.

'I didn't see the Colonel downstairs,' said Guttman.

'He's gone.'

A British euphemism apparently. 'I am sorry.'

'Oh, I don't mean that sort of departure. He's gone back to England. When war broke out, he booked the first sailing home.' Stephenson smiled. 'He acknowledged that his fighting days were over, but was still determined to do his bit.

Said he'd be damned if he'd spend the war in a Washington armchair.'

'Well, so far so good,' said Guttman, thinking of the war. Poland had fallen, of course, but since then the European front had been quiet.

Stephenson looked at him without his usual calm. 'It's the lull before the storm, I assure you. As soon as winter lifts, the *Wehrmacht* will be on the move. I fear they'll be in Paris by summer.'

The mood had turned sombre. Stephenson seemed to want to lighten it, for he reached over and opened a small floor cabinet, and extracted two bottles of Straub beer. He found an opener in the desk drawer and popped the caps off. Handing one to Guttman he said, 'Helps to wash the ham down, don't you think?'

They each drank and then Stephenson said quietly, 'You were about to tell me about the other so-called suicide.'

Guttman had made up his mind. So he told Stephenson about his relationship with Bock, simply and without drama. He didn't discuss his larger worries, and he was careful not to reveal anything simply for the sake of it — he didn't mention Nessheim, for example, or give any indication that he'd had a man on the ground, inside one corner of the German-American *Bund*. But what he did come clean about were his own suspicions and where they'd led him — through Bock, to the German-American *Bund*. There seemed no danger doing that, and anyway, Bock wasn't around to complain.

'Fascinating,' said Stephenson. 'But tell me, did you ever think that Bock might have been playing you off against his masters back in Berlin? Or worse still, that he was working on their orders and only pretending to be working for you?'

Guttman smiled. 'Even I got that far.'

Stephenson tried to look embarrassed. 'My dear fellow, I wasn't suggesting — '

'I know,' said Guttman, waving a hand to show he wasn't bothered. 'But you see, that possibility only made me even more suspicious of the Germans. Because if Bock were working for them, then he was under orders to plant a red herring so big that it would keep my attention far from where it ought to be. But if he was on the level — and this is the paradox — it would have the same effect. There isn't any evidence the Reich was behind the attempt to seize the Armory.'

Stephenson finished his beer and put the bottle down. 'So what does it all mean, do you think?'

'I can't be sure. I only know *something* is happening — the connections don't make sense otherwise.'

'We're not paid to believe in coincidence, I suppose,' said Stephenson, looking thoughtful.

'No, but equally, I'm not looking to see a conspiracy around every corner.'

'Yes, but let's think about it. What would this conspiracy consist of?'

Guttman finished his sandwich and chewed for a minute. He cleared his throat before speaking. 'It has to help the Nazis, of course, but not be known — why else the secrecy? It's a 'project' all right, but I don't think it involves saboteurs. We've already caught some of those, and we've drawn a pretty good bead on the others.'

'And whatever this is mustn't be known because — ?'

'Look at it backwards. I ask myself, what's the one thing the Nazis want to avoid?' He realised Stephenson was staring at him. 'It has to be America's entry into the war.'

'Agreed.'

'So what could the Nazis do that would ensure America stays out? Something that if it got discovered might precipitate what they're trying to avoid. So it has to be completely secret.'

They both looked at each other, hesitant to say out loud what each was thinking. 'What leads have we got?' asked Stephenson, seemingly relieved to break the silence. Guttman noticed the 'we'.

'That's the problem. Werner's dead, Bock's dead, and Schultz won't talk. That leaves the Cummings connection, which seems to me the weakest link of the bunch.'

'Any progress there?'

Guttman hesitated only momentarily. To hell with it, he decided. 'I can't do the surveillance I'd like. The usual stuff — wiretaps, mail intercepts — is out of the question.'

Stephenson raised a tactful eyebrow. Guttman explained, 'She's very well connected. And as far as the Director goes, the original info came from an untrustworthy source.'

'Who's that?' asked Stephenson, looking puzzled.

'You,' said Guttman.

To his credit Stephenson laughed.

'And there's another thing. Mrs Cummings is a friend of the President's. So it's not as if you could go over Hoover's head to the White House, even if you wanted to.'

Stephenson pondered this for a moment while Guttman stared at the books behind him — T. E. Lawrence's *The Seven Pillars of Wisdom*, *My Early Life* by Winston Churchill, Michael Arlen's *The Green Hat*.

Stephenson said, 'Still, she's all we have, isn't she?' Seeing assent in Guttman's eyes he continued, 'It seems to me we need somebody inside this salon of Mrs C. Not an informant — there's too little likelihood of finding one in time, at least not one we can trust.'

'What do you mean by 'in time' anyway? You have a deadline in mind?'

'Two actually: one unknown, one fixed. The unknown one is how long Britain can hold out. If we make it to next autumn we could have a chance, however gloomy it looks now. But we need a friend in the White House. The fixed one is July.'

'What's in July?'

'The Democrats Convention. That's when we'll know if FDR's going to run again. But as I was saying, an informant's unlikely to come our way. We need someone undercover, don't you think?'

Guttman suddenly felt as if he'd been pressed against a wall. He said stiffly, 'The Director has a policy against putting agents in undercover.'

Stephenson's eyes widened. 'But you . . . ' he started to say, then seemed to think better of it. He said quietly, 'Just a thought, you know.' He paused to let it sink in, then said, 'Why don't we have coffee downstairs?'

19

Late February 1940
Washington D.C.

He was staring dully at the stack of papers on his desk when a voice at the door said, 'Don't look so excited,' and Guttman came into the room.

It was only Nessheim's second day, but Guttman had put him to work already, sitting him down in a small room near his own office on the Fourth Floor. It had a desk and an old walnut bookcase that held files stacked sideways. The one window was small, with frosted glass panes which meant there wasn't any view.

It was an odd little nest within the FBI headquarters, since in most other respects the floors allocated to the Bureau were just many-times-over versions of the Chicago and San Francisco quarters Nessheim was used to, a series of offices running off corridors, interspersed with larger open spaces for typists and clerks. Drone work (such as the inspection of fingerprint evidence), went on elsewhere, in the Old Southern Railway Building on 13th Street.

'I'm riveted,' said Nessheim.

Guttman laughed. 'You're such a typical field agent. If you're not out and about, talking to an informant, carrying a gun, you feel you're not working. But cheer up: I've had a .38 issued to you, and tomorrow you start your new duties. I'm sending you over to the White House. I'll still need you over here, but only afternoons, and not every one.'

'What will I be doing?' asked Nessheim, slightly puzzled. He felt as though he was reverting to the days when Purvis had to teach him how to wipe his nose.

'We need to review the President's security. I want you to check the credentials of all the people who see the President on a regular basis. Everyone — from his maid to the Secretary of State. I'm afraid it means reading a lot of paper and making phone calls.'

'A desk job in other words.' That had not been Guttman's promise when he'd tracked Nessheim down in Wisconsin.

'To you paperwork isn't real work, but to me, more work gets done with a file than a gun.'

'You said I'd be undercover.'

'You will be.'

'In the White House?'

'That's only part of your duties. The rest will come in time.'

Nessheim was willing to challenge Guttman now; after all, he hadn't wanted to come back in the first place. 'Who says?' he asked.

'I say. Since I'll be the only person who knows what you're up to.'

'Yeah, yeah. You and Mr Hoover are the only people in the know.'

'*I'm* the only person in the know.'

'You always say that,' he began, then stopped

short and stared at Guttman. 'You didn't mention Mr Hoover this time.' Guttman was nodding. 'You mean . . . ?'

'Yeah,' was all Guttman said. He was pretending to look at papers at his desk.

'Did he know I was at Camp Schneider?' Nessheim demanded. When Guttman didn't answer he said, 'You better level with me, Harry.' It was the first time he'd used Guttman's first name, but he felt entitled. 'If I'm going out on a limb for you, then I think you owe me an explanation.'

Guttman didn't answer this, saying instead, 'If anybody asks what you're working on, you say you're working on extremists. Okay? Not Fascists, not Communists. Extremists.'

'Is somebody likely to ask?'

Guttman shrugged. 'Who knows? It might be Mr Hoover himself. He's been known to pop in on the spur of the moment. Keeps us on our toes, I guess.'

I'll bet it does, thought Nessheim. One thing he had picked up from his first days in the Chicago bureau was the pervasive influence of its Director. The FBI was like an immense family-owned company, whose patriarch still controlled every aspect of the business.

Guttman looked at his watch. 'Let's go out and grab a beer. Where are you staying?'

'A motel out in Virginia.'

'I live that way myself. I can give you a lift to the trolley in Rosslyn.'

★ ★ ★

They drove south to the edge of the Potomac. The small heater inside the Buick blasted out tepid air, which slowly melted the thin glaze of ice on the windshield inch by inch. Moving west along the river bank they reached the industrial end of Georgetown, where an enormous set of smokestacks belched white smoke over the river bluff. A factory shift was ending, men in overalls emerging to shiver after their heated immersion inside.

Washington was not as Nessheim had expected. The Federal architecture seemed formal and heavy, based on Greek and Roman models that may have made sense to an overwhelmingly rural America in the past, but which now seemed stolid, almost lifeless — at least compared to the vibrancy and free-for-all building styles of Chicago and New York. And there was less grandeur to the rest of the city than he'd dreamed of — actually there seemed no grandeur at all. This time of year Washington was especially stark: a collection of low houses, most on low ground, bordered by a river and basin of muddy water, with blasting winds and few hills for shelter.

Guttman parked next to an unprepossessing shack overlooking the river, which was only half-frozen here. A sign on the building said *Steamers*. Nessheim looked at it dubiously.

'Come on,' said Guttman, hopping out, and Nessheim followed him inside.

The place looked deserted. It was a greasy spoon with a lunch counter and a short-order grill that turned into a makeshift bar each evening — a holdover from Prohibition days, Guttman explained, when thirty seconds' warning could have the shot glasses hidden behind the counter and anodyne cups of coffee poured when the cops walked through the door.

They sat down at a rickety table against the far wall, and after a minute a fat man with a wart the size of a nickel on one cheek came out of the back. 'What can I get you?'

'Two Huerichs,' said Guttman. He turned to Nessheim. 'I assume you like beer?'

Nessheim nodded as the fat man delivered two bottles and no glasses. He took a pull; it was cold and rich with hops. 'Not bad,' he said.

'So where exactly are you staying?'

'A tourist court just outside of McLean.' It was pretty awful, full of travelling salesmen and truckers. But it was cheap.

'Sounds delightful.'

'I've started to look for an apartment. They seem kind of expensive.'

'Housing's at a real premium in this town these days. Nobody says, 'Go West young man,' any more — the world and its aunt seem to be coming here instead. It's where the gravy train is.'

He looked at Nessheim. 'But that doesn't solve your problem. There comes a point when a guy needs a place of his own.' He added sympathetically, 'I bet you're living on White Tower hamburgers and milkshakes every night. Not that you're gonna get fat any time soon.' He looked down regretfully at his own paunch, then drank the rest of his beer in one long swallow.

'Let me make a call or two.'

And when Guttman dropped him half an hour later at the trolley stop on the west side of the Potomac, Nessheim realised he still didn't know what he was really supposed to be doing, undercover or not, or why he had let himself be persuaded to stay in the Federal Bureau of Investigation.

★ ★ ★

It took him an hour to get to the White House in the morning, enough time for his excitement to build. He was surprised to find himself feeling this way — ever since he had almost drowned in the Atlantic he had not really looked forward to anything.

He remembered reading an article in *Colliers* about people who had survived near-death experiences. They were quick with preachy homilies — *It taught me to live to the full, Every day counts, You never take anything for granted again.* The odd thing for him, however, was that it had only been after his rescue that he realised what a close call he'd had — when he'd actually been in the water he had refused to contemplate his hopeless situation. And the emotion stirred by this retrospective recognition was not gratitude, but an anger that had simmered during his long stay in the hospital and come to a boil on his release. For when he went back to Wisconsin to convalesce, he hadn't absolutely decided to kill his Uncle Eric, but he wouldn't have bet against it. Each time he thought about his miraculous escape from death, the more enraged he felt about his uncle's betrayal.

Yet just as Nessheim had cheated death, it seemed now death was cheating him — as soon as he got home he learned that Uncle Eric had little time left to live. The big barrel-chested German he had known all his life was wasting away; his 250-pound frame couldn't have weighed half that on the day Nessheim went to see him.

Nessheim's aunt had fixed up a room downstairs, off the parlour, where Eric lay on the bed under a pile of heavy blankets. A lunch tray, soup and a roll, lay untouched on the bedside table. Even with the fire roaring next door, enough to make Nessheim sweat, his uncle was shivering from cold. When Aunt Greta went to fill his water bottle, he looked at Nessheim and smiled weakly.

'So Jimmy, how is the government these days?'

'It's okay. A job's a job.'

'Still verking for the Treasury counting honest people's money?'

Nessheim tried to smile. 'Actually, I don't work there any more, Uncle Eric. I'm with the Federal Bureau of Investigation. You know, the FBI.'

He watched his uncle's reaction carefully, but weak as he was, Uncle Eric still looked absolutely astonished. 'Really?' he said, his eyes as big as saucers. He tried to sit up against the pillow propped behind him but couldn't manage it. 'Since when?'

'A while back,' said Nessheim.

'Does your mother know?' His concern seemed entirely genuine.

'She does now.'

Uncle Eric nodded. 'Better she should know and worry, than not know and worry anyway.' He paused, and took a couple of shallow breaths. 'You like it there?'

'It's not too bad,' he said.

Uncle Eric sighed. 'You know my views. I have never been shy about expressing them.' He smiled wanly. 'But maybe this is not such a bad thing. My own country after all is at war. I hope to God yours can stay out of it.' He wriggled a shoulder against the mattress.

'Can I get you something?' asked Nessheim.

'Nah, it's just an ache. Plenty more where that came from. You know, I am no friend of the English, but I think they had a point in standing up to Hitler.'

'You do?'

'Like many Germans, I have been pleased to see Germany rise again, proud that we no longer live on our knees. But that doesn't mean you have always to have your own way. And the pact with Moscow. Bah,' he said, making a face. 'Not that it will last. But to get in bed with the Bolsheviks is not something I can excuse, whatever the Führer's reasoning. To have England as an enemy and Russia as a friend is madness. Who knows where it will lead?'

'More war,' Nessheim said quietly.

Uncle Eric nodded. 'Not that I will have to see it,' he said, and though he wriggled his shoulder again in obvious pain, he seemed pleased by the thought.

★ ★ ★

Uncle Eric died ten days after New Year's, with Nessheim now confident it wasn't he who had betrayed him after all.

At the funeral in the Bremen Lutheran church the local German community was out in force. When the service ended, Nessheim saw his old girlfriend Trudy in the churchyard, holding a toddler by the hand, then noticed a bulge at her belly. Number two on its way. He tried to catch her eye, if only for old times' sake, but she seemed determined not to catch his. Her husband, Alex Burgmeister, took her by the arm and steered her in the opposite direction.

The next day his mother found him in the barn. 'Jimmy! Come quick,' she shouted. 'There's a man on the phone and he's calling all the way from Washington.'

Twenty-four hours later he was on a train, but heading east. The conversation he'd had with Guttman over the party line had been awkward, made uneasier by his awareness that the neighbouring farmers might be listening in as an assistant director of the FBI tried to persuade him to stay in his employ.

'I told you, I don't want your job,' he remembered saying right away.

'It's not just a *job*,' Guttman had said caustically. He'd continued, 'I'm not trying to keep you in work for the sake of it. The bastards have murdered Bock.'

'I'm sorry,' he said reflexively, wondering why the *Bund* had killed Bock.

'Sorry *schmorry*. I need you back here.'

'I can't do that.'

Guttman barked down the line, 'What do you want me to say, Jimmy — that your country needs you? Okay, it does. Read the papers, you fathead, can't you see there's a war on?'

And wisely Guttman had waited while Nessheim thought about this. Could he live with himself if he simply walked away? Guttman might be flattering him, Guttman might be full of baloney, but there was a core truth to the appeal he was making.

'Okay,' he said at last.

Before Nessheim had the chance to change his mind, Guttman said quickly, 'This time don't cash your sleeper ticket in. You're going to need all the rest you can get once I've got you started.'

20

The White House seemed surprisingly small —
a compound, really, rather than the palace-sized
building and grounds Nessheim had expected.
Following Guttman's instructions he went to the
West Gate where a policeman checked his name
on a clipboard, then phoned through. A young
woman in a smart crêpe suit, cinched in at the
waist to accentuate her figure, and black high
heels came out to escort him in.

'I'm Dinah,' she said confidently, leading him
into the building. 'It's still a bit new here; the
rebuild isn't finished yet.' Her voice sounded
Southern. Nessheim had never thought of
Washington as anything but a northern city, not
since the Civil War. But the natives spoke in the
soft tones of Virginia.

Dinah opened a door and looked in. Over her
shoulder he could see two rows of cubicles and a
small sofa to one side.

'The boys aren't here,' she said, and walked
to the corner cubicle. 'There's your space.' He'd
been given a filing cabinet, a stack of yellow
legal pads and a bunch of pencils, freshly
sharpened. To Nessheim it said *desk job*, and
his heart sank.

'This should do you,' the woman said.

'I hadn't realised the office wasn't in the White
House,' he said. He felt like a kid on Christmas
morning who finds his stocking empty.

314

The woman gave him a look. 'This *is* the White House.'

'The President lives here?' he said with disbelief.

'No. His residence is in the main mansion next door. This is the Executive Wing. It's where he works — most of the time anyway. His office is just down the hall. Speaking of which, are you ready?'

'Ready for what?'

'To meet the President. He knows you're here and wanted to say hello.'

'You're joking,' he said.

'No,' she said levelly, making it clear she didn't do jokes.

'Can I have a minute?' he asked, suddenly feeling panicky. Christ, was his tie straight? Should he comb his hair? He looked down at his shoes and wished he had polished them more carefully. And his suit, a blue cotton one he'd bought the summer before in Chicago, suddenly seemed dowdy.

'The President's waiting,' Dinah said a little impatiently.

'Okay, okay,' he said, and took a deep breath. He followed her out of the office, then around a corner. Ahead of them was a mahogany door with a brass handle — that must be it, he thought, wishing his heart would stop pounding.

Dinah stopped by the door and turned to Nessheim. 'Ready?' she asked, which made him even more nervous. He gave a little nod and she rapped sharply, then to Nessheim's surprise she opened the door without waiting for a call to come in.

The room before him was very slightly oval-shaped, its sides two narrow ellipses, like the finest crescent moons. The walls were painted white, and light poured through three tall windows at the far end, behind a large desk. Next to it sat a wheelchair — a normal kitchen chair, Nessheim realised, with two small side wheels affixed.

Behind the desk a high-backed padded chair had been turned to face the windows. Nessheim almost jumped when the chair slowly started to swivel round. He took a deep breath, wondering if he should speak first or wait for his commander-in-chief to greet him.

Gradually the man sitting in the chair came into view. He had big shoulders and a bald head and his face was familiar. But not from newspaper photographs or newsreels, Nessheim realised, just as the man raised one arm and pointed a long finger at him.

'*Bang!*' the man shouted, and this time Nessheim did jump.

Behind him the woman burst out laughing and the man in the chair guffawed. It was Mueller.

'Gotcha, Mr All-American,' Mueller said with satisfaction. He was grinning, but it was not a friendly grin. 'The President's up in Hyde Park. He'll be real upset to have missed you.'

★ ★ ★

After that, Nessheim was known as the President's Boy by the other FBI agents stationed in the White House. There were five of them in all, including Mueller. Other than his old enemy, they seemed a decent bunch; Nessheim accepted both the nickname and their mild ribbing with good humour.

It was unclear, however, what the small contingent of FBI agents actually *did*, since the rival Secret Service, though stuck in a large office in the basement, were present in far greater numbers. Each time FDR left the White House, one of the Bureau agents tagged along, grudgingly tolerated by the Secret Service detail. The inevitable friction between the two competing agencies was aggravated by Mueller, who as head of the FBI contingent, didn't conceal his disdain for what he called 'Treasury gonads' — the Secret Service remained part of the Treasury Department, an anachronism stemming from its nineteenth-century origins chasing counterfeiters.

Nessheim wasn't part of any of this — he had other duties, and he reported to Guttman. This annoyed Mueller. 'Just what is it you're supposed to be doing?' he'd asked.

The problem was, Nessheim couldn't have told Mueller much about his work even if he had wanted to. As instructed by Guttman, he began reviewing the security arrangements around Roosevelt. The ground had been laid for his arrival: on his first day, the doorkeeper in the mansion showed him the log books for Presidential visitors — there was half a shelf of them, dating back to the first day of Roosevelt's presidency in March 1933. Then Nessheim talked with a man named Hackmeister, who was in charge of the White House switchboard. Apparently, the President was virtually addicted to the instrument. 'I bet half his day is on the phone,' said Hackmeister.

Finally, Nessheim met the President's two full-time secretaries, a striking woman named Missy Le Hand, and a quieter one named Tully. The two kept their own records of the President's visitors, though frequent ones to the Executive Wing weren't always noted. 'If I marked every time Mr Hopkins came to see the President,' Le Hand explained with a laugh, 'he'd have three volumes just by himself.' It was odd to see iconic names recorded in such a humdrum way — Hopkins, Corcoran, Morgenthau. Hopkins even lived there in the White House, it turned out, and Felix Frankfurter had been resident for months a few years before.

What most struck Nessheim, however, was the actual lack of real security around the President. This was not through Secret Service or FBI laxness, but due to FDR himself. He refused point blank to have guards stationed in his living quarters in the mansion; at night he would not allow guards inside the White House at all. Even more worrying from a security angle was Roosevelt's delight in shaking off his security men, especially in the afternoon when he liked to escape from his office and go for a drive. Although he always had a chauffeur, he often did the driving himself, using the retainer only to help haul him out of the modified driver's seat.

These escapades gave both his Secret Service and FBI minders absolute conniptions. Mueller's views of what the President got up to during these afternoon jaunts were relentlessly salacious. 'He's got to be playing away,' he would say. 'Who wouldn't with a wife like that? Those choppers — can you imagine how they'd feel on your ding-a-ling?'

Reuters, a young agent so green he made Nessheim feel like a seasoned veteran, piped up. 'But Mule, he's in a wheelchair, for Christ's sake.'

Mueller shrugged. 'From what I hear, that doesn't stop the guy. Something's still working down there.'

Mueller's disdain for Roosevelt was not singular; even as his second term was coming to a close, the President attracted abuse from many of America's citizens. There were sackloads of hate mail, full of anonymous death threats, though their sheer volume stripped them of the urgency they were intended to inspire. The critics were not all Americans: Mueller had come in one morning, talking about a radio programme he'd listened to the night before. 'You should have heard this guy in Germany last night going on about the President. I heard him on short wave. He sounds like a Limey.'

'What was he saying?' asked Reuters.

'Nothing nice, believe me. He calls the President Rosenfeld.' Nothing new there, thought Nessheim. Uncle Eric had done the same.

But Mueller aside, Nessheim's job soon assumed a pedestrian normality which he wouldn't have believed possible — not for someone working in the White House. After a week, his work had settled into a routine of reviewing the files and meeting with the President's administrative staff. At lunch he ate in the local coffee shops with the other FBI agents; none of them mingled with the agents from the Secret Service. Nessheim didn't ever meet the President, who was often away, and his acquaintance with the man he was supposed to help protect was confined to a couple of sightings from behind, as FDR was pushed in his bespoke wheelchair along the portico that linked the Executive Wing to the mansion. The 'glamour' of working in the White House had worn off swiftly, and not for the first time Nessheim wondered what Guttman really had in mind for him.

21

Two weeks after starting at the White House, Nessheim took a trolley car one Thursday after lunch to Washington Circle. It took forever; when he got off and followed the conductor's directions to Dumbarton Avenue he had to run, straight into a harsh western wind that was keeping winter alive. Even so he was late, and found Guttman pacing impatiently on the cobblestoned sidewalk. It was a narrow street, shaded by lines of mid-sized maple trees.

'I'm sorry,' Nessheim panted. He realised he was getting out of shape.

'I'd better assign you one of the pool cars. You're going to be moving around too much to rely on the trolleys.' Guttman gestured to one of the townhouses set back from the sidewalk. 'Let's go in.'

The house was tall and thin, its brick painted a milky yellow, with dark blue shutters on its windows. The ground level was occupied by a garage, with an adjacent flight of steps that ran up to the front door. They climbed them and Guttman knocked.

A young woman answered the door. She was dressed for business, in a short wool jacket and a calf-length skirt. Her face was striking rather than pretty, with deep-set eyes but a small crooked nose, and her dark straight hair was cut in a forbidding bob. But she smiled politely enough, and led them through to a sitting room, where a small wood fire was burning on an iron grate. A door at the far end was half-open, revealing a book-lined study.

The woman said to Guttman, 'Justice Frankfurter is waiting for you in there.'

'Take a seat,' Guttman said to Nessheim, pointing to a stuffed armchair by the fire. 'I won't be long.' He went into the study and closed the door behind him.

Nessheim sat down awkwardly, then saw the woman had stayed in the room. She was quite tall, he realised, thin, almost wiry. Now she sat down behind a small desk by the room's front window.

'Don't mind me,' she said. 'We're a little short of room, so I have to make do with this for my office.'

He nodded, but inwardly he was annoyed. Why had he been brought along if he was being excluded from the meeting?

The fire crackled, and an ember suddenly shot out above the guard, landing on the carpet. He reached down and flicked it back towards the hearth, then looking up saw the woman staring at him.

'Your nose looks out of joint,' she declared, eyeing him carefully.

'What do you mean?' He leaned back in his chair and stared at her.

'Just what I said.' She gestured at the closed door. 'Were you expecting to be in there?'

'I don't expect. I'm just the bottle washer.'

'Oh, I thought maybe you were the bodyguard,' she said tartly.

'G-men don't need bodyguards,' he said, trying not to smile.

'Of course not. How dense of me. So what are you here for?'

'To protect you, of course.'

She laughed and her face broke into a smile, surprising because up to now her countenance had been severe. She said teasingly 'Do you really need to carry a gun in your line of work?'

'That depends.'

'On what?'

You couldn't brush this woman off, he realised. 'On whether you need one.'

'You're ducking the question,' she said confidently. He shrugged, thinking of Danny Ho. Suddenly she seemed to realise why he might not want to answer. She said, 'I'm being tactless aren't I? Sorry.'

'Don't worry about it. Most agents never have to fire their weapon. It's just the luck of the draw.'

'So to speak,' she said. When he grinned, she seemed to regain her confidence. 'I know your name's Nessheim, but do you have another one?'

'Jimmy,' he said. 'And yours?'

'I'm Annie Ryerson.'

'Are you from around here?'

'Is anybody? I've been here two years — I started for the Justice last winter after his appointment was confirmed. You don't sound very local yourself.'

'Small-town Wisconsin,' he said.

'Me too. Small-town, that is.'

'So what brings a country girl to Washington?' He was making conversation, but he found himself interested, and she looked like she was enjoying herself.

'Small-town, not country. I grew up in New England.'

'I've been there.'

'To see the colours in autumn?' she asked. There was a hint of gentle mockery.

'Nope. I was working in Vermont.'

'Right,' she said, but her tone was chilly enough that he wondered if he'd said something wrong.

'You know it there?' he added mildly.

'It's where I grew up. So, where were you at law school?'

'I wasn't.'

'Aren't all FBI men lawyers?'

'Not all.'

'Where'd you go to college then?'

'Northwestern. But I didn't finish.' He felt he was being checked out by an examiner. He said sharply, 'They taught me to read but I had to leave before they let me put it into practice.'

'I wasn't trying to be nosey.'

'Sure. Where did you go?' Somewhere snooty, he decided. Vassar, or Bryn Mawr. He felt slightly disappointed.

'I didn't go to college,' she said coolly. 'Things got in the way.'

'Money things?' he said.

'Something like that.'

'Me too. Dad owned a store. He lost it in my junior year,' he confessed.

'I'm sorry.' It sounded genuine. 'Mine's hanging on. Just.'

He was surprised, and realised he had pegged her wrong. 'General store?'

She nodded. 'There used to be six in town. Now there's only three.'

It seemed incongruous, sitting in this fancy sitting room, to be talking about small-town storekeeping. But as their conversation continued, Nessheim found it completely natural. Something about this woman attracted him. She wasn't obviously sexy, some men wouldn't even have found her pretty, but he found himself wanting her to like him. He told her the story of his father's financial decline, and he liked how she listened sympathetically but without a trace of pity. When she talked in turn it was clear she knew the same territory of near-despair, but she didn't harp on the hard times, and made him laugh describing her father, whose Yankee parsimony she sketched in simple, devastating tones. Then she changed the subject.

'Where in Vermont were you working?' she asked.

'Near Woodstock,' he said, and she looked startled.

The door of the study opened, and Guttman and the Justice emerged. Nessheim got to his feet. Glancing at his watch, he was astonished to find an hour had passed.

Guttman spoke first. 'Agent Nessheim, this is Justice Frankfurter.'

A little man, not much more than five feet tall, stepped forward. He said, 'Pleased to meet you,' then vigorously shook Nessheim's hand. The voice was warm, with a hint of New York. His grey hair was combed straight back, revealing a broad forehead, beneath which jutted a wrinkled, prominent nose. He wore spectacles, but behind them he had deep thoughtful blue eyes that also managed to sparkle, as if life sobered and amused him in equal measure. His elfin stature belied an obvious energy that made Nessheim feel he had suddenly been thrust into a more active orbit.

Frankfurter said, 'Nessheim, eh? A German name.'

'That's right,' said Nessheim.

'Where do you come from?'

'Wisconsin.'

Frankfurter chuckled. 'I meant where in Germany.'

'Oh,' said Nessheim. 'A few from Bavaria, the rest from the North.'

Frankfurter nodded. 'I came from Vienna myself — back when Austria was its own master. Though I suppose Herr Hitler would say it should always have been part of Germany.'

'I'm on your side with that one,' said Nessheim softly.

Frankfurter turned to Annie. 'You know, I think Mr Nessheim here would enjoy one of your aunt's soirées. Don't you think?'

'He might,' she said neutrally.

'Why don't you ask Sally to invite him?'

'What's your address?' Annie asked impersonally. It was as if her easy chatter with Nessheim just minutes before had not taken place.

'Actually — ' he began, then stopped, not knowing what to say.

'Jimmy's only just arrived in town,' Guttman interjected. 'He's looking for a rental — a room rather than an apartment. He may not be in D.C. that long.'

Frankfurter said, 'I might be able to help with that. Some of my ex-pupils stay in a house that belongs to a friend of mine. He's a widower, no children, and it's a big place — so it makes sense for him to have boarders. Let me give you his name and address. Better still, I'll give him a call.'

Nessheim's heart sank at the prospect of more boarding-house life. Another landlord to add to his list, no doubt a 'character'. Communal facilities — the joy of other people's shaving kit on the basin each morning, a shared telephone and a shared kitchen. The smells of linoleum floors washed down with carbolic soap.

His feelings must have shown, for Frankfurter said reassuringly, 'I think you'll like it there.'

★ ★ ★

When they left Guttman seemed in high spirits; he was whistling. Nessheim still felt disgruntled.

Guttman said, 'Well done. You got an invite lots of people would kill for.'

'I'm not big on parties.' Stacey Madison had dragged him to countless shindigs all over Chicago, but it was not something he would have done on his own.

'I want you to go to this one.'

'Are you telling me it's part of the job?'

Guttman said without hesitation, 'Yes.'

'Why don't you go in my place?' Nessheim said half-facetiously.

Guttman gave a thin smile. 'Not my cup of tea, as you very well know.' He stopped suddenly on the pavement, waiting until Nessheim turned and looked at him. He saw Guttman's point: his boss was a burly balding figure in a suit that didn't fit, a tie that was loosening at the knot, and dark-brown Florsheims which, though polished to a high shine, managed to look as though they'd been worn by several other pairs of feet.

'It's not exactly mine either, Harry. What's so important about this lady anyway?'

Guttman was serious now. 'This girl's aunt is called Sally Cummings. She knows everybody. Her own political sympathies are a little suspect.'

'Is she a Pinko?' He hoped he wasn't back to tracking Communists.

'More like brown-ish — as in Brownshirts.'

'Really?' He wondered if Guttman had been watching too many movies.

'That's why I want you to get as close to her as you can.'

'I'm not sure her niece even liked me,' he protested, thinking of how Annie Ryerson had turned frosty.

'Make her like you then,' said Guttman shortly, and Nessheim saw he wasn't joking.

'All right, I'll go to the lady's soirée, or whatever it's called. But I can find my own lodgings.'

Guttman shook his head. 'Sorry. That's part of the job too.'

'How?' Nessheim found himself growing impatient.

Guttman had drawn alongside Nessheim now, and they were walking east towards the centre of D.C. The senior agent said disarmingly, 'I learned long ago that you can't explain a hunch. But don't look so glum. The Justice assures me that it's not your average boarding house.'

* * *

It wasn't, Nessheim soon realised, unless one's idea of an average boarding house was a three-storey brick home in newly fashionable Georgetown. His bedroom was on the top floor, with a view of a tall beech tree and the lawn that constituted the back yard. The room was small and low-ceilinged, and he shared a bathroom with someone he only heard down the hall, but it was quiet and homey, with small rugs on the wooden floor, prints of Washington landmarks on the wall, and a bookcase full of English detective novels.

He slept well on his first night there, and came down to breakfast to find two men at a long table having a furious argument — so fierce in fact, that Nessheim wondered if they were going to come to blows. The bigger of the two, light-haired and with a handsome face that reminded Nessheim of Gary Cooper, acknowledged Nessheim's presence with a nod, and passed him a big jug of black coffee, before starting to shout again at the other guy. 'You think that because it's quiet over there for now,

329

someone's going to wave a magic wand and the Nazis will just waft away.'

'They may withdraw.'

'Try telling that to the Poles. Or the Czechs for that matter. No one in their right mind thinks Hitler would give up an inch of territory — what about *Lebensraum?* The whole point is he wants more space. Christ, the bastard wants the whole world if we let him.'

The fair-haired man looked up at the wall clock. 'Damn, I gotta go.' He added mildly, 'See you at Sally's tonight.' He went out of the room.

Nessheim sat in silence, a little stunned by this exchange. The remaining man was unusual looking: he had a long face, with a thin brittle-looking nose and high cheekbones, and eyes the colour of a watery sky; his hair was brown, short on top but bushy on the sides. Though he sounded entirely American, there was something foreign about this mix of features that Nessheim couldn't place. He wondered if he was a Finn, thinking of the immigrants he'd known in Wisconsin. They'd usually first come over to work in the tin and ore mines of Northern Michigan, then moved south to find less punishing jobs.

'What's the matter?' the man demanded.

Nessheim realised he had been staring at him. 'Are you two guys friends?'

'Sure.'

'Oh,' said Nessheim doubtfully.

'What, you think we're enemies because we argue?'

' 'Argue''s an understatement.'

330

'Nah. We're always like that. You'll get used to our ways. Think dialectic.'

'I am. It's synthesis that's lacking here.'

'Hah,' said the man appreciatively. He wiped his mouth with a paper napkin. 'I'm Dubinsky. Welcome to the House of Youth.'

'How's that?'

'It's just a joke the Justice made.'

'You mean Frankfurter?'

'Who else? I'm his law clerk this year, but we're all connected to him. Aren't you?'

'He's the one who recommended this place.' Nessheim didn't add that he had met the man for all of ninety seconds.

But Dubinsky wasn't listening. 'When the Justice was young he lived in a boarding house on 19th Street — Walter Lippmann was his roommate for a while. The talk there was pretty highbrow, and so were the visitors — Oliver Wendell Holmes used to drop in on his way home from the court. Some wag labelled it the House of Truth. The Justice said if they had truth on their side, at the very least we have youth.'

'How many of you live here?'

'Just four,' said Dubinsky, 'and that's including you. Otherwise, there's me, and Plympton — you just saw him in full flow.'

'Is he a clerk for the Justice too?'

'Nah. He was his student at Harvard Law, and the Justice put him onto Harry Hopkins. That's when Hopkins ran the WPA. Now that he's at Commerce, Frank's moved with him. Not much change to his job — he's away at least half the time. Hopkins isn't well, so he sends Frank.'

'Who's the fourth?'

'Miss Davidson, though don't get too excited. She's fifty if she's a day and there's a reason she's a Miss — face like a moose pat. She typed for the Prof years ago, though she works at the Treasury Department these days. You won't ever see her because she doesn't 'take breakfast'.' He said this in the voice of an old woman, and Nessheim laughed. Dubinsky too suddenly looked up at the clock on the kitchen wall. 'Got to run, we've got draft opinion reviews at ten. But I'll see you around.'

Nessheim soon got used to the arguments at breakfast, which were the norm rather than the exception — and found he fit into the House of Youth easily, thanks to Dubinsky, who was friendly and a mine of useful information: there was a cleaner but no cook in the house, and Dubinsky told Nessheim how to eat cheaply in the neighbourhood and which Chinese laundry would wash his socks and underwear as well as do his shirts. Plympton was friendly too, but less in evidence. When he was present at breakfast the arguments with Dubinsky were always fierce, but Nessheim realised it was a purely verbal form of take no prisoners. No one hit anybody, no one stalked from the room.

His own working days were busy, as he went through the security files of the President's voluminous acquaintances. Often in the afternoon Guttman called him over to the Bureau's headquarters, where most of the time he was set to work looking at yet more files — those of

German sympathisers rather than White House intimates, and the less interesting for their distance from power.

But sometimes Guttman just wanted to shoot the breeze. Nessheim supposed it was a way of getting to know his boss, but he couldn't really make the man out. Guttman was friendly enough, but tight-lipped about what he hoped Nessheim would discover. It was as if he didn't trust Nessheim, and there was even an occasional glint of resentment.

Once when Nessheim tossed a wadded-up ball of paper towards the waste-paper basket in the corner, Guttman reached out and caught it in mid-air with one hand.

'Not bad,' said Nessheim.

'Some of us played ball, too. Even if we weren't all-American.'

'You played football?'

'Yeah, though just the first two years of high school. Why, you think city kids don't play the game?' he asked sarcastically.

Nessheim felt awkward. 'Not at all. And I wasn't real all-American. Second team — not that big a deal.'

Guttman snorted. 'Bull. If you'd spent high school with your nose smushed against the cinders of P.S. 57's track, you'd understand why I'm impressed.'

'Why'd you stop playing?'

Guttman looked sheepish. 'My mom. She was scared I might get hurt.'

For once Nessheim felt more experienced than Guttman. 'She was right.'

Two days later, an embossed card arrived at Nessheim's new residence. It read *At Home*, and invited him to cocktails at the home of Mrs Sally Cummings a week from Friday.

22

Sally Cummings's house was called Belvedere and was located in the northern part of Georgetown, off Wisconsin Avenue, a neighbourhood of large houses and large lots. A formal gravel drive came up from the street through gates set in the high laurel hedge that ran along the front of the property; a good hundred yards of lawn stretched between this entrance and the house. Even by the local spacious standards, the Cummings house seemed exceptionally large — a three-storey Georgian pile of rosy brick. There was a Plantation-style portico at the entrance, fronted by two columns the height of the house.

The front door was half-open as Nessheim approached, and he saw a grand staircase inside, with a banister of polished oak. As he entered the hall, a maid in uniform came up and took his coat, just as a stylish, imperious-looking older woman swept in from a side door. She was elegantly dressed in a long red silk evening gown. There was a large diamond ring on her wedding finger, and she wore a double-strand pearl choker. 'I think I haven't had the pleasure,' she said with a questioning smile. 'I'm Sally Cummings.'

She was in her sixties, Nessheim guessed, but well-preserved, with wide cheekbones and a full jaw. A mass of blonde hair was swept back in a leonine mane. He thought she must have been a beauty in her youth, then he realised she still was. Her eyes were friendly but searching, and she extended a hand with the confidence of a politician.

He said, 'How do you do? I'm Jimmy Nessheim. Your niece invited me.'

'Ah, the gentleman from the FBI. Friends of Annie's are always welcome here. And how is Mr Hoover these days?'

'I'm told he's very well, ma'am.'

Sally Cummings smiled. 'I haven't seen J. Edgar for years. I suppose that must mean I've been keeping my nose clean,' she said with an easy laugh. 'How long have you been in D.C.'

'Three weeks, Mrs Cummings,' he said.

'Call me Sally. Everybody else does,' she said tolerantly, making him feel welcome and patronised at the same time. 'Washington is not a stuffy city — you'll get used to all of us soon enough. Now, why don't you go and help yourself to a drink?' she said, dismissing him gently and moving forward to greet more newcomers at the door.

A Negro butler in a white jacket and black tie stood still as a statue by the door Mrs Cummings had emerged from, holding a tray of highballs. Nessheim took one and sipped it — he was surprised by how much bourbon it held. He moved awkwardly through the doorway into a large sitting room. It was ornately furnished, with cherry tables and several sofas; immense canary-coloured drapes were pulled across most of the floor-to-ceiling windows. At the far end there was a large portrait of Sally Cummings above the mantel of the fireplace. Perhaps twenty people were already there, talking in small groups. Nessheim didn't know any of them, though he thought the portly man standing by a sofa and gesturing with his hand might be Senator Taft from Ohio.

'What on earth are you doing here?' It was Dubinsky, suddenly at his side.

Nessheim had been asking himself the same question. 'Miss Ryerson invited me.'

'Miss Ryerson? Hah. Plympton will get a kick out of that.'

A maid in a black uniform and white apron stopped with a tray. Dubinsky grabbed one of the canapés — a cheese cube with a slice of pimento olive, held together with a toothpick. He levered the combo off with his finger and popped it into his mouth. 'Now tell me, who do you know already?'

Nessheim looked around the room. 'Not a soul.' He couldn't see Annie anywhere.

Dubinsky gave a pedagogical shake to his head. 'I didn't mean know-know. I meant — Do you recognise anybody? Look over there,' and he pointed to two men by the fireplace. 'That's Congressman Horton from Kansas, *not* a big fan of FDR. He's talking to Senator Vandenberg — you've heard of him?' he asked hopefully.

'Even I have heard of him,' said Nessheim. People said the senator from Michigan was going to run for President — and keep America out of the war.

Dubinsky pointed out other famous guests (it

337

was indeed Senator Taft), including Senator McNary, Governor Price of Virginia, and the owner of the *Washington Post*, Eugene Meyer. A couple of foreign ambassadors were huddled in one corner talking to a one-armed man whom Dubinsky claimed ran the Federal Mint. The names tripped off Dubinsky's tongue in a foggy swirl of high ranks and titles; soon Nessheim simply nodded, only half-listening. 'And later,' Dubinsky concluded, like a parent promising a treat to a child, 'you might get a surprise.'

'Is that so?' said Nessheim.

Frank Plympton spied them from across the room, and made his way over, carrying a highball high in his hand. He wore a dark blue worsted suit and starched white shirt, with a striped Brooks Brothers tie. 'Hi boys,' he said.

'Where have you come in from?' asked Dubinsky.

Plympton suppressed a yawn. 'Caro-lin-ah,' he said, in a good approximation of a mush-mouth accent.

'And how are our Southern brethren?'

Plympton shook his head wearily. 'If you let 'em, they'd have slavery back tomorrow. If you're coloured and clever down there, you've only got one option.'

'What's that?' asked Nessheim.

'Head North,' said Plympton.

A tiny dapper figure in a three-piece suit appeared at Plympton's elbow. It was Frankfurter. 'Gentlemen,' he said brightly. He nodded pointedly at Nessheim. 'I see you followed my suggestion, young man. I hope you're keeping these fellows up to scratch.'

'I think it's the other way round, sir.'

Frankfurter shook his head. 'Don't get fooled by sophistry posing as wisdom. Isn't that right, David?'

Dubinsky nodded. 'It is. Tell me, sir, is there going to be a draft?'

'Which sort? Military or Presidential?' asked Frankfurter, raising an eyebrow.

'Both,' said Dubinsky.

'I expect the Congress to pass legislation this summer instituting conscription. None too soon, in my view; if we're going to go to war we'll need plenty of men in uniform.'

Dubinsky said quickly, 'And the second kind of draft?'

'I couldn't comment on the President's inclinations — even if I knew them. But I have to say, there isn't any candidate I can see who will have the guts to face our foes — that is, before we have no choice except to fight. And if we wait until then, we'll be entirely on our own. No, I think the President will soon start to feel overwhelming pressure to stand again.'

Dubinsky was unyielding. 'I can't see why Hitler would want to pick a fight with us if he controlled all of Europe.'

Frankfurter shook his head. 'We've had this argument too many times before, and you know my answer — world domination is why. That man is never satisfied. It's just the nature of the beast.'

He turned to the side as Sally Cummings and another lady came up and joined them. 'Why

339

Lucy Rutherford,' Frankfurter announced to the other woman, 'how nice to see you. It's been years, hasn't it?'

'Lovely to see you, Felix,' she said in a clear soprano voice. 'I think I was still a Mercer when we last met.'

'Let me introduce you to the boys,' Frankfurter said. When it was Nessheim's turn to be introduced, he found himself staring into a pair of riveting blue eyes. 'Pleased to meet you, Mrs Rutherford,' he said awkwardly.

She shook hands lightly and laughed. 'Call me Lucy, please. It keeps the years at bay.'

As she turned to talk with Frankfurter more, he tried not to stare at her. For she was stunningly, classically beautiful. Her flowing black taffeta dress was set off by a diamond and aquamarine necklace. The effect was understated, elegant — in a word, thought Nessheim, classy. Not for the first time he wondered what he was doing there.

He stood uneasily at the edge of this circle, then watched as across the room a little boy, dressed in corduroy overalls, ran towards Annie Ryerson. She lifted him into the air and hugged him.

'Who's the kid?' he asked Dubinsky.

'That's Jeff. He's Annie's boy.'

'Oh,' Nessheim said, and his voice was flat. He didn't know why he felt disappointed. He barely knew the woman. 'I didn't realise she was married.'

'She's not any more. It's a sad story. Her husband was a flier who crashed during a training flight. That's when Annie came to Washington to live with her aunt.'

'Is Ryerson her married name then?'

'No. Her husband's name was Martin. Born *Martini* — I don't think her parents were that happy about it. That may be why she went back to her old name.'

'Who looks after her boy when Annie's at work? Mrs Cummings?'

Dubinsky snorted. 'Hardly. Mrs O'Neill does — that's her over there.' In the corner of the room a middle-aged woman in a housekeeper's uniform — neat blouse and a heavy black skirt — stood waiting patiently while Annie talked with her little boy.

'Right,' said Nessheim, and when Dubinsky turned to talk to Plympton, he edged towards the door, in search of a bathroom, but also just wanting to get away for a minute. Out in the hall the butler directed him to a small door under the staircase. It was occupied, so he looked around. He didn't want to go back into the drawing room just yet. An apron-clad maid was standing in the back corridor that ran behind the drawing room, holding glasses of champagne carefully on a tray she balanced with one hand — he could see the bubbles from twenty paces. She was looking at him.

'Bathroom?' he mouthed over the volume of noise from the party.

She smiled, and gestured with her head further along the corridor. As he came past her she said, 'Second door on the right.'

When he emerged a few minutes later he

heard the clink of a spoon against a glass, and suddenly the noise in the drawing room died down. He started to head back but stopped when he saw a woman near the doorway, blocking his path. She was standing behind a wheelchair, which held a man in a suit.

A voice came clearly through from the drawing room. 'Sorry to interrupt when everyone's having such a good time, but I have an announcement, one which Sally has kindly given me permission to make this evening here in her house.'

He recognised the voice. It belonged to Frank Plympton. Why was he giving a speech? Nessheim had supposed that, like Dubinsky, Plympton was here because of his association with Frankfurter, but he must know Mrs Cummings very well to be speaking like this.

'A poet said that April is the cruellest month, so with that thought in mind I figured March would have to do,' Plympton said. People tittered politely. 'And anyway, seasons shouldn't affect what I have to say tonight.' He paused for a second. 'Those of you who know me will understand that for all my weaknesses and faults, I have one undeniable strength — I'm in love with a helluva gal.'

There were a few appreciative noises. Plympton went on: 'And that's what makes me so proud to say tonight that not only am I in love with this wonderful girl, but she's unwise enough to claim she loves me too. If Cole Porter's right to say it's only natural to fall in love, he's also right to say, *Let's do it.*'

Nessheim wondered who was Plympton's lucky lady — surely not Mrs Cummings, who still beautiful or not, had a minimum of thirty years on the fellow — and then he heard Plympton say, 'Annie Ryerson has said yes to me, and we'll be married later this year. Stay tuned for the date of the big day. But in the meantime please join me in a toast to my beautiful bride-to-be — and a toast to our future happiness.'

Someone shouted, 'To your happiness,' and Nessheim heard the clink of glasses. Why had no one told him Annie was engaged? Don't be a jerk, he told himself, you barely know the girl. But he felt something promising had soured, like fresh milk that had inexplicably curdled.

He looked at the couple ahead of him, stationed back from the open door to the drawing room, where they could not be seen by Plympton's audience. He saw with a start that it was the same woman to whom he had been introduced not ten minutes before. Lucy Rutherford — that was it. He could see the shoulders of the wheelchair's occupant, and when the man tipped his head back as Lucy Rutherford whispered something in his ear, Nessheim recognised the profile — the strong sharp jaw, the wire-rimmed spectacles, the cigarette held in a dark ivory holder, the clenched teeth which suddenly flashed a galvanised grin. Nessheim's heart started beating faster.

And then he saw Franklin Roosevelt's hand reach up from the arm of the wheelchair, and grasp the wrist of Lucy Rutherford. He squeezed it with unmistakable affection. It was a gesture more intimate than sex.

The hand withdrew, Lucy Rutherford grasped the handles of the wheelchair, and the pair manoeuvred through the open door into the drawing room. Nessheim waited a discreet minute or two, then followed them in.

He felt as if he'd been punched twice in rapid succession. He wanted to go, but Dubinsky was beckoning him. Grabbing a glass of champagne from a waitress's tray, he went over and found him talking to a dimple-chinned young woman who worked at the Department of Agriculture. She asked Nessheim what he did, and when he told her she started talking about her uncle, who was some kind of big shot in the Justice Department. He tried to pay attention to what she was saying, but his mind was still reeling from what he'd just seen. He told himself it didn't necessarily mean anything — Lucy Rutherford might be FDR's cousin, for instance, or just a very old friend. But he didn't believe that for a second.

As Dubinsky started talking to the woman again, Frank Plympton came by, looking jubilant after his announcement. He slapped Nessheim lightly on the back. 'Having a good time?' he half-shouted, for the party was noisy now, fuelled by champagne and the news of the forthcoming nuptials.

'Sure I am,' said Nessheim. 'Congratulations.'

'Thanks. I'm a lucky guy.'

Nessheim wanted to agree, but sensed it

would come out churlishly.

Dubinsky had struck out with the Agriculture woman, who'd moved on to a senator's legislative assistant. He gave a resigned shrug. 'She didn't seem interested in my association with the land's most eminent jurist. Vandenberg's guy looks like he's more the ticket for that young lady.'

'None of this *obiter dicta* for her,' said Plympton with amusement. 'Power versus intellect — power wins hands down.'

'Have you set a date yet?' asked Nessheim.

'No. It probably won't be until fall.'

'That late?' asked Dubinsky.

'Yeah, well, summer is a busy time when you're working for Harry. I get to do all the travelling in the heat that he doesn't want to do.' He added softly, 'Anyway, the world should be a clearer place by autumn.'

Nessheim understood. If a guy was going to be in uniform in six months' time, he might want to give a girl the option of changing her mind. Especially if she'd already lost one husband.

'Where will it be?' asked Nessheim, trying to be polite.

'Right here, probably. Sally said she'd host the reception, and spring for a marquee. I guess this is as much home for Annie as anywhere else — Woodstock's got too many memories.'

So Annie was from Woodstock. Is that why she had flinched when he said he'd worked there?

He couldn't see her anywhere in the crowd, as half the world and their uncle came by to congratulate Plympton. Nessheim began to feel like a spare part, so he went to say goodbye to Sally Cummings. Halfway across the room he found his way blocked by an older woman in a Schiaparelli gown and long white gloves, who was taking a light for her cigarette from a friend. Inhaling, she blew smoke over her friend's shoulder, and said in a throaty smoke-filled voice, 'So Sally's got her way at last. Frank's quite a catch for the niece, don't you think? If I were twenty years younger I might even be jealous.'

The friend laughed, then moved aside to let Nessheim through. Reaching Sally at last, he found her busy talking with one of the ambassadors, but she reached out and gave his hand a quick shake. *Come again*, she mouthed.

Out in the hall he was waiting for the maid to bring his coat when Annie came out of the drawing room.

'Jimmy, you're going already? I haven't had a chance to talk to you.'

'I've had a swell time. Congratulations.'

'What are you doing on Sunday?'

He shrugged a shoulder. 'Not much. Even Mr Hoover gives us Sunday off.'

'Why don't you come over here?' He must have looked hesitant for she explained, 'Sally's going to her place in Virginia on Sunday — she keeps a horse at Five Forks. But I'm staying here, and I'm going to take Jeff for a walk in Rock Creek Park — with Frank and Doobs. It was beautiful during the snow. Then we can all come back and have lunch. Why don't you join us? I bet you're starving at the House of Youth.'

346

That was true. Breakfast was the only meal provided, and there was no cook, which meant he ate cold cereal every day. He hated to think of the rest of his usual diet: lousy lunchtime hoagies from a shop near Lafayette Square, dinner most often in a diner off M Street — meat loaf, pot roast, macaroni and cheese.

But still he hesitated. 'I'd love to, but — '

'No buts. See you here at ten. Wear boots — it's wet by the creek.'

★ ★ ★

It was dark outside when he left. As he reached the sidewalk at the end of the drive a car pulled up, its brakes squealing like a cut pig. The front door flew open and the driver got out. It was Mueller.

'What the hell are you doing here?' the agent demanded. He was red-faced and looked agitated.

'Visiting friends.'

'These are friends of yours?' demanded Mueller incredulously. He pointed at Belvedere. '*There?*'

'Fraid so,' Nessheim said mildly.

'Is the President inside? The bastard gave us the slip.' Another car had pulled up behind Mueller's, with two men inside, who kept the engine running. Nessheim recognised them from the White House Secret Service detail.

Nessheim knew he should tell Mueller the truth — it was Mueller's job, after all, to protect the man. But nothing untoward was going to happen to the President inside Mrs Cummings's house.

He said, 'I didn't see him myself. But then, we're not as close as we used to be.'

Mueller shook his head in disgust and turned towards the Secret Service men, who had got out of their car. 'Nessheim says he ain't inside.'

The two men returned to their car. When its headlights came on, the beams shone directly on Mueller and Nessheim, spookily magnifying their silhouettes against the laurel hedge. Nessheim said to Mueller, 'Gimme a lift, will ya?' The House of Youth was only half a mile away, but it was cold now, and his coat was San Francisco-bought and thin.

He could see Mueller shake his head in the harsh sodium light. 'Another time, Mr All-American. I need to find Rosenfeld.'

23

Spring came, the cherry trees blossomed all over the city, and suddenly the phoney war in Europe became real — on 9 April, Germany invaded Norway and Denmark. Nessheim told himself he wasn't surprised by the sudden onslaught, but deep down he was. He had been lulled as much by the easy life he had been living in Washington as by the deceptive peace 4,000 miles away.

He had returned to Belvedere as requested by Annie that weekend. He, Dubinsky, and Plympton had gone with Annie and her son Jeff on a long walk in Rock Creek Park, which was refreshingly uncrowded on the Sunday morning. Nessheim was made to feel welcome — Dubinsky and Plympton seemed to view his residence in the House of Youth as an admission card to their set. If no match intellectually with these high-powered Frankfurter acolytes, Nessheim was nonetheless an object of interest, for his work suggested both action and intrigue. Dubinsky especially seemed interested, even asking to see Nessheim's gun.

Plympton was more detached, but Nessheim couldn't help liking him. More relaxed than Dubinsky, and projecting the self-confidence of someone who has done well at an early age, he didn't talk a lot about himself. It took Dubinsky to fill in Plympton's background for Nessheim: he had graduated *summa cum laude* from Stanford, where he had also been the number one player on the varsity tennis team — he would have played doubles at Wimbledon one summer had he not twisted an ankle. Then on to Harvard Law School, where Plympton had made Law Review and caught the eye of Frankfurter. Through his recommendation (it was said the then-Professor had been consulted on almost a thousand important appointments in the Roosevelt administration), Plympton had stepped into a job as aide to Harry Hopkins, one of the architects of the New Deal and head of its most inspired creation, the WPA, which had given work to millions of unemployed Americans.

Yet while Dubinsky's gee-whiz adulatory account threatened to put Plympton on a pedestal anyone would want to knock down, the man himself had enough foibles to make resentment impossible: drinking so much rye and ginger ale in a bar on G Street that on the way home he puked out the back window of Nessheim's borrowed pool car; confessing that what scared him most about his upcoming wedding was the prospect of the groom's speech.

Soon Nessheim was a regular at Sally Cummings's evenings, and on weekend walks with Annie and the others — Jeff always ran out to greet him, ever since Nessheim had carried the little boy one day on his shoulders. The walks became a ritual he looked forward to, especially for the conversations it allowed with Annie. As

newcomers to Washington, they shared an
outsider status, and they talked to each other
more about their lives growing up in small towns
than their lives in the capital. Because she was a
good listener, Nessheim told Annie more about
himself than he ever had before. He realised he
trusted her, which seemed strange since she was
attached to another man.

Annie made no pretence of liking the city, or
of being impressed by her aunt's network of
powerful friends; what wearied her most about
the Friday soirées, she liked to say, was the effort
required to remember who was the junior and
who was the senior senator from Nebraska. She
did not seem especially close to her aunt, and
there was more than a hint of mistress and maid
to their relationship, since in addition to working
part-time for Frankfurter, Annie had formal
duties at Belvedere, functioning as an unofficial
secretary. Once Nessheim had heard Sally call
for Annie from upstairs. 'Annie, Annie *now*,' she
commanded. The tone was not the charming one
she deployed at her parties.

When he next saw Guttman he had to admit
that for all the time he spent at Belvedere, he had
learned nothing of consequence about Sally
Cummings, who despite a surface cordiality
didn't really give him the time of day. Their one
substantial encounter had been about Annie, and
was more admonitory than friendly. She'd
cornered him one evening.

'How nice to see you again, Jimmy. I'm glad
you've become a regular. You're very good with
little Jeff.'

'He's a nice boy.'

'Yes, and it will do him good to be part of a family. Hopefully Frank won't be travelling so much in future. Even Mr Hopkins agrees he does too much.'

Nessheim nodded, but she wasn't finished. 'It's been good of you to keep Annie company too.'

'A pleasure,' he said, but he could see she wasn't listening.

'Annie's very fond of you.'

'Likewise,' he said, stiffening.

'The thing is, I'd hate for you to grow too fond of her.' She gave a smile that could have melted ice. 'Since she's spoken for.'

'Of course,' he said, but he was blushing like a schoolgirl. Sally patted him once on the shoulder and moved away.

The next weekend Dubinsky had work to do at the court, and Plympton was away, so Nessheim went alone with Annie to walk with Jeff. When they got back to Belvedere the boy stayed in the kitchen to eat the sandwich left for him by the cook, and Annie suggested they go upstairs to her 'office', which turned out to be a small converted bedroom along the hallway. It was a cosy space with cerise-coloured curtains held back by scarlet ties, and a soft fuzzy carpet the colour of a light grey cat. There was an antique desk in one corner, with a Windsor chair next to it, positioned at an angle to give a view of the stables out back. A small sofa with plump cushions sat against the near wall, with book-lined shelves above it, full of American classics (Hawthorne, Longfellow) and French novels sumptuously bound, many of which looked as if they'd actually been read.

'What a beautiful room,' Nessheim said politely.

'Thank Aunt Sally for the effortless good taste,' she said. 'She tells me I'm learning but still have some way to go.'

Annie perched in the Windsor chair while they talked, and sitting on the sofa Nessheim soon lost all track of time, until he heard a car pull up behind the house.

'Golly,' he said, looking at his watch and standing up. He had been invited by Dubinsky to a party given by one of the court clerks, and had arranged to meet him first at the House of Youth.

He looked out the window. There was a turnaround for deliveries to the kitchen door at the back of the house, and a long midnight blue Hudson sat in the middle of it. As a chauffeur in uniform held open the car's back door, a woman got out.

'It's Mrs Rutherford,' he exclaimed.

A look of alarm spread across Annie's face.

'Could you wait a minute before you go?' she asked.

'I guess so,' he said.

He was surprised Lucy Rutherford was visiting when Sally was away. Odder still, Annie made no sign of going down to greet her. He sat down while Annie made a stab at continuing her story. He heard someone coming up the stairs, then the door to the adjacent room closed softly.

A minute later the noise of another car came

from the turnaround out back. He resisted the temptation to look, but he couldn't pretend he was listening to Annie any more; after a moment she gave up the pretence of conversation too. They sat there awkwardly, while someone moved around downstairs. Then some kind of machinery started up.

'What's that?' he whispered to Annie.

'The elevator,' she said, avoiding his eyes.

It stopped with a jarring noise on their floor, and Nessheim heard its door open. Then there was the unmistakable sound of a wheelchair moving into the corridor. There was a tap on a door, the squeak of its hinges, and a click of its shutting again.

Annie motioned for him to get up and they walked quietly out into the corridor and down the main staircase, virtually on tiptoe. He felt like a teenager sneaking out of his girlfriend's house.

When they reached the hall, out of earshot, the absurdity of the situation must have struck home, for the trace of a smile appeared at the corner of Annie's mouth.

Nessheim said, 'Is that who I think it is?'

She gave him a look, as if to say, *Don't ask*, which merely confirmed his suspicion.

'It's hard to believe,' he said wonderingly.

'What do you mean?' she asked, but she saw his unpersuaded eyes. 'I lost track of the time,' she said plaintively. 'You were meant to leave ages ago.'

'Does Sally know what's going on?' he asked.

'Of course. You think they'd use the house

without her permission?' She seemed about to smile again.

'How long has this been going on?'

'It started up again a few months ago.'

'Again?'

'Years ago, Lucy and the President were very close. According to Sally, it only stopped because Eleanor threatened to divorce him. His mother was going to cut him off if that happened, and his political career would have been destroyed.'

'So much for true love,' he said. 'Tell me, how does it work? Does someone from the White House phone and say, 'Is the room upstairs available this Thursday?''

'Don't be stupid. Lucy's one of Sally's oldest friends. And it's not as bad as it seems. I don't think he and Eleanor have been man and wife for a long time.'

Nessheim felt a long way from Bremen, Wisconsin. It seemed incredible to be standing in one of the capital's grandest houses, calmly discussing the extramarital shenanigans of the President of the United States as they took place upstairs.

'How many people know about this?' he asked.

'Not many — we make sure the staff are gone when they meet. But there's Sally, obviously. And of course the two principals in the case,' she added tartly.

'What about the chauffeurs?'

'I don't know how they can be sure of anything. His chauffeur helps him out of the car, but the President wheels himself in — he's got

355

the strongest arms. There's a ramp that gets him into the back door. Lucy's driver goes and parks on the street after he drops her off, then comes back and collects her. For all he knows, it could just be a social call on Sally.'

'Does Frank know?'

She hesitated, which gave him his answer. 'What about Dubinsky?' he added.

'He'd only know if Frank told him, and I swore Frank to secrecy. I hope I can trust you too. It would be disastrous if it got out.'

Disastrous for whom, Nessheim wondered? He didn't believe any newspaper would print scuttlebutt about the President. Even Walter Winchell, who was perfectly happy to fish in the dirtiest sewer, wouldn't dare suggest the President was an adulterer.

She saw the doubt in his face. 'Please,' she said.

'I'm an FBI agent, Annie. We're meant to protect the President, along with the Secret Service. That's what I'm supposed to be doing every day at the White House.' He pointed upstairs. 'Ensuring that he's safe.'

'No one's going to hurt him here, Jimmy. Because nobody knows he *is* here.'

She had a point, and he had to wonder in any case just whom he would tell. Mueller was out of the question. And what would Guttman do with this information? If he were to go up to the Fifth Floor with it, God only knew what Hoover would do with the news. Even Nessheim had heard about the Director's personal files, full of the secrets of the mightiest men in the land.

'You're putting me in a difficult position, Annie.'

'I'm not trying to.' She looked upset. 'It's my fault — if I'd kept track of the time none of this would have happened.'

He wondered why he didn't want to reassure her. Maybe because it was the first time he felt he'd mattered to her. He relented at last. 'I'll keep it to myself.'

She made a show of relief, exhaling theatrically with a great big *whew*. He laughed out loud at the gesture, and she leaned forward and put two fingers on his lips to keep him quiet. Without thinking, he kissed her fingers. Annie blushed, her cheeks turning as vivid as an apple polished for a teacher, and she pulled her hand away.

He was heartened, though, to see that her eyes stayed on his. Then she smiled, like a woman with a closetful of secrets who has just acquired another one.

24

When Nessheim entered Guttman's office the next afternoon, he found Fedora sitting in one of the two chairs that faced Guttman's desk. His hat was in his lap, but there was no mistaking the strawberry birthmark that stretched across his cheek.

'If it isn't the Camp Counsellor himself,' said Fedora.

'You gentlemen know each other from Vermont,' said Guttman. It wasn't a question.

'Among other places,' said Nessheim.

Guttman pointed at Fedora. 'Jack here's going up there again. We're having another look at Camp Schneider to make sure there isn't anything we missed.'

Fedora turned to Nessheim. 'You want me to try and find the tape recorder if I can?'

Nessheim ignored this. 'If you go into Woodstock, check someone out, will you? Her name's Annie Ryerson. Apparently she was married to an army flier who got killed in a plane crash out west. His name was Martin.'

'What do you want to know?' asked Fedora. 'You sweet on her or something?'

Nessheim flushed. He looked at Guttman. 'Since she's Mrs Cummings's niece, I'm just making sure.'

Guttman nodded. 'Have a sniff round, Jack,' he said.

When Fedora left, Guttman turned to Nessheim. 'So what have you got for me?'

'Not much,' he admitted. 'Sally Cummings rides in Virginia at the weekends. Her niece is alone then, so I sometimes take a walk with her and her little boy.'

'How touching,' said Guttman with a voice that could have pickled an onion.

'You told me to get as close as possible.'

'To Mrs Cummings, not the niece and her kid. You want to babysit, I'm sure I can find something for you.'

Nessheim thought about Roosevelt and his little visits — that would take the angry look off Guttman's face. But one day he might need an ace up his sleeve, so he held his peace and asked instead, 'What exactly am I supposed to find out about the lady?'

Guttman pushed away a yellow legal pad and sat, elbows akimbo, with both hands clasped on the desktop. 'I believe Sally Cummings is in the loop on *something*. She gets letters from one Lady Dove, an Englishwoman with Nazi sympathies — she may even be a German agent. Cummings herself used to sleep with the German Ambassador, and though he wasn't a Nazi I am starting to think the Nazis have someone planted here in Washington.'

Of course they have, thought Nessheim. The country was probably swarming with spies, and Washington was the obvious hub. 'Did this Nazi plant kill Bock?' Nessheim asked.

'Could be,' said Guttman. 'At first I thought it was Schultz's people — since it was Bock who recommended you. But when I talked to Schultz in Sing Sing it was clear to me that he had no idea Bock was dead.' Guttman continued, 'I don't believe Bock's death had anything to do with the *Bund*, though I do believe Schultz knows more than he's letting on. I think Bock did too, and it got him killed.'

'You think they know what this planted agent is up to?'

'Maybe. I don't know for certain,' said Guttman tersely. 'Now you can see why I keep going on about Sally Cummings. We haven't got any other leads. Bock's dead, and Schultz won't talk.'

'Wait a minute,' said Nessheim. 'You told me Bock was homosexual, right?'

'Yeah. That's how I got to him in the first place. He was arrested in the brothel a few years before — with the same kid who got murdered with him as a matter of fact. Why do you ask?'

Nessheim remembered arriving at Camp Schneider, and Beringer's intimate inspection when Nessheim had stood in front of the urinal. And how, too, when Beringer had gone to New York City for a few days, Mrs Schultz had sneered, telling Mrs Grumholz that Beringer had gone to see his new *männlich Freund*. His male friend.

He looked at Guttman. 'Because you've been talking to the wrong German.'

★ ★ ★

Nessheim's train came into Penn Station half an hour late due to snow on the tracks in southern

New Jersey, so he had only twenty minutes to switch terminals. He caught a cab on 34th Street, arriving at Grand Central just in time to buy a ticket.

In Ossining, he walked from the station and was met by the Warden at the front gates. 'I've arranged for you to use a room in my office quarters,' he said. 'That will give you privacy and none of the other inmates will know about it.'

'Is he having trouble with them?'

'No. There are plenty of *Bund* sympathisers here, and they stick together. They seem very well-organised.' The Warden looked at his watch. 'You'll have to excuse me — the priest has come down sick, so I have to find a backup. We've got an execution tonight.'

A guard escorted him across the yard. It looked like a deserted playground until Nessheim noticed the sharpshooters in the towers at both ends. The guard pointed out the Death House across the yard, a low windowless brick building. Through its open doorway Nessheim caught a glimpse of the chair itself, an oversized wooden construct, with straps hanging from each arm.

'Who's buying it tonight?'

The guard shrugged. 'Some schmo who strangled his wife.' He pointed towards the electric chair. 'He's next door, in what we call the Dance Hall. They move you there when your time's been fixed. That way they haven't got far to take you to turn on the juice.'

Nessheim was surprised. He remembered the movie he'd seen the year before — the long tense walk Jimmy Cagney had taken to the chamber, then his last-minute panic as he realised his time had come. Melvin H. Purvis was supposed to have been an adviser when they filmed it.

They entered one of the prison's original buildings, a soot-covered brick edifice the size of a warehouse, with iron bars in every window. Inside they walked down a corridor until the guard stopped and opened a door. 'All yours,' he said. 'Give a shout if you need me — I'll be waiting out here.'

The prisoner was already in the room, sitting behind a table, wearing a uniform of roughly cut grey fatigues. Nessheim almost didn't recognise him. Gone was the insouciant air, the groomed hair (now cut to prison regulation), the sartorial touch of a boater hat. In prison uniform, Beringer seemed smaller, older, and worn out. Even his moustache was frayed.

He saw Nessheim and did a double-take. Then he shook his head. Nessheim grinned. 'My name's Lazarus,' he said, sitting down across the table from Beringer.

The German remained silent.

'See something green, pal?' said Nessheim lightly.

Beringer shook his head and seemed to emerge from a dream. 'You know full well why I am surprised, young Rossbach.'

'I know and sorry to disappoint you. How did you actually get onto me anyway?'

Beringer looked a little more alive now, and Nessheim was confident that at the very least they'd have a conversation.

'We were of course slightly suspicious of you

to begin with,' Beringer said. 'You had been working for Jews, none of us had ever met you, the reference from Herr Bock was carefully couched — he knew of your family, or perhaps it was his family which did, but he didn't vouch for you personally. Yet you were good value, you did the work, and you didn't seem curious at all.' Beringer looked at Nessheim with amusement. 'Frankly, I think the view was that you were rather stupid. Certainly that was mine.'

'What changed things?'

'You were seen outside the post office, tearing up a letter. We retrieved the pieces and discovered it was from your mother. You had told us your mother was dead.'

Nessheim could see Beringer was enjoying this. The German said, 'We made inquiries after that. It helped that Wisconsin is full of *Bund* followers — you will know that yourself. We were astonished that someone with your background could betray us. At any rate, it did not take long to discover that young Jimmy Rossbach was born with a different name — Nessheim, *ja?*'

Nessheim tried to shrug but failed. 'Yes, but how did you know I was a federal agent?'

'The local *Bund* leader told us. Not that he held much affection for you.'

Oh, my God, thought Nessheim, Alex Burgmeister, the farmer's middleman and husband of his old girlfriend Trudy. How could he have forgotten that she'd known? Because I trusted her to keep my secret, he reflected.

Nessheim composed himself. 'Anyway, I'm still here. So are you, though unlike me, you'll be

363

staying put for a while.'

'You have come all this way to tell me that?'

Nessheim stared into the German's eyes. 'You know about Herr Bock?'

Beringer nodded, but his lips pursed and he rubbed a tense finger against them, as if to keep himself from responding.

'You may not know the whole story,' Nessheim went on. He could see Beringer was interested, since his eyes lifted momentarily. 'He didn't kill himself.'

He could tell Beringer was waiting for more. 'Bock was dead before he entered that room.'

'He was murdered then?'

'Yes. We thought at first it was by members of the *Bund*.'

Beringer shook his head. 'No. It may have crossed Schultz's mind, but we didn't kill him; I give you my word.'

Nessheim continued to stare at Beringer, until finally he said, 'I'm really here to make a deal with you.'

Beringer looked thoughtful. But then he shook his head again. 'I can't see how helping you will help me.'

'Because your goose is cooked if you don't. If America stays out of the war, you'll be deported back to Germany as soon as your sentence is served — I can guarantee that. Before you arrive there, German officials will receive a letter explaining how close you were to Emil Bock. The Nazis think he was working for us, you see. That's why we're confident it was they who killed Bock.'

'Salacious gossip. Calumny.' Beringer had enough spirit in him to show off his English vocabulary.

'What? That we think the Nazis killed Bock — I don't think so. Or do you mean what we plan to tell the Nazis about you? You're right — it's salacious stuff. A homosexual and a traitor; the first is indisputable, and the second will seem a logical conclusion to them. You know better than most how they operate.'

Nessheim could see Beringer was struggling. The German asked, 'And if America is in the war, do you still propose to deport me?'

'Of course not. You'll be interned. I'd say it could be a long war, too, don't you think? Easily five or six years, maybe much longer. You'll be behind bars for more than a decade. At your time of life, that can't be a welcome prospect.'

Beringer sat silently, turning his head and looking out the barred window. It was too high up for it to afford a view of anything but the sky. He sighed and put a fist under his chin. Nessheim reached into a jacket pocket and took out a pack of Lucky Strikes, then pushed the cigarettes and a box of wooden matches across the table.

Beringer looked down at the smokes and smiled. 'Is that the extent of your bribe?'

'I have to start somewhere.'

Beringer filched a cigarette out of the pack, lit it, and took a deep drag. Exhaling, he said, 'What's really on offer then?' He was all business now.

'You serve a few months more, while we

365

collect new 'evidence' that makes it clear your role in the Armory plot was minimal. We arrange an appeal, and a friendly New York City judge cuts your sentence to time served.' Nessheim gave a complicit laugh. 'You still get deported, but not to Germany. Canada or Mexico — the choice would be yours.'

'And in return?'

'You tell me what you know.'

'What, about the *Bund*? They're no threat to anyone, whatever you think. Schultz might have been, but he was never on terms with Kuhn. Not that I'm telling you anything you don't already know.'

He was actually, but Nessheim wasn't going to admit it. 'That's true,' he said, gauging how best to proceed. 'It's not local plotting we're concerned about though.'

Beringer nodded but said nothing. Nessheim sensed Beringer was hooked on the prospect of freedom in four months' time — and there were plenty of Nazis in Mexico.

Beringer said slowly, 'My knowledge is not very great.'

'I'll be the judge of that,' said Nessheim. 'We are concerned about a conspiracy — though exactly what it's about we don't know. But we're pretty sure that someone from the *Bund* was once involved — Werner, Max Schultz's brother-in-law.'

'No one's seen him for several years.'

'I know. We believe he was killed in Austria.'

'Killed? By whom?'

'The same people who killed Bock. People

366

either part of or aware of this conspiracy.'

Beringer looked shocked by this idea, then angry. 'I was fond of Bock,' he said flatly. 'There was no reason to kill him. He was loyal to the Reich, I'm sure.'

Nessheim was not about to disabuse him. He waited. Beringer said, 'How do I know you will live up to your side of the bargain?'

'You don't. But we will.'

Beringer dropped his cigarette on the floor and stubbed it out with his shoe. He seemed to have made up his mind. 'As I said, I only know a little.'

As he began to speak, Beringer looked over Nessheim's shoulder, as if better to remember. 'It was several years ago in Michigan. I was living in Detroit then, in the same neighbourhood as Schultz. We were both very active in the *Bund*. One night Werner showed up at Schultz's house, slightly tipsy. He was looking for Freda, his sister and Schultz's wife — Werner used to cadge money from her. Small sums; Schultz wouldn't allow her to give him more.

'This time he wanted a lot of money: he said he was going back to Europe for a visit. Perhaps it was the prospect of his brother-in-law's departure, but to my surprise Schultz was happy to lend it to him. It was 200 dollars, I believe. Schultz never thought much of Werner, but that night he invited him to join us in the kitchen where we were drinking. Werner had already had a snoutful, but he drank some more. He hadn't said why he was going back to Europe; I rather assumed he was going to Berlin for the

Olympics. Instead he and Schultz started talking about old times. It was then Werner mentioned Jahnke.'

'Jahnke?' asked Nessheim.

'That's right,' said Beringer, too involved in his story to explain. 'Werner was saying how canny the old boy had been, how Jahnke had brought a secret weapon to America. 'Secret weapons' — everybody always talks about secret weapons. It's all this Mars nonsense with spaceships. It's about as real as the *Katzenjammer Kids*.'

Nessheim nodded as Beringer continued, 'Anyway, Schultz asked Werner how a 'secret weapon' was going to help the *Bund*'s cause when Jahnke was back in Germany, thousands of miles away.

'Werner was unfazed. I remember him saying very clearly, 'Don't be so sure. The secret weapon I am talking about is not a device. It's a man, though he was just a boy when Jahnke brought him over.' Schultz smirked at this, and Werner said crossly, 'He's even got a code name.''

'Did Werner say what the code name was?'

'He was called *Dreiländer*.'

25

Back from Sing Sing, Nessheim was heading for Guttman's office when he ran into Fedora.

'Anything at the camp?' Nessheim said.

Fedora looked at him mockingly. 'The tape recorder was gone. The locals must have cleared out the loft. Somebody's got a government-issue machine they won't know what to do with.'

Nessheim started to move around him but Fedora put out a restraining hand. 'I looked into the broad you asked me about.'

'And?'

'Nothing much.' When Nessheim took another step he said more sharply, 'Except what she told you is so much bull.'

'What do you mean?'

'Just that this famous dead pilot hero hasn't ever been her husband.'

He waited, satisfied that he had Nessheim's full attention. 'That's not all. Mr Martin — who was born 'Martini' by the way — isn't even dead. He may have knocked up your girlfriend, but he didn't marry her.' He pulled an index card out of his inner jacket pocket and looked at his scribbled notes. 'The Wop's married all right, but his wife's name is Barbara Castor, born 1916 in Tacoma Washington. That's where they're living now, according to latest reports. With two children he's happy to call his own.'

He put the card back in his pocket and looked

at Nessheim with feigned innocence. 'What's the matter, pal? Have you been hoping to put your wick in her wax?' He gave Nessheim a playful punch on the shoulder. 'Don't worry — you'll get there. You just need to be patient. Sounds like there could be a long line of guys ahead of you.'

Nessheim grabbed the lapels of Fedora's chocolate pinstripes and pushed him until he held him against the wall.

'Hey, take it easy, sailor.' Fedora wasn't resisting, and he didn't seem alarmed.

'*What the hell's going on?*' It was Guttman, barking from his doorway down the hall. 'Nessheim, let him go. And both of you come into my office right now.'

Reluctantly, Nessheim released his hold on Fedora's pinstripes, and the man brushed both lapels, as if he were flicking off dust. They trooped down the corridor and followed Guttman into his office, then stood while Guttman faced them from behind his desk.

'Jesus wept, I can't have agents fighting in the hallway. What's all this about?'

Nessheim gestured for Fedora to do the talking, and he did, reporting in clipped tones what he'd discovered in Woodstock while Guttman listened in silence.

When Fedora had finished Guttman scratched his bald head, pondering. 'So Martin's the kid's daddy?'

Fedora nodded. 'That's right. But he wouldn't marry her. He went and enlisted — bingo, he's miles away in boot camp while she's figuring what to do. She was only seventeen. Her parents are the strict Yankee type. The old man runs a store — the kind where your credit gets cut off if you're three hours late paying the grocery bill. God knows what they were going to do, except make the kid sweat for her sins. Then she disappears — nobody could tell me what happened, and nobody knew where she'd gone. They said the parents never mention her.'

The aunt, thought Nessheim. Sally Cummings had stepped in, scooped her up, and brought her down to D.C. along with a cover story of the tragic death of the young father, leaving a poor widowed mother. And it had worked. Until now. *I should have left it alone*, Nessheim thought.

The phone on the desk rang, like a shrill announcement. Guttman picked it up and immediately looked tense. 'Yes, Mr Hoover,' he said. Fedora stood up to leave, and looking at Nessheim, mouthed three words. *Watch your back.*

'Yes, sir. Tomorrow at four,' Guttman said and hung up.

Nessheim noticed he was sweating. 'So what was that about out there?' Guttman demanded, pointing to the hallway.

'He got my goat. I'm sorry.'

'You ought to be.' He shook a disapproving head. 'Now tell me about New York.'

'I saw Beringer. He talked.' He waited for Guttman to react; when he didn't, he said, 'He told me there was an agent planted over here. Code name *Dreiländer*. He came here as a boy. His last contact was this guy Werner, but before

371

that Jahnke was his link with the Nazis — and Jahnke brought him over.'

'Who's Jahnke?'

'I was hoping you'd tell me.'

'I'll have Records check him out. There might be something there.'

Nessheim had expected Guttman to be more excited by his news. He said impatiently, 'Don't you see? If we can find out where Jahnke was, that could lead us to *Dreiländer*. Isn't that what we're looking for?'

Guttman shrugged. 'Sure,' he said, but it seemed a token acknowledgement. 'This Annie woman, how well do you know her?'

'Why are you asking about her?'

'She could be important. I find information more credible when we've found it ourselves. I'll check the files for this Jahnke fellow, but I think the priority should be closer to home. Here in Washington.'

'I don't understand.' Why had Guttman sent him to New York if he was going to dismiss his findings out of hand?

'The only lead we have that's current is this woman Sally Cummings. And we need to see the letters to her from Lady Dove. The problem is the Director would run a mile before he'd let me make an intercept. But I bet her niece can get at them.'

'But if we can find out where Jahnke took — '

'Look, you did well to get the name, and I said I'll have it checked out. But right now the priority has to be getting a look at these letters.'

'Why would Annie Ryerson agree to rifle

through her aunt's correspondence? I can't ask her to do that.'

'Not on the basis of friendship — I understand that. But you've got better ammo than affection.'

'What do you mean?' asked Nessheim.

'You've said she's marrying this young buck from the New Deal with future senator written all over him. Does this husband-to-be know that Annie's dead husband is A) not dead and B) never was her husband? I bet he doesn't know a thing. A few choice words telling her beau what really happened to Mr Martini and ten years from now Miss Ryerson will be a spinster, with what people politely call an *interesting* face, still working for two grand a year for Justice Frankfurter.'

'That's awful rough.'

Guttman said, 'Jack was right — you *are* sweet on her.'

'I barely know her. I just don't think it's my job to engage in blackmail.'

'You don't get to pick your spots, kid.'

'Don't call me kid,' said Nessheim, starting to get angry.

'You don't get to pick your spots,' Guttman repeated.

'I won't do it.'

'You won't do it?' Guttman asked with feigned astonishment. 'Anything else you feel disinclined to do? Is your White House office not big enough, Nessheim? Feeling sore because your meals aren't served on a tray?'

'It's dirty.'

'Dirty? Yeah, of course it is; so are lots of things we get paid to do. What can I tell you? You want to be a white knight on a charger, join the Red Cross. But don't ever tell me our motives aren't clean. The methods may sometimes stink, but never the motives.'

'Is that what you tell yourself when you look in the mirror?'

'Actually, I try not to. You should try shaving in the dark, Nessheim; you don't see the blood that way. I'm trying to stop something happening that's a hell of a lot more important than your delicate sensibilities, kid.' Guttman looked disgusted.

'I won't do it,' said Nessheim, and he stood up. He didn't know what would happen now, and he wasn't sure he cared.

26

When Guttman did up his tie the following morning, he noticed the fold of skin at the base of his throat just above his collar button, the same small valley he had noted thirty years before in his father. It was another sign of his own ageing, and he wondered dimly what would follow next. Hair in his ears? Hair on his back (well, more hair actually). Stiffness in his joints — forget it, he already had that. He had spent so much time over the last few years tending his invalid wife that he hadn't paid attention to the creeping signs of his own degeneration. So why was he bothering now?

Because it's just not going my way, he decided, and thought of how Nessheim had stalked out of his office. He had been wrong to bring the kid back, he thought, though the reasons for his doubts had changed. He no longer believed Nessheim had an ounce of *Bund*-ish sentiment in him; instead there was a streak of piety that had no place in the emotional armoury of an agent of the Bureau. Nessheim wanted his work to be a grand vocation, a calling more than a job. Guttman liked to think he was as moral as anyone — his job was going after bad guys — but he would never have worn a white hat. It was not a crusade.

Since he had a meeting with Hoover that afternoon, Guttman put on his suit jacket carefully, making sure the flaps to his side pockets were out. Now all he had to do was go to his wife, waiting patiently in her wheelchair next door, take her into the bathroom for the extended morning ablutions, get her dressed (a good half-hour some days), make her breakfast (she said she was getting tired of Quaker Oats but he hadn't found a palatable alternative yet), settle her in the living room with the newspaper and the book of her beloved crosswords, then wait for the day help to arrive. Then he could drive to his office, where other people would say his working day began.

★ ★ ★

At eight-thirty, Marie brought him the early post — from within the building, from field offices (Detroit, Albuquerque), and a few bits from what he no longer thought of as the real world. One from this last bunch caught his attention, a card in an envelope marked *Private: Harry, could you give me a call? I've got something. Bill*

He rang Stephenson at 'The Club' but was told the Canadian was out. He would have called him again, later that morning, but an agent had been shot and wounded trying to stop a bank robbery in Kansas, and though this was not part of Guttman's normal responsibilities, the relevant assistant director was away and he had to stand in. There was national press interest (though Louis B. Nichols would deal with that), but he had to talk with the SAC in the Wichita office, who sounded green and scared on the phone. First Nessheim, then this guy, thought Guttman, who never liked holding someone's hand. No one had ever held his.

Lunch was Pastrami on rye which Marie brought in without his asking — 'You'd have forgotten,' she said when he seemed surprised at the paper plate, with its dollop of mustard and dill pickle. Then another phone call, from Milwaukee, where the SAC said a local congressman who'd raised questions about the prosecution of a brewing magnate for bribing safety inspectors was threatening to visit the Bureau field office when he was back in Wisconsin for summer recess. Hold him off, Guttman advised, hoping the congressman would forget about it by then.

And through all this he was trying to prepare mentally for his four o'clock meeting with the Director.

When the time came and he took the elevator up to the Fifth Floor, he was apprehensive. Then Tolson came up behind him in the hall, striding hard.

'Hi, Clyde,' he said.

Tolson, usually affable, just nodded curtly. That was ominous.

When he entered the Director's office, Hoover was at his desk. Guttman noticed that the drapes on the windows had been drawn. They looked new — and heavier. Steel-reinforced no doubt.

Hoover stood up. He was wearing a silk tie with polka dots. Probably a freebie, thought Guttman. He had learned over time that the Director had no compunction about accepting presents. Restaurant meals, hotel rooms (separate suites for him and Tolson), free bets at the track, drinks and meals on the house at the Stork Club during visits to New York, and seemingly half his wardrobe.

'Have a seat at the table, Mr Guttman,' Hoover said.

Guttman knew now he was in hot water. Hoover usually called agents by their surnames, in a kind of grown-up adaptation of prep-school practice. The politer prefix of 'Mr' spelled trouble.

Helen Gandy appeared in the doorway. Her hair, Guttman happened to know, was washed and dried every seven days by an Italian woman in Maryland, and each day she wore an identical navy blue dress and low pumps. She was entirely loyal and entirely without initiative; that Hoover hadn't had to call for her now meant her appearance had been prearranged. Another bad sign.

'Show her in, please, Miss Gandy,' Hoover instructed gravely.

The woman who entered the room a moment later had dark shoulder-length hair, and a face that hovered between expectation and experience. She was holding a Manila envelope and on her wrist was a clunky, oversized watch. A man's watch. Hoover adopted the gentle voice he put on with younger women. 'Thank you for coming in, Dinah. This is Mr Guttman. Do you recognise him?'

Her eyes surveilled Guttman impassively then shifted back to Hoover. 'Yes, sir. This is the man

I watched on two occasions in Bethesda and once in a diner near Franklin Park.'

'And he wasn't alone?'

'No, sir. He was with a man later identified as Emil Bock of the German Embassy.'

'Can I have that, please?' asked Hoover, and she handed over the envelope. 'That will be all, Dinah.'

As she left the room, Guttman wondered what the hell was going on. It was no secret Bock had been his source — did they expect him to have maintained contact by letter?

Hoover placed the Manila envelope on the table. 'Mr Guttman, your performance in recent months has been troubling to me. You've risen high in the ranks of this organisation and have important responsibilities, so I was willing to overlook some of your recent deficiencies — in particular, your subverting of our campaign to prosecute traitors who went to fight for a foreign power in Spain. I can't help but think that at least some of the misinformed press coverage of our arrests of these men should be laid at your door.'

'I never talk to journalists, Director,' said Guttman.

'So you say. In any case, I've not asked you here to discuss that. Now, look at this, please.'

Guttman took the envelope and undid the thin string wrapped around its protruding clasp. Inside were two glossy photographs. Both showed Guttman on a park bench, sitting in bright sun next to Emil Bock. In the first he was handing a slim envelope to Bock; in the second

Bock was taking out its contents, a large wad of dollar bills. Twenty-dollar bills actually, thought Guttman.

He looked up to find Tolson and Hoover staring at him in silence. But he knew it would be fatal to speak first.

Hoover said, 'Can you explain what's going on in the photograph?'

Just what it looks like, he wanted to reply. He said, 'I am giving Emil Bock 1,000 dollars, Mr Hoover.'

'Why?'

'To hand over to Max Schultz of the German-American *Bund*.'

'Did he?'

'I hope so — that was the point of it. I wanted him to win the confidence of Schultz.' He stopped there; it was crucial to keep Nessheim out of this. He could defend giving Bock money, but he couldn't make a case for Nessheim's undercover role — not when it had been explicitly forbidden by Hoover.

Tolson spoke up in his alto tones. 'Was this the only time you gave money to Bock?'

Guttman shook his head. 'I gave him 500 dollars on two other occasions.'

'Were they receipted?'

'By Bock? No.' Guttman wished he could loosen his tie.

'And you don't even know for sure that he gave the money to Schultz.'

'Schultz is in Sing Sing, doing twenty-five to thirty-five, so I consider it money well spent.'

Tolson ignored this. 'What about internally?

Were the payments receipted by you?'

'They were,' he said carefully, 'but not in the normal ledger. On each occasion I dictated a note for the working case file stating what I'd done.'

'Why there?' Tolson could be relentless — unlike Hoover, whose patience often ran out before all the questions got asked.

'Because no one else would see the working file until the case was closed. I didn't want it showing in Accounts where it might raise questions.'

'Exactly,' said Tolson, as if Guttman had walked into a trap.

Hoover was pursing his lips disapprovingly. When he spoke, his jaw jutted aggressively. 'Have you got anything else to say for yourself?'

Guttman still didn't know what was going on. Did they think he was skimming money? He hesitated, then finally asked, 'Why has this come up now? Those pictures were taken almost a year ago.'

'Dinah misplaced the film. She only found it last week.'

'How convenient.' He regretted this as soon as he'd said it.

Hoover looked angry. 'It's of no relevance when this came to our attention. What matters is that there has been a serious breach of the FBI code. It's true that from time to time we feel obliged to pay informants. It's not a practice I am happy with, though where circumstances warrant we have no choice. But it must only be done with absolute integrity, and following

381

Bureau procedures. Any deviation will not be tolerated — from you, or from anyone else.'

Hoover was in highest dudgeon now; Guttman had seen it often enough. 'I consider this a very serious violation of Bureau standards. There will be an internal inquiry that Mr Tolson will chair; you will have the opportunity to present your side of things in full. But until then, you are suspended from duty, effective immediately.'

Stunned, Guttman managed to protest: 'Mr Hoover, I'd ask you to wait for the inquiry's verdict before taking away my responsibilities. I have an investigation underway of the greatest importance; I'm convinced there's a Nazi plot to destabilise the highest elected office of this country.'

Tolson actually laughed. But Hoover was still furious. 'So the first time we hear about it is when we're about to suspend you. As you would say, *how convenient*.'

'What about my reports? What happens to them?' He was thinking about Nessheim; it was critical now that Nessheim stay with the Bureau. Once suspended, Guttman wouldn't be able to do anything.

Tolson was prepared for this. 'The White House crew will keep reporting to Mueller, and for the time being he'll report to me. Same for the field offices — I'll alert them as soon as we're done here. As for your own staff in the building, they'll report to Louis B. Nichols.' Realising Nessheim would straddle this divide, Guttman said nothing.

Tolson looked at Hoover. The Director leaned forward and clasped his hands together on the desk. 'Mr Guttman, someone will collect your personal effects from your office. The guards are next door; they'll escort you from the building.'

Part Four
1940

27

15 May 1940
West Pomerania, near the Polish border

It was a bleak view from the house. A quarter of a mile of rough headland lay between it and the coast, where Schellenberg could see the steely grey of the Baltic. He sensed a storm brewing.

He shivered and moved closer to the fire. It might be May, but this late in the afternoon the air had turned sharp, almost winter-like. The turf bricks in the hearth glowed like coal, but without the same emitted heat. He had been shown into this vast drawing room by an ancient butler in a frock coat, who had then closed the large oak door and disappeared, leaving Schellenberg to stare at the antique furniture and the oil paintings hanging in heavy gilded frames and wonder why Heydrich had asked him to meet here.

Despite its size, the house could not disguise its dilapidated state — gutters on the roof line were hanging by a thread, and the windows' paint was flaked from the harsh salt air. An aura of decay hung over the grounds as well: the iron railings running either side of the tall gates at the beginning of the drive had been stripped, ready to be molten for military use, and the pale cows Schellenberg had spied in the fields as his car approached were transparently milk-less. Still, even the fading of its grandeur could not disguise the fact that this estate must have once belonged to an immensely wealthy family.

The door opened and the old butler came in, bearing a tray, which he put down on a mahogany side table. It was midway between teatime and drinks, a no-man's-land for refreshments. Schellenberg noted that the tray held two glasses, a half-full bottle of whisky, and a soda siphon. As the butler left the room another man entered, and the servant lowered his head deferentially.

'Good afternoon,' said the man, coming across and extending his hand. He was much older than Schellenberg, and was dressed in a well-worn tweed suit and a wool tie the colour of sage. He was of average height, with silver hair slicked straight back and a trim Van Dyke beard. 'Welcome to Kernshagen. It is a pleasure to meet you.'

Shaking hands perfunctorily, Schellenberg said sharply, 'Where is the *Obergruppenführer?*' In a room of such refinement this sounded jarringly rude, but his driver had taken four hours to reach the coast. They were only 100 miles from Berlin, on the edge of the Pomerania Bay, but the roads had been full of troops, reinforcements moving towards Belgium and France. For all the mechanised efficiency of the *Blitzkrieg* in the west, most of the soldiers he'd seen had sat in horse-drawn carts.

The man said, 'The *Obergruppenführer* is two hours east of us, I'm afraid. In Poland — or should I call it eastern East Prussia now?' His expression was amused, though his eyes seemed to take everything in. He added quietly, 'But he's given me orders to pass on to you.'

'I see,' said Schellenberg, but his back was up. His summons had been couched in urgent terms; Schellenberg had not come this far to be fobbed off with a surrogate; he could have stayed in Berlin for that.

'Who are you?' he demanded of the man, who looked too old to be in the army.

'Forgive me,' he replied, bowing his head. 'My name is Jahnke.'

Schellenberg stared at him open-eyed.

Jahnke said cordially, 'Let us have a drink, Herr Schellenberg. There is some whisky on the tray, which you won't often see these days outside Berlin. It's a taste I developed during my years in America, though the whisky is Scotch — Johnnie Walker. I took the precaution of importing three cases last year. It's a luxury that will not, I fear, be available again any time soon.'

Schellenberg felt embarrassed and impatient all at once. 'Thank you, but I should be getting back. If you would be so kind as to give me these orders . . . '

Jahnke gave a tolerant smile. 'Of course. But your driver is right now being fed by Bertha in the kitchens. It's not up to me how you deal with your men, but in my experience an empty stomach makes for a bumpy journey home.'

He said this with such charm that Schellenberg felt ashamed for his churlishness. 'A whisky would be most acceptable,' he said, realising how pompous this sounded. I've changed, he thought unhappily.

They sat down in captain's chairs by the fire. Jahnke half-filled Schellenberg's glass with Scotch, then added soda from the siphon. Schellenberg noticed that Jahnke's own drink was the size of a sherry doled out for a maiden aunt.

Schellenberg took a long pull on his drink, and emboldened said, 'Why is Herr Heydrich in Poland?'

'He's with the Führer.'

'I see,' was all Schellenberg could manage. How inappropriate his little sulk at Heydrich's absence now seemed. Still, he was puzzled, since surely the Führer's attention right now lay in the other direction. 'I am surprised he's not visiting the Low Countries.'

'One might think so,' Jahnke acknowledged with a nod, 'but then, the situation there seems almost a fait accompli. I believe the Führer is assuming France will fall within a few weeks.'

'There is still England to think about,' Schellenberg found himself protesting.

Jahnke looked unfazed. 'He seems to think that is only a matter of time as well. The British may surrender once they see the Continent is lost, along with half their army on the French coast. If they don't, then we'll invade. One hopes that can be avoided.'

Schellenberg did too. He was already involved in the plans for an invasion — not from a military planning point of view, but rather how to handle both British intelligence and their police once the island had been subdued.

Operation Sea Lion was an operation that Schellenberg wanted to remain hypothetical.

Then Jahnke said, 'It's not Poland that is occupying the Führer's attention, but east of there.'

Russia. Inevitable, of course, since everyone knew the alliance between Hitler and Stalin was never going to last. But surely now was not the time to wage war against yet another country, especially one so big.

'Nothing immediate,' said Jahnke reassuringly, reading Schellenberg's thoughts. 'But the Führer likes to look ahead.'

Was there a hint of scepticism in his voice?

Jahnke changed the subject. 'Heydrich said you were in England last summer. What did you make of them there?'

Schellenberg thought about his trip with Irene — it seemed an age ago. He'd had only one piece of business; otherwise the role of tourist had been perfectly authentic, though they'd gone under Dutch names and Dutch passports. 'I found them a curiously passive people. Polite, restrained, and not at all eager for war.'

'And yet?' asked Jahnke persistently, and Schellenberg realised the man would not be satisfied with clichés.

Schellenberg said, 'I believe there is a toughness beneath their veneer of civility. *Thank you very much; After you; Do excuse me, madam*,' he mimicked in his best English accent, and was glad to see that Jahnke looked amused. 'But the fact is, they won't be pushed around. They're desperate to forestall an invasion, but not if that would mean dishonour. Their new Prime Minister is very keen on honour. The playing fields of Eton and so on.'

Jahnke smiled. 'I think you'll find Mr Churchill went to Harrow, but it's much the same thing.'

Schellenberg did not mind the correction; he was slightly in awe of this veteran of the espionage world.

'Fortunately,' said Jahnke, 'we have some friends in England of our own.' Schellenberg was surprised; seeing this Jahnke added, 'The *Obergruppenführer* has kept me in touch with developments.'

Schellenberg nodded. It made sense that Jahnke knew whom he had met with in London. Schellenberg said now, 'It went without a hitch. But . . . ' and he hesitated.

'Yes?'

'I worried that our meeting could have been watched.'

'What made you think that?' Jahnke's manner was no longer quite so easy.

'I felt I might have been followed. There was someone with a camera — I saw him on Piccadilly, and then once across the street at my hotel.'

'Could they have detected you entering the country?'

'I don't think so. Our passports were unimpeachable.'

'There's an alternative explanation, of course. They might have spotted you because they were following the lady.'

'But her cover seems rock solid — her husband is famous for his pro-Soviet sentiments.'

'They might be following her on account of that,' Jahnke suggested. He chuckled. 'Though I'd like to see their faces when they found a suspected Communist meeting up with the head of German counter-espionage.'

Schellenberg did not share his amusement.

The door opened and the butler came in, then went to the fireplace where he started to poke the glowing turf. 'Thank you, Staatz,' said Jahnke gently, and the old man put the poker down and shuffled out of the room.

Jahnke turned to Schellenberg. 'Staatz is what the English call a 'retainer'. Serfdom was abolished in Pomerania in 1808 — Staatz's great-great-grandfather was one of those 'freed'. Frankly, it was a change in name alone. Staatz is the eighth generation of his family to serve the estate.' He sipped his whisky with an air of abstraction, then said quietly, 'Tell me, how is our friend at the Reichsrundfunkhaus?'

Schellenberg hesitated before replying. Only the week before he had been to the state broadcasting centre, out at its vast modern headquarters in a suburb of Berlin. It hadn't been his first trip, nor, he thought with a sigh, was it likely to be his last. For the man he'd visited — the foreign broadcaster William Joyce — was proving a nightmare.

Schellenberg said now, 'He's a bit of a handful, to tell you the truth. Fame has gone to his head.'

'Are you worried he won't do as he's told?'

'Not really. I don't see that he has any choice. He can hardly go back to England now. They'd hang him.'

Jahnke seemed satisfied with this. But then he said enquiringly, 'Something else is worrying you, Herr Schellenberg?'

Normally Schellenberg would have resented the intrusiveness, but he realised he wanted to unburden himself. Jahnke could not be more different from Heydrich — the apprehension Schellenberg always felt in the company of the *Obergruppenführer* was entirely absent now. Perhaps that was it; he felt that he could have an honest conversation with this worldly-wise man. It had been a long time since that had seemed possible.

'When I first interviewed Joyce, I wanted to be sure he had not been in recent contact with our English friend.'

'Naturally. And?'

'He said he hadn't, but I wasn't sure I believed him. If he had written to her, and the British are onto her, then the channel of communication to our *Dreiländer* friend could be compromised.'

Jahnke did not look worried. 'It's conceivable, I grant you, but very unlikely — and it would require unprecedented trans-Atlantic cooperation. But there's something else nagging at you, isn't there?'

Schellenberg saw no reason to dissemble. 'Werner,' he said bluntly.

'It will be four years ago this summer, won't it?'

So Jahnke knew. The memories that continued to haunt him came in a distasteful rush: the drive along the forestry track, the short hike to the clearing, the propping of the body against a tree and wrapping the hand around the butt of the gun.

He shook his head to clear the image, and found Jahnke's eyes on him. Sympathetic but dispassionate, they seemed to understand. 'It was necessary,' said Jahnke softly. 'He had been indiscreet.' When Schellenberg lifted a questioning eyebrow, he added, 'With Ambassador Luther — as you know.'

Schellenberg nodded. 'I hope Luther was the only one.'

'You think Werner talked to others?'

'What about the man at the embassy — Emil Bock?'

Jahnke said, 'Werner didn't know Bock. And in any case, Bock himself can't talk to anyone now — German or American.'

Schellenberg was still worried. 'Are you confident that ultimately Bock was one of ours?'

Jahnke rubbed his beard, musing. 'If I have learned one thing after forty-five years in this peculiar business, it's that there is no 'ultimately' for any secret agent. In this case, however, the beauty of it is that it didn't matter — whether the Americans thought Bock was theirs or ours is of no consequence. That's the whole point of diversions — to divert. That's all. And intentionally or not, Bock did his job magnificently. Remember that the American domestic intelligence people are not very experienced with this kind of penetration. Thanks to their famous Hoover, they are only conditioned to look for Reds under their beds.'

Schellenberg was cheered by this. 'I understand they even have a Jew running their counter-espionage,' he offered with a laugh.

He was slightly disappointed when Jahnke didn't laugh as well but looked sober instead, saying, 'Over the years I have found the Jews to be many things, but stupid is not one of them. When we have managed to rid the world of their race I imagine the average intelligence level will diminish markedly. Some Party members would probably think that's not a bad thing,' he added drily.

'So you think the *Dreiländer* is safe?'

Jahnke got up and fetched the bottle of whisky from its tray, tipping it until a quarter of an inch was added to his glass. He stood and sipped, staring out the long window towards the iron-coloured sea. 'The *Dreiländer* I knew was still a boy, though always at heart a loyal German. I thought I was teaching him, but I realise now just how much he taught himself. He could act a part effortlessly.'

He was still staring out to sea, talking to himself as much as to Schellenberg. 'I simply can't believe the Americans will find him. They may find strands — how he's contacted, who else is unknowingly involved. But they won't put it together; the Americans are a lucky people, but this would require exceptional intelligence as well as luck.'

He turned and looked down impassively at

Schellenberg. 'Besides, I have never believed in leaving things to chance. If the Americans somehow discover what we have in mind, they will find that it is just the beginning of a maze, not the end point. And as with any maze, there will be many possible paths to follow: just choosing one will take them long enough for our man to accomplish the task.'

Jahnke looked pointedly at his watch. 'Your driver will have been well fed by now,' he declared, and clapped his hands. The door opened and Staatz appeared.

'Fetch Herr Schellenberg's coat, please. His car is waiting outside.' Jahnke turned and faced Schellenberg, and the smile on his face was bitter-sweet. 'It has been a pleasure meeting you, Herr Schellenberg. I have heard much about you; now I know why. So: your orders.'

And he extracted a small buff envelope from his coat's inner pocket. It was sealed but not addressed. Jahnke said, 'Read it in the car. It won't take you very long.'

And before his driver even reached the gates of Kernshagen, Schellenberg slit open the envelope with his penknife, curious to see what Heydrich wanted him to do. As he looked at the thick cream-coloured sheet, he hoped that what had been conceived of so long ago (almost twenty years, in fact, when Schellenberg was still a schoolboy) was finally coming to fruition. He felt a surge of excitement, and a little fear, as he read:

Sag dem Dreiländer, dass er zuschlagen sollte!

It couldn't be clearer: *Tell the* Dreiländer *to strike now!*

But these weren't Heydrich's words. Schellenberg looked with awe at the signature at the bottom of the page, signed in ink the colour of deep carmine:

Adolph Hitler

28

Nessheim had spent the rest of the day wondering when he would be fired. He told himself he would reinstate the plans he had made after the Armory raid in New York. Back he'd go to Wisconsin, then out West to collect his car and personal possessions before . . . what? He wondered. He supposed with several years at the Bureau under his belt he could become a policeman in some small town, but contemplating a life spent issuing speeding tickets and sending drunken teenagers home was enough to lower his spirits. He realised that for all his disaffection from his run-in with the *Bund*, he had enjoyed coming back to work for the Bureau.

At the White House the next morning as he parked his car he saw Fedora leaving from the west gate. He stayed in his car until he saw the other agent reach Pennsylvania Avenue, since he didn't want a second bust-up which would give Guttman another reason to fire him. But Nessheim wondered what Fedora was doing there, especially when Nessheim entered the Executive Wing office and found Mueller in inexplicably high spirits, talking almost manically as the other agents arrived for work.

Nessheim spent the morning in the Mansion, reviewing the presidential schedule with Missy Le Hand and Miss Tully, glad to be away from Mueller. When he returned to his cubicle he found a message from the switchboard to call Guttman. He dialled the Bureau HQ and got Marie, Guttman's secretary.

'Mr Guttman wants to see you.'

'When?' he said warily.

'This evening.'

'At his office?' he asked, thinking he'd rather quit than get summoned to be fired.

'No, he wants to see you at home. Let me give you the address. It's in Virginia.'

Christ, he thought as he scribbled down the address Marie read over the phone. She added, 'Mr Guttman asked that you keep this meeting confidential.'

'Understood,' said Nessheim, but he didn't.

★ ★ ★

Guttman's house was on a street of ranch houses on the edge of Arlington. They were brick residences, single storey and recently built, and the neighbourhood seemed well-heeled — there were good cars in most of the driveways, and even at dusk Nessheim could see the lawns were tended, the trim on the houses neatly painted. Yet the development ended abruptly next to several empty lots; the developers must have run out of cash. He parked there, away from the houses — he had a sixth sense that something wasn't right.

Guttman answered the door, wearing corduroy trousers and an open-necked shirt. He looked tired, his face pale under its five o'clock shadow.

'Come on in,' he said, and Nessheim entered a little foyer, and followed Guttman into the sitting room. It consisted of three armchairs, tidily arranged, and a sofa the colour of chartreuse, with big stuffed cushions. There were a few prints on the wall, and a framed photograph of the Empire State Building.

Guttman moved over to a maple credenza by the window. 'Drink?' he asked, and before Nessheim could reply, he took out a bottle and poured two stiff shorts into stubby glasses. 'Water?' he asked again, and when Nessheim nodded he took the glasses into the kitchen next door.

Nessheim followed him; an overhead bulb with a yellow shade cast a liverish light on the dim linoleum floor. Nessheim was impressed to find a refrigerator humming in one corner, but the sink was a low ceramic basin, and the cupboards were warped. Through the kitchen was a small dining alcove, with a small plaster Jesus on a wooden cross in the corner that Nessheim couldn't help staring at.

'My wife's Catholic,' Guttman said.

'Sorry,' said Nessheim, dumbfounded.

'What, sorry that she's Catholic, or sorry that I caught you looking?' Guttman said with a tired laugh. 'You Catholic?' he asked.

'Lutheran.'

'My wife's a Polish gal,' Guttman said. 'My

401

own people were Poles, so we had that in common. Just not our religions.'

'Where is she now?' asked Nessheim.

'She's right through there.' He jerked his thumb at the wall. 'I hope she's asleep.'

They went back to the living room and sat down, Nessheim taking the couch.

'Good whisky,' he said, taking a sip.

'A present from the Director himself — Johnnie Walker Black,' said Guttman. He added as a sour afterthought, 'Back when I was in favour.'

'Why, what's happened?'

'You haven't heard?' Guttman seemed genuinely surprised. 'I thought word would have got around. I've been suspended.'

'What for?'

'I'll come to that,' said Guttman. But before he could go on, there was a thud from another room. Guttman got up and hurried to the back of the house. Following him discreetly, Nessheim found his erstwhile boss kneeling down in the bedroom. His wife appeared to have fallen out of bed.

'Can I help?' asked Nessheim.

Guttman glared at him, then his face relented. 'If you wouldn't mind,' he mumbled.

Mrs Guttman was a bird, small with arms like fragile wings sticking out from her cotton peignoir. Her eyes were closed as Nessheim bent down and gently helped Guttman lift her onto the bed, where Guttman hastily covered her with the sheet and blanket. It was only as her husband tucked a pillow under her head that she opened her eyes, and finding Nessheim in her field of vision, they widened. She had been a pretty woman once, Nessheim thought, and her eyes still held a twinkle. She said distinctly, 'Thank you.' Then her face creased into a smile.

Back in the kitchen, Guttman opened the icebox and took out a half-eaten tube of liver sausage, then retrieved a heel of bread from a covered crock. 'Hungry?' he asked, and Nessheim shook his head. Guttman smeared the pâté-like sausage on the bread with a butter knife and took a big bite. With his mouth half full he said, 'My wife isn't very well.' He stopped chewing. 'She's got multiple sclerosis — what they used to call 'creeping paralysis'.'

'I'm sorry,' said Nessheim. He was at a loss to say anything else, so he was quiet for a moment, then continued, 'You were saying you've been suspended.'

Guttman nodded as he chewed. 'They escorted me from the building without so much as a by-your-leave.'

'Who do your people report to now?'

'The Justice staff report to Louis B. Nichols; Mueller keeps the White House bunch.'

'What about me? I could be either.'

'Yes,' Guttman said, close-mouthed as a poker player drawing only one card.

'Do I get a choice?'

'Why choose?' Guttman's expression had gone into neutral.

Nessheim suddenly understood. 'I could hide between the pair of them, couldn't I?'

'For a while. It might be long enough.'

Long enough for what?

Guttman went on, 'I can only operate by proxy now.'

Nessheim was suddenly conscious that the dynamic between them had changed. Guttman was in no position to give orders any more; he was asking Nessheim for help.

Nessheim said, 'What is it you want me to do?'

'Let's go sit down. This may take a while.'

★   ★   ★

When he left Guttman's house it was dark. Here in Virginia the stars dotted the sky like fairy lights on a Christmas tree, but there was no moon and the street was black as fresh tar. The pool car — a Ford that had been serviced the month before — was reliable, and started up with a low roar, and the headlights were brighter than those of his own pickup truck, still sitting in California. He hoped Devereux was looking after it, though he doubted he was going to see it again any time soon.

For the first time Nessheim had felt Guttman was levelling with him, especially when Guttman told him what he really thought was going on. Nessheim welcomed the confidence, not having had it before. And as he listened to the man he had found himself starting to share Guttman's sense of urgency. By the time the older agent had finished talking, Nessheim made it clear that he would do what he could to help — though there was a tricky moment when, feeling obliged to reciprocate Guttman's new openness, he told him about President Roosevelt's secret rendez-vous with Mrs Rutherford. Fortunately, after some initial astonishment, Guttman had seemed to forgive Nessheim his failure to report this news before. Not that Guttman was in any position to do otherwise; Nessheim was the last string he had left to pull.

With Guttman suspended, Nessheim was the only one in a position to find the *Dreiländer*.

I have no choice, thought Nessheim. Like it or not, it was up to him.

29

When Nessheim entered the Executive Wing office the next morning, Dinah greeted him breezily. There was no sign of Mueller. Nessheim worked desultorily until eleven o'clock examining the recent logbooks of the White House Mansion; it was impossible to concentrate. Then he phoned Marie.

'Mr Nichols was asking after you,' she said.

'Oh?'

'I explained you were working for Mr Mueller now.' She sounded as if someone else was in the room with her.

'Right,' he said. 'Listen, Marie, I need to come over and check some files for Mr Guttman. If I came by at five, do you think that would be okay?'

'Of course, Mr Finsterwald,' she said. Finsterwald? Someone *was* in the room with her. 'If you could come an hour later, that would be ideal.'

'See you at six, Marie.' He looked at his watch. If he got moving he should be just in time for his earlier appointment. Not that it was scheduled.

He was just getting up to leave when Mueller walked in. 'You,' Mueller said, pointing a finger. 'I want a word.'

They went out in the corridor. Mueller asked, 'So what's the story with the Hopeless Hebrew?'

'What do you mean?'

Mueller frowned. 'Don't play hayseed with me, Nessheim. If I've heard the news so have you — your boss is no longer your boss.'

Nessheim shrugged. Suddenly Mueller started to sing, to a tune from *The Wizard of Oz*: 'Ding dong, the Heeb is dead/ The useless Heeb, the Heeb is dead.'

He stopped suddenly, and looked at Nessheim. 'What I can't understand is why you're not reporting to me.'

'I don't know,' Nessheim said blandly.

'Who *are* you reporting to?'

'Louis B. Nichols,' he said, confident that Mueller wouldn't challenge this — Nichols was an assistant director.

'It doesn't make much sense — with you over here most of the time.' He sounded angry. 'I wouldn't count on its lasting, pal. In the meantime I'm keeping an eye on you.'

Nessheim shrugged again, but his stomach was churning. The last thing he needed was to have Mueller checking up on him. 'Anything else, Mule?' he said, trying not to bait the man, or to show the fear he felt.

★ ★ ★

He made it seem pure coincidence, and she bought it. She would have picked up little Jeff from nursery school twenty minutes before, and he managed to time his arrival at the corner of Wisconsin Avenue perfectly. Nessheim didn't look in her direction, but he didn't need to.

'Jimmy!' Annie called out.

407

His face was a pantomime of surprise as he turned to find her standing, holding Jeff's hand, only 50 feet down the sidewalk.

'Hi!' he said, sounding surprised. I should be in Hollywood with Purvis, he thought without pride. Jeff let go of his mother's hand and scooted towards him, beaming.

'Hey, sailor,' he said, bending down and ruffling the little boy's hair.

'We're on our way home,' said Annie. 'But what are you doing here? Shouldn't you be at work protecting the rest of us?'

'I was conducting a gunfight in the neighbourhood.'

'Did you plug him?' asked the little boy.

'Jeff! What a way to talk,' said Annie.

Nessheim laughed. 'How do you know it was a him? Ma Barker was as tough as any man.'

'Which way are you going?' asked Annie. She was wearing a pale blue dress and clutch coat that highlighted her dark hair.

'Beats me,' confessed Nessheim. 'I was through for the day and just taking a walk.'

'Walk with us then,' said Annie, and they set off. While Jeff babbled on about robbers and guns, Nessheim talked with Annie — it was small talk, about where Frank was (in Montana, talking to the owners of silver mines), and about Justice Frankfurter's cold, and then, briefly but gloomily, about Europe, where the German advance was now engulfing western Europe — France was falling, the British Army was being pushed back on every front.

When they reached the gates of Belvedere, he

stopped. Jeff piped up, 'Aren't you coming home with us?'

Perfect, thought Nessheim. 'Well . . . '

'Mom, please,' the boy pleaded.

'Why don't you come in?' she said. 'Sally's at Five Forks today.'

'We got cake,' said Jeff.

'Cake?' said Nessheim with mock-astonishment. 'What are we waiting for?'

★　★　★

With Sally Cummings in Virginia, the staff were also away, except for Mrs O'Neill, who whisked Jeff off to have cake and a mug of milk in the empty kitchen, while Annie and Nessheim went upstairs. She had put china cups and saucers and a full teapot on a tray with a strainer, and Nessheim dutifully carried it up to the landing. Next to the newly installed lift, the door to the adjacent bedroom was open, and looking in he saw Shaker-style furniture and a two-poster bed.

They went into Annie's study next door, where she took the tray and put it down on her desk, motioning him to sit on the small settee against the wall. She seemed in such a good mood that he hesitated before spoiling it. But there was never going to be a good time for this. So he plunged in as soon as she had poured out the tea and sat down behind her desk.

'Annie, you know at the FBI I'm what they call a special agent.'

'Yes, Jimmy,' she said like an indulgent mother. She added with a laugh, 'We call you

'The G-Man' behind your back.'

'I bet you do. But you probably don't know that I work in counter-espionage.'

'For Mr Guttman, right? The man who came to see the Justice.'

'That's right. You know what counter-espionage is.'

She gave him a look. 'I saw *The Lady Vanishes*, Jimmy. I hope your work is not quite that exciting.'

'Hitchcock has nothing on us. The thing is, I'm working on detecting Nazis who may be here in the States.' He was keeping it vague; there was no point alarming her yet — that would come soon enough.

'Okay,' she said equably.

He paused, unsure how to proceed. 'Some of them are in contact with other sympathisers — by letter, I mean. The people receiving these letters may be entirely innocent, but we have to make sure.'

There was still a half-smile on her face but she seemed to sense his seriousness. 'Okay,' she said again, slowly.

'Your aunt is one of these people receiving letters.'

'Are you trying to tell me Aunt Sally is a Nazi spy?' she asked, laughing a little nervously.

'Of course not. But we think an English-woman she corresponds with may be.'

'And who's this English lady, Jimmy?'

'Her name is Lady Dove.'

She stared at him with a look of incredulity. 'Are you serious? Lady Dove a *spy*? Justice

Frankfurter, and Doobs and Frank — anyone who's been to Oxford knows Lady Dove. She's no spy — at least not for the Nazis! God, Jimmy, her husband is a Socialist.'

'I'm not thinking of Sir Henry Dove,' Nessheim said, and he found his voice sounding shaky even to himself. 'Her *first* husband is now a major figure in the British Fascist movement — people call him Oswald Mosley's right-hand man. And we have evidence that Lady Dove's sympathies are also with Hitler.

'Believe me,' he said, trying to sound soothing, 'we're not saying your aunt's doing anything wrong. But we do think she might be being used by Lady Dove. And unless we know what Lady Dove is telling her, we won't be able to help.'

Annie considered this for a moment, then said briskly, 'I see — you want to read her letters. Lady Dove's to Aunt Sally. That's what you're asking, isn't it?'

He didn't want to look her in the face. She went on, with almost analytic detachment, 'Yes, that's what you're asking for. And since Aunt Sally's not about to grant such a request — you know as well as I do what she'd think of that — you've decided to sidle up to her niece instead.'

'Hey now . . . ' he began, wanting to pre-empt the anger he sensed behind the precision in her voice.

'Come off it,' she said, suddenly impatient. 'Though why you think I'd actually help you spy on my aunt is incomprehensible.'

She said this so definitively that he waited,

hoping she might add some softening words. She sat there, looking at him, as if seeing him afresh for the bastard he was starting to feel he was.

But he had no choice. 'Part of my job involves reviewing security arrangements, and that means checking into people who know the President.'

His tone must have been a giveaway, for she looked alert again, viewing him with wary eyes. 'And . . . ?' she asked.

'It means we learn all sorts of stuff about people. Most of it is completely irrelevant, but we hear about it all the same. That makes it kind of tough.'

'Makes what kind of tough?' she asked.

'In my case, learning things about people I actually know. That's unusual — normally, it's just a file, you can't even put a face to it.'

'You know my face well enough by now, Jimmy.'

Her lower jaw was moving and she was clicking her teeth nervously. He said, 'We talk to friends and relatives, and sometimes go back to the person's home town.' The words were sticking in his throat like magnets to an iron bar.

There was a long pause, and then she said, 'So you know.'

He nodded.

'He's just a little boy, Jimmy. I don't care if my name is mud, but I can't have it sticking to him.'

'We wouldn't do anything to hurt him,' he said urgently.

'But you'd tell Frank, wouldn't you? That would ruin everything.'

'Frank doesn't know?'

412

'Frank doesn't know,' she said dully.

Nessheim remained silent. Guttman had been right. But how could you marry a man under such a canopy of lies?

Annie said, 'I'm glad to know this is official business. I'd hate to think you were acting like such a sleazeball of your own accord.'

The words hit home. Part of him wanted to make his excuses, tell Guttman that all bets were off, re-tender his resignation, and go and try to make an honest living somewhere else.

But then he thought of what it was that Guttman feared was really happening, and of the man's helplessness, confined to his little ranch house on the edge of Arlington with his sick wife. 'Annie, please, I — '

'You don't have to be polite, Jimmy. In the circumstances, it would seem more than a little ridiculous. I'll go get the letters.'

He nodded dumbly and said nothing; having shown an iron fist, it was too late to hold up a velvet glove.

'Wait here,' Annie said, and she left the room. He heard her walking down the corridor, towards her aunt's suite of rooms at the back of the house. He sat there, feeling about as virtuous as a customer in a whorehouse, waiting for the girl he'd picked.

When Annie came back she was holding a stack of tissue-thin blue writing paper, held together by an oversized paper clip. She handed them over with an expression of distaste.

'Thanks,' he said. Annie was heading for the door when he said, 'Please don't go. I may need you to explain things I don't understand.'

She sat down silently. He began reading the letters — there were almost three dozen. The first one began formally:

Dear Mrs Cummings,
How nice it was to meet you this past year, and I do hope you will let me know when you are next again in England . . .

Sally Cummings must have replied promptly, for the next letter was dated five weeks later and thanked Sally for her reply. After this, the letters came at a rate of roughly every two or three weeks, and very quickly they shed their formality for an established intimacy. The tone of the Dove letters was chatty, high-spirited, and a little naughty, which didn't alter even when war broke out.

For this was a correspondence between two society ladies with a shared penchant for people, parties, and prolific gossip. None of the letters was remotely traitorous, and Lady Dove's sympathies, whatever her unsavoury associations in the past, seemed entirely patriotic, leavened only by a keen eye for the absurd.

We're much more hungry than afraid, she wrote pluckily to Sally two months into the conflict, explaining that:

Louisa the cook discovered that the cat had eaten the bacon ration, so being a practical Polish girl she used the uneaten rinds and powdered eggs to make a quiche for a lunch

I was giving (why one's social life should evaporate because of Herr Hitler is beyond me). Among my guests was the Home Secretary, a grim little Scot named Anderson. He lapped up the quiche without batting an eye, then asked — this is the God's truth — if he could have the recipe for his wife.

In the same vein, she recounted how the local wartime bureaucrats had switched round all the Oxford street signs, intending to confuse future German invaders, but succeeding only in getting her new cleaning lady completely lost. Blackouts were in force but the evenings never dull: her friend Jorge the manager of the Mitre reserved a dozen oysters and half a lobster for Lady Dove and her friend Nancy — *You'll remember her, the one with the handsome husband who ran off with a Soho dancer.*

Jorge had produced a bottle of Chablis as well, and later the two ladies had weaved their way down the blacked-out High Street, then sat in the dark in the Principal's Lodgings, listening to the broadcasts from Berlin:

Lord Haw-Haw indeed — we laughed until we cried. How Herr Goebbels would have been annoyed at this reaction.

Yet even in the early letters there was another focus — references to a shared 'project' — which slowly came to dominate the correspondence.

'Do you know what she means here?' he asked

Annie at one point, holding up an airmail page. 'I wouldn't dream of reading her letters without her permission.'

'Don't you want to know what they say about Frank?'

'Not in the slightest. I already know Sally thinks the world of Frank.'

'Oh, she does. But I don't understand what project he's helping her with.'

'What do you mean?' she demanded, as curiosity vied with scruples.

'Just this,' and he read from one of the letters:

. . . I think you're quite right to think that telling the whole story would not have the desired effect. Honesty is by no means always the best policy. Even the finest men would run a mile, and it would be too cruel if a mistake in early life, however bad, created an immovable obstacle. As well as scare him off the project for good!

He looked up to find Annie looking uncomfortable. She didn't say anything, so he read from another:

How sweet that he has confided in you, little knowing how much you've done to steer him in this direction . . .

He thought at first that Annie wasn't listening, for she was looking out the window, as if there was another voice outside which she'd rather hear. But a tear was forming in one of her eyes.

'What's wrong?' he asked as gently as he could, though by now he had a good idea.

She shook her head.

Then finally he read from a long letter which had been written in March, not long after Nessheim had first visited Belvedere:

How good he has gone public at last, and it sounds a marvellous occasion — senators, Presidential assistants, even a jewish Justice (you must allow me my little prejudice or two). But seriously, well done you — I'm only miffed this damn war kept me from seeing the fruits of our labour.

This time when he looked up, he saw tear tracks on both her cheeks. She wiped them with her fingers, leaving her cheek shiny. She said, 'What do *you* think she's talking about, Jimmy?'

'You and Frank — you're the project.'

'What did you think it was, a big Nazi plot?'

'I'm so sorry,' he said, sitting back in his chair with the sheaf of letters in his lap.

'So, do you still think my aunt's a spy?'

'No,' he said quietly.

Annie nodded absently, no longer willing to look at him. She said, 'And I thought you were such a nice guy.'

'You've got Frank, and he *is* a nice guy. He's got a great future.'

'Sure he does. Shares in Plympton Holdings are always rising.'

'You make it sound like a business decision.'

She said impatiently, 'That's right, Jimmy, just

417

like you — I'm all business. But I'm not the only employee I have to think about. My boy is four years old. He needs more security than I can give him.'

'I hope it's about more than security.'

Annie shrugged. 'I think you've got what you wanted, Agent Nessheim. You should go now. You must realise you're no longer welcome here.'

30

Nessheim went to see Stephenson the Canadian next, feeling sickened by what he'd forced Annie to do, especially since all it had uncovered was her aunt's tawdry scheming to marry her off to Frank.

Guttman hadn't really briefed him adequately about this meeting in a Georgetown club. 'Tell him everything you know,' Guttman had ordered, and when Nessheim had raised an eyebrow, he had said emphatically, 'He's one of the good guys, Jimmy.'

Now upstairs in a small study, Nessheim and Stephenson sat across a desk, gauging each other. Stephenson was tall, probably in his fifties, carefully but casually dressed in a rich blue blazer and tie. Nessheim couldn't help noticing his hands, which were intertwined on the desktop. They were large and long, with fine fingers that could have gripped a basketball or equally — for the man was hard to place — played a Beethoven sonata.

'Harry said he was sending you in his stead,' said Stephenson. The voice was North American, but tinged by an English softness.

'That's right. I report to him.'

Stephenson looked at him knowingly. 'You mean you used to report to him. I know what happened.'

There was something presuming about this

419

which Nessheim didn't like. Guttman had told him to trust the man, but Nessheim felt uneasy.

Stephenson went on, 'He said he'd been suspended. I can't say I'm surprised; Harry never struck me as a Bureau type.'

Nessheim stiffened.

Stephenson unlocked his hands and waved one of them airily. 'Oh, I don't mean because he's a Jew. They're not my favourite kind of people, to tell you the truth; they do like to look after each other. But that's neither here nor there. It's just that you'd have to agree Harry doesn't really fit the Hoover mould. I know he's got a law degree, but a night school on the Lower East Side isn't exactly what the Bureau has in mind, is it?' His long straight nose crinkled with disapproval.

'I didn't even graduate from college, Mr Stephenson, so I'm in no position to look down at Mr Guttman's qualifications.'

Stephenson was unperturbed. 'I wouldn't have thought he was an easy fellow to work for. And the Bureau must have had good reason to suspend him. I'm meeting with Hoover later this week, so I guess I'll find out then.'

Nessheim looked at the books on the wall behind Stephenson, growing increasingly angry. Why had Guttman trusted this prick? He was tempted to get up and leave, whatever Guttman's orders, and he was damned if he'd tell this man anything — even about Lady Dove's gossipy letters. How he regretted coercing Annie as he had. Had this jerk talked Guttman into that?

420

'You look uncomfortable, Agent Nessheim,' said Stephenson. 'Why's that?'

There was no reason not to say. He squared his shoulders. 'My understanding was that you and Agent Guttman saw things the same way. 'Things' being a threat to the security of both our countries — I think you know what I'm talking about. I see now Harry misread that, and by proxy so have I. The fact that you don't like the man is, in your words, neither here nor there, but the fact that you've misled him all along is . . . ' he searched for a word and finally spluttered, 'the shittiest thing I've seen for a long time.'

He was disconcerted to find Stephenson smiling. 'What's so funny?' Nessheim demanded, starting to rise to his feet. 'If you'd like to bring that hyena smile of yours outside I'll — '

'No, no, no,' said Stephenson, who was now laughing. 'Sit down, Agent Nessheim, and I'll give you a beer. I was *testing* you, young man. Can't you see that?'

Unpersuaded, Nessheim sat down again reluctantly, and Stephenson said, 'Harry trusts me, you're right. And I trust him. My only concern was whether I could trust you. If it weren't so important, it wouldn't matter, but I had to be sure.'

'Sure of what?'

'Sure of you. Look, your Director does not see eye to eye with Agent Guttman — that's not exactly a state secret, now is it? Hoover would rather be chasing clapped-out veterans of the Spanish Civil War than digging into Nazi sympathisers who may be plotting to kill the President.'

Nessheim waited, still leery. Stephenson said, 'When Harry told me he had been suspended — and what the reason was — I realised someone had it in for him. I had to make sure that this someone wasn't you — and that you were really on Harry's side. And unless you're John Barrymore's brother, Agent Nessheim, you gave me my answer. I'm not seeing Hoover later this week, by the way; that was a red herring to see if you'd flinch. Now, let me find that beer while you look at this file.'

The file was named *Dubinsky* and Nessheim went through it with astonishment, leaving the bottle of beer Stephenson placed on the arm of his chair untouched while he read the contents. When he'd finished he looked up at Stephenson and said, 'I'll follow this up right away.'

Stephenson nodded. Nessheim said, 'This would fit the bill for the *Dreiländer*.'

'What?' The Canadian leaned forward in his chair.

Nessheim told him about Beringer's revelation that a Nazi agent had been planted as a boy years before.

Stephenson said, 'You know about Werner?'

'Yes. Beringer said he'd taken over contact with the *Dreiländer*.'

Stephenson nodded. 'Then you probably also know that Werner disappeared. Only to turn up dead in Austria, in a region known as *Dreiländereck* — three lands, after its proximity to three different countries, Italy, Yugoslavia, and

Austria. It seems likely the plant may have come from there — since that was the name he was given.

Nessheim said, 'But the original contact here wasn't Werner. A man named Jahnke brought the boy to America — '

Stephenson interrupted: 'Do you know who that is?'

'Not really. I gather he was involved in German espionage efforts over here during the last war.'

'He works now with von Ribbentrop, which means the German Foreign Office. He's linked closely to Heydrich as well — who's the head of intelligence for the Nazis. And we know a senior German intelligence officer named Schellenberg saw Lady Dove last summer in London. Taken together, it would confirm that this sleeping agent has probably come alive.'

'But we don't know where Jahnke planted this agent originally. Much less where he is now.'

'I don't think we can help you there. We don't have any information about Jahnke when he lived in America.'

'I'm going to find out what we know at the Bureau.' He said this more in hope than expectation. 'The other thing I need to tell you is that we've seen the other end of the Lady Dove–Sally Cummings correspondence.'

'Well done,' said Stephenson.

Nessheim shook his head. 'I haven't got good news. Unfortunately, this famous project they kept writing about turns out to be nothing more than a joint effort to get Sally Cummings's niece married. Lady Dove knows the guy in question.'

He told himself there was no reason to explain Annie Ryerson's complicated past.

'What a pity,' Stephenson said. His frustration was obvious, but then he pointed hopefully at the file in Nessheim's hand. 'Maybe our answer's in there.'

★ ★ ★

Marie had stayed late for him — it was six-thirty when he made it to the Justice Building. She was a big-shouldered French Canadian woman, rising forty, with reddish hair that wasn't its original colour, and a feisty manner. Yet right now she looked scared. Nessheim dreaded making his request, since he knew it was going to make her even more frightened. Before he could say anything she came out from her desk and shut the door to the corridor behind him.

She spoke in a half-whisper. 'Mr G says if you need to see him tonight, you're not to come while it's still light. In fact, it's best if you go there after midnight.'

'That late?'

'He'll have a light on in the kitchen — that's in the rear of the house. The back door will be open.'

'I need your help before then, Marie.'

She didn't say anything.

'I need to see a file, but it's in Records. Here,' and he handed her a slip of paper with Jahnke's name on it. 'It'll be Historical, Marie, not Active. I'd go myself, but they'd want Harry's signed okay on the request. I haven't got that.'

'What makes you think they'd let me have it instead?'

He didn't have an answer. 'Harry told me you'd help, Marie. I'm not trying to get you in trouble.'

She went over to her desk and brought out a stack of forms — FRs, he realised, File Requests. She took a pen out of a holder and he watched as she wrote in flowing ink *Harry Guttman* on the signature line. Seeing him look wide-eyed, she said, 'Relax, I do this all the time. Harry never remembers to sign anything.' She added sharply, 'Including your termination request last fall.'

'Won't Files know he's been suspended?'

'Yeah. But he'll have had a backlog of FRs. The Fifth Floor will want to see everything he's pulled. Don't look so worried — they *will* see everything he's pulled. Except this.'

Someone was coming down the hall, a heavy tread. 'Get in there,' whispered Marie urgently, pointing to Guttman's own office. He moved quickly and she had half-shut the door behind him when he heard a voice in the anteroom.

'Hello, Marie. You're working late.'

'Hi, Mr Tolson. Just clearing up a few odds and ends.' Nessheim stood behind the half-closed door. He stared at Guttman's desk as he listened. It held a tacky-looking pen set and a stained blotter, but otherwise had been swept clean.

'If it's for Mr Guttman I'll need to know what they are.'

'Of course, Mr Tolson. I was making a list, actually, just like you said I should. I'll bring it up in the morning. It includes his FRs and all the correspondence from field offices.'

'Good. I also want to double-check his direct reports. Would Harry have a list of them on his desk?'

For an awful moment Nessheim thought that Tolson might come through the door. There wasn't going to be much he could say to explain his presence.

Then Marie said, 'I don't think so, Mr Tolson. To be honest, if it was anything administrative, I'd have it out here. Mr G tended to prefer it that way.'

Tolson laughed, a thin cackle. 'I'm not surprised. I know what his desk looked like. The thing is, the Director has split Guttman's reports between the White House detail and Louis B. Nichols. There's a little confusion about one guy who seems to have fallen through the gap. Do you know this Nessheim character?'

Marie paused. 'Is he the young fellow who played football?'

Tolson said, 'I didn't know that.' He sounded irked.

'You played yourself, didn't you, Mr Tolson?' asked Marie with a palpable coo to her voice.

'A bit,' said Tolson. 'I was all-Conference my last year.' Nessheim could almost see the man's chest puff out.

'Golly,' gushed Marie.

'Anyway, I need to have a word with this Nessheim guy. Get a hold of him for me

426

tomorrow, will you, Marie?'

'Of course, Mr Tolson,' she said.

Nessheim waited, then suddenly the door swung open and Marie was gesturing for him to come out. 'Holy Mother of God,' she exclaimed.

'What's wrong?' he asked. 'You were terrific.'

She was literally shaking. 'I left the FR on top of my desk, with your name and Mr Guttman's. I thought any minute Mr Tolson would look down and see it. How was I going to explain that away?'

'Thanks a million. I better go and get the file.' He reached down for the form.

'Not so fast,' she said. 'Nichols may be down there — if the reception clerk mentions your FR is from Guttman, he'll be onto you right away. I better go.'

'I can't let you take the risk, Marie.' He knew he was asking too much. If Guttman's suspension became permanent, she might still survive, but not if she were linked to Guttman's misdemeanours.

Marie shook her head. 'Spare me the Sir Galahad stuff, okay? I'm doing this for Mr G.' She scooped up the signed form and went out the door.

She was back ten minutes later, holding a file. 'No problem — Mr Nichols had gone home, and I know the night clerk. But read it now, will you? I want it back in place before I leave for the night.'

He took the file and went into Guttman's office, closing the door behind him. He read quickly, and soon discovered that most of the file concerned Jahnke's activities during the war, about

427

which the contents were long on speculation and short on facts.

Kurt Jahnke had been born in Germany in 1882, the son of a wealthy landowner in Pomerania, which stretched across northern Germany and western Poland, just under the Baltic. That much seemed indisputable.

Then he had emigrated to the States where reports variously suggested he had enlisted in the army, been a policeman, worked for German intelligence, and made a fortune. When war broke out in 1914 he had become a staff member of the German Consulate in San Francisco, though according to the field office's reports he had travelled extensively — until America's entry in 1917, when the consulate had closed and he had either disappeared (one report) or resurfaced in Mexico City (another). He had next turned up in Germany after the Armistice, taking over the family estate in Pomerania after the death of his father.

With Hitler's rise Jahnke had re-entered the intelligence arena, though the file was unclear whether this was due to ardent Nazism or his friendship with Rudolph Hess. He was currently said to be running a small intelligence-gathering operation on behalf of the Third Reich's Foreign Office, one subordinate to the Nazi Party's own espionage and counter-espionage organisations.

That was the bulk of the file, but at its rear there were several typed notes appended to the main account. One was labelled *Jahnke: Earlier History*, which included a paragraph that made Nessheim sit up:

Prior to his service at the Consulate, Mr Jahnke established an undertaking business that specialised in the shipment of dead members of the Chinese community in the San Francisco area back to China. Previously the transportation of coffins outside the continental United States had been proscribed on health grounds, but Jahnke provided zinc-lined coffins which met government regulations.

Jahnke is believed to have sold this business very profitably in 1914 to a local Chinese syndicate.

One of Nessheim's early assignments at the Bureau's San Francisco office had been to investigate this very business, then run by a Chinese family named Wong. He remembered the scam: bodies were duly interred in zinc-lined coffins and shipped westwards for China, but 15 miles out the cargo was intercepted and pine coffins substituted for the far more expensive zinc ones. The latter were then taken 15 miles back and used all over again. It had taken two months to bust the racket, and his colleague in the last three weeks of the investigation had been Jake Mueller.

Nessheim tried to work it out. If Jahnke had come back to America in 1915, any boy he brought with him then would now be well over thirty years old. That was plausible; what didn't make sense was the idea that in 1915, when

Adolph Hitler was an unknown corporal on the Western Front, Jahnke would have been part of a conspiracy to plant an agent who could be counted on to do the Nazi's bidding twenty-five years later.

Nessheim felt deflated. How could there be a plot if there was no one to enact it? He glanced idly at the other notes. Most speculated on the supposed targets of Jahnke's sabotage efforts during the last war: an explosion in Philadelphia and another on Black Tom Island in New York Harbour, a counterfeiting scheme in Baltimore that would have swamped the Eastern Seaboard with phoney dollar bills, even a plan to start a bordello near Capitol Hill where clients including congressmen would be secretly photographed and blackmailed. Whatever the truth of any of these schemes, Jahnke remained an elusive figure.

There was only one more item, a handwritten note in ink and the last page of the file:

After his departure from San Francisco in 1917, Subject was reportedly spotted twice in the city in subsequent years — in 1924 and then in 1928. Both sightings were reported by Huan Deng Lee, member of one of the famous Six Families that effectively run Chinatown, and an occasional Bureau informant.

Another hand, this time writing in pencil, had added in brackets after Deng Lee's name: *Reliable?* Nessheim hoped so.

31

Most days, when Nessheim came back to the House of Youth after work, he changed clothes, switching his suit for khaki trousers or even jeans and a V-neck sweater, and taking off the holstered .38 he wore each day. He would put the pistol in his second drawer, under the stack of Chinese-laundered shirts, and hang his jacket in the closet.

But this evening he kept his suit on, and his gun. He was getting used to being surprised about people he had thought he understood, and he wanted to be prepared for the worst.

Dubinsky's room was down the hall; it overlooked the street in front, and was furnished for a long-term inhabitant — a comfortable sofa, a big bed, watercolours on the wall. Nessheim had only been in it once before, to return Dubinsky's copy of *The Grapes of Wrath*.

He knocked, then entered when he heard a mild 'Come in.' Dubinsky was at his desk, positioned by the window. Dusk was falling, the shadows long, but Nessheim could see a woman outside, walking on the sidewalk in a short-sleeved shirt. May already felt like summer in this heat-drenched town.

The law clerk seemed surprised to see him. 'Hi, Jimmy, what's up?'

'I wanted a word.'

Dubinsky's expression remained friendly, but

now was curious too. 'Sure thing. Take a pew. I'd offer you a drink, but my house is dry.'

Nessheim didn't smile. Dubinsky said, 'Hey, what are you doing Decoration Day weekend?'

Nessheim shrugged, not wanting to be distracted. 'Don't know.'

'Sally's going to have a big shindig out in Virginia on the day. You want to come along?'

'Can I use my real name?'

There was an almost imperceptible pause, then Dubinsky laughed. 'Why, isn't 'Nessheim' legit?'

'It is. But actually that's what I wanted to ask you. Is 'Dubinsky'?'

'What makes you say that?' Colour was draining from his cheeks.

'Immigration have examined their records thoroughly but can't seem to find you. The English authorities have checked for the last twenty years, and your parents couldn't have gone there from Germany, not with you in tow. There's no record of it.' Stephenson's people had done a lot of work.

Dubinsky bristled. 'Why are you poking into my life like this, Jimmy? Who do you think you are?'

'A friend. But also an agent of the Federal Bureau of Investigation. Doobs, you can get mad as you like, but I'm trying to do this the easy way. Otherwise, three agents will come out to the house tomorrow at sunrise, pull you out of bed, and take you to Bureau HQ in your pyjamas. It's your choice.'

Dubinsky's eyes were moving around the

room, almost dancing. The relentless affability was gone, and he looked for a moment as if he would explode.

Then he sighed, almost in relief, and said, 'It's not what it looks like.'

'What's not?' Nessheim wasn't going to try guessing.

Dubinsky gave a sigh. 'My passport's in a different name. It's in the name of von Leyser. My father's name.'

'That's a long way from Dubinsky,' said Nessheim, recognising the aristocratic significance of the 'von'.

'My mother and Ernst von Leyser divorced in 1920 — I was only eight years old. I was raised by her and my stepfather in England.'

'Your stepfather was called Dubinsky?'

'No. His name was Rosenberg. A Jew. As was my mother.'

'Was?'

'She died in 1926.'

Nessheim was unswayed. 'But when did you decide to go under her name?'

'I wanted nothing to do with my father once the Nazis came to power. He's a general in the *Wehrmacht*. I called myself by my mother's maiden name when I came to America eight years ago. It seemed the right thing to do.'

Nessheim ran a hand through his hair, thinking. Then he said, 'How do I know all this is true? With the war on in Europe, it's not as if I can prove it either way.'

Dubinsky lifted both hands and Nessheim realised he wasn't going to learn anything more

433

by asking questions. It was time to go and see Guttman. 'All right,' he said, standing up. 'That's it for now. We'll need to talk again.'

'I'm telling the truth, Jimmy. Honest.'

Nessheim shrugged, which Dubinsky seemed to take as a positive sign. 'Are you going to Sally's tonight?' he asked.

'Nah,' said Nessheim, relieved that Dubinsky didn't seem to know about his conversation with Annie. 'I've got to pack. I'm going to be out of town for a few days.'

'Going anywhere nice?'

'Not really,' he said. Much as Nessheim liked the place, right now California was not his idea of nice.

* * *

He drove carefully through Georgetown and over the bridge into Virginia. At this time of night there were almost no cars on the road, and he was certain he wasn't being followed. But he was mindful of Mueller's words — *I'm keeping an eye on you* — and he realised the surveillance might be at the other end, waiting at the hive instead of following the bee. So he went past the street where Guttman lived, and turned onto a parallel road in the development. Cutting the engine and lights, he sat in his car for a good five minutes. Nothing moved on the street.

The night was cloudless, and a silver moon hung like a lamp in the sky, casting too-revealing light. He got out and put on his overcoat, not because it was cold — the late spring air was like

434

a warm bath — but because his coat was dark. He walked along the line of low brick houses, trying to gauge the distance down the street. Then behind one house he saw a light in the distance — at two in the morning, the only light on in the neighbourhood.

Moving off the sidewalk, he walked along the side of a two-storey house with a brick porch in front. He entered the back yard, praying no dog would bark. Almost stumbling over a tricycle on the lawn, he made his way to the rear of the lot, where a low chain-link fence separated the property from Guttman's.

He hopped the fence. In the moonlight Guttman's yard looked meagre, a square of lawn that needed mowing, and an apple tree which looked starved of water. He made his way to a back deck of pine planks, one of them loose. In the shadows he felt around for the handle to the back door. He had to give it a good yank, but then he was in the house.

He stopped, listening carefully. The air was filled with a rhythmic rumble. Thunder? There had been no sign of rain. The light he'd seen was in the dining alcove, and through the doorway he could make out the figure of Guttman in the living room. He was dressed in shirtsleeves, reclining against the chartreuse sofa's cushions, and snoring to an orchestra of his own.

Nessheim walked through the alcove to the living room. When Guttman didn't stir he tapped him on the shoulder. Guttman took several seconds to respond. Then his big sloping shoulders jerked and his eyes opened in alarm.

'You scared me, kid,' he said, looking embarrassed.

'I didn't want to wake your wife by knocking.' Nor alert anyone watching the house.

Guttman stood up, tucking his shirt in. 'Let's go to the kitchen.' There he took a big bottle of fizzy-looking water out of the fridge. He found two jelly glasses and filled them, then handed one to Nessheim, who took a swig and made a face.

'You don't like celery soda?'

'Not much. Must be an acquired taste,' he said, handing back the glass.

They returned to the living room, Guttman clutching his glass. He reached down onto the coffee table, then handed Nessheim a phone number written on it.

'What's this?'

'My new number — I had another line installed this afternoon. I may be paranoid, but I can't take a chance on the old one's being tapped. You have to be able to call me and talk securely.'

'How do you know they won't tap the new line as well?'

'Because they don't know the new one's there. I had it installed in my wife's maiden name. The phone company won't alert them about some unknown installation out in Virginia. Believe me, I know the competence limits of our organisation. Now, did you see Stephenson?'

'I did. I told him about *Dreiländer* and Jahnke, but he wasn't able to help us much. But he did give me a file. It was about Dubinsky, one of the lodgers in my house.' Nessheim told how he had then tackled Dubinsky about his name change, and related Dubinsky's explanation. 'If he's lying then he knows his cover is blown. We need to act fast.'

'No, we don't,' Guttman said quietly.

'What do you mean? I'm not sure I believe him.'

'I would.'

He watched Guttman, and gradually understood. 'You don't say,' Nessheim remarked drily at last. 'So how long have you known Dubinsky?'

Guttman tried out a look of wide-eyed innocence, but seeing Nessheim's cold stare, he relented. 'I should have told you. Sorry.'

There was a pattern here, of activity behind the scenes when Nessheim got sent on stage. He was getting awfully tired of not knowing who was working the props behind him. 'What was Dubinsky supposed to do?'

Guttman shrugged. 'Make you feel welcome in the House of Youth.'

'Is that all?' He recalled how Dubinsky had suddenly stopped coming on the weekend walks with Annie to fetch her son Jeff; the law clerk had pleaded demands of work. It now looked very convenient.

'Yeah. I didn't actually do the asking. The Justice did.'

Nessheim tried to keep his cool. 'Does Dubinsky work for the Bureau?'

'Nah,' said Guttman, still looking sheepish. 'He just wants to. Justice Frankfurter keeps recommending him. And he knew about the name change — he said it's one of the first things Dubinsky told him, back when they met at Oxford.'

'That doesn't mean he should believe him.'

Guttman was more confident now. 'The Justice knows plenty of people in Germany. The story's solid.'

'Had you met Frankfurter before we went to his house?'

Guttman nodded. 'Something wrong with that?'

'No, I guess you Jews stick together. I shouldn't be surprised — everybody else does: the Italians, the Irish, the German-Americans in the *Bund* — '

'What did you say?' Guttman looked furious. Nessheim raised a hand to calm him down, but Guttman was not appeased. 'Listen, *schmuck*. Jews aren't trying to kill Nazis, and Jews aren't after German-Americans, and Nazis aren't the refugees. If Jews stick together at a time like this, there's a reason.' His eyes blazed.

'I'm sorry, Harry,' said Nessheim.

Guttman exhaled, and an awkward silence ensued. At last Guttman broke it.

'Okay, now — did you talk to the girl?'

'I've seen the letters,' Nessheim said without enthusiasm. He explained what he'd found.

'You mean it was all about plotting their engagement? I don't believe it.'

'It's disappointing, I know,' Nessheim said. 'But there's some good news. I found the Jahnke file. He had a business in California shipping back the coffins of dead Chinese to China. Then during the war he was a spy for the Germans — that's how he came to the Bureau's attention. He returned to Germany, but the file said he was spotted two different times in San Francisco in the twenties.'

'Where does that get us?' asked Guttman.

'If he brought a boy over and kept an eye on him, then it must have been out there. He never stayed anywhere else long enough.'

'It seems a little thin to me.'

'I think I should follow it up.' Guttman frowned, but Nessheim persisted. 'We don't have much choice — now that you've vouched for Dubinsky and we know Sally Cummings is nothing more than a matchmaker.'

'I'd still rather you stuck around,' said Guttman. But he didn't even pretend it was an order. When Nessheim didn't reply, Guttman leaned back against the sofa with his mouth open, looking exhausted. He's going to start snoring again any second now, thought Nessheim. But then the open mouth started moving. 'I better make a long-distance call.'

32

Late May 1940
San Francisco

'I was meant to be back east by now,' said SAC Morgan, as he stood by the window. Nessheim remembered Morgan had started as a cop in Philadelphia. Behind him Nessheim could see lights on a freighter in the Bay, heading for Oakland. It was nine-thirty at night, and there was no one else on the floor except for the late receptionist.

Nessheim had phoned him from the Oakland terminus that afternoon, then on Morgan's instructions waited until the office was deserted. He'd killed time sitting on a bench near the Embarcadero, trying to concentrate on what he needed to do here, and not think about what had happened in the last week, especially with Annie.

As the train sped through Ohio he had written her a letter he'd posted when switching trains in Chicago:

Dear Annie,
    I am heading out to California, following leads, as they say at the Bureau.
    I'm so sorry — though an apology looks pretty thin on the page. I feel worse than you could know about what I put you through. I know that may sound like the boss who

440

says it hurts him more than the man he's firing, but our friendship came to mean a lot to me.

Maybe some day you will let me explain.
Yours sincerely,
Jimmy

Now Morgan came back to his desk, looking down at the papers on it with distaste. 'Harry said it was urgent. Though from what I understand, Harry's not in any position to call the shots these days.' It was clear he was doing Guttman a favour that might never be repaid. 'I don't want you talking to the other agents while you're here.'

'Not even Devereux?' His friend from his time out here. When Morgan shook his head, Nessheim said, 'He's got my pickup truck. I was hoping to collect it.'

'Another time.'

Nessheim sighed. It wasn't as if he could afford to come 3,000 miles at the drop of a hat.

Morgan sat down on his padded swivel chair and used his long legs to push it nearer the desk. He took his keyring out of his trouser pocket and unlocked a drawer, then brought out a file. 'I've done some digging into this guy Jahnke and there isn't much to show for it. I'd have thought there was more in D.C.'

'Just enough to send me out here. The HQ file mentions an undertaking business Jahnke started, shipping Chinese stiffs back to their homeland. He sold it to some Chinamen who were crooked — their zinc coffins never got to

China. You may have forgotten, but you had me and Mueller work on it.'

'I remember.' He looked intently at Nessheim. 'And I remember Mueller.'

'I thought maybe there would be some back trail to Jahnke through the business.'

Morgan had half a smile on his face. 'Funny you should say that. It's the one lead in the file that doesn't look completely cold. Let's take a little trip to Chinatown.'

★　★　★

They walked north, the night air cool and salty from the Bay. The business district lay like a series of deserted canyons underneath the concrete cliffs of commerce, but as Morgan and Nessheim turned west and climbed Sacramento Avenue the streets grew more residential — and more Chinese. They were one street over from Clay, where he'd chased the trio of bank robbers in what seemed an age ago. He hadn't thought about that day in months, but now it came again, close as his breath.

At the corner of Grant, Morgan looked at his watch. 'We need to kill half an hour. How about a bowl of noodles?'

They went into the nearest restaurant, a single room brazenly lit, with low tables and cheap kitchen chairs. At the back you could see a couple of cooks standing over the stovetop, holding woks that hissed and spat from the fierce gas flames. They sat down and Morgan ordered a bowl of chow mein and a bottle of beer from the Chinese waiter. Nessheim was too tense to feel hungry and asked only for egg rolls and tea.

Almost at once, the waiter came back and put a bowl of noodles the size of a tureen in front of Morgan. He reached for the soy sauce. 'Have you liked working for Harry?'

Nessheim picked his words with care. 'Let's just say it's been eventful.'

Morgan slurped some noodles with a Chinese soup spoon. He wiped his chin with his napkin, then said, 'Harry's not exactly what he seems, now is he?'

'How's that?' asked Nessheim.

'Everybody knows he's smart — do you know a Jew in the Bureau who's dumb? And they see this short dumpy guy and assume he's the resident thinker. Don't get me wrong — Harry *is* smart, but he's tough too.'

'Yeah?' It seemed unlikely.

'Let me tell you a story. I first met Harry when he came down to Philly — I was still a cop then. It was a mail fraud case, but with some muscle involved. The conmen had crossed state lines, and we hadn't got anywhere, so my Chief of Police decided to call in the Bureau. It was still pretty new then — I don't even think it was called the FBI.

'Anyway, I was pissed off about having the Feds called in over my head, and even more so when this fat, sloppy Yid comes into my office. I brief him, and we go out to find some of the crooks — this was in south Philly, which can be a rough part of town. I'm thinking I've got to look

443

after this guy, who's heavyset but otherwise a pretty unimpressive physical specimen. And then, all of a sudden we spot one of the guys we're looking for, and I go to collar him, and out of nowhere he whacks me with a roundhouse I didn't see coming.

'*Boom*, I'm out on the sidewalk, figuring my jaw's broken and what the fuck? when suddenly I look up and the fat little Heeb hits the guy with a right hand like I've never seen. Never! The crook is not only down on the sidewalk with me, he's out completely cold. I mean KOed completely.

'I get up, we cuff the jerk, a paddy wagon shows and we throw him in, and then we keep walking. Unbelievably, Harry's exactly the same as ten minutes before, short and squat and smiling kind of nervously, as if nothing's happened at all. But if you'd seen him tag the other guy, you'd never forget it. And after that I looked at him in a different way, and you might even say we were friends.'

'Were?'

Morgan looked at him hard. 'Nessheim, if I can get you out of my hair and go back east, Harry and I will be friends again.'

★ ★ ★

They walked down Grant Avenue, which was growing crowded with a mix of Chinese and sightseers. Morgan was moving quickly now, with such long-legged speed that Nessheim could barely keep up. Ahead of them on the left

444

he could see the brick bulk of the Episcopal church looming.

Morgan wheeled to his right, towards an open doorway, and stopped. Nessheim could see a couple of Chinese customers standing inside. It was night-time but inside the scene was identical, as if neither the passage of several years nor the difference between day and night could alter it. The same thin wire holding the unfolded strips of dough; the same Chinese girls filling flimsy cardboard boxes with the finished article. The sickly smell of the finished fortune cookies — sweet and cloying, like unpleasant perfume.

Morgan walked straight through the room to the back. Nessheim remembered the small concrete paved yard behind the building, but Morgan didn't open the back door. He walked instead into the tiny kitchen where the last time Nessheim had almost retched at the sight of putrid chicken necks sitting in a saucepan of greasy water. The room was as tiny as he remembered but Morgan walked to one corner, kicked a garbage can out of the way, then reached down and pulled at a large square of the linoleum flooring, which immediately gave way. Beneath it sat a panel of plywood, roughly a yard by a yard, and when Morgan stomped on one corner it flipped into the air, revealing an opening with an iron ladder leading down.

He followed Morgan cautiously down the ladder, and found himself in a cellar, which was half-lit by a high small window that was just above the street level outside. Crossing the bare room Morgan pulled open a large door, and they entered a dank corridor with whitewashed sides and faded wall lamps.

They walked slowly along until Morgan stopped at an open doorway on the left. He gestured for Nessheim to come and have a look. In a space the size of Sally Cummings's drawing room, a dozen men sat around a long table, each with a stack of coins and bills. The table was covered by a green baize mat which had Chinese numbers and characters etched in red; at one end an old man sat, reaching with a curved bamboo stick for some of the black-and-white buttons that lay scattered in front of him.

'Fan Tan,' Morgan explained. 'One of the old Chinese games.' They kept going along the corridor, and came in semi-darkness to a heavy wooden door. It was locked, and Morgan banged on it with his fist. A slit no bigger than a mail slot opened at face level, and Nessheim could just make out a pair of eyes. Bolts were shot, a key turned in a lock, then the door slowly opened. A stocky Chinese man with a pockmarked face and a white short-sleeved shirt stood in the doorway, holding one hand up to block their way. 'What you want here?' he demanded. Nessheim wondered why his face seemed familiar.

Morgan held up his own hands to show his peaceful intentions. 'I want to see Tang Hui,' he said. 'Tell him Mr Morgan's here.'

'You wait,' the man said, and walked away down another dim corridor. There was something almost medieval to this subterranean nest. Nessheim could imagine people imprisoned here for years in lightless cells, with the world outside none the wiser.

Morgan pointed to the door the pockmarked man had just opened. On their side it was lined by heavy metal studs, each the size of a belt buckle, spaced only inches apart. 'When this is locked from the inside, it takes the cops half an hour to break it down. You can't use an axe because of these studs. By the time they get through you'd think you were in a nunnery.'

The pockmarked man returned. 'Follow me,' he said shortly. He led them through two more heavy doors, each with the same viewing slit at head height. Then suddenly he stopped by a final door and, opening it, motioned them to go in.

They stepped into what must have been another gaming room, for though empty now of tables it was very large, probably fifty feet long and half that wide. It reminded Nessheim of the visitors' room at Sing Sing where he had met Beringer.

In a far corner an old Chinese man sat in a yellow wing chair. He wore a silk smock, scarlet with gold embroidered dragons. Next to him was a low stool, which the pockmarked man went and sat down on. Nessheim wondered if he was there to translate; then Morgan said quietly, 'Tang Hui's English is pretty good, but his hearing's not — he must be eighty years old. Let me do the talking.'

'Tang Hui,' Morgan said loudly, approaching the old man.

The figure in the wing chair looked up. His face was the colour of caramel milk and wrinkled as a walnut. Wisps of white hair ran down from his lower lip and hung like fuzzy strings beneath his chin. His eyes, black and the shape of almonds, studied Morgan carefully. Then Tang Hui gave the slightest of nods.

'I need to ask you about someone from a long time ago. It's nothing bad for you — the man I want to know about is in another country now.'

Tang Hui did not reply. Morgan continued: 'He owned the coffin business before the last war. It sent many Chinese people to lie in peace. His name was Jahnke — Kurt Jahnke. He's a German. Do you remember him?'

There was a long pause while Tang Hui stared at Morgan. Then he lifted an arm and pointed at the younger man on the stool. 'This is my son. Soon he will have to be the family memory. But I remember the man Jahnke.'

'What can you tell us about him?'

The old man flipped his palm up in a gesture of indifference. 'What is there to tell? He start the business and it did very well. It was a time when life was very difficult for Chinese businessman. Jahnke had the advantage. I believe he sold it for a very large sum.'

'I thought he sold it to you,' said Morgan.

'No,' he said. 'It was bought by the Wong brothers. They got in trouble with the authorities. Then the Six Families stepped in. It was important for the community to know the business would continue. That is no surprise: I too would like my bones to rest in Canton.'

'Do you know what happened to Jahnke after that?'

'No.' The answer was quick, too quick.

Morgan pressed him. 'You never saw him again?'

Tang Hui looked down at his son on the stool. Nessheim realised that he was avoiding answering the question.

'I think not,' said the old man at last, turning his head to look at Nessheim.

Morgan sighed, and Nessheim decided to speak. 'Do you know where this man lived back then?'

Tang Hui's eyes widened involuntarily.

Morgan said sharply, 'It's worth your while helping us, Tang Hui. We could always take another look at this business.'

Tang Hui shook his head. 'There is nothing for you to discover. I assure you, the coffins that leave the harbour here arrive untouched in China.'

Nessheim intervened again. 'We are not here to cause you problems. The difficulty we face comes from long ago, not today.' Risking Morgan's ire he went on, 'But it is very serious. This man wants to hurt this country, maybe even hurt the President.'

Tang Hui examined Nessheim's face as if it were a map of uncertain provenance. Nessheim stared back at the almond-shaped eyes, and said calmly, 'I am telling you the truth.'

The old man kept his gaze fixed on Nessheim. Then his face broke into a smile, revealing a line of crooked yellowing teeth. 'Jahnke made a joke to me about his home. He said, 'Some people want a place to go to when they die. I want a place to live more.''

Morgan gave Nessheim a baffled look. Tang Hui said, looking only at Nessheim, 'Do you know where I mean?'

'I do; I've even been there. Thanks,' he added, but the son was already rising to escort them out.

They followed him back along the corridor, past the various gaming rooms, which were now teaming with gamblers. Finally they clambered up the short iron ladder and re-emerged into the back of the fortune cookie factory. The pockmarked man replaced the false cover on the floor and followed them through to the front, where the same shift was tending the miniature assembly line, the girls packing boxes with the still-warm cookies.

They had almost reached the door when the pockmarked man called out from behind them. 'I have not forgotten you.'

Turning around they saw him standing about ten feet away, anger in his face as clear as his scars. It took Nessheim a moment to realise it was him and not Morgan the man meant. And now he remembered why the man looked familiar, how this man had tried to keep him from coming into the factory after Danny Ho. *What you want?* the man had shouted. He could hear the words again.

'I know you too,' he said mildly.

The man reached back to his rear trouser pocket, then suddenly came out with a hatchet, its blade curved to a menacing point. Beside him, Morgan tensed and stepped back, ready to draw his gun. Seeing this, the pockmarked man stayed where he was, though he was shaking his weapon in fury.

'You killed my cousin Danny Ho,' he said harshly, glaring at Nessheim and spitting the words out like bitter pills. 'Do not come back here again, or next time you will be the one who dies.'

33

Nessheim spent the night in a hotel off the Tenderloin, kept awake by rowdy sailors, drinking and chasing whores, and by more than one police siren. Morgan had picked the place, telling him that no one would think to find him there.

Once Nessheim had explained where he was going next, Morgan had been helpful, though grudgingly. 'I suppose you'll want the use of a car. You'll have to pay for the gas.'

Nessheim skipped breakfast and crossed the Bay Bridge by eight-thirty. Fog had swept in from the west side of the peninsula, but it lifted almost immediately once he reached the eastern side of the Bay. He took Route 50 south, skirting Oakland and touching the base of the foothills, where it was already warm, and summer had turned the meadow grass a gorgeous gold. Near Hayward he turned east and drove through the Castro Valley, then climbed a series of switchback roads. The little Dodge struggled a bit, and at the top Nessheim pulled into a cut-out and let the car cool down. A breeze off the Pacific reached him, unimpeded this high up, but the temperature was already in the seventies, and he remembered how quickly the heat came when you moved away from the ocean.

He rolled down the hills mostly in neutral, to keep from paying more of Morgan's charge for gas. He had no clear plan in mind — how do you locate a foreigner who moved away over twenty years before? — but he knew where he would start.

Down in the flat, he stopped to check his oil and fill the radiator on the edges of Livermore, about ten miles further east. Here it was hotter, 85 degrees in the shade he guessed, and though not even summer the land was bone dry, the twisted trunks of the sycamores and oaks mimicking their roots straining for water underground.

He found the bar easily enough, spotting the lot out back where Mueller had parked his car. But the sign outside was gone, and two of the front windows were broken. He pushed at the old saloon door, but it was bolted from inside; when he peered through the glass, he saw dusty tables and several overturned chairs.

It had seemed his best bet, the watering hole for the local *Bund* meetings where Mueller had got drunk and a Jew's application to join had been vetoed. He'd hoped that at the very least he could procure from the owner names of local German-Americans who might be able — and willing — to say they knew Kurt Jahnke all those years ago.

He wondered where to try next. Tax records? Would the clerk at the Town Hall let him see them? Probably, with a Bureau ID. But records might not go that far back, and the clerk might just say no. Nessheim didn't have time for court orders, nor could he have got one without an authorisation that he didn't dare seek. There was a safer bet, which would not involve his indicating what he was looking for.

The Livermore library was in a small adobe building sitting next to a branch bank. On a Tuesday at midday it was virtually deserted. Behind the front desk, a bored woman in her twenties directed him to shelves in a far corner. The phone books were low down; when he kneeled he saw they went back to 1910, and he felt more hopeful. With reason, for he found the 1913 edition had a K. Jahnke listed on 4th Street.

He went into a drugstore down the street, where he sat at the chrome-lined counter of its soda fountain and ate a hot dog and a pile of Jay's potato chips, washed down by a Dr Pepper drawn from the soda fountain tap. A few locals sat in the booths — store owners, a trio of farmers in blue jean overalls, and two gossipy-sounding housewives. After an initial inspection of this stranger in their midst they barely looked at him again.

When he paid the bill he asked the soda jerk how to get to 4th Street, then went out into the hot midday sun and drove along the main drag for a quarter of a mile before turning down a quiet shady street — 4th. This must have been the oldest part of town, for the houses were Victorian, high-gabled constructs of thin white pine, painted pale colours to keep their insides cool.

The house he was looking for turned out to be the biggest on the block, with three storeys and a big porch that ran along its three front sides. But it was not in good shape: a missing rail in the porch's balustrade had not been replaced, the daisy-filled grass in its yard needed cutting, and an apple tree had been allowed to grow its own way for years.

He walked up onto the porch and found lace curtains over the windows which made it difficult to see inside. As he moved towards the door, ready to knock, he looked behind the house, where the lot extended to a shaggy cedar border. A small vegetable plot sat in between with a scarecrow standing in the middle. Then the scarecrow moved.

It was a woman, raw-boned and skinny, probably in her late fifties. She wore a straw hat, a man's long-sleeved shirt, and rubbed her back as she stood upright, a wooden trowel in one hand. 'Help you?' she called out to Nessheim.

He came off the porch. 'I hope so.' He walked to the edge of the square of overturned soil. 'I'm looking for a man who used to live here years ago. I think he owned the house, but I'm not sure.'

'What's his name?'

'Jahnke. He's German.'

'You don't say,' she said, with a hint of dryness. She had hazel eyes and must once have been a pretty woman — good bones, as Nessheim's mother liked to say — but years of sun meant cracks ran like railway lines across her face, and her hands were chafed the colour of strawberries.

'Lot of German folks around here?' he asked.

'Too many for some,' she said.

'My name's Nessheim,' he said, thinking he had better get any awkwardness about that out of the way.

'Mine's Koehler,' she said with half a smile. 'This man you're looking for, you say he lived here?'

'I think so. It was a long time ago. I believe he left when the last war broke out.'

She wiped the sweat on her forehead with the back of her wrist. 'I don't know about you, mister, but I think it's pretty darned hot. You want a glass of lemonade?'

Inside, the house was shabby but clean. The front parlour had been dusted to within an inch of its life, but a floorboard was split and the skirting needed realignment. In the kitchen there was a coal stove, dormant this time of year, and a small electric hot plate. No fridge, but when she fetched a pitcher of lemonade from the larder and poured him a jelly glass full, it was refreshingly cool.

They stood in silence for a minute, drinking, the woman leaning with her back against the sink. 'I've only been here eight years. Me and my husband had a place outside Dublin — apples and asparagus. But you know how it is: two bad years in a row and it's gone. We came here, but my husband died.'

'I'm sorry,' he said simply. He would have liked to hear her story, but there simply wasn't time.

'Me too,' she said flatly, then drained her glass. Putting it in the sink she said, 'I think I heard about this fellah you're looking for.'

'Really?'

'I didn't know him, but the people here before me bought the house from him — I don't own it, you see. I just rent it from them. They said he'd fixed the place up like a palace. Had a player piano in the parlour, and Tiffany glass in the lamps that came all the way from New York. He was the first one in town to have an automobile.'

'Did these people know him well?'

'They must have. They had twin boys of their own, but then they raised the other one too.'

'What other one?' he asked.

She looked at him patiently. 'They adopted Jahnke's boy when he had to leave.'

Nessheim almost dropped his glass. 'Did Jahnke ever come back to see his boy?' He tried not to sound too interested.

She grimaced. 'I'm not sure. All the boys moved away after their parents died. They were strange people — more German than American, if you ask me. We had a strong chapter of the *Bund* around here, and the old man was one of its leaders. Swastikas, Nazi salutes — the whole shebang. He liked to boast that one of his cousins in Germany was the head of their secret police.'

'The Gestapo?'

'Yeah, that's right — I forgot the name.'

'Are the sons like their old man?'

She nodded grimly. 'Worse by all accounts. One of them's living over in Yosemite Lakes; I haven't seen him in five years. I don't know where his twin is. They make sure I pay the rent, but they send Ed Heiserman to come collect it.'

'What happened to the adopted one?'

'I don't know. Ed said he was in San Francisco, but Ed's seventy-three next week, so who knows?' She took his glass and placed it next to hers in the sink. 'I better check my lettuces now. Hope I've been some help.'

Out on the porch he thanked her for the lemonade. 'What's the name of these people?' He tried to sound offhand, but one of his knees was trembling.

'It's German too, naturally.' She chuckled. 'They're called Mueller.'

★ ★ ★

He was relieved to know the truth at last, but also frightened — very frightened, and not just for himself. He was carrying a secret which he could trust no one with except Guttman, who was almost 3,000 miles away. If anything happened to Nessheim now the secret would be lost, and the world would be changed. He had seen a newspaper at the hotel that morning. The British Army had been crushed in France, and now huddled forlornly on the beaches of Picardy and Pas-de-Calais. It was hard to see how Britain could stave off the *Wehrmacht* if it lost half its soldiers. The pressure on the new Prime Minister, Churchill, to negotiate with the Germans would be immense, and if something happened to his one remaining ally — Roosevelt — it would surely be impossible for the British to fight on.

As he drove back into the main street of

Livermore, he tried not to look over his shoulder every other second. He told himself he couldn't have been followed here; if he started worrying about that, his fears would overwhelm him. He parked outside the drugstore where he'd had lunch, and located a phone booth at the back of the store, near the shelves of Epsom salts, Pepto-Bismol, and other mild medicaments. Shoving a nickel in the slot, he got an operator right away, and waited impatiently as she took her time placing his call.

There was no answer at the Virginia end. It was late morning on the Eastern Seaboard, and Guttman wasn't going to work these days, so where was the man?

Nessheim waited half an hour, buying a pack of Juicy Fruit gum in the store and walking the length of the old-fashioned boardwalk along the main street's storefronts. When he tried phoning again, he heard the local operator speak and an unfamiliar female voice reply 3,000 miles away.

The operator came back to Nessheim. 'They said no.'

'*What?*'

'They won't accept the call.' Her voice was infuriatingly prim.

'Make it station to station. Tell them it's urgent.'

He heard the operator try again; it sounded half-hearted. 'Sorry,' she reported back to Nessheim. 'Still no go.'

'What the hell is going on?' he said.

'You don't need to cuss,' the operator said, and cut off the connection.

459

Nessheim felt panicky and isolated, like a man visiting a deserted island whose dinghy has been washed away. Then he thought of Morgan. He wasn't going to risk another collect call, but he had just enough change for three minutes.

Fortunately he got the SAC right away.

'Where are you?' Morgan asked.

Nessheim ducked the question; he knew too much right now to trust anybody. 'Coming back to town. Listen, can you send a message to Guttman? Marie, his secretary, can get hold of him.'

'I've already had a message from him,' said Morgan. 'Harry says Stephenson's struck gold, whatever that means, and you're to return to Washington right away. But you're not to go back the way you came out.'

'How's that?'

'Otherwise you'll be greeted in Chicago.'

'What's happened?'

He could hear Morgan take a deep breath. 'They're on to you, pal. Somehow they know you're out here.'

'Who's *they*?'

'Whoever's out to get you. I don't know more than that, and I'm not sure Harry does either.'

'Listen, can you please call Harry and tell him — '

Morgan interrupted him immediately. 'Not on your life. I took Harry's call, and now I've taken yours. That's all I can do.' He waited a second for this to sink in, then added, 'Tolson also called. He wanted to know where you were. I said I hadn't seen you — in fact, I barely remembered you ever worked in the Bureau here. I can't do more than that.'

'But I know who — ' he said, trying again.

'Save it for Guttman,' ordered Morgan. 'I can't do anything more. You understand?'

'Sure,' he said bitterly.

'Harry expects to see you tomorrow.'

It was the 28th of May. If he caught that evening's train it wouldn't get in until the 30th — Decoration Day. And since he couldn't go via Chicago he might not get back until the 31st.

Nessheim said, 'Sure he does. And pigs will fly.'

There was a long pause, then Morgan said, 'People already do.'

34

The first time Nessheim saw an aeroplane had been at the county fair in Green Lake, Wisconsin. It had been parked outside the vast oval dirt track where the trotters ran; you could see it from the grandstand where he'd sat with his father, waiting for the first race. A biplane, it started from a grass strip a farmer had cut, racing away in the distance until by some miracle it had left the ground. It climbed to a few hundred feet, then banked and turned back to pass over the grandstand. It was then that Nessheim saw a man standing on the top wing, waving. He'd never forgotten the thrill of that sight, but although Nessheim had seen plenty of planes since then, he had never flown in one himself.

Leaving Livermore, he knew he had until seven p.m., and he just made it. He left the Bureau car in the airport parking lot, with the keys shoved under the front seat, and ran to the terminal, a new stucco building painted a bilious green. Finding the ticket counter for United Airlines he was glad he had kept his local chequing account, since there was no way he had cash for the $137 his ticket was going to cost.

There was just one problem: United Airlines flight number 4 was full.

He listened with disbelief as the woman behind the counter, whose name tag said

Maureen, told him he could always fly down to Burbank and hope there'd be a seat going for the east coast on the day's last flight. She didn't sound optimistic. Otherwise, he would have to wait until the next day.

He looked at his watch: it was six forty-five. The flight was leaving in fifteen minutes, and unless he acted fast it would be leaving without him. He didn't know what Stephenson could have discovered that made Guttman want Nessheim back in D.C. so fast, but he couldn't reach Guttman to argue.

He considered his options. He could show his FBI ID and try to bluster his way on, hoping to occupy an empty air hostess's seat or the jump seat in the cockpit. But he would need to invoke higher authority — SAC Morgan at the very least, who had made it clear he was heartily sick of helping Nessheim.

But then he found an easier solution. Seventy-five bucks persuaded a young lawyer for a shipping company, half-cut from waiting at the terminal's bar, that he would be happy to stay an extra day in the city of fog. There was a slight hiccup when Nessheim offered a cheque in payment, but here his FBI identification card did come in helpful, convincing the lawyer that his cheque wouldn't bounce.

Five minutes later, holding his small canvas bag, Nessheim went outside in the early-evening breeze and crossed the tarmac, eyeing the plane apprehensively, ducking as the propellers started up and whipped the air around his head. The plane seemed big enough — maybe too big when he thought of what it had to do to get off the ground. As he climbed the steps to its open door, he only hoped that Guttman's sense of urgency was not misplaced.

The plane was a new model DC-3, a sleeper service, and inside he found it shaped like a giant cigar tube, with facing pairs of seats, four rows on the left side and three on the right, where the galley occupied the missing space. A pretty gal in a blue jacket and matching skirt led him to his seat and asked him if he'd like something to drink.

At take-off, he looked out the window as they accelerated down the runway, hoping they weren't about to end in the Bay. It seemed to go on for ever, the aeroplane straining to gain speed, until its nose lifted and the wings shuddered, and he could feel the wheels leave the ground. They hovered for a minute, dangerously low, then soared quite sharply upwards. Any parallels with the Pullman he'd normally take stopped when he thought of how this 'train' was airborne, floating through air with none of the reassuring connection of rails.

They climbed through cloud just as he spied the peaks of the High Sierra in the distance, reddish crags highlighted by the setting sun and topped by snow. The plane shuddered and shook, then the turbulence subsided and they levelled off. A few minutes later, the pilot came back and shook hands with everyone, announcing that they were flying at 23,000 feet.

'Is the co-pilot flying the plane?' a woman passenger asked nervously.

'What co-pilot?' he said, and everybody laughed.

Nessheim had a bourbon and ginger ale with his meal, which was served on china with silver cutlery and a linen napkin. He ate chicken fricassee and potato croquettes and string beans, all served hot. There was even strawberry pie with ice cream for dessert.

When the hostess took away his tray, she explained that the seats would be turned into beds after dinner, and that Nessheim had the upper bunk, which unfolded from the ceiling. He decided that if he were going to die on his way east, at least he would do so in comfort.

But he could not relax, because he was angry with himself. He should have seen it before — it was obvious now, looking back: Mueller's connections with the *Bund* chapter out in Livermore, and his casual reference to growing up 'down the road' in Dublin; his prejudices — how he hated Guttman the Heeb, with no time for the Chinese or Negroes either. Plus the fact that he had listened to short-wave broadcasts from Germany.

Mueller must have killed Bock, probably because Bock's friendship with Beringer linked him to Werner — who would have been Mueller's contact with the Nazis once Jahnke had left America. In Austria Werner had been murdered as well — another man who had knowledge of the *Dreiländer*'s identity.

He was surprised that as a boy 'Mueller' had been allowed by the Nazis to adopt his new family's German-sounding name, and surprised too by the way the grown Mueller had felt free to

465

spout vehement anti-Roosevelt views. But in Washington, of course, Mueller had the best kind of cover, working for the FBI. And it had got him to the White House, within striking distance of the President. No wonder Mueller had been happy to take a job most senior agents wouldn't touch.

After dinner the hostess drew the curtains around each set of bunk beds. Nessheim stripped to his skivvies and climbed up. He found it impossible to sleep and was wide awake when they hit the runway with an enormous thump at Salt Lake City. No one got off, no one got on; twenty minutes later, refuelled, they were again rolling down a runway and, as Nessheim held his breath, implausibly rising into the air.

He must have dozed off, for when they came over the east side of the Front Range in Colorado they encountered sudden turbulence that made him sit up with a start, convinced the plane had crashed. Up and down they went. Each time they achieved some equilibrium, the plane would shake and drop and bump, and Nessheim would be convinced they were falling out of the sky again.

He hated being so scared. He knew how unlikely it was that they would crash, and he had never had a fear of heights. What was the problem? Then he realised: if he did go down Mueller's secret would go down with him. Why hadn't Guttman answered the phone? And why hadn't Nessheim thought to write the answer to the question on a postcard and mail it to Guttman?

He fell asleep at last. He was only dimly awake at their next stop. 'We're in North Platte,' he heard a hostess tell someone in another bunk. Refuelling only, so he couldn't get off. He remembered the town from his jaunt west along the Lincoln Highway. He wondered if the surly farmer was still on the land west of there, and the girl — *Ain't you gonna kiss me?* It seemed another lifetime now.

He woke when morning came and they drifted through Iowa, descending slowly towards Chicago. He got dressed and did a basin wash in the bathroom at the rear of the plane. When he returned the bed had been put back in the ceiling and he sat down again. There was nothing to do but wait, and in Chicago they weren't allowed off even to stretch their legs.

At Cleveland he had to change planes, to a daytime version that was seats only. He had almost an hour and tried calling Guttman again, but there was no answer. This time he took the precaution before boarding of mailing a note to Guttman at his home. He wrote elliptically in case Guttman's mail was being opened on Hoover's orders.

Speak to a woman who owns the old Jahnke house on 4th Street in Livermore. Her name is Koehler. She knows the family who bought the house from Jahnke, and says Dreiländer was 'adopted' by them when Jahnke left town.

J

467

He landed in Washington just after two-thirty in the afternoon, having added Akron and Pittsburgh to the itinerary of intermediate stops. He called Guttman's house and the phone was answered right away — again by a woman.

'Is Harry there?' he asked.

'Who's calling?'

'Tell him it's Rossbach,' he said, using the alias from Camp Schneider.

'Could you hold on a minute, please?'

He waited impatiently, looking through the window as two men in blue shorts and T-shirts pushed long-handled carts holding the passengers' bags. At last the woman picked up the phone again. 'Mr Guttman says on no account go to the office. He wants you to meet him at the bar by the Potomac tonight at ten.'

'I can come out right now.'

'No, that won't be possible.'

He said sharply, 'Let me speak to Mr Guttman, please.'

'I'm sorry, that's not possible either.'

His voice hardened. 'Tell him I need to speak to him now.'

'I don't think you understand, sir. I was talking to Mr Guttman on the other phone line. He's in New Jersey — he won't be back until after supper.'

★ ★ ★

He had six hours to wait so he went to the House of Youth. None of his colleagues at the Bureau knew where he lived, so there was no

468

reason to think Mueller would be coming for him there, or anyone else. And despite the pull-down bed and munificent service in the air, he realised he was drained from the last twenty-four hours. His 'one' flight east had entailed seven sets of take-offs and landings.

He took a taxi, making it clear to the driver before they'd even left the airport that he didn't want to talk. Nessheim had him drop him off a block away and took his time walking to the house, checking the tree-lined street carefully for any waiting, occupied cars.

The coast was clear. He went into the house and back to the kitchen, where messages were left for the lodgers. There was nothing for him, just a note pinned with a tack on the table for Plympton. He hesitated, then unpinned the paper.

Frank,
We've all gone out to Sally's in Virginia. Call and say what bus you're catching and I'll come pick you up in Burke. See you tomorrow.
Doobs

So Plympton was away, but would be back in time to join the gang in Virginia for Decoration Day. Good, thought Nessheim. He wouldn't have to duck their company while he sorted out what to do, since there was no longer any chance that Nessheim would be invited, too.

★ ★ ★

469

He left the house at nine, half an hour after sunset, grateful it was dark. He was going against the flow of traffic — residents of Washington were leaving town for the one-day holiday, so it only took him twenty minutes to reach the river and find the sign, *Steamers*. This time the bar was crowded, full of the white workers from the next-door factory already celebrating their day off. The man with the nickel-sized wart was behind the counter, pulling beers; next to him a fat woman with dyed blonde hair was serving Sloppy Joes on hamburger buns, and slabs of freshly fried fish, gleaming with grease, which she slathered in mayonnaise and stuck between the mountainous halves of large soft rolls.

He saw Guttman in a corner, sitting by himself with two full bottles of beer. Spying Nessheim, Guttman got up and disappeared into the back. Nessheim found him outside, sitting at a solitary picnic table. In the darkness of the bar's back yard, he was eerily highlighted by light spilling like paint from a window upstairs, where a noisy private party was going on.

'You made it,' Guttman said.

'I called you from the coast but some woman wouldn't accept the call.'

'That was the helper — she didn't know who you were.' He looked bone tired, but there was life in his voice again. 'I've been to Princeton and back — 320 miles round trip.'

He sounded so triumphant that Nessheim didn't interrupt with news of his own discovery. Guttman explained, 'Princeton's got a little centre where they monitor foreign broadcasts in

English. The prick who runs it wouldn't help me over the phone, so I went there myself. Have a look,' he said, taking a piece of paper from his jacket's inner pocket.

Nessheim took it and put it down on the table. In a patch of light he peered at the paper, which was part of a typed transcript:

Announcer: *This is Germany Calling, Germany Calling, Germany Calling.*
Lord Haw-Haw: Tonight I want to speak directly to our American friends, who must be looking with concern on events of Europe. There are those in that country who would like to join in the unfortunate war now spreading across all of this continent, but I think we can see through them easily enough. Money-men, financiers, lackeys of the House of Rothschild — the usual predators who profiteer from the misery of common men at war.

We in Germany have no fight with the United States. After all, there are more people of German descent in that new country than of any other nation. Those descendants of Aryan stock will understand at once that the Reich bears no ill will towards its far-western neighbour.

As this momentous Decoration Day

in America approaches, I say to those of you who listen with open minds and decent hearts, that the best way ahead for America is peace, not war.

The transcript ended:

Before I bid you goodnight, I have a few messages for special friends. Spectre, watch the moon ascending. Donegal, continue as before. Dreiländer, the time is right.
To all of you, goodbye. May peace be with you and the United States.

Nessheim looked at Guttman, whose face was half in light and half in shadow. 'Dreiländer.'

Guttman nodded. 'That's right.'

'How did you know where to look for this?'

'Stephenson. It was all his doing.' Guttman seemed happy to credit the Canadian. 'We were trying to figure out how the Dreiländer would receive his orders. His contact Werner was dead, Jahnke's in Germany, and the letters from Lady Dove don't lead anywhere. So I wondered if they could be using radio sets — the Nazis we arrested in New York last year were using them to contact Berlin.

'But Stephenson said nah, it'd be too risky — if the Dreiländer got caught with a transmitter-receiver the game would be up. But that's when Stephenson had a eureka moment

— *why not a normal radio broadcast?* There's nothing suspicious about listening to the radio, and what safer way to reach the *Dreiländer* — since only he will understand the message?'

Nessheim said, 'You can listen to German broadcasts here on short wave.' Mueller had.

'Exactly. They've got this guy Lord Haw-Haw giving propaganda talks in English. Stephenson says his real name's Joyce; he's American-born but lived in England for years. So I went to Princeton to go through the transcripts, and this is what I found.' Guttman stabbed a stubby finger at the paper. 'I figure that's the trigger — *the time is right*.' Then his face fell, and he sighed. 'What I don't know is who the message is for.'

Nessheim could contain himself no longer. 'I do.'

'You do? Why didn't you say so?' asked Guttman in astonishment.

'The Dreiländer is Jake Mueller.'

'*Mueller?* Are you sure about this?'

'I am.' Nessheim told Guttman about his discovery in Livermore, then looked at him anxiously. 'What do we do now? There isn't enough proof to bring charges against Mueller. You and I may know it's him, but what real evidence do we have? Just a long chain of coincidences.'

Inexplicably, Guttman was smiling happily; Nessheim wondered if the drive to Jersey had been too much for him.

Guttman said, 'I've got good news and bad news, kid.'

473

'Get the bad out of the way.'

'Mueller's discovered that the President's been using Cummings's house as a rendezvous. I don't think he knows what FDR is doing there, but he's on to something.'

'How the hell did he find out?'

'It doesn't matter — in a way it even helps. Let me tell you the good news. Mueller's in Canada with Eleanor Roosevelt — way out in Calgary. That buys us some time.'

'Are you sure?'

'Yeah. Marie talked to him yesterday on the phone — I told her to make up some excuse to call him. I don't trust the bastard either, though I never had him down as a Nazi.'

Harry the Heeb, thought Nessheim. He said, 'Mueller will be back at some point. How do we protect the President then?'

'By that time Hoover will know. He wants to see me first thing on Friday morning. I want you there too. In fact, I *need* you there. You can tell the Director everything you've discovered out in California. After that, he won't let Mueller within a million miles of FDR.'

'We've still got no real proof.'

'We don't need to.' Guttman gave a great sigh of relief. 'Until you showed tonight, all I had for Hoover was this Haw-Haw stuff — but I couldn't have told him who the transmission was going to. When he hears Mueller's cousin is the Chief of the Gestapo he's got to have another think, even if he doesn't accept that Jahnke planted Mueller years ago. After all, what if I went to the press, like your old hero Melvin

474

Purvis? Can you see Drew Pearson's column asking why the FBI hired a leading Nazi's cousin and let him guard the President?' He shook his head. 'No, Hoover will have to act. And we can take our time to build the case against Mueller.'

Nessheim finished his beer and put the empty bottle on the picnic table. 'What do you really think of Mr Hoover? I mean, did you used to like him?'

Guttman looked thoughtful. 'I don't really know how to answer that. He hired me, and I've been at the Bureau a long time — twelve years; I started only four years after he took over. Back then he was still a person. But the truth is, liking Mr Hoover doesn't come into it. Not that he gives a damn if you like him or not, either. I respect him — he's done a lot. The Bureau was nothing until he got here. To that extent, I'm grateful to Hoover, as any American should be.'

Nessheim tried and failed to suppress a yawn. Guttman said, 'Anyway, you should get some rest. Take it easy tomorrow — it's a holiday after all. Whatever you do, don't go into the office.'

'Okay,' said Nessheim.

'Before you go, tell me about the aeroplane; I've never been on one. Were you scared? Jesus, I would have been.'

'Nah,' said Nessheim, trying not to think of the fear he'd felt when they hit turbulence over the Front Range of the Rockies. 'It was a piece of cake.'

35

He got back to the House of Youth after midnight. On the kitchen table there was a message for him, taken by his landlord.

Miss Ryerson asks that you please go to Belvedere at noon tomorrow.

What did Annie want? Was she coming in from Virginia to give him the audience he had requested? If so, she probably just wanted to lambaste him again for his probes into her past. He didn't allow himself to hope she might have something else to tell him.

The upstairs hallway was pitch dark, and Nessheim was glad to know that Mueller was in Canada. He jammed a chair under his room's door knob, nonetheless, and slept with his .38 tucked under a second pillow on his bed. During the night he woke once, and wondered what had stirred him. Was that the faint noise of a footfall on the stairs? He strained to listen but it had stopped. He fell asleep again, convinced he had imagined it.

He slept late, almost until ten, excusing himself with the thought that it was only seven a.m. out in California. When the sun came through the window he got up and took a bath, shaved, and dressed. He wore a jacket despite the sunny warmth of the day because he didn't know if he was dressing for business or not. And that way he could wear his gun and holster. You never knew.

He timed his walk perfectly, reaching the Belvedere gates exactly at noon. They were closed but when he pushed they gave way, and he walked up the drive, feeling like a penitent rather than a guest. The house looked stark and cold, despite the increasing warmth of the day. He went round the back, where he rang the back doorbell. After a minute he heard steps on the kitchen's hard tile floor, then the door opened.

'Jimmy! How good to see you. Come on in.' It was Frank Plympton, dressed for the weekend — a blue short-sleeved cotton shirt and khaki trousers.

Nessheim was embarrassed. Would Annie have confided in Frank what he had written to her from the train; would she have said the 'G-Man' was sweet on her? Even if she had, Frank was being friendly, perhaps out of a victor's magnanimity.

Nessheim took a hesitant step into the kitchen. Plympton said, 'You looking for Annie? Come on upstairs.'

They went through the deserted spic-and-span kitchen, its big range cold and gleaming from polish, then out into the hall and up the grand staircase. Frank was talking, but Nessheim barely heard him. What a mistake this was. He didn't know what he would say to Annie now, especially with Frank present. Was there some way he could pretend he'd never sent the letter? No. Was there some hole he could crawl into instead? No again, and with each step he was abandoning all chance of making his excuses and getting out of there.

They reached the landing upstairs, and went past the elevator and the first guest bedroom to the open door of Annie's converted office. He took a deep breath and followed Plympton in. Annie wasn't there. He was disappointed, and relieved.

Plympton said, 'I'll go find where she's got to, Jimmy. Have a seat.'

Nessheim perched uneasily on the Shaker chair Annie kept in a corner between her desk and the window. He felt slightly depressed, since clearly Annie didn't want to have a heart-to-heart, not if Plympton was around.

He heard Plympton coming down the hall from the bedroom. 'In a minute,' Plympton said, as he re-entered the room. He added cheerfully, 'I'm sure you'll be happy to wait.'

'What do you mean?' said Nessheim, with a robustness he didn't feel.

'Don't you know?' said Plympton. His voice was still friendly.

'Frank, if this is about Annie, then let me explain.'

To his surprise, Plympton seemed amused. 'I saw your letter,' he said. 'It's in the drawer over there.'

'Then you know there's been nothing — '

Plympton cut him off. 'Kind of nice, I thought. Reading it, I realised that a message from Annie would make you come running.' He looked at his watch. 'Won't be long now.'

As they sat awkwardly in silence — Nessheim

on the Shaker chair, Plympton on the swivel chair behind the desk — he wished Annie would hurry up.

'Pretty warm today,' Plympton remarked, opening one of the desk drawers. 'Take your jacket off, why don't you?'

'That's all right,' said Nessheim. He would feel too self-conscious, sitting in his shirtsleeves with a holstered .38 hanging from his shoulder.

'They'll be saddling up just about now,' said Plympton, looking at his watch. It was expensive — a Bulova, which Annie had given him as an engagement present. Nessheim knew this because she had shown it to him and Dubinsky first, asking if they approved.

Then he thought about what Plympton had said. 'Who's 'they'?' he asked.

Plympton looked at Nessheim with curiosity. 'Sally and the others, of course.'

Plympton was still rummaging in the drawer as Nessheim looked out the window. The garage was empty — usually there were two cars in it. Sally would have the big Plymouth in Virginia, but with Annie here, he'd expect to see the other one — a Buick — which she would use to drive Plympton out to Five Forks. He was about to ask where the Buick was when Plympton said, 'Take your jacket off, Jimmy.'

His tone made Nessheim look over. Plympton was standing by the desk now, screwing a four-inch silencer onto the barrel of a .22 calibre pistol.

'Jesus, Frank. Is that thing loaded? Be careful.'

'Of course,' said Plympton calmly and swung

the pistol until its barrel, elongated by the silencer, was aimed right at Nessheim. 'Stand up, Jimmy, but keep your hands away from your body. Then I want you to take your jacket off. Very carefully.'

'What's this about?' Nessheim demanded.

'Go on, do it. And I have to warn you: if your hand so much as brushes your holster it will be the last thing you ever touch.'

Plympton said this so cheerfully that Nessheim was too stunned to react, but when the man impatiently waved the pistol Nessheim stood up right away, keeping his hands in the air. Taking painstaking care not to touch his .38, he pulled back both lapels of his jacket as if he were packing them in a suitcase, and wriggling first one shoulder, then the other, let the jacket fall in a heap on the floor.

'Good. Now we're going to do the same with the pistol. Take your hand and pull the holster strap down your arm. If you touch the gun I'll shoot.'

Plympton said this in the tone of a grown-up warning a small child not to play near the fire. Nessheim did as he was told.

'Now drop the whole shebang onto the jacket.' Nessheim did this, too, though the protruding butt of his .38 missed the coat and landed with a thud on the floor.

Plympton frowned and moved from behind the desk. Without looking he kicked the holster and gun across the carpet towards the door to the hall. He motioned Nessheim to sit down again in the Shaker chair. Once he had,

Plympton moved back and squatted to pick up the Smith & Wesson .38, all the while keeping his gun trained on Nessheim. Reaching for the shelf of the bookcase, he put Nessheim's pistol down. Then he stood facing him, keeping his distance.

'Take it easy, Jimmy,' he said gently. 'It won't be long now.'

And suddenly Nessheim understood what was going to happen. He couldn't believe it at first; it upset everything he and Guttman had agreed the day before, overturned all their carefully deduced conclusions.

This empty house was perfect for a meeting that wasn't meant to be observed — like this one. But also for another, more intimate one. They weren't waiting for Annie, and Plympton wasn't jealous or angry with him. He had a different agenda.

'I've got it, Frank,' he said abruptly.

Plympton looked surprised but not discomfited. 'You do?'

'We're waiting for the President and his friend Mrs Rutherford.'

'Clever boy.'

'Do you mean to kill them?' It seemed best to get the cards out on the table.

'I do, Jimmy. Though they won't ever think it was me. It's your name that will go down in history.'

'You think *I'm* going to pull the trigger?'

'Of course not. But it will look that way. Distraught by news of Annie's engagement, so crazed with jealousy that you're out of your mind, you commit a double homicide. Then sanity returns and you decide to turn the weapon on yourself. The tragedy of your suicide will be lost in the outpouring of grief about the double murder. I mean, no one remembers that John Wilkes Booth was a pretty good actor, now do they?'

'And where are you meant to have been while all this plays out?'

'I wasn't feeling well when I got back from Montana. I overslept and didn't find Dubinsky's note. I came here in the hopes of seeing my fiancée, arriving just after the catastrophe.' Plympton spoke with such sincerity that Nessheim momentarily wondered if he actually believed the scenario was true.

'Is that why you're using a silencer?'

Plympton looked down at the extended barrel of his gun. 'I prefer the European term — suppressor. It's especially effective with a low-calibre bullet. The neighbours might recall hearing it later, but it won't be enough to alarm them at the time.'

'And then what happens to you?'

He paused. 'Who knows? In the aftermath, I might as well marry Annie. Her aunt's awfully well-connected, and any scandal attached to her role as the President's procuress is going to be swept under one hell of a carpet. *FBI Man Goes Berserk* — that will be the story, and the explanation that becomes common currency in future. You won't hear much about Lucy Mercer Rutherford.'

'Why are you going to do this? I don't understand.'

'Don't you?' Plympton seemed to survey Nessheim afresh. 'Think about it. Belgium's fallen, Holland's fallen; any day now, France will surrender. That leaves only the English, who are a tougher nut to crack, and won't give up right away. The best way forward is to get them to see that their position is hopeless, and let them make peace — on our terms, of course. But as long as they think there's any chance of America coming in on their side they'll try and tough it out.

'Six weeks from now the Democrats will nominate their presidential candidate. A movement to draft Roosevelt is gaining momentum; believe me, I know — Hopkins is one of its spearheads. But if Roosevelt isn't around to be nominated, then Garner will get it, and he'll keep America out of the war. So will the Republican candidate — Wilkie might make pro-war noises, but I saw a Gallup Poll the other day that only gave him eight per cent of the vote. It doesn't matter who gets elected in November provided it isn't Roosevelt.'

Plympton gave a small smile. 'At that point even the English will see the writing on the wall. They're not lunatics, and they'll sue for peace.'

'Doubtless,' said Nessheim, but he was thinking of how Plympton had phrased something. 'You said *our* terms a minute ago. Are you telling me you're German?'

'*Ja*,' he said with a schoolboy's grin.

'How did you get to be called Plympton then?'

'My 'father',' and there was nothing filial in his tone, 'owned a saloon in California. His real name was 'Plumholtz', but he changed it when

483

he bought the bar during the last war. Better for business not to have a German-sounding name.'

'Don't tell me,' said Nessheim, suddenly recalling his evening in the same establishment with Mueller and the members of the local *Bund*. 'The bar was in Dublin.'

Plympton looked startled again. 'Dubinsky mentioned you'd gone to California. You were digging into *my* past while you were out there?'

'Another agent took me to a German party there a couple of years ago.'

'That must have been Mueller.'

'You know him?'

'I knew anyone who was German and lived near Dublin.'

'So Mueller's been working with you?'

'Of course not,' said Plympton, looking offended by the suggestion. 'Mueller's an idiot.'

'But Jahnke wasn't, I suppose.'

Plympton looked stung. 'You don't know anything about him.'

'I know he brought you over as a boy. I understand Mueller was adopted. Did Jahnke bring him over from Germany too?'

Plympton nodded. 'Yes, though not with any specific instructions.'

'So Mueller was just cover for you?'

'Yes. Herr Jahnke never failed to cover all eventualities. He's a very clever man.'

'I'm sure,' said Nessheim. 'But Mueller wasn't very discreet. He hung around with the *Bund*.'

'Big surprise — idiots love idiots.' Plympton gave a regretful sigh. 'Sadly, the *Bund* demonstrates what happens when people are transplanted:

they're inevitably enfeebled by their new environs. That's the failing of this country — its premise that it's a melting pot hides a fatal weakness.'

'You're going back to your Fatherland then?'

Plympton shook his head. 'It's too late for that. I honour my country, and do its bidding, but there's no point pretending I could ever feel at home there. That was all sacrificed when my mother had me sent over here.'

'So this country has weakened you too?'

Plympton didn't like that; for the first time his face showed irritation. Nessheim backed off. It was important not to press gratuitously. He'd been taught that during a training session on hostage-taking, an increasing phenomenon in which bank robbers ended up surrounded, but holding a gun to a terrified teller's head.

'Why the code name?' Nessheim asked. 'Why *Dreiländer*?'

Again Plympton looked startled. Then he regained his composure. 'My birth name was Seitz — my parents were Austrian, from Villach. It's *Dreiländer* territory — you know what that means?'

'I know German — think of my surname.'

'Pity you don't honour it more,' Plympton said lightly.

Nessheim said, 'That's also where Werner was killed. The Nazis shot him in the head at point-blank range.'

'Did they? I can't say the news comes as a surprise. Werner was something of a loose cannon.'

Nessheim made a stab in the dark. 'Like Bock?'

'What do you know about that?' Plympton seemed happy to tell Nessheim things, less happy to discover Nessheim already knew some of them. It was important to keep him off guard that way; Nessheim sensed his only chance lay in Plympton's thinking the FBI was on to him.

'I know it wasn't suicide, though it was meant to look like it. Not everybody at the Bureau is as dumb as you think Mueller is. But why did Bock have to die?'

'He'd served his purpose, by making you think the *Bund* was full of conspiring masterminds.' He gave a deprecating laugh. 'But there was always a chance he knew more than he should. I had standing orders to remove anyone who might know of my background. I'm sorry about the coloured boy, but it seemed the best way to make the suicide look genuine. Thank God they were the only people I had to kill,' said Plympton, as if he should be the one Nessheim felt sorry for. 'The ex-Ambassador, Herr Luther, didn't trust Werner; he thought he might be reading his cables. And since Luther knew about me from Werner, I was worried I'd have to kill him, too. Fortunately Berlin recalled him first.'

Nessheim felt like a rat in an experiment on overfeeding, his mind racing to keep up. Plympton said, 'What else do you know about me?' He now seemed genuinely curious, student-like, in the same way he had formerly asked Nessheim lots of questions about the Bureau.

'I know that you're a big feature in the letters of Lady Dove to Mrs Cummings.'

'I bet I am.' Plympton sounded genuinely pleased.

'Is that why you went to England five years ago?'

'Partly. I wanted to see the Justice too. I don't share the Party's hatred of the Jews. If it was up to me, I'd evict them all from Germany — Madagascar seems to be the latest idea. But as long as they're not in the country I haven't got a problem with them.'

'That's big of you. So you got to know Lady Dove when you were there?'

'Of course — Werner told me she would be my contact with Berlin if war broke out. He seemed to know he was being pushed aside, though I doubt he had any idea they were going to kill him.' He gave a shake of his head and whistled through his teeth. 'God, she was a lousy lay. I guess I was supposed to think it was a privilege screwing her.'

'Maybe she thought *you* were bad in bed.'

'I don't get complaints,' Plympton said.

It was the first sign of vanity in the man, and Nessheim wondered what Annie made of Plympton's prowess. As if reading his thoughts, Plympton said with a wry smile, 'Cheer up, fellah. I never had Annie, if that's what you're wondering. Not my type.'

'How romantic.'

Plympton laughed. It was the same easy laugh as before. He said, 'She's a good girl and I'll do my duty. We may even have kids. But that was not the attraction, if you get my drift.'

'What was the lure then?'

'Don't be silly,' said Plympton, as if he were disappointed in Nessheim. 'How else could I get close to him?' He shook his head. 'I know you didn't finish college, Jimmy, but I figured you to be a little brighter. I mean, you had the answer sitting in your hands — Annie told me you forced her to show you the letters Lady Dove wrote to Sally. But you didn't get it — you thought they were just about putting me and Annie together.'

'Weren't they?' It didn't matter in the slightest now, but he still wanted to know.

'Of course not. They told me how the order would come. Then all I had to do was listen to the short-wave radio.'

Nessheim remembered now. Lady Dove had mentioned listening to the propaganda broadcasts from Berlin — how they had amused her and her friend. That must have been the tip-off to Frank that the order to strike would come over the air. He said firmly, 'It seems a pretty roundabout way to give you orders.'

'Intentionally so; it was safer that way. With Werner gone, there was no one else to give me away. Though as it turned out, you could have got there if you were a bit sharper. Thank God you're not.'

But Nessheim ignored him, thinking what this meant. 'So Sally was the conduit. Does that mean she knew all about this . . . this plot?'

'Well,' Plympton began, but stopped when there was the sound of a car in the drive.

488

Nessheim glanced out the window and saw a large Plymouth pull into the turn-around between the kitchen door and the garage. He looked back at Plympton, whose voice for the first time betrayed his tension. 'Don't even think of shouting for help, or I'll shoot you right away.'

They didn't have long to wait. There was the noise of steps in the kitchen below, then in the hall on the stairs. Then the sound of the door closing in the room next to them.

They sat in silence, as Nessheim tried to imagine the scene in the adjacent room. Did Lucy Rutherford sit patiently waiting or would she be nervous, pat her hair as she looked in the mirror, and reapply her lipstick?

Only moments later there was the sound of another car out back. A door slammed, but when Nessheim saw the tension in Plympton's face he didn't dare take another look out the window. This time it took longer, and he thought he even heard voices downstairs — perhaps the President had his chauffeur wheel him in. A light hydraulic whine filled the air; the elevator was moving. The elevator door emitted its faint hiss and then Nessheim heard what he knew must be a wheelchair move across the hallway carpet. There was no knock on the door, just the noise of it opening and clunking shut.

It won't be much longer now, Nessheim thought, and he watched as Plympton stood listening intently, his back to the door to the hall. Presumably he would give the lovers time to get undressed; that way they would be even more vulnerable when he came through the door. He would have shot Nessheim by then, through the temple probably. Then he'd come back after killing Roosevelt and his mistress, remove the silencer, wipe the gun clean and wrap Nessheim's inert hand around it, then let the gun fall to the floor next to Nessheim's body. The set of fingerprints would tell an irrefutable story.

Nessheim had been here before: he remembered the cold water of the Atlantic as *The Braunau* had motored away. He felt the same impotence now, and he had no doubts about Plympton's determination. If he tried to do anything, he would merely accelerate the disaster that was about to happen.

Suddenly he noticed a shadow on the carpet in the hallway. Had it been there before? Could someone be lurking in the hall? The President's chauffeur, perhaps, though why would he be standing just outside the room of the illicit lovers? Anyway, thought Nessheim gloomily, the chauffeur wouldn't be armed. Plympton would shoot him too before he opened the connecting door and went into the next room.

Then he saw the toe of a shoe edge an inch or so into the open doorway. He averted his eyes, and made a point of returning Plympton's gaze. Though he resisted the temptation to glance past him, he was gradually aware of a figure coming into view.

Plympton suddenly spoke, in the tones of a vet proposing to put down a client's dog. 'This will be painless, Jimmy, if you let it be. You won't feel a thing. I'm going to come closer now, and then

I'm going to tell you to shut your eyes.'

'No, you're not,' said a woman's voice.

Nessheim looked behind Plympton and saw Annie standing in the doorway. She had picked up Nessheim's .38 and was pointing it at Plympton's back.

'Don't turn around, Frank. I've got the gun.'

'Darling, it's not what it seems. I found Jimmy here. That's his gun, and I took it off him. I think he means to shoot the President.'

'I don't think so. I heard what you were saying, Frank.' There was a slight waver in Annie's voice.

'I don't know what you think you heard, darling; I was telling Jimmy here what I thought he planned to do.'

Nessheim noticed Plympton was moving each shoulder. It was distracting, which must have been the point. Fortunately Annie understood this. 'Stop moving,' she said sharply, and Nessheim saw she had a firm grip on the gun.

'Sure,' said Plympton, suddenly standing still. 'Whatever you say.' His gun was still pointed right at Nessheim's forehead, and he said with the same easy insouciant voice, 'You've got me covered, Annie, but I've got lover boy here covered as well. If I hear your trigger starting to move I'm going to make sure Jimmy goes first.'

The lines were drawn. Annie seemed to hesitate, and for a moment Nessheim thought she was going to lower her weapon. He had to take the risk and speak. 'Annie, if he's going to shoot me, then let him — just be sure you shoot him too. Otherwise, he's going into the room next door to kill the President. Do you understand?' She looked stunned. 'Do you understand?' he repeated sternly, trying to administer a verbal slap in the face.

She nodded and he was glad to see her tighten her grip on his gun.

'Annie,' said Plympton, and he was rolling his shoulders again. 'Why on earth did you come back?'

She hesitated before speaking, and her voice was brittle. 'I was worried you wouldn't have found Doob's note; I was going to come round the house. I wanted to make sure you were coming to Five Forks.' She added, suddenly forlorn, 'I didn't expect this.'

'I bet you didn't,' said Plympton, and now each time he moved a shoulder he was turning slightly, so that he was no longer standing with his back facing Annie but at an angle that was gradually widening. Nessheim saw that Plympton was using the cover of talk to disguise the fact that he was moving. It was Danny Ho all over again, but Nessheim was watching the re-enactment without a gun in his hand. He felt paralysed, like a mouse cowering beneath a reared-up snake.

Plympton was saying, 'You've managed to stop whatever you think was going on.'

Annie looked mystified and Nessheim realised Plympton was about to make his move.

'Shoot him!' Nessheim shouted and he jumped straight out of his chair at Plympton, hurtling into him just as he fired. There was a muffled bang and Nessheim's head hit Plympton in the stomach. As he threw his arms around the man to bring him down there was another explosion, much louder. Plympton fell down with Nessheim on top of him, dropping his gun. When Nessheim lifted up his head to throw a punch at Plympton's jaw he realised there was no point. Plympton wasn't moving. His mouth was open, lips pronouncing an unspoken *Oh* of surprise. It was the startled look of a dead man, and when Nessheim pulled his arm free from underneath Plympton's back, he found blood running all over his hand.

Annie was standing stock-still, staring in disbelief at the gun she still held. Nessheim got up slowly, feeling inexplicable pain in one side. It was then that he realised Plympton had fired too, and that blood was seeping through his shirt, low down, just above his pelvic bone.

Then all hell broke loose. He heard a door smashed open downstairs and people shouting in the kitchen.

'Give me the gun!' he shouted at Annie. The pain in his side was becoming intense.

She looked at him as if she had never seen him before.

'Quick,' he insisted. 'Give it to me.'

She handed it over. He held the pistol by the barrel and winced — the barrel was hot. He put his hand on its grip and moved it around, trying to make sure his prints obscured any of hers. Then he remembered the trigger and put his finger carefully inside the guard, placing it on the thin slip of metal.

He looked over at Annie and found her staring

at him. He said, hearing his own urgency, 'They'll be here any second. Whatever they ask, you have to say I shot Frank.' He could hear people pounding up the stairs. 'Do you understand?' he demanded again.

Seconds later a man burst into the room with his gun drawn. When he saw Plympton on the floor he pointed his gun at Nessheim, who let his fall to the floor as he raised his hands straight up in the air. From next door he heard a shout of surprise — agents had gone in there without any pretence of knocking. The interlocking door opened, and Reuters, the young FBI agent from the White House detail, was standing there, his gun drawn.

Through the doorway Nessheim caught a glimpse of Lucy Mercer Rutherford, sitting up in the two-poster bed in a lilac robe, a look of absolute terror on her face. The President was in the Shaker chair in the foreground, and he was dressed — except for his socks and shoes. The door closed as soon as Reuters saw that another agent was covering Nessheim.

'Let me explain,' Nessheim said to the Secret Service man.

'Save it,' said the agent. 'You're going to get to tell your story more than once.'

Epilogue

September 1940
Washington D.C.

It seemed strange to be parking right in front of Guttman's house.

Nessheim had listened to the radio on his way from the airport and was glad to hear that the polls said Roosevelt was leading in all the key states. His re-election seemed certain. It wasn't time for a novice in the White House, Nessheim thought, much less an isolationist. Germany had yet to invade England, and its air assaults, though severe, had not brought Great Britain to its knees. It looked as if the recalcitrant English might finally get some help from the U.S. Not that much admittedly, but it was a start, and it certainly made clear whose side America was on.

He got out, still feeling a little stiff. It had been a luxury to fly from Chicago, and the fear he had felt on his first trip on a plane had not recurred. He had enjoyed the flight, marvelling at the height they had reached and the fact that he was so far above the clouds.

He had come back without reluctance because Guttman had said he wanted to talk to him about his future. He had almost died twice working for the man, yet somehow this intensified rather than attenuated their bond. Not that he would continue working for the FBI;

although he had not yet submitted a letter of resignation, it was only a matter of time.

'Jimmy,' said Guttman warmly as he opened the door and shook his hand. He didn't seem as fat, and he was wearing a new suit and a handsome crimson tie. There was an air of energy about him that reminded Nessheim of their first encounter in Chicago.

Guttman's suspension had been rescinded the day after Frank Plympton had been shot dead in Belvedere. Hoover had wanted his assistant director's cooperation in making sure word never leaked about the attempt on the President's life. The tacit price was Guttman's reinstatement, and a bargain had been struck. When in late June Hoover announced the creation of a new Special Intelligence Section, he also announced that Guttman would be its head.

Mueller had been transferred, after arguing that it was not his fault that a distant cousin was the head of the Gestapo, and that he had no reason to suspect his childhood acquaintance Frank Plympton of anything other than practising the Washington art form of social climbing. Sally Cummings, on the other hand — she, thought Nessheim, was the One Who Got Away.

In the immediate aftermath of Plympton's attempt Cummings escaped particular notice, sharing the shock at what had almost happened, and tending to her niece, who was distraught. And when Guttman finally felt he could ask her for an interview, Sally Cummings had gone to see Hoover instead. After half an hour, the Director had emerged, proclaiming that Sally was innocent of any wrongdoing. Almost simultaneously he'd asked Miss Gandy to arrange an urgent meeting with President Roosevelt at the White House, where Guttman imagined the guest bedroom of Belvedere would have featured in the conversation.

As they walked into the living room Nessheim spied Isabel, Guttman's crippled wife, through the open door of their bedroom. When she smiled shyly at him he felt in a peculiar way that he was on home ground.

In the living room Guttman had set two glasses out. 'Celery soda?' he asked, but before Nessheim could decline he laughed, then went to the kitchen and came back with two bottles of beer.

'So how have you been?' asked Guttman.

'Okay,' said Nessheim slowly. 'My dad died.' It had been the month before, while Nessheim had been driving back from San Francisco after collecting his stuff. His father had dropped dead behind the house, as he was walking towards the barn. Nessheim only just got home in time for the funeral.

Guttman's face sobered. 'I'm so sorry, Jimmy. How's your mom?'

Nessheim shrugged. 'Not too bad. She's selling the place and moving into town. She's got a part-time job in a general store there, so she's keeping busy.' He had offered to stick around on the diminished homestead, with the implicit promise of making another go of it on the land, but his mother had vetoed that right away, saying she didn't want to keep living in a house full of memories.

'Your trip West go okay?'

'It was fine.' Morgan had departed by the time he had arrived, and Nessheim had paid a purely courtesy call on the new SAC, who knew nothing about him. His old friend Devereux was getting married, and had bought a new Chevrolet, so he didn't seem to mind the loss of Nessheim's pickup truck. They'd had lunch in Chinatown on California Street; Nessheim hadn't even caught a glimpse of the fortune cookie factory.

Guttman was pursing his lips, usually the prelude to a proposition. 'You thought about what you're going to do next?'

'A little.' Nessheim wasn't going to volunteer much.

'What if I told you I had a terrific assignment lined up? It suits you to a T. The only downside from your point of view is that you'd still be reporting to me.' He smiled, but he was watching Nessheim closely.

'Harry, no offence, but I don't think D.C. is my kind of town.'

'Who said the job was in Washington? It's on the coast.'

'San Francisco?'

'Try Hollywood,' said Guttman.

'You want me in the movie business?' Nessheim laughed, thinking of Melvin Purvis.

'I do actually,' said Guttman. 'But no, I can't see you on the silver screen myself. You'd be working in a studio.'

Great, Nessheim thought, he would be making the pro-FBI propaganda movies Hoover had already persuaded the studio moguls to produce. No thanks, he thought. But before he could open his mouth, Guttman drained his glass and stood up. 'Think about it, then we can talk some more,' he said. He was looking out the picture window towards the street. 'I've got to go out for a while. You sit still — there's somebody coming who wants to see you.' This time the smile was for himself. 'I think you'll want to see them too.'

★   ★   ★

When the bell rang, Nessheim opened the front door.

'Hi,' she said. He'd always liked the coolness in her voice, the way she didn't gush.

'Hi, Annie,' he said simply. He'd tried writing to her, once from California, then after his father's death, but he had never mailed the letters.

They went into the living room, where after a moment's awkwardness while he took her coat and hat, Annie sat on the sofa and he took the big wing chair.

'It's good to see you,' he said, and though she gave a wan smile, she did not say it back to him. She wore a patterned cotton dress and jacket, and her hair was longer, swept back from her face. It softened her appearance, highlighting the attractiveness of her face, and the power of her surprisingly green-blue eyes.

There was so much to say that he couldn't. 'Are you still working for the Justice?' he managed to ask.

She nodded. 'He's been very understanding. Though I don't think he's invited to Aunt Sally's evenings any more.'

He'll survive, thought Nessheim. He said, 'I thought *you* sent out the invitations.'

'I don't send anything out for Aunt Sally any more.'

'Don't tell me she fired you,' he said lightly.

'Pretty much. And told me to find another place to live. I had two weeks to do it.'

He was stunned. 'What happened?'

'This was one scandal she didn't think I could live down, I guess.'

'She should talk.' Sally had a lot to answer for, not that anyone could prove it. And Hoover had cleared her, to Guttman's fury. 'She's the one who set you up — why should she be angry with you?'

Annie just shrugged.

'Does she know . . . ' and he hesitated.

'No. I didn't tell her that. I haven't told anyone.'

'Good,' he said.

Annie said, 'And since she thinks it was you who killed the Golden Boy, you shouldn't expect any more invitations to Belvedere, either.' She laughed, and he was glad it was more happy than harsh.

He nodded, feeling he couldn't tell her that her aunt's involvement in the affair had been more than social. It seemed pointless as well as cruel to do so.

'So where are you living?' he asked. 'And who looks after Jeff?' He assumed Sally wouldn't let

500

Mrs O'Neill continue to help out.

'Jeff's started school, which makes things easier. I drop him off before I go to the Justice's, then collect him in the mid-afternoon on my way home. It's a long ride on the bus for me, but I can read.'

She hadn't answered his first question. 'But where are you living?'

She pointed over his shoulder, and he turned and looked out the living room's picture window. 'See the yellow house,' she said, pointing. He looked across the street and saw a tidy bungalow with a summer awning still over its front steps.

'It belongs to an old lady named Mrs Jupiter. Jeff and I have the apartment in her basement. It's not Belvedere, but the rent's less than Aunt Sally spent on canapés. Mrs Jupiter's a nice old thing and I do a few chores for her around the house. It's worked out pretty well.'

What a coincidence, he was about to say when the penny dropped. Annie said, 'Harry came to see me about a week after . . . the shooting. By then Sally made it clear I had to find another place to live. I think at first he wanted to make sure I hadn't been in league with Frank, though I also had the feeling Harry knew you hadn't pulled the trigger.'

'He's sharp,' said Nessheim.

'Yeah, but he's a nice man, too. He caught me at a bad moment; I hadn't any idea where to go next. I was even considering Vermont — God help me, I was that desperate — and Harry couldn't have been nicer. He put me in touch with Mrs Jupiter.'

The old softie, thought Nessheim, a little taken aback.

'But what are you going to do?' she asked. 'Harry's itching to have you back.'

'I don't know,' he said. 'I'm thinking of signing up.' He reasoned that if he enlisted there was more chance he could bluff his way through the medical than if he waited to be drafted. Not that he would tell Guttman any of this.

'In the army?' She looked concerned and also disappointed — or was he kidding himself?

'I might as well — we'll all be drafted soon enough. It couldn't be the navy; I get seasick just seeing a boat.'

'I thought that FBI agents could be exempted from the draft if they wanted.'

He shrugged.

'Does Harry know about this?' she asked.

'No, and I'd be grateful if you wouldn't tell him.'

She shifted on the sofa, sitting up with her hands on her knees. 'You know, I was hoping you'd be coming back to Washington.' She was looking down at her clasped hands. 'I've missed our talks.' She paused and looked away from him as she spoke next. 'I've had a lot happen to me, but I never felt I really shared it with anybody.'

'Me neither,' said Nessheim truthfully.

She said, 'When Harry first came to interview me, you were still in the hospital. I asked after you, and he said he thought you'd probably be going home for a while. That was his way of letting me down gently, I guess.'

'I figured you'd never forgive me.'

'For what?'

He was flustered. 'A lot of things, I guess. Forcing you to show me Lady Dove's letters. And then — with Frank, you know . . . ' He found himself stumbling so he stopped talking.

Annie looked thoughtful. 'I've been thinking a lot about Frank lately. It's not as if I can pretend now that I really knew him.' She gave a small sigh. 'He was always pretty aloof. Kind-hearted, and he was good with Jeff — well, up to a point. He couldn't take the rough with the smooth very well. I realise now he had a lot on his plate,' she said, then softened, her voice full of regret. 'I guess knowing that he wasn't really in love with me just makes it worse.'

'That will get better,' he said gently.

'Maybe,' she said, though she didn't sound convinced.

Guttman would be coming back soon, Nessheim sensed, and he didn't know what to say. Impulsively he asked, 'Can I write to you? You know, once I'm in the army I'd send you a letter maybe.'

She looked at him appraisingly. He was about to tell her he understood if she'd rather he didn't, when she said coolly, 'Like the letter you wrote from the train?'

'I meant every word of it.' He had to force himself to return her gaze. It suddenly seemed terribly important what Annie said next.

'Okay then, write me another one. I might even read it.'

Acknowledgements

Kate Elton of Random House encouraged me to write this novel, and I am enormously grateful for her continued support. Special thanks to Georgina Hawtrey-Woore for her advice and patience, Susan Sandon and Emma Mitchell. I would also like to thank my agent Gillon Aitken, Clare Alexander, and especially Andrew Kidd for his invaluable comments on earlier drafts.

My gratitude is owed to Julian Turton and Olivia Seligman for introducing me to the *Dreiländereck* and for their careful reading of what resulted; Jocelyn Turton for correction of my German; retired Special Agent Larry Wack for answering my questions about the 1930s FBI; Jeanette Thomas for help with the geography of Washington D.C.; Professor Emeritus Larry Hill of Texas A&M University, David McCormick, Sir Ian Kershaw, Stephen Glover, Jon and Ann Conibear, and Sara Nelson for her friendship.

Among my family, I would like to thank Willard Keeney for sharing his extraordinarily deep knowledge of American transport history; Bill and Polly Billings for lifelong (my life, that is) hospitality in Woodstock Vermont; and my brothers, Daniel Rosenheim and James Rosenheim. Laura and Sabrina Rosenheim also helped, as did — most of all — their mother.

We do hope that you have enjoyed reading this large print book.

Did you know that all of our titles are available for purchase?

We publish a wide range of high quality large print books including:
Romances, Mysteries, Classics
General Fiction
Non Fiction and Westerns

Special interest titles available in large print are:
The Little Oxford Dictionary
Music Book
Song Book
Hymn Book
Service Book

Also available from us courtesy of Oxford University Press:
Young Readers' Dictionary
(large print edition)
Young Readers' Thesaurus
(large print edition)

For further information or a free brochure, please contact us at:
Ulverscroft Large Print Books Ltd.,
The Green, Bradgate Road, Anstey,
Leicester, LE7 7FU, England.
Tel: (00 44) **0116 236 4325**
Fax: (00 44) **0116 234 0205**

Robert Danziger receives an unexpected call
from a childhood friend, Duval Morgan.
Duval, after twenty years in an Illinois state
penitentiary for the rape and assault of a
young nurse, is now out. Robert has returned
to his native city of Chicago to start afresh.
Duval is from a past that Robert would rather
forget, but after reluctantly agreeing to meet
him he's astonished to find him proclaiming
his innocence. Duval gradually spends more
time with the Danziger family, befriending
Robert's wife Anna and young daughter
Sophie, and Robert wonders what his old
friend really wants . . . When Anna, a lawyer,
takes up Duval's cause, Robert is reluctant to
encourage her, and, just as Anna's investiga-
tions into the rape case start to make
progress, Duval disappears . . .

KEEPING SECRETS

Andrew Rosenheim

Jack Renoir has a big secret: as a young boy he had witnessed his uncle's brutal murder on his Californian apple farm. Now he's a man who makes his living discovering other people's secrets while making sure he keeps his own. But when a beautiful young English-woman walks into Jack's life he doesn't realize she is going to turn his carefully constructed world completely upside down. As his defences dissolve he agrees to start a new life with her in England — and that is when his troubles really start.

STILLRIVER

Andrew Rosenheim

Michael Wolf felt he had escaped his past —
Stillriver, the small town in Michigan where
he grew up, his troubles with his father, the
petty jealousies and competitiveness of his
younger brother, and most of all the disaster
that ended his relationship with Cassie, the
love of his life. However, Michael is forced to
return to Stillriver when he is told of his
father's brutal murder. He finds the town's
new prosperity only partly masks old hurts
and humiliations. But when he discovers that
Cassie has also returned to Stillriver, he is
thrown into total turmoil while trying to solve
the mystery of his father's death.

DRY SEASON

Dan Smith

On the banks of a sprawling river, in a Brazilian backwater, lies Sao Tiago — a town for people with nowhere else to run . . . and it's where Sam, a former priest has ended up. Scarred by what he saw, after leaving England to help people, he cares for nothing except drinking and fishing on the great river. But when, one night, he finds himself fighting to save a man's life, it's just the start of a battle with Sao Tiago's dark heart. Sam, entangled in the affections of an ex-prostitute and a predatory landowner's wife, finds that life is cheap; love can be deadly. Now he must face his past in order to forge the chance of a future and survive in a town without a soul.

FROM BLOOD

Edward Wright

Shannon Fairchild shelved her PhD to clean homes — rebelling against her academic family. But when her parents are tortured and murdered, Shannon, consumed by guilt, vows to find out who was responsible. Ringing in her ears, her mother's dying words 'find them and warn them' remain a puzzle to her. Then she discovers a history of radical political activism linking her parents to a fatal bombing in the 1960s. The two masterminds behind the attack have been deep underground and evading the FBI ever since. When Shannon sets out alone to track down the notorious fugitives, she finds that her past — and future — is irrevocably linked with theirs. Now begins a race against the clock to find her parents' killers — before the killers find her . . .